BOOK OF NIGHT

BOOK OF NIGHT

HOLLY BLACK

DEL REY

7 9 10 8

Del Rey
20 Vauxhall Bridge Road
London SW1V 2SA

Del Rey is part of the Penguin Random House group of companies
whose addresses can be found at global.penguinrandomhouse.com.

Penguin
Random House
UK

First published in the US by Tor Books in 2022
First published in the UK by Del Rey in 2022

www.penguin.co.uk

A CIP catalogue record for this book is available from the British Library.

Hardback ISBN 9781529102376
Trade Paperback ISBN 9781529102383

Printed and bound in Great Britain by Clays Ltd, Elcograf S.p.A.

The authorised representative in the EEA is Penguin Random House Ireland,
Morrison Chambers, 32 Nassau Street, Dublin D02 YH68

www.greenpenguin.co.uk

Penguin Random House is committed to a sustainable future
for our business, our readers and our planet. This book is made
from Forest Stewardship Council® certified paper.

For everyone who has ever come to New Year's Eve at my house

I have a little shadow that goes in and out with me,

And what can be the use of him is more than I can see.

He is very, very like me from the heels up to the head;

And I see him jump before me, when I jump into my bed.

—From "My Shadow" by Robert Louis Stevenson

BOOK OF NIGHT

PROLOGUE

A ny child can be chased by their shadow. All they need to do is run straight toward the sun on a lazy afternoon. As long as they keep moving, it will be right behind them. They can even turn around and try to chase it, but no matter how fast their chubby legs pump, their shadow will always be a little bit out of reach.

Not so with this child.

He runs across a yard dotted with dandelions, giggling and shrieking, his fingers close on something that shouldn't be solid, something that shouldn't fall *before* he does onto the clover and crabgrass, something he shouldn't be able to wrestle with and pin in the dirt.

After, sitting in the mossy cool beneath a maple tree, the boy sticks the tip of his penknife into the pad of his ring finger. He turns his face away so he doesn't have to watch. The first poke doesn't go through the skin. The second doesn't either. Only the third time, when he presses harder, frustration overcoming squeamishness, does he manage to cut himself. It hurts *a lot,* so he's ashamed of how tiny the bead of blood is that wells up. He squeezes his skin, to see if he can get a little more. The drop swells. He can sense the shadow's eagerness. His finger stings as a dark fog forms around it.

A breeze comes, shaking loose maple seeds. They spiral down around him, coptering through the air on their single wing.

Just a little drink every day, he'd heard someone on the television say about their shadow. *And it will be your best friend in the world.*

Although it has no mouth and no tongue and there is no wetness at its touch, he can tell that it's licking his skin. He doesn't like the feeling, but it doesn't hurt.

He's never had a best friend before, still he knows that they do things like this. They become blood brothers, smearing their cuts together until it's impossible to tell where one ends and the other begins. He needs someone like that.

"I'm Remy," he whispers to his shadow. "And I'll call you Red."

1

HUNGRY SHADOWS

harlie's ugly Crocs stuck to the mats on the floor behind the bar, making a sticky, squelching sound. Sweat slicked the skin under her arms, at the hollow of her throat, and between her thighs. This was her second shift today; the afternoon guy quit abruptly to follow his boyfriend to Los Angeles and she was stuck with his hours until Odette hired a replacement.

But as tired as Charlie was, she needed the cash. And she figured she better keep busy. Keeping busy meant keeping out of trouble.

There'd always been something wrong with Charlie Hall. Crooked, from the day she was born. Never met a bad decision she wasn't willing to double down on. Had fingers made for picking pockets, a tongue for lying, and a shriveled cherry pit for a heart.

If her shadow had been one of those magic ones, she was pretty sure even that thing would have run away.

But that didn't mean she couldn't *try* to be different. And she was trying. Sure, it had been hard to keep her worst impulses in check these past ten months, but it was better than being a lit match in a town she'd already doused in gasoline.

She had a job—with a timesheet, even—and a stolid brick of a boyfriend who paid his share of the rent. Her gunshot wound was healing nicely. Little successes, but that didn't mean she wasn't proud of them.

It was on that thought that Charlie looked up to see a test of her resolve walk through the double doors of Rapture Bar & Lounge.

Doreen Kowalski's face looked hot and blotchy with crying—she'd obviously tried to fix her makeup, but had wiped her mascara so hard that it winged out to one side. Back in high school, she wouldn't have given Charlie the time of day, and she probably didn't want to tonight either.

There are countless differences between the lives of people with money and people without. One is this: without the means to pay experts, it's necessary to evolve a complex ecosystem of useful amateurs. When Charlie's dad got what the doctor told him was a skin cancer, he drank a fifth of Maker's Mark and asked a butcher friend to cut a divot out of his shoulder, because there was no way he could afford a surgeon. When Charlie's friend's cousin got married, they asked Mrs. Silva from three blocks over to make their wedding cake, because she loved to bake and had fancy pastry piping doodads. And if the buttercream was a little grainy or one of the layers was a bit overbaked, well, it was still sweet and just as tall as a cake in a magazine, and it cost only the price of supplies.

In the world of shadow magic, Charlie was a successful thief, but to the locals, she would always be a useful amateur, willing to palm a wedding ring or retrieve a dognapped pit bull.

Charlie Hall. Drawn to a bad idea like a moth to a wool sweater. Every hustle an opportunity to let her worst impulses out to play.

"I need to talk to you," Doreen said loudly, reaching for Charlie as she passed.

It'd been a slow night at the lounge, but Odette, the ancient, semiretired dominatrix who owned the place, was sitting at a table out front, gossiping with her cronies. She'd notice if Charlie chatted to one person for too long, and Charlie couldn't afford to lose this gig. Bartending at Rapture was a lucky break, given her track record.

It'd been arranged by Balthazar, who ran a shadow parlor out of the basement, speakeasy-style, and had good reasons to keep an eye on her—not the least of which was that he wanted her to come back to work for him.

And as Charlie looked over at Doreen and that familiar excitement stirred in her, she felt the precariousness of her commitment to the straight and narrow. Like a strategy for success that's only the word "profit" with a lot of exclamation points.

"Can I get you a drink?" she asked Doreen.

Doreen shook her head. "You have to help me find Adam. He disappeared, again, and I—"

"Can't talk now," Charlie interrupted. "Order something to keep my boss off my back. Club soda and bitters. Cranberry and lime. Whatever. It's on me."

Doreen's wet, red-rimmed eyes suggested that she'd have a hard time waiting. Or that she'd had a few drinks before she arrived. Maybe both.

"Hey," one of the regulars called, and Charlie turned away to take his order.

Made a cosmopolitan that spilled ruby red out of the shaker. Topped it with a tiny pellet of dry ice that sent smoke wafting up, as though from a potion.

She checked on another table, a guy who was nursing a beer, trembling fingers applying a third nicotine patch to his inner arm. He wanted to keep his tab open.

Charlie poured a shot of Four Roses for a tweedy guy in dirty glasses who looked like he'd been sleeping in his clothes and told her he didn't like his bourbon too sweet. Then she crossed to the other end of the bar, pausing to make a whiskey-and-ginger for Balthazar himself when he waved her over.

"Got a job for you," he said under his breath. With his flashing eyes, light brown skin, and curls long enough to be pulled back into a disreputable ponytail, he lorded over his shadow parlor, making the town's corrupt dreams come true.

"Nope," Charlie said, moving on.

"C'mon. Knight Singh got murdered in his bed, and the room was trashed. Someone made off with his personal folio of magical discoveries," Balthazar called after her, unconvinced. "This is what you were best at."

"Nope!" she called back as cheerfully as she could manage.

Fuck Knight Singh.

He had been the first gloamist ever to contract Charlie's services, back when she was just a kid. As far as she was concerned, he could rot in his grave, but that still didn't mean she was going to rob it.

Charlie was out of the game. She'd been too good at it, and the collateral damage had been too high. Now she was just a regular person.

A drunken trio of witchy-looking twentysomethings were celebrating a weeknight birthday, black lipstick smeared over their mouths. They ordered shots of cheap, neon green absinthe and winced them down. One must have recently gotten her shadow altered, because she kept moving so the light would catch it and project her new self onto the wall. It had horns and wings, like a succubus.

It was beautiful.

"My mother haaaates it," the girl was telling her friends, voice slightly slurred. She gave a hop and hovered in the air for a moment as her shadow wings fluttered, and a few patrons glanced over admiringly.

"Mom says that when I try to get a real job, I am going to regret having something I can't hide. I told her it was my commitment to never selling out."

The first time Charlie had ever seen an altered shadow, it had made her think of a fairy tale she'd read as a child in the school library: *The Witch and the Unlucky Brother*.

She still recalled the story's opening lines: *Once upon a time, a boy was born with a hungry shadow. He was as lucky as lucky could be, while all the ill luck was bestowed on his twin, who was born with no shadow at all.*

But, of course, this girl's shadow wasn't lucky. It looked cool and gave her a bit of minor magic. She could maybe get three inches off the ground, for a couple of seconds at a time. A pair of stacked heels would have taken her higher.

It didn't make the girl a gloamist, either.

Manipulated shadows were the specialty of alterationists, the most public-facing of the four disciplines. Alterationists could cosmetically shape shadows, use them to trigger emotions so strong they could be addictive, and even cut out pieces of a person's subconscious. There were risks, of course. Sometimes people lost a lot more of themselves than they bargained for.

The other gloaming disciplines were more secretive. Carapaces focused on their own shadows, using them to soar through the air on shadow wings or armor themselves. Puppeteers sent their shadows to do things in secret—in Charlie's experience, largely the kind of foul shit no one wanted to talk about. And the masks weren't much better, a bunch of creeps and mystics intent on unraveling the secrets of the universe, no matter who it hurt.

There was a reason they got called glooms, instead of their proper title. You couldn't trust them as far as you could throw them. For example, no matter what gloamists said, they all trafficked in stolen shadows.

Charlie's boyfriend, Vince, had been robbed of his, probably so some rich fuck could have his third go-round at an alteration. Now he cast no shadow at all, not even in the brightest of bright light. It was believed that shadowless people had an absence in them, a lack of some intangible thing. Sometimes people passing Vince on the street would notice and give him a wide berth.

Charlie wished people would get the hell out of her way too. But it bothered Vince, so she glared at every single person who did it.

When Charlie circled back, Doreen said, "I'll take a ginger ale, to settle my stomach."

Odette seemed distracted by her friends.

"Okay, what's the problem?"

"I think Adam's gone on another bender," said Doreen as Charlie put the drink in front of her, along with a cocktail napkin. "The casino called. If he doesn't come in on Monday, they're going to fire his ass. I keep trying his cell, but he won't answer me."

Charlie and Doreen had never been particularly friendly, but they knew some of the same people. And sometimes knowing someone for a long time seemed more important than liking them.

Charlie sighed. "So what is it you want me to do?"

"Find him, and make him come home," Doreen said. "Maybe remind him he's got a kid."

"I don't know that I can make him do anything," Charlie said.

"You're the reason Adam's like this," Doreen told her. "He keeps taking on extra jobs that are too dangerous."

"How exactly is that my fault?" Charlie wiped down the bar area in front of her for something to do.

"Because Balthazar's always comparing him to you. Adam's trying to measure up to your stupid reputation. But not everyone's a born criminal."

Doreen's partner, Adam, was a blackjack dealer over at the Springfield casino and had started working for Balthazar part-time after Charlie quit. Maybe he thought that dealing with whatever sketchy shit went on at the tables prepared him for stealing from glooms. She also suspected that Adam had thought that if Charlie could do it, it must not be that hard.

"We can talk more after my shift," Charlie said with a sigh, thinking of all the reasons she ought to steer clear.

For one, she was the last person Adam would want to see, in any context.

For another, this was going to result in zero money.

Rumor had it that Adam had been spending his extra Balthazar-dispensed cash rolling bliss—that is, getting your shadow tweaked, so you could stare into space for hours as awesome emotions flooded through you. Adam was probably lying on his back in a hotel room, feeling real good, and definitely wouldn't want Charlie dragging him home before that wore off.

Charlie looked over at Doreen, the last thing she needed right then, sitting at the other end of the bar, playing miserably with her stirrer.

Charlie was just reaching for the seltzer pump when a crash made her look up.

The tweedy guy, with the "not-too-sweet" bourbon request, was now on his hands and knees next to the empty stage, tangled in a swag of velvet curtain. One of the goons from the shadow parlor, a man named Joey Aspirins, stood over the guy as though trying to decide whether to kick him in the face.

Balthazar had followed them up the stairs, still yelling. "Are you crazy, trying to get me to fence that? You setting me up to look like I'm the one that stole the *Liber Noctem*? Get the fuck out of here!"

"It's not like that," the tweedy guy said. "Salt's desperate to get even part of it back. He'll pay real money—"

Charlie flinched at Salt's name.

Not a lot rattled her, after everything she'd seen and done. But the thought of him always did.

"Shut up and get out." Balthazar pointed toward the exit.

"What's going on?" Doreen asked. Charlie shook her head, watching Joey Aspirins shove the tweedy guy toward the doors. Odette got up to talk with Balthazar, their voices too soft for her to overhear.

Balthazar turned, catching Charlie's eye as he was walking back to the shadow parlor. He winked. She ought to have raised her eyebrow or rolled her eyes, but the mention of Lionel Salt had turned her stiff and wooden. Balthazar was gone before she'd managed to react.

Last call came soon after. Charlie wiped down the counter. Filled a dishwasher with dirty shakers and glasses. She counted out her drawer, peeling the money for Doreen's drink off her tips and slipping it in with the rest of the bills. Rapture might exult in its strangeness, might have its walls and ceiling coated in Black 3.0, paint so dark it stole light from a room, and might have air thick with incense. Might be the kind of place locals came to glimpse magic, or kink, or if they got tired of sports bars with kombucha on tap. But the rituals of closing were the same.

Most of the rest of the staff had already left by the time Charlie got her coat and purse out of Odette's office. The wind had kicked up, chilling the sweat on her body as she walked out to her car, reminding Charlie that it was already late autumn, barreling toward winter, and that she needed to start bringing something warmer to work than a thin leather coat.

"Well?" Doreen asked. "I'm freezing out here. Will you find him? Suzie Lambton says you helped her out, and you barely even know her."

The job probably wouldn't be too hard, and then she'd have Doreen off her back. If Adam was blissed out somewhere, she could always steal his wallet. That would send him back home fast. Take his car keys too, just to show she could. "Your brother works at the university, right? Office of the bursar."

Doreen narrowed her eyes. "He's a customer service representative. He answers phones."

"But he has access to the computers. So can he fix it so my sister has another month to pay her bill? Not asking him to cancel the debt, just delay it." Orientation fees, student technology fees, and processing fees were all due before the loan money showed up. That wasn't even counting the junker Posey would need to get back and forth to campus. Or books.

"I don't want to get him into trouble," Doreen said primly, as though she wasn't trying to persuade a criminal to find her criminal boyfriend.

Charlie folded her arms across her chest and waited.

Finally, Doreen nodded slowly. "I guess I could ask."

Which could mean a lot of things. Charlie opened the trunk of her janky Toyota Corolla. Her collection of burner phones rested beside a tangle of jumper cables, an old bag of burglary supplies, and a bottle of Grey Goose she'd bought wholesale off the bar.

Charlie took out one of the phones and punched in the code to activate it. "Okay, let me try something and see if Adam bites. Tell me his number."

If he answered, she told herself, she'd do it. If he didn't, she'd walk away.

She knew she was just looking for an excuse to get into trouble. Wading into quicksand to see if she'd sink. She texted him anyway: *I've got a job and I heard you were the best.*

If he was worried about not being good enough, then the flattery would be motivating. That was the nature of con artistry, playing on weakness. It was also a bad way to train your brain to think about people.

"Let's see if he responds and—" Charlie started to say when her phone pinged.

Who is this?

Amber, Charlie texted back. She had several identities that she'd built for con and never used. Of them, Amber was the only gloamist. *Sorry to bother you so late, but I really need your help.*

Amber, with the long brown hair?

Charlie stared at her phone for a long moment, trying to decide if this was a trick.

You really are as good as they say. She added a winking emoji and hoped ambiguity would allow her to sidestep any of his questions.

"I can't believe he's texting you. What is he saying?"

"Take a look," Charlie told Doreen, handing over the phone. "See? He's alive. He's fine."

Doreen bit her fingernail as she read through the messages. "You didn't say you were going to flirt with him."

Charlie rolled her eyes.

On the other side of the parking lot, Odette, swathed in an enormous cocoon coat, made her way to her purple Mini Cooper.

"You really think you can get him to tell you where he's staying?"

Charlie nodded. "Sure. I can even go there and hog-tie him, if that's what you want. You'll have to do me a better favor for that, though."

"Suzie says asking you for help is like summoning up the devil. The devil might grant your wish, but afterward, you're out a soul."

Charlie bit her lip, looked up at the streetlight. "Like you said, I barely know Suzie. She must be thinking of somebody else."

"Maybe," Doreen said. "But all that stuff you did—even back in the day, the stuff people said—you've got to be angry at someone."

"Or I could have done it for fun," Charlie said. "Which would be pretty messed up, right? And since I am doing you a good turn, it'd be polite not to mention it."

Doreen gave one of those exhausted sighs that mothers of little kids seemed to have welling up in them at all times. "Right. Sure. Just bring him home before he winds up like you."

Charlie watched Doreen go, then got into her Corolla. Buckled her seat belt. Tried not to think about the job Balthazar was offering, or who she used to be. Thought instead of the ramen she was going to boil when she got home. Hoped her sister had fed the cat. Imagined the mattress waiting for her on the floor of her bedroom. Imagined Vince, already asleep, feet tangled in the sheets. Shoved her key in the ignition.

The car wouldn't turn on.

2
KING OF CUPS, REVERSED

The wind whirled down the tunnel of Cottage Street, stinging Charlie's cheeks, sending hair into her face.

Her Corolla still sat in the parking lot of Rapture. No matter how many times she twisted the key or slammed her hands against the dashboard. Jumper cables hadn't done a thing to resuscitate the car, and tow trucks were expensive.

She'd considered calling Vince, or even a cab, but instead she'd gotten the vodka out of the trunk and done a couple of sulky shots straight out of the bottle, standing there feeling sorry for herself. Looking up at the sky.

The last of the leaves had turned brown; only a few still hung on branches, drooping like sleeping bats.

A car had slowed at the stop sign. The driver called out a vulgar proposal before he hit the gas. She flipped him off, although it seemed unlikely he noticed.

It was nothing Charlie hadn't heard before anyway. She saw herself reflected in her car windows. Dark hair. Dark eyes. A lot of everything else: breast and butt and belly and thigh. Too often, people acted like her curves were some engraved invitation. They seemed to forget that everyone gets born into bodies they can't just kick off like slippers, figures they can't transform as though they were shadows.

Another gust of wind sent a few leaves into the air, although most clotted together along the edges of the road.

And that was when Charlie had decided it would be a great idea to hoof it the mile and a half home.

It was a nothing walk, after all. A stroll.

Or it would have been, for someone who hadn't been on her feet all day and half the night.

The term "pot-valiance" occurred to her, too late.

She passed a darkened bookstore, in the window a fall display of pumpkins with plastic vampire fangs jammed into their carved mouths. They rested toothily beside horror novels and a decorative dusting of candy corn, their orange bodies just beginning to sag with rot.

The whole street was shuttered. Pulling her coat tighter, Charlie wished that Easthampton was like some of the surrounding college towns—Northampton or Amherst—full of enough tipsy students stumbling through the late-night streets to justify at least one pizza place staying open after the bars closed, or a coffeeshop for up-all-night overachievers.

All the quiet gave her too much time to think.

Alone on the dark street, Charlie couldn't escape Doreen's words. *But all that stuff you did—even back in the day, the stuff people said—you've got to be angry at someone.*

She kicked a loose chunk of cement.

When she was a kid, Charlie had been a mop of black hair, brown eyes, and bad attitude. She'd gotten into one kind of trouble after another, but along the way, she learned she was good at taking things apart. Puzzles, and people. She liked solving them, liked figuring out how to get at what they were hiding. To become what they wanted to believe in.

Which made her consider the Adam thing again. It couldn't hurt to play it through. Distract herself from the night.

Charlie fished out her phone and typed: *There's a volume in the Mortimer Rare Book Collection at Smith College that I'm sure contains something important. I can pay you. Or we can work out a trade.*

Gloamists were always on the hunt for old books detailing techniques for shadow manipulation. They'd been known to kill one another over them. She was offering Adam an easy job.

It had to be somewhat tempting.

For ten years, she'd stolen things for one gloamist or another. Books and scrolls and occasionally other, worse things. For ten years, she'd kept her identity secret. Kept a low profile, worked off and on in restaurants and bars to give her cover, and used Balthazar as her go-between. A little over a year ago, she'd put down a deposit on a house. Convinced Posey to apply to colleges.

Then she'd blown it all up.

It seemed like there'd been a furnace inside Charlie, always burning. A year ago she'd seen how easily she could turn everything to ash.

Adam wasn't writing back. Maybe he was asleep. Or high. Or just not interested. She shoved the burner back into her bag.

Out of the corner of her eye, Charlie thought she saw the oily slide of something in the space between one building and the next.

It took her mind off her past, but not in a good way.

People talked about disembodied shadows walking the world the way they talked about Slender Man or the girl with the cheek full of spiders, but Charlie knew Blights were more than a story. They were what was left over when the gloamist died and the shadow didn't. Quite real, and very dangerous. Onyx worked on them, and fire, but that was about it unless you were a gloamist yourself.

Her real phone chimed, drawing her thoughts back to the present with a start. It was a text from Vince: *All okay?*

Home soon, she texted back.

She should have called him, back at Rapture. He would have picked her up. He probably would have been nice about it too. But she didn't like the idea of leaning on him. It would only make things worse when he was gone.

A sound came from down the street, by where Nashawannuck Pond ran into Rubber Thread Pond, across from the abandoned mill buildings. Someone was there.

She walked faster, shoving her hand into her pocket to wrap around the handle of a folding tactical knife attached to her keys. It had kept an edge despite her using it to open cereal boxes and chip putty off old windows. She didn't have much of an idea how to use it to defend herself, but at least it was sharp and had an onyx handle to weaken shadows.

A flicker of movement drew her gaze down an alley. A light on outside one of the shop doors illuminated a heap of stained clothing, white bone, and a wall spattered with black spots of blood.

Charlie stopped, muscles tensing, her stomach lurching, as her mind tried to catch up. Her brain kept supplying her with alternatives to what she saw—a discarded prop from a haunted house, a mannequin, an animal.

But no, the remains were human. Raw flesh torn open, shredded along with clothing as though whoever did this was desperate to get to the person's insides. Charlie stepped closer. The cold contained the smell, but there was still a charnel sweetness to the air. The man's face was turned to one side, eyes glassy and open. His rib cage was broken and partially removed, jagged pale bones rising above the mess of flesh like a circle of silver birch trees.

And against the wall, there was the movement again. His shadow, which ought to have been as still as his corpse, was shredded and wafting in the breeze, as though it was torn laundry on a line. As though a strong gust might blow it free.

The man's face was so changed by death that it was the clothes she noticed first, tweed, wrinkled and a little dirty, as though he'd been living rough in them. This was the man Balthazar had thrown out of Rapture's parlor. The guy who'd proposed selling something of Salt's back to him.

Two hours ago, she'd been setting a Four Roses in front of him. Now—

There was a sound at the opposite end of the alley, and Charlie looked up with a sharp inhalation of breath. A man in a long dark coat and hat, with eyes as dark as bullet holes, was staring at her.

There was something wrong with his hands.

Really wrong.

They were entirely made of shadow, right to the scarred nubs of his wrists.

He began to walk toward Charlie, his footsteps sharp and distinct on the asphalt. Half her instincts were telling her to run, the other half wanting her to freeze because running would ignite the predator's desire to give chase. Was she really going to fight? The knife in her hand seemed ridiculously small, little better than cuticle scissors.

Sirens wailed in the distance.

At the sound, the man paused. They watched one another, the corpse between them. Then he stepped back, slipping around the corner and out of her line of sight. Charlie felt light-headed with shock and horrifyingly sober.

Forcing herself to move, she stumbled out of the alley and fast-walked toward Union. If she was near the body when the police arrived, they were going to have a lot of questions—and weren't likely to believe a story about some guy with shadow hands. Especially not from Charlie, who had been hauled in twice before the age of eighteen for confidence schemes.

Her legs were carrying her forward, but her mind was reeling.

Ever since the Boxford Massacre twenty years ago, when the world had become aware of gloamists, Western Massachusetts had been lousy with them. The Silicon Valley of shadow magic.

From Springfield with its shuttered gun factories and boarded-up mansions to the universities and colleges to the idiosyncratic farms of the hill towns, polluted rivers, and the marshy beauty of the Quabbin Reservoir, the Valley was cheap enough and close enough to both New York and Boston to be a draw.

Plus, it had an already high tolerance for weirdos. There were goats available for mowing lawns. A gun club that ran an annual Renaissance faire. You could buy an eighteenth-century bedframe and a hand-thrown pot in the shape of a vagina and score heroin from a guy at a bus station—all within a fifteen-minute travel window.

These days you could add on stumbling into a shadow parlor and getting an alterationist to remove your desire for any of the aforementioned vices, or adding on a new one. Rolling bliss was skyrocketing in popularity. The more gloamists there were, the more the towns were changing, and there wasn't enough onyx in the world to stop it.

And yet, for all that, this murder seemed uniquely awful. Whoever or what-ever had done it would have needed incredible strength to crack open a body like a walnut.

She shoved her trembling hands deep into her pockets. Her familiar route had become strange to her, full of jagged shadows that moved with each gust of wind. Her nose seemed to catch the scent of spoiling meat.

Two more breathless blocks, and then she was heading up her driveway, hands trembling.

The bell over the door jangled as she entered into the ugly yellow kitchen of their rental house. A frying pan and two dirty dishes sat in the sink. There was a plate domed with another near the microwave. Their cat, Lucipurrr, nosed it hopefully.

Heading toward the living room, she found Vince asleep in front of a tele-vision turned down low, his big body sprawled on their scavenged couch, a paperback resting on his stomach. When she looked at him, she felt a stab of longing, the uncomfortable sensation of missing someone who hadn't yet gone.

Her gaze went to where his shadow ought to have fallen. But there was noth-ing at all.

When Charlie had first met him, her eye had noted something off, as though he was always a little out of focus, a little blurred at the edges. Maybe she'd been distracted by being drunk, or by his being hard-jawed and clean-cut in a way guys attracted to her never were. It wasn't until she saw him the next morning, silhouetted in a doorway, seeming as though light was streaming through him, that she realized he didn't have a shadow.

Posey had noticed right away.

Now Charlie's sister sat on the worn gray shag rug, squinting at a grainy moving image on her laptop, a spread of cards in front of her. She had on the same pajamas that she'd been in when Charlie left, the cuffs scuffed and dirty. No bra. Her light brown hair twisted into a messy bun on top of her head. The only adornment she wore was an onyx-and-gold septum ring, which she never removed. Posey took all her Zoom calls with the camera on her end off, at least partially so she didn't have to dress up for them.

She sounded entirely professional, her voice soothing as she continued her tarot reading, barely seeming to notice Charlie. "Nine of Wands, reversed. You're exhausted. You want to give a lot of yourself, but lately you feel as though there's nothing left to give—"

The person on the other end must have started spilling their guts, because Posey cut herself off and just listened.

When they were kids, their mother had dragged them to lots of psychics. Charlie remembered staring at dusty velvet pillows and beaded curtains in the front room of a house off the highway, Posey's head on her lap, listening to their mom getting lied to about her future.

But even if it was a scam, their mother had needed someone to talk with, and it wasn't like she was going to open up to anyone else. Psychics were therapists for people who couldn't admit they needed therapy. They were magic for people who desperately needed a little magic, back before magic was real.

And while Charlie didn't believe Posey had powers, she did think that her clients got someone who treated their problems as important, who wanted to help. That seemed worth a fifty-dollar donation and a subscription to her Patreon.

Charlie went back out to the kitchen and uncovered the plate. Vince had cooked egg tacos, with sliced avocado on the side and twin splashes of Tabasco and sriracha. From the plates in the sink, it looked like he'd even made some for Posey. Charlie ate hers at the rusty folding table in the kitchen while she listened to her sister talk.

"King of Cups, also reversed. You're a smart woman, but sometimes you make decisions you know aren't the best."

A shiver of leftover adrenaline made her put down her fork for a moment and take a few ragged breaths. She tried to focus on her sister's voice, on the familiarity of the story Posey was telling.

The majority of people who called for readings had problems to do with love. Maybe they wanted to know if they had a chance with somebody in particular. Or maybe they were lonely and wanted someone to tell them it wasn't their fault they hadn't found the right person. But most often it was because they were in a relationship that had gone bad, and part of them wanted to be told that it would be worth all the suffering, while another part of them wanted permission to get out.

Most of their mother's visits to psychics had been about relationships. The Hall women fell in love like they were falling off a cliff. They were terrible at picking men, as though there were some kind of ancestral curse that started with Nana's marriage to a guy so awful that she was still in prison for shooting him in the back of the head while he was in his BarcaLounger, watching TV. It lasted through Mom making Charlie and Posey sit quietly in the back seat of a Kia while she drove around trying to catch their father cheating, through a stepdad who broke Posey's wrist and an ex-boyfriend of Charlie's so desperate for money to pay a gambling debt that he convinced her to file tax returns for dead people and give him the cash from the refunds. Posey said that a guy had to have a hole in his head, his heart, or his pocket for one of the Hall women to go head-over-heels for him.

Maybe that was true. Maybe there needed to be something missing in a man, so that Charlie felt she could pour herself into that absence and heal him like an elixir. Or maybe it was only that Charlie felt as though she'd lost something too, and loss sings to loss.

Vince was a dependable guy. Tough, hardworking. The halting quality to the way he told stories about his family made it clear he was uncomfortable sharing much about his past, but she'd been sizing up marks for long enough to make some good guesses. The calluses on his hands were new, and he had the kind of straight teeth that were the result of braces. Knew the kind of stuff you learned in college but didn't have any debt. He'd come from money.

Charlie wondered if they'd turned their backs on him after he lost his shadow. She'd tried to ask, but his answers were evasive. And she hadn't tried *hard,* because she wasn't sure she wanted to hear about that better life, and how far he'd fallen from it.

After all, he was willing to look the other way when the real Charlie Hall emerged, the one attracted to trouble, prone to bleak jags where she barely got out of bed. The one who'd spent years trying to blot out the ouroboros of her thoughts with too much alcohol, too many men, and a string of heists. People said that a person without a shadow didn't experience emotion as fully or deeply as other people. Maybe that's why it didn't bother Vince, what she was and what she'd done.

At home with Vince, she tried to be both fabulist and fabulist's creation, a woman whose past as a con artist was long over and who wasn't fighting down the urge to go off the rails again.

And if he was slightly too good a listener, if she sometimes suspected that he could hear the hurt, feral part of her yearning to lash out, at least he didn't push her away.

"Come on," Charlie said, poking Vince's leg with her foot. She wanted him to come to bed with her, needed his breath in her hair and the weight of his arm across her to protect her from thinking about white bone or drying gore or men with shadows for hands.

Vince opened his eyes. Stretched. Turned off the television. He had that tall man's habit of hunching a little when he stood, like he was trying to be less intimidating.

"Did you find the food?" he asked, passing her on the way to the bedroom, his fingertips sliding across her back. She shivered greedily, inhaling the perfume of bleach that still clung to his skin from work.

"You're a good guy," she told him.

He smiled in answer, confused but pleased.

Vince paid his bills. He took out the trash. He was kind to the cat. And if he longed for another life, he was with Charlie now. It didn't matter what was in his heart any more than it mattered what was in hers.

3
THE PAST

When Charlie was thirteen, she told her mother she'd had a visitation. Mom had gotten deeply into crystals and divination after her divorce and had a friend who got "messages from angels," so it wasn't like the idea came from nowhere. Charlie claimed that the spirit of a witch who had died during the Inquisition had started speaking to her, and then through her.

It wasn't a good plan, in retrospect. But Mom wouldn't listen to her any other way. And Charlie was desperate.

Enter *Elvira de Granada*—a character half based on an anime seen late at night and half on bullshit from grocery-store horror novels. But Elvira could say all the things that Charlie Hall couldn't. Elvira could spit out all the pent-up rage that filled an already-scarred heart.

The problem was that Mom really, really, *really* needed to be convinced that her new husband was a bad guy—and fast. Travis was mean and hated Charlie and Posey.

But he wasn't stupid. When he smacked Posey—for *nothing*, for just jumping around and annoying him and refusing to go to bed on time—he did it when Mom wasn't there to see, and instead of acting like nothing happened, he claimed Charlie hit her sister and that Posey was covering.

Charlie got punished, of course. And so did Posey, for lying.

From then on, Travis knew he had the upper hand. He told their mother that she needed to set more boundaries with the kids, that their dad had let them get away with "bloody murder," that they were sneaky, lied for attention, and stole from his wallet, and if Mom didn't do something soon, they would never respect her, plus they'd probably wind up in prison.

When he hit Charlie, she didn't even try to tell.

Mom was fascinated by the idea that her daughter might be a medium. She was astonished when Charlie told her facts about relatives, although they were just things she'd remembered or stories she'd overheard. Occasionally, they were straight-up lies about dead people that seemed impossible to disprove.

But even Elvira de Granada couldn't convince Charlie's mother that Travis was no good. Charlie's mother decided that Elvira was bitter and distrustful on account of being tortured to death. And that's when Charlie came up with *Alonso Nieto,* warlock. Unlike Elvira, he wasn't just accused of witchcraft—he admitted to being a practitioner.

It turns out that men have more authority, even when they're not real.

Mom *loved* talking to Alonso. Charlie had thought she'd been convincing when playing Elvira, but with Alonso, Mom wanted to be convinced.

Charlie knew she had to be careful, all the same. If Alonso was going to successfully persuade Mom to leave Travis, the warlock needed to give them something concrete.

It didn't hurt that Travis's badness was starting to leak out. When they were first married, he made a big show of telling Mom how perfect she was and how great their life was going to be, but he couldn't keep it up. Now, when they argued, he'd start in with comments about her weight and about how she wasn't that smart. Flowers and date nights faded away, and so did a big chunk of his contribution to their finances.

Charlie knew she had an opportunity, but she needed help. So she let her little sister in on the plan.

Posey had been confused by Elvira and Alonso, although happy *someone* was talking shit about the stepdad she hated. Still, it had clearly creeped her out to see her sister possessed. Now that she knew it was a game, though, everything was different.

Professional psychics usually specialize in one of two types of readings, although neither sister knew that at the time. The first kind was a cold reading, the kind that Posey would go on to do as a phone psychic, making up things on the spot, based on observations. The second kind of reading was hot.

During a cold reading, the psychic might study how often a client looked at their phone, whether their finger had a pale patch of skin from the removal of a wedding ring, the newness of their shoes, or the visibility of their tattoos. On the phone, the psychic had to rely on their word choices, their accent, and the level of agitation in their voice. A good cold reading was the convincer that allowed the client to relax and start supplying information.

A hot reading was something else. It involved doing research on a person ahead of time. Some celebrity psychics even bugged their intermission halls or sent out assistants to eavesdrop on audience members at performances.

That's what Charlie intended to do, a hot reading.

With Posey's help, they went through Travis's pockets. They figured out the password on his computer and scrolled through his browser history, his emails, his Facebook messages. They located his stash of porn, which was *gross,* but contained nothing weird enough to sink him. It turned out that he wasn't flirting with anyone else or embezzling money. Travis was evil, and also boring.

Though Charlie didn't do great in school and had been long ago sorted into the group of kids who were never going to college, she read a lot and she paid attention. She was smart.

But smart kids can still be plenty stupid.

Charlie decided that since she couldn't find anything on Travis, she'd *create* evidence. She made a new Facebook page with his name and picture, then started flirting with women. Soon that became texting on a burner phone. Managing being Travis part of the time and Alonso the rest of the time was exhausting. It was playing pretend on steroids.

But rather than getting tired of it, she found herself frustrated by all the time she had to spend as Charlie Hall, who was still a kid with a lot of math homework. She looked forward to improvisation, when it seemed like all the right words came out of a part of her that she didn't even know was there.

Even though she was able to fake up evidence, she wasn't sure it would be enough to convince her mother. She enlisted Posey to manipulate their environment. To flash lights in rooms on the other side of the apartment, turn on the stove, and leave little things where their mother could find them. To show off Alonso's power. They reinvented the Victorian spiritualism movement from first principles.

Charlie had stumbled into one of the headiest delusions that existed— Alonso told Mom that she was important, special, chosen. He was vague on the details, but the details didn't matter.

It wasn't long before Mom was on the hook. In fact, sometimes it seemed to Charlie that her mother was more interested in Alonso than in her, more excited to spend time with him than with her kid. Sometimes Charlie felt like the most important thing about her was being a vessel.

After a bad night where Travis yelled at Charlie to clean up her room and, when she didn't do it to his satisfaction, ripped her copy of *Howl's Moving Castle* in half, she decided it was time. Three days later, Alonso told Mom to look in the glove compartment of Travis's car, where Posey had already planted the burner phone.

After that, things started moving very fast.

Mom looked through the messages on the phone and saw the promises "Travis" had made to these women and the awful stuff he'd told them about her. Travis denied it all, becoming more and more furious when he wasn't believed.

Sucks to be you, Charlie thought with satisfaction, remembering how many times her mother had believed him instead of them.

Charlie was glad when they moved out, gladder still when her mother filed for divorce, thrilled to be moving into their small new apartment, even if money was tighter than ever. But Charlie was a little afraid of what she had done. It was a heavy weight to know that she had committed a betrayal so big that if her mother found out, Charlie might never be forgiven.

And she was in no way ready for her mother to introduce Alonso to her friends. Charlie refused to go. She cried and insisted that she didn't want to, that she didn't like letting him talk through her anymore.

She was teetering on the cusp of adulthood. Three-quarters child, one-quarter yearning. Her dreams were confused kaleidoscopes of swanning through the sets of TV shows, drinking cocktails that looked like vodka martinis and tasted like Sprite, wearing lipstick and pumps covered in red craft glitter, and marrying someone who was half pop star and half stuffed animal.

She knew she had to stop pretending to be Alonso before she got caught, but she didn't know how to stop without disappointing her mother.

Just let him come through. This will be the last time. I promise, honey.

Her mother convinced her to talk to the friends once, and then a second time. By the third visit, Charlie could tell that some of them had grown skeptical. Rand, a portly man with a beautifully waxed mustache, tried to trip her up with historical questions, and Charlie panicked. She talked too much. On the car ride back, she could feel her mother's gaze on her, disheartened and on the verge of disillusionment. Charlie's whole body felt as heavy as lead.

The third time, she didn't protest going, although her mother seemed conflicted. Still, Charlie had looked up historical facts, and between those and Alonso's probable ignorance about things like antibiotics and gravity, she thought she could push through one more time.

More important, Charlie had remembered what worked on her mother. Charlie didn't need to convince them of anything.

She needed to make them *want* to believe.

And so instead of answering their questions, she spun a jagged-edged fantasy. She knew all her mother's friends well enough to guess who hoped her sculptures would be featured in a magazine, who wanted love, who wanted her children to move closer.

Alonso told them what they wanted to hear, with a kick in the ass.

You have already met the man you are destined to be with and you know who he is and why you're not together.

Your children will be at their happiest near a lake, but they will resist this knowledge.

Your work will be celebrated after your death.

And then Alonso told them he had fulfilled his purpose, and that he would finally be allowed to move on. After solemn and tearful goodbyes, Charlie let her whole body go limp. She fell to the floor and pretended unconsciousness for a full minute—until she worried they were going to call an ambulance.

Even her mother's most skeptical friend plied her with cookies and herbal tea after that.

She never had another "visitation."

Sometimes her mom looked at her strangely, but Charlie tried not to notice. And Posey, jealous of the attention Charlie had gotten, started reading tarot cards and cultivating a thousand-yard stare.

While Charlie felt as though she had been left with only the least interesting parts of herself and lost the rest.

4
MORE COFFEE

Bright morning light flooded the kitchen. Lucipurrr was in the sink, paws balanced on a dirty plate, licking the leaky faucet.

Charlie poured coffee, noting the shine of Posey's bloodshot eyes and the restless way her leg moved under the table. She was still in the pajamas she'd been wearing the night before, adding unicorn-shaped slippers, their fur a stained gray.

"Did you stay up all night?" Charlie asked, although the answer was obvious.

"I found a new channel to follow." Posey's tone suggested she expected Charlie to argue with her. On the message boards Posey frequented and in the videos she sought out, dangerous advice was passed around on quickening one's shadow, the first step to becoming a gloamist.

Most of the mainstream articles written about shadow magic were about alterations—clickbait like *Is Magic the New 1%? Hollywood Actress Starts New Shadow Trend. Rip Out Cravings for Junk Food at the Root. Most Useful Shadow Alterations for New Moms. Is Removing Desire the New Lobotomy?* In those stories, gloamists were the providers. The dealers. The grocery stores of magic. The Old Saint Nicks of magic.

Celebrities had their shadows altered more frequently now that the trend had caught on, changing them like other people might change their haircuts, dressing up for the Met Ball with shadows in the shapes of dragons or swans or large hunting cats. They had their emotions triggered to better prepare for roles, or to be able to write more evocative songs.

And if a few people starved to death, or threw themselves off bridges, or had so much of themselves removed that they seemed to float through their days, that was a small price to pay. When shadows withered or burned up or failed to graft, the wealthy could always buy new ones.

But dig a little deeper into the morass of links and articles, past the gloss of general interest, and you got to theories about how people became gloamists. Legitimate sources weighed in with a measured manner. A scientist from the Helmholtz Research Centres was quoted in a now-viral interview in *The New Yorker* as saying "Shadows are like the shades of the dead in Homer, needing blood to quicken them." But it seemed as though every wellness influencer and would-be wizard had a hunch to sell. YouTube and TikTok became crammed with bogus tutorials. *How I Woke My Shadow with Pain, Shadow Quickening After Fistfight, Magic Ability Discovered After Drowning, Safe Asphyxiation Techniques with Plastic Bag—Guaranteed Results*. And in the depths of 8kun, the ideas were much weirder and much worse.

Charlie could remember before, when actual magic had seemed impossible. And then the confusion when no one seemed to be sure what was real and what wasn't. But Posey had gone from a childhood belief in magic into an adulthood where magic was real—just denied to her.

Charlie vividly recalled coming home to a bathtub half filled with melted ice and her sister sitting on the floor, wrapped in a towel, her lips blue with cold. "I should have stayed in longer," Posey had told her, teeth chattering. Charlie begged her not to try anything like that again.

Instead, Posey had gotten a piece of fishing line to tie to a tongue piercing and begin the slow and painful-looking process of splitting her tongue. Apparently once you got used to using the muscles on both sides simultaneously, it trained your brain to a "bifurcated consciousness." The second thing every gloamist needed, after a quickened shadow.

As far as Charlie could tell, all Posey got out of it was a slight lisp.

Charlie yawned and checked the messages on both her phones. On her real phone, there was an invitation to a barbecue from Laura, her closest friend from high school, who these days had three kids and not a lot of time. A plea to bartend at another friend's backyard wedding. Spam from a shop with a sale on onyx charms.

She took out her burner and texted Adam, giving things another try:

Can we meet up? Somewhere private. I don't want us to be spotted together.

This was the tricky bit, getting him to bite. Once he told her where he was, he was screwed.

Then Doreen could go scream at him and drag him home.

If only it could be that easy for Charlie to fix things for Posey. But there was no con or heist, no scam she could think of that would help.

Tomorrow?

With her car out of commission, that was going to be tight. *Sure,* Charlie typed. *I can come over in the morning, before class.*

No mornings.

She ground her teeth in frustration. If she didn't know when he was going to be there, then she'd have to stake out the place. And since she was pretending to be Amber the gloamist, it made no sense for her to even have some other job. Charlie decided to go for vague. *I have a thing until midnight. I can meet you after.*

He sent her a thumbs-up and a winking emoji. When he followed up with the number of his hotel room at the MGM in Springfield, she felt a little guilty, as though she was scheduling a rendezvous.

You're not doing anything wrong, she told herself.

Okay, she was doing *something* wrong, just not what it looked like.

"Have you been paying attention to what I said at all?" Posey demanded.

"Definitely," Charlie lied.

Posey rolled her eyes and kicked the leg of Charlie's chair with a slippered foot. "There's this video where people take ayahuasca and are guided through waking their shadows. Everyone on the message boards are flipping out over it. I know someone with a lake house over by Lake Quinsigamond, and he wants a bunch of us to re-create it—if someone can get the DMT."

Charlie raised her eyebrows. "That's the stuff that makes you vomit all night. And grosser stuff."

Posey shrugged. "Can you get it?"

"DMT?" Charlie said, trying to decide how bad an idea it really was. "I don't know. Ask around Hampshire College. If someone is dealing it locally, they're dealing it there. Or maybe when you start at UMass you can see if someone can synthesize you some in the bio lab."

Charlie's sister had spent the last few years bingeing Reddit threads, watching videos, and chatting with other gloamist hopefuls until dawn. But lately things had gotten worse. Posey had started staying up for days at a stretch and not leaving the house for weeks. Despair seemed to be chasing her heels as her shadow refused to quicken. She'd gone so deep down the rabbit hole that Charlie worried it had become an oubliette.

That was why it was so important for Posey to go to school. At UMass, she could study umbral science with actual professors instead of yutzes from the internet. Maybe she'd even discover some other interest.

The only problem was the number of forms and fees and surprise charges. While Charlie had gotten together most of the money for this last bill, she didn't have it all. But she could get it once Doreen's brother came through and bought them a little more time.

So Charlie fell back on the family tradition of mostly ignoring the situation and occasionally, guiltily, suggesting that her sister try to go to bed earlier. Acting like her problem was insomnia.

Like they didn't both know Posey was drinking buckets of coffee and soda and maybe popping Adderall to stave off exhaustion. At least that would serve her well in undergrad.

Charlie had a sinking feeling that her sister already had an idea about where she was going to get DMT, and that it'd involve boosting something. Most likely, *Charlie* boosting something.

Posey's cell pinged, and as she checked it, Charlie devoted herself to the drinking of her coffee. She was going to need it.

"Mom pulled the Seven of Cups today," Posey muttered, holding up her phone so Charlie could see the photo of their mother holding a tarot card.

The card of a daydreamer, a searcher. Their mother was living in a long-stay motel with a new guy, but there was always a new guy. She liked to have Posey weigh in on her fortunes, since divinations were free for family.

Charlie ignored a familiar stab of guilt, dulled by time but never totally gone. "What are you going to tell her?"

Posey scowled. "What do you care? It's not like you believe I know what I'm talking about." At her tone, Lucipurrr looked up from the sink and hissed.

"That's not fair," Charlie said. "And you're upsetting the cat. She hates it when people fight."

Posey ignored her. "There's a reason they cut shadows off people and sell them. Everyone wants magic. It's not just me."

Charlie glanced automatically toward the bathroom where Vince was showering. She lowered her voice. "I wasn't criticizing you. Stop being so fucking paranoid."

When Charlie was a kid, someone had given her a box of tricks for a birthday. A handkerchief that pulled inside out to change colors. A hat with a false bottom. A stack of marked cards. She'd practiced night after night. But in the end, it was just another kind of fakery. A different way of lying.

Of course, Charlie knew what it was like to want magic.

Posey dragged her laptop over. "Let me show you something."

Charlie took another sip of coffee and started to make a pile of the mail scattered over the table. Catalogs, electric bill, propane bill, cell phone bill, another letter from the hospital marked in red, and three from a collection company. The total crept higher each month, with interest. Plus, she was going to have to resuscitate a 1998 Toyota Corolla, before it got towed. But first, Posey.

"Think about all the things that have been covered up," Charlie's little sister said. "Testing radiation on dead babies, forcing companies to poison the stuff used to make bootleg alcohol during Prohibition. And not just our government, or any government. Companies. Institutions. If there was a way to quicken a shadow, they'd hide it from us."

Posey turned around the screen of her computer to show a video of teenagers sneaking around a hospital. Underneath, the file claimed to be undoctored surveillance footage. The kids' eyes glowed in the green infrared light. It was creepy, seeing them giggling beside sleeping patients, snipping with their fingers like they were playing Rock, Paper, Scissors—and only picking scissors, over and over and over.

"What are they using all those shadows *for*?" Posey asked. "They must have a way to wake them."

Charlie frowned at the screen, unimpressed. She didn't think much of shadow robbers. They were the sloppy stickup artists of the magical crime world. And she figured shadow dealers were selling to people who'd lost their shadows through excessive alteration, or used them for experiments. If someone really knew how to quicken a shadow, it seemed unlikely to Charlie they'd just sit on that information when the world would be full of money ready to rain down on them.

"You ever heard of shadows ripping?" Charlie asked, partially because she wanted to know, and partially to change the subject.

Posey scowled. "What?"

"I saw one—last night—that was—I don't know—it looked like it had been through a shredder or something. And there was a man who . . ."

Posey stared at her so oddly that Charlie let the last sentence trail off. Posey, who believed everything, didn't appear to believe her. Charlie wished there was a way for her to prove the shadow had come from a tattered plastic bag. That the man had been wearing gray gloves. But Charlie knew what she'd seen.

"Someone must have been trying to cut it off," Posey said finally. "They say it's like having your soul cut away from your body to lose a shadow." She dropped her voice to a whisper. "And you know Vince—"

"Oh, come on, stop," Charlie said, cutting her off. "He has a fucking soul."

"There's something wrong with him," Posey said. "He couldn't do that grim shit job of his if there wasn't."

Vince cleaned hotel rooms after something happened involving a lot of blood or a body—a stabbing, a shooting, an overdose. His boss handled dispatch, farming out the work to three freelancers who worked off the books: Winnie, an older woman with grown children who had been a professional clown before she started this. Craig, who said he was doing it for a year to learn what gore looked like before he applied to Tom Savini's school for special effects makeup. And Vince.

"You're one to talk about shit jobs," Charlie said.

Posey ignored her. "He's too quiet. And I think he's been lying about speaking *French*."

Charlie gave a weird snort-laugh, surprised by the ridiculousness of the accusation and the seriousness with which Posey spoke. "He's done what now?"

Posey scowled. "We were watching television and there was an episode where one of the characters said something in French and he grinned before the show explained what any of it meant. It wasn't just *bonjour* or whatever, either; he understood an entire French joke."

"So he took it in high school. So what?"

Posey shook her head. "No one remembers the language they took in high school."

"I've got no idea what bothers you about him," Charlie said, throwing up her hands. "And I don't think you do either."

"I guess he's good-looking, but you *know* there's something missing there. You text other guys behind his back." Posey grabbed Charlie's cell phone off the table. "See? *Oooh, Adam, let's meet somewhere private.*"

"Give me that!" Charlie grabbed it out of her hand.

"Admit it, what you like best about Vince is how much he's willing to put up with."

Before Charlie could explain, Vince's heavy step announced him. His hair was wet, his shirt tight over the thick, muscled part of his upper arms, his gray eyes tinted greenish from the yellow walls.

Posey got up, then pushed past him, laptop tucked under her arm. She wasn't gentle either, shoving her shoulder against his chest.

Vince raised his eyebrows. "She finally heading to bed?" he asked, and went to pour coffee from the pot.

"Hopefully," Charlie said, forcing her gaze away. She wondered how much he'd overheard and if he'd confront her. What he might admit, if rage loosened his tongue. Would he tell her that he wished he was somewhere else, with someone else? That he was just marking time? Would he stop being so careful?

Charlie Hall, imp of the perverse. Appreciated a relationship for being simple and still tempted to see if she could make a complicated mess of it.

Impulsively, she picked up her phone and searched for questions in French. "*Voulez-vous plus de café?*" she asked, stumbling over the pronunciation.

He stared at her in confused alarm, which was understandable since she'd just spouted gibberish. "What?"

Charlie shook her head, feeling ridiculous. "Nothing."

"We better go look at your car," he said, taking a deep swallow from his mug.

She bit her lip. "Okay. Yeah."

V ince drove a white van, rusty parts covered with house paint. It was easily as old as Charlie's car and equally likely to give up the ghost at an inconvenient moment, although it hadn't so far. She swung herself up into the passenger seat. An old Dunkin' foam coffee cup rested in the center console, next to a phone charger with the prepaid phone he always used plugged in and a yellowed paperback entitled *Cry of Evil* with a lady on the cover holding a gun in a sexy but unlikely position. A tree-shaped air freshener hung from the mirror, only adding a layer of lemon oil to the aggressively bleach, vinegar, and Lysol smell of the back.

Vince's gaze was on the road. Charlie studied his profile. His jawline. His hands on the wheel.

"Last night," she said. "I think I saw a dead body."

He glanced at her. "Is that what you and your sister were arguing about?"

"We weren't—" she started, then stopped herself. "Posey just needs someone she can shout at. She's wired from all the caffeine, irritated from not enough sleep. And there was a video of kids breaking into a hospital that bothered her."

Vince didn't look as though he entirely believed her. "Where did you see the body?"

"On my way home."

He glanced at her, frowned. "Walking?"

"I was fine," she said as he pulled into the empty parking lot of the bar. "It was just weird. I never saw anyone dead before."

He must see bodies all the time, at his work. But he didn't try to one-up her by pointing that out.

He didn't tell her that she shouldn't have been out alone or try to make her promise that she wouldn't do it again either. He never told her how to act, or what to wear—which was, for the record, an extremely boring black v-neck t-shirt, black jeans, and checkerboard Vans—and that was good, of course. But there was a part of her that kept wanting to squabble. Like Posey, maybe she needed someone to yell at. Maybe she wanted to be yelled at.

Charlie tried to swallow the impulse.

She turned to sit with the door open, letting her legs dangle out of the van as Vince opened up the hood of her Corolla. He started poking at the insides, then went around to try to turn the car on. It didn't so much as shudder.

"Can you tell what's wrong?"

"Starter, I think," he said, frowning.

It made her twitchy to sit by and watch, even though she knew next to nothing about cars. "You need me to do anything?"

He shook his head. "Not at the moment."

She watched him work, the bend of his body. The sureness of his hands. And the way he seemed to defy the sunlight, casting nothing on the ground.

Charlie had known a local girl who'd sold her shadow. She'd been a pole dancer, over at what locals unkindly referred to as the Whately Ballet. She finished her shift around the same time as Charlie, so they ran into each other sometimes at the few eateries open all night.

"He paid me *five grand*," Linda had confided in a whisper, her expression hard to read. "And it's not like I was using it."

"*Who* paid?" Charlie had asked, taking a bite of very oily fried eggs.

"I'd never seen the guy before. Bought a lap dance, and that's when he made the offer. At first I laughed, but he was serious. Said there was someone who wanted a shadow just like mine."

The diner had been dimly lit and Linda was sitting. From that angle, it hadn't been obvious anything was missing.

"Do you notice that it's gone?" Charlie had asked, frowning at the blurred edges of her own shadow.

Linda had taken a slug of her coffee. "You know when there's a word and you feel like it's on the tip of your tongue? It's like that. There was something inside me that isn't anymore, but I don't know what. I'm not sure I miss it, but I feel like I should."

Every time she thought of the conversation, it made her wonder if it was how Vince felt too. But when she'd asked him about it, he'd told her he couldn't remember what it had been like before. And when she'd asked him if he wanted a new shadow, he said he didn't need one.

Charlie picked up her burner phone and scrolled through the local news, looking for some mention of a body found in Easthampton. Nothing, even though the local crime beat at the paper was so sleepy that shoplifting and drunk students got reported. Who was the dead guy? And had he really stolen a book from Lionel Salt?

That rich bastard's name stood at the top of lists of donors to museums and charities and hot chocolate runs. Kids swapped stories of seeing Salt's car creeping along different roads—a matte black and silver Rolls-Royce Phantom Mansory Conquistador—a car whose name guys in high school had delighted in saying in its entirety so often that it lodged in the head like an earwormed song.

But most people hadn't been inside Salt's horror show of a house or watched him poison someone in the hopes of stealing a quickened shadow. If there were a different set of rules for the rich, Lionel Salt operated without rules at all. Just thinking about him made Charlie nervous.

She turned her mind back to the dead guy. He'd ordered bourbon and paid with a card. Which meant there'd be a receipt in Odette's office with his name on it. If she knew who he was, she'd be able to ask around. Find out more about what he thought he'd been doing.

Her phone buzzed, and it took her a moment to realize it was her burner. Adam. *We haven't talked payment.*

This was why Adam needed Balthazar as a go-between, not just for anonymity, but because Balthazar would have nailed down the cash immediately.

Since she wasn't planning on paying him anyway, she could have promised any amount. But she figured she'd take the opportunity to find out just how much bliss he'd been rolling. *Can we work something out?* she texted.

The reply came quickly. *What kind of connections do you have?*

Charlie frowned. She'd expected him to bring up bliss, not whatever this was about. *I know people,* she wrote.

He took a moment to respond, and when he did it was a long message: *I have something that I need to move Somehting big but I don't want anyone to know it's me making the deal. Act like its you and ill get your thing for free.*

A job like the one she was offering could have gotten him a grand, easy. Twice that, if the client was desperate. What could Adam have that he needed to hide? He was, by all accounts, not a particularly skilled thief. And he had Balthazar to move things for him.

Sure, she wrote. *Who are you making the deal with?*

He typed his message back fast. *All you'll have to do is talk on the hotel phone. I'll tell you what to say.*

Charlie noticed Vince watching her and shoved her phone guiltily into her pocket. "How did you learn about cars?"

"I told you my grandfather was strict, right?" Vince said, his attention returning to the guts of the Corolla. "He taught me lots of stuff. He believed in the improving power of work, no matter how old you were. He didn't believe in excuses. And he had a limo that broke down sometimes."

"So he was a livery driver?" Charlie asked. "He let you ride in the back sometimes?"

He shrugged. "Dropped me off the first day of high school. Everyone stared at me like I was somebody."

She tried to picture him back then. Had he been a gangly kid who ate two lunches and never filled out? The boy who sat in the back of the class and read comics? The track star? Nothing fit.

"You wouldn't have liked me," Charlie told him, bumping the toe of her sneakers against the van door. "I was a weird kid."

Her boobs came in at ten, cresting over the tops of her Walmart bras. Between that and her home life, she'd kept her head down until high school, when she found ways to make herself look scary. Oversized clothes, lots of eyeliner, and hair that hung in her face. Frankenstein boots that she wore until the soles peeled off.

Vince gave her a heavy-lidded look and she wondered if he was going to make a joke.

"I like weird," he said instead, and went back to disconnecting something on the car.

He had no idea.

A few moments later, Odette's shiny purple Mini Cooper pulled into the lot. She got out, a voluminous black caftan billowing around her. The faded facial tattoos on her papery skin and the heavy silver piercings along her lips, cheek, and all the way up her ears made it clear that she'd been a badass while they were still in diapers.

She strode over to them, giving a wave with a gloved hand that had metal claws attached to the tips of the cloth.

"You're a tall drink of water," Odette said, looking Vincent up and down. Her gaze didn't travel to the asphalt, to his missing shadow.

Vince wiped a hand on his pants and stuck it out. "Vince," he said. "You must be Odette. Heard a lot about you."

Charlie wondered what her boss saw when she looked up at him. He had dirty fingernails from working on the car. A lot of dark blond hair covering his face. Gray eyes that looked hollow in the wrong light. Handsome, in that broad-shouldered, hard-jawed way that seems to defy decadence. Handsome enough to annoy her when people looked at him, and then at her, and drew unflattering conclusions.

After a beat, Odette gave him her hand as though she were a queen bestowing it to a knight. "All bad, I hope."

"Awful," he agreed, giving her a lopsided smile.

Odette winked at Charlie. "The quiet ones always do surprise you," she said. Then she headed inside.

Vince was almost done with the repair when a Lexus parked behind Rapture, as far from them as possible. A white-haired man in mirrored sunglasses got out. He had a sport coat on and immaculate boat shoes.

"Is that guy lost?" Vince asked.

"He's probably a client," Charlie told him. Odette still had a few.

"Huh," Vince said.

The man had to pass by them on his way to the main entrance. He kept glancing in their direction nervously.

"Some of the guys have been tied up by her for four decades," Charlie whispered. That was a decade and change longer than she'd been alive.

"Rich," Vince said.

"No doubt," Charlie agreed. "It's funny. None of them are ever what I expect. He looks like a regular businessman, the kind of guy who'd have a winter house in Florida, brag about his grandkids, vote Republican. Have a puppeteer on staff for corporate espionage but be too nervous to look them in the eye."

Vince squinted at the man. "He's wearing a Vacheron Constantin watch. South of France, for the house. He can afford it."

Charlie frowned. "I hope she hits him extra hard."

Vince turned back to the engine, and Charlie watched flies buzz around the lot. As the afternoon stretched late, it came to her that it was odd for Vince to know about a watch so fancy that she'd never even heard of it.

Maybe his grandfather with the limo knew about rich people. Or maybe Vince took stuff people left in hotel rooms. The idea that he might have secrets bothered Charlie, even though she had plenty. But he wasn't supposed to be like her.

"Tell me about some of Odette's other clients," he said. "While I work."

Vince loved gossip, even about people he didn't know. If you met him, silent and six-foot-whatever, you wouldn't think it. But he'd listen, and comment, like the stories mattered. He remembered the details.

Sometimes she wished he wouldn't. It made her worried he was going to see through her patter and figure out the real reason she'd left the game.

Charlie had spent so many years in it. Robbing libraries, museums, antiquarian book fairs. Lied and charmed and conned, picked pockets and locks, and even once trapped a Blight in an onyx binding box. She might not have been magic, but she'd cross-pollinated the magical world like a bee.

Gloamists didn't have spells, per se, but they had notes on techniques and experiments done by glooms through the ages. At first, there was a movement to digitize and share them in a large online free library, until people began to upload hacked versions.

The library was formally dismantled after a copy of the *Cosmometria Gnomonica* was uploaded, detailing a way for gloamists to gain power by pushing past previous limits by feeding an open stream of life energy to their shadow. Thirty gloamists died before it became clear that the critical last part, which explained how to calculate how much was too much and cut off the supply, had been deleted from the PDF version.

Ever since, gloamists guarded what they had and were suspicious of anything they couldn't authenticate. Which led to hiring people like Charlie to get originals.

It was scary work, dealing with people who could rip out a part of her. Once, caught, a gloamist altered Charlie's shadow so that she was so filled with terror that she trembled in her closet for the better part of a week. Not only that, but cons required her to become other people. When she came up for air between jobs, Charlie wouldn't quite know who she was. She'd get another tattoo, as though it could root her in place. She'd get drunk. Maybe she'd find someone to break her heart. Burn through a chunk of cash, squirrel the rest away, and then do it all over again.

It ended when she stole a volume for Vicereine, the head of a local gang of alterationists who called themselves the Artists. A nineteenth-century memoir, not easy to get off the puppeteer in Albany who'd lifted it from some guy in Atlanta. Charlie had taken a month to worm herself into the right position to get her hands on it.

Then, Charlie's boyfriend, a cowardly shitlord named Mark, tried to sell it out from under her. He made a side deal with another gang for far less than the book was worth. Like Posey, he wanted a quickened shadow and was willing to believe that gloamists could help him.

Charlie could have told him that she'd discovered what he was trying to do and dumped his ass. But no, Charlie needed to make her point by circling it in fire.

When he tried to make the exchange, Mark discovered that the book was blank. Charlie had carefully removed the cover and replaced the insides with a college-ruled notebook from Target. For the insult, they cut off Mark's shadow and all the fingers of his right hand.

He'd been a musician.

Charlie tried to tell herself that he deserved it, and that it wasn't her fault. But that didn't stop her from crashing hard into depression and self-loathing.

Back then she was working at Bar Ten, and after her shift, she'd lie in bed until she had to work again, too exhausted to move. Eventually, she lost her job. Started burning through her savings. A couple months later, Mark and his brother shot up her car while it was stopped at a light. Only one bullet hit her, but that was plenty. Two hit the guy in the passenger seat, a hookup, who died immediately.

It haunted her that Posey could have been sitting in his place.

Mark and his brother went straight to prison, where they were rotting to this day.

All of it because Charlie had needed to show off. To exact revenge. Charlie Hall, at her best when doing her worst. Whenever she tried to create something, it broke apart in her hands. But blowing something up? There, Charlie had an unerring instinct for greatness.

No more stealing magic, she told herself as she recovered. No more gloamists. No more cons. No more living her life with the volume turned up to eleven. No more putting the people she loved in danger. She'd lost her nerve.

Not long after the bandages came off, she hooked up with Vince. When she'd noticed him next to her at the bar, her first impulse had been to move as far away as possible. He had a hard jaw, big hands, and angry eyebrows. He was hunched over his drink like he wanted to punch it. She'd had a bad day in a bad month in a worse year and was exhausted by the idea of getting hassled.

But he waved down the bartender when she was being ignored and interposed himself between her and the press of the evening crowd. When he spoke, it was to ask her the sort of questions that didn't demand much.

She liked his deep voice and the strangeness of his eyes, so pale a gray that they seemed barely a color at all. She appreciated that he hadn't hit on her. And he wasn't bad looking. Objectively, he was far hotter than the guys to whom she was usually attracted—pretty, sad, skinny, whippet-faced fast-talkers. Objectively, he looked like he could snap them in half.

Maybe she needed something different. A nicotine patch of a man. Something to draw off her worst impulses, at least for one night.

Outside the bar, he'd traced the tattoo of roses and winged beetles along her throat, his fingers gentle. But when she'd twined her arms around his neck and kissed him, he'd pressed her against the rough bricks with all the fervor she could want, his height and the strength of his arms suddenly a real and previously unknown advantage.

She took him home, and in the morning, he was still there. He made coffee and brought it to her on the mattress, along with toast that was only slightly burnt at the edges. Maybe she loved him a little right then, although she would have never admitted it to herself. He was looking for a place, he said. Did she know anyone with a room to rent?

But Charlie never let herself forget that Vince's life with her was a kind of exile. He kept a picture of himself with another woman, one he never talked about, in his wallet. That first night she'd looked through it and found ten dollars, a driver's license from Minnesota, and the photo, worn thin from the touch of his fingers.

Every now and again she'd pickpocket him again, to check. It was always there.

5

INSIDE OUT

Although they managed to drive the Corolla home—slowly—it made an alarming clunking noise, and Vince thought he needed a part that it was too late to get. He offered to drop her back at Rapture for her shift, but he wasn't likely to be back from his cleaning job in time to pick her up.

Charlie arranged for her friend Barb to give her a lift home, not wanting to be alone on the street again. Barb was a line cook at a vegan restaurant in Northampton that stopped seating at eleven on Fridays; by the time they got the last table turned over, the kitchen clean, and the next day's food prepped, it was close enough to one in the morning for the timing to work out.

Standing outside, huddled in her coat, Charlie watched Balthazar leave with Joey Aspirins. She couldn't help thinking of the nameless murdered man and his tattered shadow. Couldn't help wondering if Balthazar had ratted the guy out to Salt. She hoped not. She wanted to keep on liking Balthazar.

When she was a kid, she'd imagined making Salt pay for what he'd done to her. But the idea of revenge was childish, and it died with her childhood. Charlie was pragmatic. People like her didn't get back at people like Salt.

Still, she couldn't help wondering about the *Liber Noctem,* this book he was apparently desperate to get back. Wondered what it would be like to have something he wanted. To have the power to take something from him.

Then Charlie reminded herself that she didn't want to wind up a corpse in an alley, and definitely not the alley just around the corner from her rental house. If she was going to get murdered, she'd like to do it in Paris. Or Tokyo.

What she did want was her sister in college and her debts paid.

Well, that was what she *wanted* to want.

You can't quit, Balthazar had told her when she informed him she wasn't taking jobs. *You're too good. This is the only thing you're good at.* Sometimes Charlie worried he was right about that second part.

Idly, she took out her phone and tapped out "Liber Noctem" into the search window. An auction notice from Sotheby's came up:

LIBER NOCTEM. Colloquially called *The Book of Blights,* each letter individually stamped into pages comprised of a nickel alloy. Created in 1831 in Scotland by its anonymous author, the book is one of the most significant documents related to the phenomenon of disembodied shadow manifestations. Rumors of an actual Blight being involved in the writing of the book are unconfirmed but add to its historical significance.

Catalogue Note: Sotheby's does not endorse carrying out any of the rituals in this book and will ask the buyer to sign papers indemnifying Sotheby's from any and all related damages.

Bidding begins at 520,000 GBP.

The picture that accompanied it was of a silvery book with elaborate clasps, like an old bible. Not exactly an easy thing to hide.

Could that be what Adam had and was trying to move? What he wanted Amber to take the fall for?

Barb pulled up in her slightly dented electric-blue minivan, startling Charlie out of her thoughts. Barb powered down the window and cracked a huge smile. "Get in, babycakes."

Charlie tossed her bag onto the floor of the passenger side and climbed up after it. Barbara Panganiban was easily her favorite of the people she'd met in the course of getting, and then losing, bartending jobs all over the Valley.

"A bunch of people are at my house tonight," Barb told her, throwing the car into reverse. Her thick black hair was pulled into an olive-colored headscarf and her cook's jacket hung open over a singlet. "I thought about saying something earlier, but I figured it'd be easier to kidnap you."

Several times a month, usually on the weekends, Barb and her girlfriend, Aimee, played host to a rotating crew of restaurant workers and other people with shifts that finished after midnight. Barb would make a giant pot of *pancit* with the recipe her grandmother handed down to her mom back in the Philippines, or defrost *arroz caldo,* and everyone else would either bring something (mostly liquor) or make something (often experimental).

Charlie used to show up regularly, back when she and Barb worked together. But then there'd been a con in Worcester, then the even weirder thing in Albany, and then she'd gotten shot. By the time she'd met Vince, her attendance had grown spotty. Still, Charlie should have thought to check the Slack where the dates were posted. If she had, she wouldn't have been caught by surprise.

"Oh, come on," Barb said. "Aimee misses you."

That seemed unlikely. Aimee was about ten years older than Barb, skinny, and so quiet that even when she spoke, it was in a whisper. Charlie couldn't tell if she secretly enjoyed the extreme extrovert energy of these gatherings, or if Aimee just loved Barb so much that she was willing to put up with her girlfriend's nightmarish idea of fun. Either way, Charlie had never gotten the impression that Aimee had fully committed her to memory.

"If you don't mind me being empty-handed." Maybe it would do her some good to have a night out. If she went home, she'd just think about whether Adam had Salt's book and if she could get it, or argue with Posey about acquiring DMT. "Vince can pick me up when he gets off work."

"Tell him to come in," Barb said. "I want to meet this mystery guy. Do you know how hard it is to find someone in the Valley that a friend hasn't already gotten with?"

Charlie sure did.

Fifteen minutes later they pulled into the crowded driveway of an old farmhouse in the shadow of Mount Tom and backing into the Oxbow part of the Connecticut River. It had been in Aimee's family and come to her after the death of a great-aunt. The place was sprawling, with the last significant updates having been done in the fifties. A finicky mustard-colored electric stove occupied a corner of the kitchen, and a burnt-orange shag rug ran through everywhere else, including the bathrooms.

They entered to music from a Sonos that at least three people were trying to control at the same time. The air smelled like ginger, fried onions, and pizza.

Aimee, in leggings and a tank that showed off tattoos of koi running down both her arms, half hiding behind butt-length brown hair, drifted over to kiss Barb. She whispered to Charlie that the drinks and food were in the dining room, and that they were out of ice.

Charlie thanked her and, deciding that she couldn't follow Barb around like a duckling, wove through the main area toward the booze. She passed Angel and Ian on the rug, playing what appeared to be chess with a mix of snack food for the pieces. Ian had a vape pen hanging on one corner of his mouth as though it were an old-timey cigar. Both of them worked over at Cosmica, a diner-style restaurant that served buffalo-meat burgers and a lot of cocktails. When Ian noticed her, his mouth opened far enough for the vape pen to fall on the board and send a cheese puff rolling into a potato chip.

She and Ian had slept together late one night, when neither of them were making good decisions. She hoped that wasn't going to make the evening awkward.

A guy was sitting on the couch, head buried in his sketchbook. She recognized him as a webcomic artist. He'd been creating a surprisingly explicit and sprawling story of a mouse warrior for years, but it had only recently started gaining a big readership. There was a rumor that he'd begun making serious money.

The long-haired man sitting next to him must have thought he was doing well, since he was trying to convince him to invest in a weed truck, like an ice cream truck but selling edibles and joints and creams. It would drive around neighborhoods and, Long Hair Man insisted, be really good for older people with mobility issues. There was some question from the people sitting nearby about whether this was legal, but the really heated debate was around which celebratory weed song the truck should play.

That led to the subject of rolling bliss, which several of them had done. "I went to this alterationist, Raven, out in Pittsfield," Long Hair Man said. "And she got me so joyed up, I almost walked out in front of a semi. Worth it, though. It was like that feeling you get when you're a kid and summer's just started combined with all the optimism of first love."

In the kitchen, Don argued with his girlfriend, Erin. They were a dramatic couple, prone to tears and shouting about which had been mean to the other first. Don was a bartender at Top Hat, a nice place, one of the first Charlie had been fired from.

She poured four fingers of Old Crow bourbon into a plastic cup and sidled past Don and Erin to get some ice from the freezer before she remembered there wasn't any. She settled for a little cold water to cut the burn. Don bent his head to hide that he was wiping his eyes.

At least it wasn't her crying in the kitchen this time.

"Charlie Hall!" José called. "Long time. You don't like us anymore?"

He was standing in a little knot with Katelynn and Suzie Lambton, who had made that comment to Doreen about Charlie being like the devil.

"Have you heard from *him*?" José demanded as she approached them. He worked at a tiny gay bar called Malebox, where he'd met his ex, the one who'd moved to Los Angeles for a guy and stuck Charlie with double shifts.

Charlie shook her head. "But Odette might have an address to send his last check on file, if you want to send him a haunted object or something. Or there's a service that ships packages filled with glitter to your enemies. They don't call it the herpes of crafting for nothing."

He gave her a wan smile but was clearly sunk in misery. "He's probably basking in the sun, happy, eating avocados off the trees in his backyard, having sex with a hot surfer every night. Meanwhile, I will *never* find love."

"I told you," Katelynn said, "I'll fix you up with my cousin."

"Isn't he the one who ate a dead moth off the bathroom floor?" José raised his eyebrows.

"As a child! You can't hold that against him," Katelynn protested.

"I should just get a gloom to cut my feelings right out of me," José declared dramatically. "Maybe then I'd be happy."

"You can't be happy without feelings," Katelynn said, pedantic to the end.

Charlie appeared to have arrived at the exact point in the night when everyone had drunk too much and become either belligerent or morose. She slung back the Old Crow. She'd better catch up.

"I heard Doreen was looking for you," Suzie said as Katelynn and José continued to argue over whether a mouth tainted by a moth could ever be enjoyably kissed. Suzie had on a billowy-sleeved dress in a yellow pattern and a large, chunky necklace. Her dark hair was pulled up into a tortoiseshell clip. She wore the kind of thrift store finds that cost more than new clothes.

Some of the people at the party might have heard that Charlie had "fixed things" for someone in a jam, or had a vaguely criminal side gig, but were light on the details. They saw what they expected to see: Charlie Hall, perennial fuck-up, who had a hard time holding down a job and was willing to make out when she got really drunk.

Suzie Lambton knew a little more. When she was at Hampshire, a professor had tried to have her tossed out for plagiarizing a paper. Charlie found the way to change his mind.

She shrugged. "Adam's in the wind. She wants me to find him for her. Convince him to go home."

"If I were you, I wouldn't get involved in his mess," Suzie told her. "When people get to a certain age, either they change or they curdle. He's pushing thirty and wants to live like he's twenty. Wants to come into work drunk from the night before, gamble, that kind of shit. I'm going on a yoga retreat next weekend. You should come with me instead."

"Too late," Charlie said, lifting her plastic cup in a salute. "To wise advice and bad decisions."

Suzie, who probably *had* plagiarized her paper, raised her glass.

Vince rolled up a half hour later, with orange juice and ice, having received Charlie's text that the party was low on both.

She went over and hugged him, burying her face in the wool of his coat. It carried the scent of leaves and cold night air. A small smile lifted one corner of his mouth, and she felt a swell of strange, bittersweet longing for someone who was already hers.

Tina, who worked at the *Hampshire Gazette* and drank like a journalist in a movie, was loudly musing about getting her shadow altered to have a cat tail. "Guys love a tail," Tina proclaimed, to protests by nearly everyone. Aimee thought Tina shouldn't consider fetishes along a gender binary. Ian wanted it to be known that he thought it was *disgusting,* and that men did not want to *molest animals.* The artist agreed it was kind of hot, but his comic was about saucy mice.

Charlie told Tina that she had maybe misunderstood what "getting some tail" actually meant.

"Mermaids, right?" Vince asked, in such a clueless just-joined-the-conversation tone that it was hard to know if he was joking, or if he'd misheard the earlier part.

It didn't matter. Everyone laughed. It was funny either way.

As Charlie poured more bourbon—with *ice* this time—she decided she was glad she'd come. She was just buzzed enough to feel an expansive warmth for the people in the room. See, she was fine being a normal person and doing normal-person things. She ate some cheese that Tina made from the milk of her own goats and which no one had the heart to tell her tasted weird, and smiled for absolutely no reason.

Then she heard Ian, speaking loudly enough to drown out the Sonos. "Hey, Vince. What's the worst thing you've ever seen at that job of yours?" His tone made it into a challenge.

Vince looked up from the winged armchair where he sat, caught midconversation with Suzie and José. The chair, Charlie noted, looked as though it had been shredded by a cat, and bits of stuffing showed along the arms.

"None of it's great," Vince said, clearly attempting to deflect the conversation.

"Yeah, but there must be something. An eyeball in the sink. Hair on the ceiling. Come on." Ian grinned in an entirely unfriendly way. *"Entertain us."*

Charlie had been feeling pretty good until that moment. Her current boyfriend wasn't sulking in a corner, or saying something obnoxious, or picking a fight, the way that past ones had. Vince was willing to listen and make the sort of encouraging noises that kept people going—catnip to the self-involved. But no matter how much any of her friends were getting along with Vince, the night was about to go bad anyway.

"Ian," Charlie said, trying to make her voice as stern as Odette wielding a cat-o'-nine-tails in her back office.

He smirked at her, and she was suddenly sure that this wasn't about being unpleasantly curious. It was about some weird feeling Ian had about Charlie.

He wanted to prove something to her, or ruin something for her. "I'm just asking a question. Getting to know the guy. I mean, if you're fuc—"

Vince interrupted him, pushing himself out of the chair. "Once I saw someone turned entirely *inside out.*"

Charlie was used to him hunching a bit, trying not to take up too much space or be too intimidating. Not with his shoulders back, the muscles in his arms tense. His voice sounded as calm as ever, but the hair stood up along her arms. "Bones and organs and fingers and toes. Everything. Like a sock. Inside. Out."

"Really?" Ian asked, impressed.

"No," Vince said, stone-faced.

People nearby laughed. Even Charlie laughed, surprised into it.

"Fine, asshole, I won't ask you about your stupid job," Ian said, moving in close. Getting up in his face, daring to get hit. When Vince didn't react, Ian gave him a shove.

Vince let himself be pushed back, but there was a barely restrained glee in his eyes she had never seen there before. "It's just a lot of picking bits of brain off walls. Nothing much to tell."

For a moment, the two men stared at one another.

A moment later, Ian blanched and ducked his head. "I didn't know you'd be so boring," he muttered.

Vince sat back down with a shrug, as though nothing had happened. As though nothing had been about to happen.

Charlie was heading over to apologize when Suzie Lambton perched herself on the arm of Vince's chair. She touched Vince's shoulder as she said something. Tossed her hair. Laughed. Vince smiled in return, one of his real smiles.

Charlie had a sudden and almost overwhelming urge to knock her to the ground.

She drank a slug of bourbon instead.

"You know, you can't make her catch on fire just by staring like that," Barb said.

Busted, Charlie looked away. "I wasn't—"

Barb laughed. "Go over and tell him he did good. It's not easy to let some little guy insult you."

"I'm sure Vince is fine," Charlie said, scowling a little. "He never gets riled."

What he did get was hit on. Vince, with hair the color of old gold, was a lot of people's type. Charlie had a gaudy kind of beauty. Nothing understated in her curves. No subtlety to her cleavage. Maybe Suzie thought she had a shot.

Suzie was pursuing a master's degree at Smith. Rumor had it that her wealthy parents still paid her rent. Was able to do that yoga move where you stood on your head. Maybe she *did* have a shot.

"Harsh," Barb said. "Abandoning him to the wolves. Well, just one wolf, but you know what I mean."

Charlie shrugged.

"Don't blame me if you wind up in a thruple."

Charlie rolled her eyes, heading for the wraparound porch outside. She needed to get some air. The intensity of her anger at Suzie bothered her. She didn't get jealous. Not like that.

It didn't make sense to long for someone who was already yours.

It's the alcohol, she told herself, as she sat on a porch swing that she hoped wasn't full of spiders.

Most of the nearby houses didn't have lights on, but a scattered few caught her eye. The soft glow of a pink night-light in a child's room. A television, the screen moving between images. A beacon burning over a garage door, waiting for someone to return. This area had all been farms once. Tobacco, probably. You still passed old drying barns on the back roads.

Out past the highway was the Connecticut River, a black snake curling around Mount Tom until it shed its skin and became the Chicopee River, then the Swift River, and finally the Quabbin Reservoir. Charlie remembered walking around there when she was a kid on a field trip at school. They went to see a fish hatchery and then climbed the observation tower. Charlie had stood at the top and looked down into the water, wondering if she could see the drowned buildings beneath the waves.

The Quabbin was a human-made reservoir, created by flooding four towns. And while the residents had relocated, their homes, shops, and halls remained. They were still down there, with whatever had been left inside. Secret, unless you knew where to look, and how.

She thought of shadows moving in the dark, as impossible to spot as drowned towns.

"You ready?" Vince asked, the door closing heavily behind him. She jumped, surprised.

His eyes looked eerie in the porch light. Silver.

"No thruple?" she asked after a moment.

He frowned at her in the same confused way he had when she'd read the French phrase off her phone. She wished she could *make* him tell her what he was thinking. Of course, it was possible he was just thinking that he was tired, annoyed with her friends, and wanted to go home.

Or it was possible that he was thinking there was something seriously wrong with her.

"Never mind." She got up from the swing and dusted off her pants.

Charlie needed to stop looking for trouble where there was none. She needed to stop looking for trouble, period.

A t home, she got ready for bed, washing her face and putting on a t-shirt. She moved to climb over Vince to her side of the mattress when he put his hand on her hip. She paused, straddling his chest.

Outside their window, the moon was a bright silver coin in the black sky, lighting the room well enough to see the intensity of his gaze. He reached up to thread his fingers through her hair.

"Your friends are nice." His mouth curved up on one side. "Mostly."

She wondered if he was going to ask her about Ian. "You were a hit."

"Because I brought ice," he said, clearly not believing her. "Everyone loves the guy who brings ice."

She could have explained how bad the previous guys she'd brought around were, and how great Vince seemed by comparison, but that didn't reflect well on either one of them. "I certainly do," she said, before realizing what that meant. She'd intended to be funny, to imply *I love ice,* not *I love you.*

But he didn't seem alarmed, and after a moment the sharp spike of panic faded. She was just drunk. Drunk people said stupid things.

"Come a little closer," he told her.

As she bent toward him, his thumb went to her cheekbone, brushing lightly over her skin. Her hair fell around them in a canopy.

He levered up to kiss her, mouth careful, as though she was something fragile and precious. Spun sugar. The wing of a butterfly. Someone who wasn't a human callus. Or a rock ready to be thrown through a window. Someone who wasn't Charlie Hall.

Maybe that was how he thought he was *supposed* to kiss girls, the way he'd kissed the girl whose picture was in his wallet. Maybe he wanted to be respectful. But every time he did it, Charlie couldn't help thinking of it as a challenge.

She reached down, hand on his chest, fingers sliding beneath the waistband of his sleep pants. She loved how his breath caught, went uneven. Loved the way that when he kissed her again, his mouth was looser, his tongue dirtier.

Pulling away, she squirmed out of her panties, kicking them to one side of the bed, not bothering to take off her shirt. Then she crawled back, on her hands and knees. He bent over her, covering her body with his. His mouth went to her throat, to her shoulder, his fingers tracing over the part of her breast just above her heart.

When pleasure hit at the base of her spine, she let it carry her past all regrets.

6
MARSHMALLOW TEST

Charlie groaned and rolled over. Coffee was brewing in the other room, the scent of it making her feel incrementally more awake. Outside, someone was using a leaf blower, the sound a steady, grating thrum. Above her, the familiar dried brown rings of a water stain from their leaky ceiling formed Rorschach-like patterns. A gun. A goat. An hourglass. In tea leaves, those would all be warnings. She rubbed her face with the heel of her hand and got up.

Her underpants were somewhere beneath the comforter. She found them and tossed them into the laundry pile, along with the shirt she'd slept in.

Naked, she flopped face-first on the mattress and took out her burner phone. She needed a better plan than the one that was just (1) go to the MGM and disappoint Adam by not being Amber, then (2) get him to go home and disappoint Doreen by being himself.

But . . . if Adam truly had the *Liber Noctem*, Charlie wanted it.

I think I can get to your place by 1:15am, she texted. *Leave a key at the desk and I'll just come up.*

Almost all hotel elevators needed keys to operate, which would mean that if she didn't have one, he'd have to come down to get her. Maybe he'd be willing to make things a little more convenient for both of them.

OK, he texted back.

See you tonight, she wrote.

As soon as she arrived at the hotel, she'd get that key. Then she'd text to say that she'd changed her mind and felt weird about going straight to some guy's room. The casino floor served drinks until four in the morning; she'd suggest they meet there. He might be tired, might get frustrated by her, but she didn't think he'd give up on a job because she asked him to come downstairs first.

Since she'd have his room key, she could just waltz in while he was waiting for her at the casino bar. So long as he didn't keep the book in the wall safe, she could find it, grab it, and go. And even if he *did* keep it in the safe, she had enough information from knowing Doreen—kid's birthday, his birthday, wedding anniversary—to guess the obvious passcodes.

Disguise wouldn't be a big deal. Charlie just wanted to look different enough that she wouldn't be noticed on security cameras, in case he got somebody at the hotel to show him the footage. She had a collection of wigs shoved in the bottom of a dresser drawer, packed in ziplocks, for just this purpose.

She tossed an auburn one into her backpack, along with a tube of distractingly red lipstick, a sparkly yet stretchy dress, and a pair of flats she could run in. Then she changed for work—a black t-shirt, skirt over bike shorts, and her trusty, ugly Crocs.

So long as her Corolla could get her to Springfield and back, she might be able to have something she never thought she would—the satisfaction of taking something away from Lionel Salt. Maybe she'd destroy it and send him the twisted melted metal remains.

After she got the book, she'd dob in Adam to Doreen and let her figure out how to get him home.

Charlie's body was on autopilot as she stirred bitters into old-fashioneds, pulled drafts, and doctored abominable Smirnoff Ices with half shots of Chambord. Up on the stage, a drag trio in sinister yet glittery Elvira-esque attire belted out songs from the nineties. Mixing drinks, she found herself glad of something to do with her hands, some distraction from the churn of her thoughts.

In the hours before a job, adrenaline kicked in. She was alert, focused. As though she only truly came awake when there was a puzzle to solve, a potential triumph outside the grinding pattern of days. Something other than getting up, eating, going to work, eating again, and then having a few hours before bed with which you could work out or do your laundry or have sex or clean the kitchen or watch a movie or get drunk.

That grinding pattern was life, though. You weren't supposed to yearn for something else.

She'd done a couple of credits at the local community college before screwing that up too. *Criminals,* her ancient and slightly doddering professor declared, *have no self-control.* There was a test, where a marshmallow was placed in front of a child. The child was told that if they can wait for the researcher to return, they will be given two marshmallows. The one-marshmallow kids were the ones who were most likely to turn into criminals, who were reckless, who sought pleasure and excitement over all else, stole when they thought they could get away with it, lied when it benefited them. Who chose the temporary thrill over the permanent gain.

Charlie poured three shots of Chartreuse that glowed the bright green of poison. Shook up a dirty martini, dropped extra olives into the cloudy brine of the drink.

Her mind went over all the things that could go wrong, and she thought of the receipts in Odette's office, one of them revealing the name of the dead guy who wanted to fence those pages from the *Liber Noctem*. If he was the one holding the rest of the book, with Adam in charge of moving it, she was screwed. It wouldn't be at the hotel. But if she knew the dead guy's name, she could hit his place next.

Maybe she hadn't changed much after all.

If someone had put a marshmallow in front of her as a child, she would have eaten it straightaway, because adults couldn't be trusted to keep their promises.

At ten, Charlie got a half-hour dinner break. It was her chance to pee and scarf something down before she was back on until one, with just one more fifteen-minute break between. Usually, she went a few blocks over to Daikaiju for ramen, but tonight she walked to the convenience store on the corner and got microwavable mac 'n' cheese, a container of sad-looking grapes, and a coconut water.

She drank the coconut water on the way back, tossing the container in the garbage before she passed through the large black double doors of Rapture. She headed straight to the break room. Although technically part of the backstage, it had a microwave and a place to sit.

Since the performers were on stage, there was no one to object to her being there. She made her way to a satiny pink sofa that looked only slightly moth-eaten. Makeup cluttered a long mirrored counter. Shimmery stage outfits hung on a garment rack that bowed in the middle as though about to collapse beneath their weight. A hook on the wall held a few abandoned garments, including a deep red satin pantsuit that Charlie coveted, waiting for their owners to come and retrieve them. A small side table next to the sofa held a dirty cream landline phone.

The main area of Rapture, including the bar and the stage, wasn't all that large. You could get perhaps a hundred people in, packed tightly together—although if you counted Balthazar's basement shadow parlor, you could probably cram in thirty more. Only one hall ran into the back, leading to the dressing room where

Charlie's mac 'n' cheese spun on the glass microwave plate. Directly across from it was the large metal door that led to Odette's office.

Just one quick peek at the receipt, she told herself. His name wasn't a secret. Charlie had run his card through the machine. She'd given him the paper to sign and the pen to sign with. If she'd been paying more attention, she'd already know.

Crossing the hall, Charlie knocked. When no one answered, she let herself inside.

Wallpaper with a pattern of gleaming golden knives covered the room. A powder-coated neon purple steel desk rested in the center, a brass lamp glowing atop it. An art deco–style bookshelf ran along the back wall, piled with stacks of papers. Beside it was a second steel door. This one was ajar, revealing Odette's dungeon.

From where Charlie was standing, it appeared to be small and well organized, with a dog cage in one corner and a Saint Andrew's cross dominating the rest of the space.

Charlie liked Odette. She liked working at Rapture. Odette let her order in dry ice, infuse vodka with Meyer lemons or ginger or peppercorns in big glass vats they kept in a cool spot beneath the stage. Charlie got paid and got decent tips, and if someone gave her a hard time, they got removed.

It was stupid to risk a good job for something that couldn't really matter. Even if she found the book, so what? So she'd take something away from Salt—but it would be nothing like what he took from her.

But even as she thought that, her fingers were digging through the receipts on Odette's desk. Charlie Hall, failing the marshmallow test. No impulse control. Curious as a cat on crack.

And there it was, Four Roses, $4.25. He'd added a fifty-cent tip, which sucked, but whatever, speak no ill of the dead. *Paul Ecco.* Charlie stuffed the receipts back into the neon purple envelope and zipped it up, repeating his name in her head. She grabbed a pen and was about to retreat back to the break room to write it on her hand when Odette came in. She startled to see Charlie.

Fuck, Charlie thought. *Fuck. Fuck. Fuck.*

"Charlotte?" Odette asked, stern as a schoolmistress. This must be the exact tone of voice she used before she slapped the shit out of someone and then charged them for it.

"Sorry," Charlie said, holding up what was in her hand. "I was looking for a pen."

"These are *my* pens, my dear." Odette looked no less irritated but seemed to believe Charlie's crime was exactly what she'd said it was.

"Sorry," Charlie mumbled again.

"And I'd prefer you didn't come back here without my explicit permission. We're decadent here at Rapture, and informal, but that doesn't mean there are no rules."

"Of course." Charlie nodded.

"*Good,*" Odette said, in a way that made it clear Charlie was dismissed.

She slunk from the room, entirely aware of how lucky she'd been.

As she ate her sad food in the greenroom, slathered in hot sauce from a packet, she googled "Paul Ecco" on her phone. No obituary, nothing in the local news. She added "book" to the search and was surprised to find that the third hit listed him as a "rare and antiquarian book dealer" at a place called Curiosity Books. The website boasted a large online inventory and some kind of physical store in one of the Easthampton mill buildings that saw customers "by appointment only." It featured some first editions, mostly science fiction and comics, and a whole section devoted to antique magic tomes.

Rare book dealers occupied an interesting position in the ecosystem of gloaming. They were the ones willing to comb through out-of-the-way used bookstores, going through piles of old musty boxes, looking for the one hidden gem. They might discover volumes that no one else even knew existed. Or they could be fences for thieves looking for the highest bidder.

Of course, it was possible that Paul Ecco was both a rare book dealer *and* a thief, but it seemed more likely that he'd been who Adam cut a deal with, to move the *Liber Noctem*. After Ecco's death, Adam would need someone else, which would have been why he'd sounded out Charlie.

If that was true, Adam had probably hung on to the book, which was good news. But why was Ecco bringing around a few pages if he'd had access to the whole thing? Had he been playing Balthazar?

Maybe she better plan to hit his place after all. Which meant finding out if anyone was home.

The old corded phone had a dial tone when Charlie brought it to her ear. She punched in the number of the bookshop. Two rings and someone answered.

"Curiosity Books." The voice was gruff, and a little too eager.

"Is Paul there?" Charlie asked, wondering what answer they'd give.

"This is him. You looking for a book?"

"An illustrated edition of *The Witch and the Unlucky Brother,*" Charlie improvised, heart pounding. Unless this was a different Paul Ecco, the person on the other end of the line was posing as a dead man. "We spoke about it yesterday?"

Yesterday, a day after he would have been murdered.

"Ah yeah," the man said. "Some boxes just came in, so I'll have to look through the inventory and get back to you. Why don't you give me your name and number . . . ?"

He paused, waiting for Charlie to supply the rest.

The problem with phones and caller ID was that he very probably had Rapture's number already, so the only thing left to lie about was her name.

"Ms. Damiano," she said, giving him Vince's surname instead of her own. "And you can ask for me at this number."

"I will get back to you *very soon*," he said ominously. "Good evening, Ms. Damiano."

Because that wasn't creepy at all.

She checked her cell. Seven minutes before she had to be behind the bar. Not a lot of time. But there was one other person who knew something worth knowing about Paul Ecco.

Charlie pushed aside the velvet curtain, took that first step onto the onyx top step—mirrored by the onyx lintel over the threshold—and then down the stairs into Balthazar's shadow parlor.

Although weakening the power of shadows for the brief period of passing over the step wasn't particularly useful, the other property of onyx was more so—it made quickened shadows solid. That was what made onyx attached to weapons particularly valuable; it meant that gloamists' shadows could be struck.

The space was low-ceilinged, with the same black, light-sucking walls as the rest of Rapture. A few people sat at tables with their drinks, heads bent in conference. One girl had her eyes shut as the gloom beside her did something to her shadow that looked a lot like stitching. A boy with a skateboard slouched low in a chair, resting his head against the wall, eyes rolling up into his head.

Toward the back was another velvet curtain. Inside, a pair of club chairs—for clients—were arranged opposite a small beat-up wooden desk where Balthazar sat. Joey Aspirins leaned against the far wall, arms folded over his chest.

"You got an appointment?" Joey Aspirins demanded, louder than was necessary.

Balthazar waved airily. "Oh, don't be silly. That's the girl from the bar. What's your name again—Shar? Cher?"

"Very funny," she said.

"Charlie!" He snapped his fingers as though it had been on the very tip of his tongue. "You've reconsidered taking on jobs. I knew you would. Welcome back into my good graces."

Balthazar had wavy black hair and long eyelashes and wore a messy black suit with a messy black tie over a wrinkled shirt. An onyx tiepin was stuck into his lapel. Word was, he used to be an alterationist and had burned up his shadow by using it too hard. He still had the cleaved tongue of a gloom and wore a silver stud at the apex of the split. He came in late, left early, and often forgot to pay the rent to Odette. He was the exact sort of skinny fast-talker that Charlie usually got involved with and then regretted.

Joey Aspirins, by contrast, was small, wiry, and sunken-cheeked in a way that spoke of ill health, maybe addiction, in his past. He wore his gray hair military-short. He had a lot of tattoos, including a few crawling across his throat, combat boots, and a wardrobe that seemed to consist entirely of white t-shirts with short-sleeve button-ups over them. When he looked at Charlie, she knew he didn't expect her to be smart. Well, she didn't think he was some kind of genius either.

Charlie put her hand on her hip. "I'm headed off break. I thought I'd ask if I could get you anything from the bar?"

"Aren't you thoughtful," Balthazar said, skeptical but not about to turn down a drink. "Perhaps that old-fashioned you make with amaro?"

"Orange peel and a cherry?"

"A couple of cherries," he said. "I like a *lot* of sweet with my bitter."

Nice line. With great force of will, Charlie didn't roll her eyes. "And I wanted to ask you something."

"You don't say." Balthazar was the picture of innocence.

She sighed. "There was a man I saw the other night on the street. He had shadows for hands. Do you know him?"

"You've met the new Hierophant," he said.

The Hierophant. The magician in a tarot deck and a position among the gloamists. Locally, shadow magicians came together to choose representatives from each discipline to sit in what they—perhaps not incorrectly—called a Cabal.

The representatives were well-known. Vicereine, famous for causing a washed-up actor to win an Oscar with his post-altered-shadow performance and having altered her influencer ex-boyfriend so that his shadow's head looked like a pig. Her gang of Artists had grown over the years to be highly influential, in part because alterations were so lucrative.

Malik was rumored to have puppeted his shadow to steal an extremely large ruby from the British Museum before they installed onyx, while Bellamy of the masks had no reputation so to speak of, which was a reputation in itself for those of the masked discipline.

Then there was Knight Singh. After his murder, they were going to have to find someone else.

The Cabal oversaw whatever adjudication was needed outside of the law among gloamists, and all of them put in a little money to hunt and trap the one thing that no gloamist wanted the daylight world to know too much about: Blights.

Whatever unlucky fucker crossed the Cabal was given the position of Hierophant.

"He didn't look very friendly when I saw him," Charlie said. "But I guess none of them are."

If the Hierophant was in the alley with the body, it was very likely Paul Ecco had been murdered by a Blight.

"That guy who came in the other night trying to get you to sell something for him," Charlie said. "How come you tossed him out?"

"You know why they call this guy Joey Aspirins?" Balthazar cut her off, nodding to his companion.

Charlie shrugged.

Balthazar's easy smile faded and she had a sense of the menace underneath. "Because he makes headaches go away. And you are one. You were good, Charlie. One of the best. Come back to work and we'll talk. Otherwise, get out."

As she went back to the bar and made Balthazar his cocktail, Charlie reminded herself Paul Ecco's murder shouldn't matter to her. His choice of a drink wasn't that interesting and his tip sucked. He was dead, sure, but lots of people died. Probably Adam was the one with the book, anyway.

As she got back from delivering the booze, she was flagged down by a guy wearing a neatly trimmed goatee and locs. He wanted to do the whole absinthe thing, with the water and the sugar cube on fire, and wanted five of his friends to do it too. Then there was a scotch drinker on the other side of the bar who wanted to debate the relative smokiness and saltiness of Speysides.

By the time Rapture was closing, Charlie had pulled her hair into two sweaty pigtails and slung a wet towel across her neck. Balthazar and Joey Aspirins were gone. The performers were sitting together in the corner with Odette, drinking pale purple aviations while Charlie pocketed her tips for the night and counted out the till.

"Is this what you thought you'd be doing with your life?" Odette was asking.

"Oh no, honey," said one. "My mother wanted me to be a doctor."

The three of them laughed as Charlie loaded the dishwasher. One of the barbacks, Sam, swept up broken glass.

That's when the doors opened. A bearded guy in a deep green fisherman's jacket walked in, his shadow in the shape of wings at his back.

"We're closed," Odette called, turning in her chair and making a grand gesture with one hand. "Come back on another night, dear."

The bearded man's gaze went to Odette and her table, then over to Charlie. "Ms. Damiano?" he asked, and for a moment, Charlie didn't understand. Then she did, and felt a flush of horror. This was the man on the other end of the phone, the one who'd pretended to be the late Paul Ecco.

"Charlie Hall," she said, pointing to herself.

This was a lounge, after all. People passed through. Used phones. She told herself there was no way her voice was so distinct that he could be sure she was the one who'd called.

But as he crossed the room, heading toward the bar, she could tell he'd made his decision. And as he walked, his shadow began to grow, feathers lengthening and then rolling toward Charlie like fog.

On the other side of the room, the performers gasped and Odette stood up so quickly that her chair fell over.

Charlie stopped moving.

The dark reached toward her with suddenly knifelike fingers. She threw herself against the shelves, making the bottles behind her shake dangerously.

And then it slid away, as though they'd all imagined it. As though nothing had happened. The man's shadow looked utterly normal, unaltered. No longer even in the shape of wings.

"*Abracadabra,* bitch," he said with a grin, leaning his arm on the scratched wood of the bar top.

7

THE PAST

Charlie hadn't thought there was anyone she could like less than Travis, until Rand came along.

He was one of Mom's crystals-and-tarot friends and had been particularly skeptical when she was channeling Alonso. He hadn't thought much of her, so she was surprised when one day Mom told her that he was waiting for her in the main room of their apartment.

"What does he want?" Charlie had asked.

"He said that he'd been doing a reading and there was something that concerned you. He wanted to tell you himself." Mom was boiling green tea in a regular pot with several pieces of quartz at the bottom, for clarity of thought. "Go on in. I'll join you in a minute."

Rand was sitting on the couch. His mustache looked even longer than it had before, twisted up with wax on both sides into a style he called "imperial" and everyone else called "hipster." He had on a tweed jacket and slacks, only slightly worn at the elbows and knees. It all combined to give him an affable look that fell somewhere between professor, old-timey saloon owner, and Rich Uncle Pennybags from Monopoly.

One of his main gambits was convincing older women that he was special and that they were special through their connection to him. Charlie had no idea that Alonso was stepping on his game.

She also didn't know that Rand was a con artist.

"Sit down," he said, patting the couch beside him.

She chose the chair that was as far as she thought she could go without seeming rude.

He gave her the fake smile that adults give kids—too broad. "Your mother probably told you that I have a message for you."

She just kept looking at him. The only good thing that living with Travis had done for her was free her from wanting to please adults.

He cleared his throat, leaned forward, and kept going. "But it isn't really a message from me, it's a message from *Alonso*."

Charlie opened her mouth to object, before she realized that she couldn't. If she did, she'd be admitting Alonso wasn't real.

"You see," Rand said, looking her right in the eye, like he knew exactly what she was thinking. "He came to me in a dream and revealed that it was important you help me. You believe in Alonso, don't you?"

Later, she would wish that she'd said many things. She wished she'd been clever enough to tell him that since Alonso spoke *through* her, she'd never met him. She wished she'd tearfully told Rand that she *hated* Alonso speaking through her and that he'd taken enough from her already. Basically, she wished she'd already become the con artist he was going to turn her into.

But in that moment, she was too scared. She felt cornered, caught. And so she just nodded.

"Good," he told her. "You're going to come with me to a party this weekend. Tell your mother you want to go."

"I'm not doing any sex stuff," Charlie told him.

Rand looked surprised, then insulted. "That's not—"

"Keeping my clothes on," Charlie said, in case he didn't understand what she meant. Her mother had told her that when guys asked you to keep a secret, it was usually sex stuff.

"All you have to do at the party is tell lies," he assured her nastily. "And you're good at that, aren't you?"

Which was close enough to a threat. When her mother asked Charlie if she wanted to go with Rand, she insisted that she did.

Much later, she would realize that her mother shouldn't have been okay with that. Twelve-year-old girls don't have any business gallivanting around with grown men they don't know particularly well. But her mother worked a lot back then and was so busy that having Charlie out of the house for a few hours on a weekend was a relief.

The party was being held in the Berkshires. Charlie sat silently in the passenger seat of his car, although he tried to talk her around. He let her choose the station on the radio. He took her through the McDonald's drive-through and let her order whatever she wanted, which was fries and a milkshake. He told her a story about her mother that was a little bit funny.

It didn't make her hate him any less, but it did mean she enjoyed the drive more.

Finally, as they drove along a tree-lined road, past mansions set acres and acres apart, she caved and asked him the question she should have asked before she ever got in his car.

"What are you bringing me to this place to do?"

"You're going to sneak upstairs at the party."

Charlie gave him an incredulous look. "You want me to *steal* something? What if they catch me?"

He laughed a little, as though her totally obvious conclusion was totally obviously wrong. "Nothing like that. Nothing *illegal*. You're going to wear a nightgown under your coat. You go upstairs, third room on the left. Don't let anyone see you. I want you to wait until I give you the signal, then stand in front of the window in the nightgown. And before you ask, it's not skimpy or anything like that. Nothing to offend your delicate sensibilities."

He was making it sound easy, but that was a lot. "Why?"

He kept his eyes on the road.

She sucked up the last of the strawberry milkshake through the straw, the sweetness of it mingling with the salt on her lips. Sucked again, to make that sound adults hated. "If you want me to do it, you better say."

Rand glanced at her swiftly, as though he'd just realized how big a role he'd given her. "Think of it as playing pretend. Stand there for a few minutes like you're a pretty princess, then sneak back out and wait for me in the car. You won't have to say anything to anybody."

He must have thought she was seven instead of twelve. "Whatever."

He parked the car near a hedge, got out, and fumbled around in the trunk. When he returned, he had a Walmart bag containing a white cotton nightgown and a blond wig.

"Go on," he said.

"Don't look," she said, and got into the back where she'd have more room.

"I don't intend to," he told her.

"And stand guard so no one else sees."

He made an annoyed sound but stood with his back against the window and his arms folded over his chest.

She scrambled into the nightgown, pulling it on over her clothes and then slithering out of her shirt. She tucked the nightgown into her jeans. The material bunched up weirdly, but it was the only way she was going to be able to fully hide it under her coat. Then she jammed the wig on her head and tried to tuck any stray pieces of her own dark hair up into it.

When she climbed out, he began twisting the end of his mustache back and forth between his thumb and first finger, like a villain in need of someone to tie to some tracks. He frowned at her jeans. "You can't wear those in front of the window."

"Okay," she said. He was clearly getting more nervous the closer to his plan they got.

"And you're not wearing the wig right."

"I don't know how to put it on," she objected. "I don't even have a mirror."

"Just . . ." He paused. "I don't know either. Give it to me."

He tried to adjust it to hide more of her hair, shoving at her hairline until he got so frustrated that he gave up. Charlie had a memory of an elderly neighbor with a wardrobe of wigs and a lot of bobby pins, but she'd bet Rand had never even heard of those, much less thought to bring some.

"It doesn't matter," he muttered, more to himself than to her.

She put back on her own coat. It was a pink puffer with ratty and somewhat matted fake fur around the hood. It had come to her secondhand, via one of her mother's friends with a slightly older daughter. They were always dropping off clothes—all of them a lot cheerier and more colorful than Charlie would have chosen for herself.

Nothing she had on was appropriate for a place like this. She was going to stick out like a sore thumb. She was suddenly filled with the terrible conviction that Rand had no idea what he was doing.

It only got worse as they approached the gates. Stone walls led to wrought iron bars with cutouts of horses on both sides.

He leaned over to the com on one side of the stone pilings, pressed a button, and gave his name. They waited as the wrought iron gates swung open.

"Won't they notice us being on foot? It's weird," she whispered to him, looking down a very long driveway at a gigantic mansion. Three stories, the top floor covered in painted shingles, and stone on the lower section. Ivy crawling around the windows and big white columns flanking the front doors.

"Don't worry so much," he said, and pulled her off the road. "I am considered *eccentric*, which helps me be able to explain anything I do in terms of my *eccentricities*. Do you know what that word means?"

"Yes," she said, annoyed. Hadn't she fooled at least some adults into believing she was a dead warlock? Maybe he should give her some credit.

He pointed across a stretch of sparsely wooded lawn that led toward the side of the giant mansion. "Go that way."

"Go where?" she asked.

He sighed and pressed a phone into her hands. "Go in through the side. Then, I told you—second floor, third door on the left. Go quickly, but don't run. Don't draw attention to yourself and don't get distracted. No matter what happens, this phone is not for you to call me on. This is for me to send you a signal. When it buzzes, you get into position and you *take off your jeans*."

Charlie's heart was racing and her fingers had gone cold with anxiety. "I don't want to go in there alone."

"I'll meet you by the side door. How's that?" He glanced toward the gate. They might be hidden from the front of the house, but if another car came through their little conference would look extremely suspicious.

"I don't think I can do this."

He put his hand on her chin, tilted her face up. "Too bad," he said impatiently. "Mess this up, and I will have a long talk with your mother. You decide which is worse."

She shook off his grip. What he wanted her to do—sneaking into the mansion, playing some trick on the people inside—felt impossible, but losing her mother would be worse. Mom would never forgive Charlie, not just for the deception, or costing her a marriage, or making her act like a fool in front of her friends, but for ruining the magic. Charlie would get sent to her father and his off-the-grid experimental homestead with chickens and a composting toilet that wasn't installed right. And his new wife would never let her stay. "I'll say you're lying."

"You got your sister in on it, didn't you?" Rand smirked. "She's still a little kid. You really think she wouldn't admit everything if your mother pressed her?"

"Posey hates Travis," Charlie said. "More than me, even."

There was something in Rand's face, some calculation that hadn't been there before. Maybe he hadn't guessed *why* she'd played the part of Alonso; maybe he'd thought it was for fun, to mess with people, or even to get something from her mother: *Alonso says you better buy me a brand-new Xbox. The spirits demand it!*

Charlie wasn't sure if she was in more trouble or less.

"Travis was a dick," he said finally.

She gave him a half smile, not a real one, but not nothing either.

And so Charlie walked across the grounds, hands in the pockets of her coat, head down. Above her, the sky was overcast. As she walked, she realized that to be really convincing she should have put on the wig upstairs. But she didn't trust herself to get all her hair into it again. And besides, it was better for *her* to be disguised the whole time. That way if Rand got in trouble later, she wouldn't get in trouble with him.

She put her hood up anyway.

The side of the house where she'd been directed had been taken over by caterers. They had a tent up and a grill going. Whole cookie trays of puffs and shrimp and other things Charlie had never seen before were being prepped and then sent inside, presumably to be put on some fancier plate.

Near the door was a small stone patio where some of the staff, in their black-and-white server outfits, were sitting and smoking. One drank coffee out of a paper cup, their breath and the hot liquid clouding in the air.

Another spoke Spanish in a low voice to a coworker. She didn't understand all the words because she didn't pay enough attention in class, but she thought he was complaining about a guy who was hot but also terrible.

Even though they were distracted, she didn't dare walk right past them. They would take one look at her and know she was in the wrong place. Her sneakers were muddy from the walk, and they were *sneakers*. With glittery laces.

But as much as she couldn't walk past them, she couldn't stay where she was either. They'd notice her lurking around the bushes eventually and then she'd have no chance. Her feeling that Rand had no idea what he was doing returned. Maybe she should take the cell phone and call her mother. If she got Rand in trouble, maybe Mom wouldn't believe anything he said.

"Hey, kid?" His voice startled her. "C'mon. Quick."

She found him holding the door open. She could see distant movement in other rooms, but no one close by. Ducking her head and not looking at anyone else, she hurried into the house.

For a moment, she was so startled by the fanciness of it that all she could do was look around. Polished wood. Cream-and-gold-striped wallpaper. Paintings in heavy antique frames with no glass protecting them.

He steered her toward the staircase.

"Remember the job." His voice was low and intense. "Third door on the left. A little kid's room. Take off everything but the nightgown. When I give you the signal—*not before*—you stand in the window. Behind the filmy curtain, so your face is blurry, okay? Got it? Not before the signal. Stand there for one minute, then put back on the coat and get the hell out of the house. Your job is not to be seen and to leave no trace."

Charlie nodded, feeling clumsy and afraid. She was sure she was going to be caught and then he would tell her mother everything anyway.

"Okay, well, don't just stand there. Go!" He turned his back on her, heading toward the party.

Charlie hurried up the steps.

The air in the upstairs hall was hushed. Crystals hung from sconces, gleaming, spilling rainbows onto the wooden floor.

Her hand turned the knob on the third door and she found herself in a massive room, the whole thing done up in pink with a bed in the shape of Cinderella's carriage at the center. The walls were muraled in vines.

Unlike in the hall, though, there was dust covering the furniture.

As though whoever had once slept in this room had been gone a long time. As though someone didn't want it disturbed.

Charlie took off the coat, placing it gently on the side of the dresser, next to a music box. At the vibration, it gave off a few eerie notes. She toed off her sneakers too, since they were muddy and there was an expanse of pale pink carpet between her and the window. Then her jeans.

In her mind, she challenged an imaginary Rand. *See? You didn't have to tell me to do that.*

When she was done, she crossed the room. But instead of going near the window, she opened the interior doors. The first led to a bathroom painted in pink as well, with a crown gathering cloth above the bathtub. A bar of pink soap rested in a little dish by the sink, but it was dried and cracked.

The second led to an enormous closet, so big that there was a sitting area with a vanity. Photographs of a blond girl were stuck to the frame around the mirror with rainbow tape. *Hailey.* There was her name, on the back of a pink soccer jersey. And there she was, arms around her friends. In another picture, riding an enormous chestnut horse. She looked happy. She looked alive.

But obviously, she wasn't.

Charlie sat down at the vanity. She understood what Rand had brought her here to do.

She imagined what he was going to say to Hailey's bereaved parent: *Look at your daughter in the window. Want to keep talking to her? Well, I'd love to help, but I am going to require a financial contribution. Yerba mate and mustache wax ain't free.*

Inside the drawers she found a comb, a hair tie, and two sparkly barrettes.

Charlie pulled off the wig and used the tie to pull her hair back so that when she put the wig back on properly, strands weren't constantly falling out. Then she took the comb to try to arrange the wig like the girl's hair in the photos.

She stared at someone who was herself and not herself. She felt a little giddy at the thought of sliding into a different life. Of trying on a different self, one that had been loved so completely that her bedroom had become a tomb, missing only its mummy.

Rand still hadn't signaled, so she went through the girl's things until she found the most nondescript t-shirt and a bag big enough for the wig and nightgown. She placed those near the door just as the phone buzzed. When she looked down at it, the screen had one word.

Now!!!!!

Charlie moved to the window, careful to keep the gauzy drape between her and the glass.

She expected to see Rand outside guiding the action, but she couldn't spot him. For a long moment she thought nothing was going to happen, that no one was going to look up. But then a woman did, and she screamed.

It wasn't a scream of horror or fear, but pure agonized grief. Charlie had never heard a sound like it.

She was glad the curtain was between them. She didn't want to have to see the woman's face too clearly.

But when she collapsed, face still upturned, Charlie lifted one hand and pressed her palm against the glass.

Better Hailey's mom believed her daughter could see her, right? Better to give her some resolution. Something.

Then, realizing it had probably been more than a minute, she stepped away from the window and raced across the floor to her things. *Get the hell out,* he'd said. Of course, because if you saw a ghost, the immediate thing to do would be to visit the room where you saw it.

Charlie yanked off the wig. She ripped off the nightgown. For a moment, clad only in her bra, Charlie had the terrible feeling that she was going to get caught like that. Then the inside-out t-shirt was over her head, her coat was back on and zipped, and she was moving toward the stairs.

But before she could go down, she heard the sound of voices coming from that direction. Turning, she moved the other way down the hall. It was a big house; there had to be a bathroom she could hide in.

She found another set of stairs, grander ones, and hurried down them to a marble-floored foyer. It was extremely exposed, and the last place that she ought to be spotted.

Darting through the closest doorway, Charlie found herself in a music room. A patterned carpet in greenish tones covered the floor, running up to a sofa that looked both too stiff and too small to be comfortable. Beside it was a stringed instrument that looked a little like a guitar and an upright piano. She was not too old to have a child's longing to press the keys, even if she had no idea how to actually play. Instead, she contented herself with running a finger over the glossy black lacquer that covered it.

"There you are," Rand hissed, grabbing her by the arm. "What's wrong with you? Please tell me you didn't steal anything. Never mind, don't tell me anything. Just get out of here."

"You're hurting me," Charlie complained, pulling against his grip.

But he held on, squeezing her arm more tightly as he pressed his keys into her hand. "Wait in the car."

"I would have gotten caught if I did what you said," she told him, angry that Rand hadn't realized she'd been *clever*. And angrier at herself for expecting him to be *fair*.

He pushed her toward the front door. "Get gone."

Charlie took a deep breath and walked out. Past the giant white columns. Down the stone steps. She kept her gaze only on the ground in front of her, so if the woman whose child she'd pretended to be was there, she wouldn't notice her and panic.

She passed the valets, feeling conspicuous. There were a few couples heading out. She overheard a man say to his wife, "He's a swindler. Why doesn't she see that?"

Charlie's face felt hot, but she kept going until she came to the gate. There, she waited for a car to pass and darted through. Another thing she'd been able to figure out on her own.

When she made it to the car, she climbed in and slammed the door. She wished she knew how to drive. She would leave him there. Maybe she'd pick him up eventually; maybe not. What could he do, call the cops?

In that moment, she felt very young, and as though she didn't want to have to be this grown-up yet.

When Rand came out to the car, she expected him to be mean, like he'd been inside, but instead he was jubilant.

"You were incredible!" he said as he pulled onto the road with a whoop. "What a rush, right? Seriously, you were a natural. I knew you had it."

"Had what?" Charlie said.

"You're like me. This is what people like us were made for. Born deceivers. Like laughing hyenas, smiles on our faces, prowling the edges of society, looking for the weak and the slow."

And when Charlie didn't say anything in return, he shoved her shoulder. "Oh, don't be like that because I scolded you in there. Tensions were high! You don't have time for the niceties when you're on a job. We're good, right?"

Charlie nodded, pleased to be praised, even by him. It made her feel as though everything was going to be okay. He was going to take her home and this would just be a weird thing that happened one time. She could go back to thinking of him as her mother's friend and avoiding him.

She could convince herself that he was wrong, and that they weren't alike.

An hour and a lot of fiddling with the radio later, they pulled up outside her apartment building.

"Here," he said, handing her a twenty. "You earned it."

"Thanks." Charlie took it and got out of the car. Together they walked up to the second floor.

Charlie's mother was putting together a puzzle with Posey on the dining room table. A box of pizza sat next to them.

"Glad you're back," her mother said. "It was getting late. Did you have a good time?"

Charlie had forgotten where Rand was supposed to have taken her, but she nodded.

"Well, thank him," her mother prompted, with a long-suffering smile directed at Rand. He smiled back, two adults teaching a child responsibility.

Anything for this to be over, Charlie thought. "Thank you," she said to Rand.

"We should do it again sometime," he said. "Give your mother a break."

Charlie went to the pizza box and got a slice, ignoring him.

Mom invited Rand to stay and eat something with them, but to Charlie's relief, he declined.

A week later, she was out in the street, trying to teach herself skateboarding. She'd been falling a lot. Her knee was bleeding when Rand got out of his car.

"I've got another job for us, my little charlatan," he said. "*Charlatan Hall.* I love it."

Charlie shook her head, feeling numb all over.

"No?" He sounded amused. "Oh, come on. I'll pay you better this time. And it's not like you really have a choice."

She stared at him, openmouthed. "You can't say anything. I know what *you* did. I could tell."

"Oh?" He held up his phone, with a picture of a ghost in the window up on the screen. "Before it would have been my word versus yours, but not now. I have proof you're a little con artist."

Charlie looked at the picture and her heart sank. It wasn't entirely clear it was her, but the figure was her height. And her mother would have known she was out with Rand that day.

"But *you* took me there. *You're* the one who lied to those people," Charlie protested.

"Oh, she'd hate me too," Rand said, still smiling. "But why would I care about that? Besides, you had fun. You wouldn't be half as good at it if you didn't."

It would be years before she understood the technique he'd used to draw her in. The quicksand of cons, transitioning from having something small on someone to having them over a barrel. You start with blackmail. A little thing, maybe, so long as a person would put in some effort to make it go away. Maybe they'd be willing to swipe something for you, fudge some numbers, change a grade, take a little cash out of the till, whatever. But that's when they were sunk. Because if they gave in, they were no longer just hiding whatever their initial indiscretion was, but what they'd done to cover it up. And the more they tried to dig themselves out, the deeper they sank.

There is nothing as instructive for learning how to get someone on the ropes as being put there yourself.

8

THE *LIBER NOCTEM*

As the gloamist spoke, Charlie froze, her back pressed against the rear ledge of the bar.

He turned his head toward Odette and the two drag performers. "Get out."

With very little power, glooms could make a puppeted shade pick a penny up off the ground. With more, they could crush your heart by reaching down your throat. Charlie's entire career as a con artist and a thief had been about avoiding facing one directly.

The performers rose and scuttled toward the back exit that led to the dumpsters, past the stage. As Odette followed them, she looked back and mouthed something to Charlie. Unfortunately, she had no idea what Odette was trying to tell her. Hopefully it was that she planned to call the police. Not that Charlie had a high opinion of their bravery in the face of magic, but maybe body cameras might rattle this guy.

"Call me Hermes. What do you got on draft?" He had a little South Boston in his voice. She guessed he was in his thirties, with dark hair and pale skin flushed red in the cheeks from wind. He had the look of a practical guy, not someone interested in magic. Not someone *with* magic.

"I guess you didn't hear the owner say we were closed," Charlie told him firmly. At the moment, his shadow was insubstantial as a moonbeam. She knew it cost them *something* to manipulate it, she just wasn't entirely sure what.

"The owner's gone," he said. "Just us now."

The etheric shape moved toward her again, so large that the whole room seemed to darken. Charlie crossed her arms over her chest.

Hermes slammed his hand down on the bar, making her jump. "Do you know what I could do to you?"

Her adrenaline spiked, making it hard to think, but she reminded herself that he had no idea who she was. Whatever had driven him to confront her, he didn't think he was talking to Charlie Hall, thief of magic. He saw only Charlie Hall, overcurious bartender. And that was how she was going to play this, with the arrogance of ignorance.

"Do to me? I don't know, what can you do with your scaaaary shadow?" she asked. "Hover a little? Look two inches taller if I don't squint? Better sense of smell?"

For a moment, she had the satisfaction of Hermes looking flummoxed. Then he snorted. "You really don't know, do you? You know nothing about nothing."

"That's me, an ignoramus," Charlie told him, proud of how even her voice sounded. "For instance, I have no idea why you're here harassing me."

The man's shade stretched like taffy—toward Charlie and then *through* a slender seam in the wood of the bar, over the sink and spare glasses and plastic containers of grenadine and simple syrup.

In all the time she'd stolen from them, she'd dreaded the thought of being caught by one of their shadows. To find out the limits of gloamist powers in the worst way possible. Ironic, to have avoided it then, only to have it happen now.

She took a step away, but the narrowness of the bar prevented her from escape. She was trapped with mirrored shelves of booze behind her, along with a register and finicky cappuccino machine.

"Paul Ecco," Hermes said, into that silence. "You might be the last person he spoke with on earth. Pretty girl like you, I bet he bragged about how rich he was going to be. Maybe showed you a rare object he was intending on selling. But, you see, that object belonged to Mr. Salt. Tell us how Ecco got it. Tell us and you can go back to your sad little life and pretend you never had a brush with death."

Lionel fucking Salt.

This was a fishing operation. Hermes had no idea Charlie knew anything. But she'd lied on the phone to test him, and that had made her look suspicious. In a year away from the work, she'd gotten sloppy. "All I did was pour the guy a shot."

He has no reason to hurt me, she told herself, although she doubted anyone who worked for Salt would need a reason. The room was quiet, as though she and the man shared a single indrawn breath.

"You know what I feed this thing?" the man demanded, stepping away from her and his shadow. "Blood. Maybe yours."

Hermes's shade *congealed* somehow. For a moment, it seemed as though he was in two places at once, so convincingly did the shadow re-create him. It appeared solid, although the umbilical cord–like connection to the bearded man's feet remained visible but blurry.

A shadow finger reached toward her and Charlie braced. When it brushed her skin, she had the sensation of something cold and a little electric, as though she was being touched by a storm. She stiffened, stumbling back as a wave of fear crested over her—too great and too paralyzing to be her own.

Charlie's heart skittered, the unreality of the moment making her dizzy.

"Okay, get that thing away from me. You win." Charlie's voice shook as she held up her hands in surrender, backing away. She bit the inside of her cheek to steady herself. "You convinced me. I'll pour you a beer, even though we're closed."

The shade didn't move. "You're a real joker, aren't you?" Hermes said.

Reaching onto the mirrored shelf, Charlie took down a pint glass. It was slippery in her fingers, her palms sweating. The shade hung in the air, drifting beside her, as she pulled a draft of their nicest IPA.

Maybe she could try the truth. Well, some of the truth. "I was walking home and I saw him. Paul Ecco, dead. I recognized him from Rapture. It looked bad, what happened to him. And then when it wasn't in the news, I guess I got curious."

"You're lying," he told her. "You knew him. You called looking for him."

"I didn't expect anyone to *answer*," she said. "And then I thought that if I asked for Paul, the person on the other end of the line would tell me what happened. I didn't expect that you would pretend to *be* him."

"I don't believe it." His anger had the edge of desperation to it, as though going back to his boss empty-handed was something to worry about.

"I never met Paul before that night," Charlie insisted, knowing it was futile as she saw Hermes's expression. He didn't *want* her to be unconnected.

She didn't think she could make it to the doors in the back, but she might have to try anyway. She wished for the stupid onyx-handled knife in her purse. Wished for anything.

"Stop trying to play me," he growled at her. His shadow seemed to be flickering at the edges, as though it was made from some dark fire. "You're in this somehow. The next time you open your mouth, you better be very careful what comes out."

He'd already decided what he wanted to hear, and he wasn't willing to listen to anything else. Either she was going to have to make a doomed run for it, or she was going to have to make him believe a good story.

Hermes wanted the *Liber Noctem* for his boss and believed that he had more than just the pages he wanted to sell, pages that she assumed Ecco's murderer had acquired. Charlie could talk about how he'd been asking Balthazar to fence the part he had, but she suspected that he'd already spoken with Balthazar, and that he'd thrown her at least halfway under the bus. After all, Hermes had seemed very certain she was the caller.

Charlie pushed the beer across the bar and made a show of sighing. "When Paul came into Rapture, he wasn't alone," she lied. "There was another man, and I heard him say something about 'a whole book.' Does that help?"

Hermes hadn't mentioned the book directly, so maybe that would convince him. That *could* have happened, if he really was moving the book for Adam.

"Are you sure the thing with him was a *man*?" Hermes asked.

"I think so," she hedged, wondering if there was someone else he was expecting to find involved. Had anyone actually talked to Ecco that night?

"Edmund Carver," Hermes said. "Was that what Paul called him?"

Charlie hesitated. If she said yes, she could tell he'd be pleased. But she had no idea who that person was, and she'd have to supply details that she didn't have. She shook her head again. "I didn't hear a name, and his shadow didn't seem—"

His shade struck Charlie in the face, hard enough to knock her off balance. Her hip hit the sink and her feet went out from under her. She fell to her hands and knees on the tile.

"Don't lie to me," Hermes said.

Charlie was conscious of many things at once—the stickiness of the floor; the overripe stink of spoiled liquor; the pins-and-needles feeling of her slapped cheek; her horror of what was happening; the baseball bat that Odette insisted they keep behind the bar, under the ice maker, just out of her reach.

Time seemed to slow and speed at once as Charlie crawled to the bat.

The bearded man's shade flickered above her, an etheric hand striking the shelf of bottles and sending them down in a rain of shattering glass.

Charlie covered her head automatically. A half-full bottle smacked her shoulder as more bottles smashed around her. Little chips of splintered glass flew up from each crash, lodging on her clothes and stinging her skin. Spilled liquor flowed over her knees in a torrent.

Charlie's fingers closed around the bat and she pushed herself to her feet, shaking with adrenaline and fear and rage.

With no good ideas, she was going to go for the bad one.

They better carve that on her tomb. The Charlie Hall credo.

She swung hard at the shade. The bat passed straight through, as though it were a ghost. The momentum made her stagger forward. She almost fell right on her ass.

Hermes cackled. He had stepped back from the bar, as though he were a spectator in what was happening and not its architect. "You're a real firecracker, aren't you? Last chance. The truth this time. Who gave Ecco the pages from that book?"

The air seemed to thicken around her.

"You wouldn't know the truth if it stuck its tongue up your ass," she told him with the best sneer she could summon up.

This time the shade went right down her throat.

She felt as though she were drowning. As though her lungs were filled with something heavier than air, something she couldn't cough up.

Panicked, she scratched at her throat, choking on shadow, her screams soundless.

Wisps of it blew from her mouth and nose, from behind her eyes. Darkness was crowding in the edges of her vision and she wasn't sure if it was the lack of air or the shadow.

For a moment, she felt as though she were standing outside herself, noting the way the edges of her lips were turning blue. Watching as she gasped, tipping her chin up as though drowning and seeking the top of the wave.

When Charlie opened her eyes, she found herself on the tiles. She could breathe again, although inhaling hurt.

Charlie looked up at the mirrored ball on the ceiling and saw a figure standing behind Hermes, arm pressed to his throat. But from their blurred shape, she couldn't identify the new person. Their arrival must have been what made Hermes call his shadow back.

She began crawling slowly over the glass-covered floor, telling herself that when she made it to the open area of the lounge, she was going to run for the back doors, hit them hard with her shoulder, and not look back.

"You've let your shadow feed for too long tonight." Impossibly, it was Vince's voice she heard. But it had gone all wrong. Soft and menacing. As oblivious to Hermes's squirming as if it were irrelevant. "There's not much of you left. Can you feel the strain, like something spooling out of you?"

The man made a choking sound, twisting his body, trying desperately to break free.

"It doesn't matter now."

Charlie almost couldn't recognize this Vince, standing in the middle of the empty club. Tightening his grip.

Then came a sound like a wet branch breaking.

She caught her breath.

Reflected in a dozen tiny mirrors, the bearded man hung limply in Vince's arms.

9
THE PAST

Charlie took to pickpocketing like it was what her fingers were made to do. At twelve, Rand set her up to study with a retired magician who had learned to lift wallets and watches as part of her act, and every Tuesday and Thursday after school, he would drop her off at Ms. Presto's house. He told Charlie's mom that it was for piano lessons.

Ms. Presto smoked, and her whole house reeked of it. It was a small place, over in Leeds, with barely any backyard. Inside, it was stuffed with antique memorabilia, including an automaton that had once graced a department store but now stood in a corner wearing a top hat, with half its face missing. "The only magicians people have heard of are men, but some of the greats were women," Ms. Presto would say, waving her cigarette around. "And let me tell you something, the best grifters were *always* the females. We know how people think. We've got the nerve. And we don't get caught."

Charlie liked the way Ms. Presto included her in that declaration. *We.* And she especially liked the idea that she might dodge any consequences.

"So the first thing you have to understand is the tap. You tap somewhere on the body of the mark while you make the lift. Maybe you bump into them if you're walking or touch their shoulder if they're sitting in a crowded restaurant. People think the tap is misdirection, but that's not it. The brain can't process the feeling of being touched in two places at once, so it only alerts the mind to the harder hit.

"Tap 'em on the shoulder and they don't feel your hand in their pocket or purse. There's no real finesse. Just grab."

Charlie thought about that. Ms. Presto gave her a cardamom hard candy out of a silver skull on her coffee table. "What if you stick your hand in a purse and there's too much stuff? Or what if it's zippered?"

"Ah, now, that's where misdirection comes in," she said. "Surprise them. Razzle-dazzle them. Or just pick an easier mark. Lots of fish in the sea. And some of them are wearing solid-gold chains."

"What about clasps?" When Ms. Presto had first started talking, it had seemed simple. But the more Charlie thought about it, the harder it seemed. It took her three tries to put a necklace on, much less take one off of someone with one hand, all while razzle-dazzling them.

"Hand on the back of the neck, a little pressure, and clever fingers," said Ms. Presto. "It's all the same. Let's start practicing."

First they hung jackets on the automaton and strapped watches onto the arms of chairs. Then, when Charlie had mastered that, Ms. Presto would walk around her house so that Charlie could pretend to bump into her, or be walking up to her in a crowd.

Finally, they were ready to go out.

One afternoon, Rand drove her to the Holyoke Mall instead of Ms. Presto's house.

"We going shopping?" Charlie asked.

Rand didn't even seem to mind her tone. He grinned like the joke was on her. "Your lesson is here today."

Ms. Presto met her in Macy's, where she was buying a pair of sneakers. "Never hurts to have a bag on you," she told Charlie. Then she smiled. "Or an old woman with you."

They walked out into the main mall.

"Am I going to watch you first?" Charlie asked hopefully.

Ms. Presto shook her head. "No point delaying the inevitable. Let's go toward the Starbucks. There's always a crowd there."

And so Charlie started the first day of on-the-job training. She slid past people in narrow aisles with an "excuse me" and a touch on the arm. It worked in Sephora, and the Apple Store. Easier than she would have thought too, but not particularly precise. She did manage to lift a wallet from a guy, but all the forays into handbags resulted in her getting random things. A key ring. A lipstick. And once, a balled-up tissue.

After five lifts, Ms. Presto bought her a Frappuccino.

"Two things," she said. "Once you got the thing, you put it in your pocket. What did you do after that?"

Charlie shrugged. "Walked away?"

"In the future," Ms. Presto said, eyeing her seriously, "you're going to take out a candy. Or some money. Whatever it is you want people to think you put your hand into your pocket for. Always keep something in there to pull out. Always. Otherwise, you're giving them two things to notice. The lift itself and the hand coming out of the pocket empty."

Even though no one had said anything to Charlie, her palms started to sweat at the thought that she'd made such an obvious mistake.

"Oh, and you don't strike me as much of a hugger," Ms. Presto said.

Charlie shrugged again. No one in her family was a hugger, except her grandmother, who she didn't get to see much. Not even she and Posey hugged.

"Get used to touching people while you talk. Hand on their arm. Hand on their shoulder. Embrace them when you see them, and again when you leave. That way when you *have* to do it, you know how to make it seem natural."

"Okay," Charlie agreed, and took a long sip of her Frappuccino. This was the one piece of advice, no matter how wise, she knew she was not going to follow.

"Good, good." Ms. Presto stood up. "I will wait for you in the Macy's. I need to return those sneakers."

"What am I going to be doing?" Charlie asked, already knowing she was going to hate the answer.

"You're going to find the people you stole from and put their things back." Ms. Presto gave her that rabbit-out-of-the-hat smile of hers and sauntered off, bag in hand, looking a lot heavier than it had at the beginning of their trip.

An hour later, Charlie had returned the keys and the wallet and had given up looking for anyone else. Rand was waiting for her outside Macy's.

"I heard you were good," he said when she got in. "Really good."

"Yeah?" she asked.

He laughed. "Don't let it go to your head, kid." But he took her to the hamburger place where you could eat as many peanuts as you wanted and let her order whatever, so she knew Ms. Presto had given her high marks.

Charlie couldn't help being pleased at the idea that she had a natural talent for pickpocketing, but what she loved best was burglary.

She loved being in spaces that belonged to other people. Walking across their carpets. Trying on their lives the way you could try on their clothes.

And it was easy, mostly. People in big, expensive houses had lots of doors, and most of the time she could find one that was open. Sometimes there was a key under the mat. Failing that, an unlatched window. She'd shimmy inside when there were no cars around. Very few people had alarm systems, and even fewer bothered to turn them on.

When Rand sent her into houses, he was usually looking for something specific. A huge sapphire ring. Antique napkin holders shaped like tiny filigree cobwebs. A signed first edition of *The Maltese Falcon* rumored to go for upward of a hundred grand. He fancied himself one of those heroic criminals in movies, the ones who never lowered themselves to stealing televisions.

But sometimes Charlie would bike across town and break into houses on her own.

When she was little, her dad had worked for a company that installed pools and hot tubs. Sometimes he'd bring her with him on those construction projects and she'd stare at the giant houses with their manicured lawns and their glistening pools, the bright blue of tropical seas in calendars.

Nowadays, when their father saw Posey and Charlie, it was to take them out for ice cream and act as though everything was fine, even though he was married again, his new wife was pregnant, and she clearly didn't want anything to do with two daughters from his first marriage.

And her father wanted his smiling, happy daughters. Wanted roses in their cheeks and for them to giggle and chorus *after a while, crocodile* to his *see you later, alligator,* the way they had when they were little and certain they would always be loved. They had to play along, or he would get stiff and mean. If they were fussy or cranky, he'd ignore them completely.

So when Charlie tried to complain about Travis or tell her father any of her worries or fears, he got annoyed and transferred his attention to her sister. And if Posey chimed in, he took them both straight home.

Their father's affection was entirely conditional, and he made no secret of it.

Those houses he'd brought her to way back when, though? Those were the houses she broke into when she was alone.

Charlie'd look through their refrigerators, making sandwiches out of whatever was there. Tuna and pickle. Kimchi and leftover pork loin. Tofu and Brie. She'd try on the clothes from their closets, lie down in their beds, and sometimes, when she was sure the people who lived there were away on vacations, she'd swim in those crystalline pools her father built, staring up at the clouds.

She'd pretend that those families were her families. That soon someone would call her inside to do her homework, scold her for not wearing sunscreen and dripping on the carpet.

It was in one of those places she watched a television program that had a gloamist on as a guest. She was explaining about shadow magic, with three models to show off her alterations. One had the shadow of a bird. The second shadow had a heart cut out of its chest. And the third wore a crown, the points rising high off the shadowed head.

When the host asked about other uses for magic, the gloom laughed. "Isn't this enough?"

"Why were you hidden from the world for so long?" the man on the television asked.

Charlie, stolen ice cream on her lap, soup spoon in her hand, listened as the woman explained how early gloamists weren't aware of one another. Each one discovered the discipline anew and lost those discoveries with their deaths. A few letters existed as proof that some found one another, and stray telegrams were exchanged in the 1940s. But things didn't truly change until the BBSs of the 1980s. Much of the contemporary practice of gloaming was developed on message boards and locked forums, when finally people all over the world with quickened shadows realized they weren't alone.

Charlie had stared at the model whose shadow had a heart-shaped hole in the chest. She wondered how it felt to be him.

When she left those houses she broke into alone, she didn't take anything at all.

10
FULL-TILT BOOGIE

L ooking at the dead man on the floor of Rapture, Charlie knew she had to do something, but the shock of violence rooted her in place.

Vince—*her* Vince, so even-keeled that he didn't react even when he got shoved—had murdered someone.

And he didn't realize she'd seen him.

If she sank back down to the floor, lying in the wet and the glass, she could pretend she'd been unconscious the whole time. Only when he touched her would she blink up at him like Snow White, the chunk of apple dislodged from her throat. Then he could make up any lie he liked about what had happened and she could nod along. *Oh, that dead guy? He must have slipped on a banana peel.*

Charlie pulled herself to her feet instead, holding on to the bar top. Made herself appear surprised he was there. "Vince? How did you get . . ."

The light turned his features hard-edged and she remembered how she'd found him frightening that first night in the bar, before he'd spoken.

He watched her gaze go from him to the dead man, take in the way Hermes's neck was at the wrong angle. Vince's face seemed horribly washed of expression.

Keep looking surprised, she told herself. *Everything is very surprising.*

"He's gone," Vince said, crossing the floor to her. "You're bleeding."

Funny that he could kill Hermes but wasn't going to call him *dead*. Went for the polite euphemism. *Gone.*

Very, very far gone.

"I'm fine," Charlie insisted, although she wasn't at all sure. Her body hurt from being struck with bottles. She could feel the sharp sting of shallow cuts and there was very probably glass in her bra. Her thoughts were absurd.

Also, there was a corpse in the middle of the floor.

A corpse whose shadow was still moving, squirming and pulling against the connection to the bearded man as if it wanted to be free.

Charlie shuddered, a visceral horror moving through her. "What . . . is that?"

"It'll settle after a couple of minutes," he said after a pause where they both stared at the struggling shadow.

"Is it a *Blight*?"

Charlie didn't understand the details of how energy exchange worked for gloamists, but she understood enough to know that the more of themselves they put into their shadow, the more it could do. A gloamist could let their shadow draw their energy directly, but they could also put pieces of themselves—memories they no longer wanted, desires that shamed them, emotions that stood in their way—into their shadow. Upon a gloamist's death, that could become a Blight. Detached shadows, cut off not just from a human, but from their own humanity. Most were little better than animals, and the gloamists made it their business to hunt them down. Others could think and reason. Charlie had seen very few, and never expected to witness the birth of one.

Vince didn't meet her gaze. "It might be."

Charlie thought of Paul Ecco's shadow, of the way that it had been shredded, as though his shadow had been destroyed separately from whatever killed him. And she considered Vince, who seemed to know a lot more about gloaming than she'd thought.

"Is it *dying*?" she asked, hush-voiced.

He nodded. "Unless it's cut free or it tears free, it'll die."

She remembered breathing the shadow into her lungs. Remembered the blow from its hand. It might be pitiful to watch the thing struggle, but she was glad it couldn't get to her. And glad it would soon be gone.

Vince shook his head. "Is anyone here but you?"

Charlie glanced toward the back room. Odette and the others had gone in the direction of the exit behind the stage, but it was possible that one or more of them had locked themselves in her office instead of leaving. "Maybe."

He nodded. "I've got to move the body into my van. You going to be okay by yourself?"

"I said I was fine." Charlie put both hands on the bar top. She felt a little light-headed, but that was all.

He nodded, like he didn't believe her but didn't have time to argue either.

Charlie went out from behind the bar, slowly and carefully stepping around the glass. Chunks of it were already embedded in the bottoms of her Crocs; it gave them an uneven fall on the floor and caused them to make a harsh sound, like tap shoes.

Glass slippers.

Gingerly, she navigated her way over to a table. There was still a tea candle burning on it, the wax gone liquid and the glass burned dark.

That was when the Blight ripped free and came at Charlie directly.

Onyx was useful in two ways for stopping quickened shadows. It weakened them and forced them to become solid, so that a knife with onyx in it could cut them no matter how translucent they appeared. But Charlie didn't have any onyx, and what hurt shadows the most was the brightest light—fire.

Charlie grabbed the candle, not caring how the hot wax splashed her wrist or the glass scorched her fingers. She swept it down toward the Blight, tossing the flame right at it. The shadow caught, and flared bright as dry brush.

For a moment, she just stared at the broken tea light, the spill of wax. Her burnt fingers.

And Vince stared at her. "Quick thinking," he said.

Charlie sat heavily in a nearby chair. Nodded.

Vince heaved up the body over his shoulder, like it was a dead deer or something. He headed for the double doors of Rapture.

Was he the first person you've killed? The words sat on Charlie's tongue. She swallowed them. His job was cleaning up crime scenes. She'd like to believe that gave him some perspective when it came to handling the dead, a reason to be so calm. But *murdering* someone, that was a whole other thing.

Her ex-boyfriend's brother—the one who eventually shot her—had been in prison for knocking over a liquor store. He'd told her about how after their first kill, people's minds don't work right. They go full-tilt boogie, bubble-brained. That's why, even if they're normally meticulous, even if they planned the whole thing, they start screwing up. They do stuff that doesn't make sense, like calmly letting in the police when their whole bedroom is covered in blood. Or renting a getaway car under their own name.

Vince wasn't acting like that. He'd done this before.

And a history with murder wasn't the only secret he'd been keeping, given the way he'd spoken about that gloamist's shadow. He knew much more about that world than he'd ever let on. As much as she'd been keeping from him, he'd been keeping a lot more from her.

She looked down at the stupid bike shorts she was wearing, at her stretchy dress, soaked with spilled booze. Beads of blood were blooming along her calves where shards of glass struck her, and when she looked at the backs of her hands, she was surprised to find they were bleeding too.

It was hard to fault Vince, though. Whatever his secrets were, she could still count on him. He was currently getting rid of a dead body for her. You couldn't get more dependable than that.

A little laugh escaped her mouth, a weird giggle.

Her gaze fell on the floorboards and her own shadow. She blinked at it twice, waiting for her vision to clear. It seemed to ripple. Had Hermes done something to it?

Puzzled, she leaned down and touched her hand to its shadow on the floor. It met her, as usual. When she pulled back, she left a small smear of blood from the cuts on her fingers behind.

Just then the landline behind the bar began to ring, making her jump.

Charlie staggered back to the bar. "Yes?"

"Darling," said Odette, sounding for all the world like a starlet from the past. "I heard a terrible crash and then everything went quiet."

"Are you still in your office?" Charlie asked, ashamed of the way her voice didn't come out as evenly as she'd intended. "He's gone, but he left a real mess. You shouldn't have stayed."

The line disconnected. A moment later, she heard the turning of tumblers. Odette sauntered back into the room just as Vince came through the double doors.

"Did the police finally come? I called them ages ago." She regarded them and the room, taking in the destruction of her club and the presence of Vincent with a somewhat stunned expression.

"No one here but us." Charlie realized abruptly that she wasn't okay after all. Her hands were shaking. She thought she might have to sit down. She thought she might not make it to a chair before she did.

Odette was talking. "Did you know that man? I tried to get the gun out of the safe in the back, but I couldn't remember the combination."

Charlie knelt down on the floor, forcing herself to take a few deep, even breaths. That was what she did when she was having a panic attack. And she suspected this was going to be a *monster* of a panic attack. "What?"

"*That man.*" Odette frowned at her. "He seemed to think he knew you. And perhaps you should move off the floor. A chair would probably be more comfortable. Cleaner, I'm sure."

"He thought I knew someone else, but I don't. I didn't." Maybe Charlie was the one whose mind had gone full-tilt boogie. "I'm good right here."

Odette sat down on a barstool. She looked at the smashed wall of liquor and gave a long sigh. "I don't understand the world anymore. I think I'm getting old."

Charlie shook her head. "Never."

"Did you see what that man did? With his . . ." Odette looked toward the double doors, the way she'd been looking when the magic rolled toward her. "With Balthazar's shadow parlor, I saw the wondrous part of gloaming, but not the awful side."

"Yeah," Charlie said quietly.

"It was *horrible*." Odette glanced toward Vince, then back at Charlie. "Do you think this has something to do with Balthazar?"

"The man was looking for a guy they tossed out the other night," she said after a moment.

"But why ask you?" Odette said, which was an entirely reasonable point.

Charlie opened her mouth, trying to find some explanation that could make sense when Vince interrupted her. "Is there a first aid kit somewhere? She's bleeding."

"Oh, of course. In my office," Odette said, rising from her barstool.

"Just tell me where—" Charlie began, but Odette cut her off.

"Don't be ridiculous. Stay." She headed into the back again.

Charlie sighed, and deliberately did not look at her shadow, which might or might not be moving. Which might or might not mean something. "I'm *fine*."

"I know." Vince squatted down next to her and ran his hands lightly over her arms, checking for cuts. His fingers were careful. Careful, like how he kissed. Not the rough, blunt pressure against a jaw.

"Vince?" she said.

He took her hand and smiled like any kindly boyfriend, one who didn't believe he'd been overheard talking about magic. Who hoped she didn't know, or wouldn't mind too much about him being a murderer.

Odette returned with the kit, cell phone tucked against her cheek. "You know that if I had called you from a goddamn Fridays you would have sent someone *immediately*." She dumped a lumpy red bag with the caduceus symbol unceremoniously beside Vince. "You think my tax money's no good because there's a whip painted on my sign?"

Vince searched through, took out a length of gauze, and then wetted it with soap and water from the bar sink. "There are a few pieces of glass I want to get out."

"You better go," she whispered to him. "Now." He had a body in his van. It seemed impossible that the police would overlook that piece of evidence.

"Just a second." He wiped off some blood.

He discovered what Charlie thought were probably eyebrow tweezers in the kit. Charlie wondered if there was emergency eyeliner in there too. Knowing Odette, very possibly.

The glass came out easily. At the sight of the shard, the gleaming blue of a

Bombay Sapphire gin bottle, Charlie felt a bit dizzy. Part of her wished she'd taken a shot of something before he started, but the last thing she needed right then was to be slow-witted.

"If the police aren't here in ten minutes, I am going to wake up the mayor," Odette purred into the phone. "Mark my words."

Charlie had no idea if Odette knew the mayor or not; it wasn't impossible.

"I'll see you at home," Vince said. He didn't stop bandaging her leg, his hands steady and sure, as though he'd done this before too, not just the murdering.

Charlie took a breath, let it out. The whole night had felt like one long tumble down a well. And she might still be falling. "Yeah, go. You have to go."

Vince rose, put his hand on her shoulder, and then headed for the door in the back.

"Where's your fella off to?" Odette asked. She was behind the bar, rummaging in the drawers, pulling out extra napkins and themed drink stirrers.

"He wants to avoid the local constabulary." Charlie pushed herself up. "What are you hunting for?"

Odette raised her tattooed eyebrows, but when it was clear that Charlie wasn't going to say anything more about Vince, she relented. "An ancient pack of clove cigarettes. I know I put some in here, maybe five years ago? Ten? I need something. My hands are shaking. Maybe I should take a gummy."

"Maybe," Charlie agreed.

"Would you like one?" Odette asked.

She was tempted but shook her head. She hadn't taken a shot, so there seemed like no point in anything less immediately effective.

Odette got a plastic bottle out of her handbag, opened it, and popped a handful of THC gummies into her mouth. In about a half hour, she was going to be either unconscious or tripping balls.

"You okay not mentioning Vince?" Charlie asked her.

"I could be," Odette said. "But I'd like it if you told me what kind of trouble he's avoiding."

"I don't know," Charlie said, inventing a whole backstory as she spoke. "He said it was from when he was a kid. We've all got stuff. What's in the past doesn't matter now."

"Oh, honey." Odette put her hand on Charlie's arm, giving her a fond squeeze. "The past is the *only* thing that matters."

The police arrived fifteen minutes later, sirens going as though they'd been in a rush the whole time, rather than moseying up fifty-five minutes after being called. Odette let them in. A detective named Juarez took down Charlie's statement that a man had pushed his way in and trashed the place. He saved his eye-roll for when Odette explained that there were no cameras because she believed in the privacy of her patrons. No one said anything about shadows or magic.

Detective Juarez told them he'd write up a report and that a photographer and someone from forensics would come over tomorrow to document the damage. Then he gave Odette his card and said he'd be in touch. Personally, Charlie doubted Odette would ever hear from him again.

11

SOME BRIGHTER STAR

Charlie got into the Corolla and turned it on, letting the warm air from the heater wash over her. Resting on the passenger seat was a bag with the sparkly dress and wig that she'd brought to get in and out of the casino hotel. So much for her easy shot at Adam and the manuscript.

The time on her dash read two thirty. Her burner phone had a cracked case and three angry texts on it, culminating in a disturbing one that warned her if she was playing him, he was going to bash her head in. She tapped out an excuse about a car breaking down, but there was no confirmation of delivery. He'd probably blocked her number.

Meanwhile, Vince was waiting for her at the house.

Charlie put her head down on the steering wheel and took a shuddering breath.

At least her car had started. She drove the few blocks home, taking the long way that avoided passing the alley where she'd seen Paul Ecco's corpse two nights ago.

Vince's van wasn't there when Charlie pulled into the driveway.

Of course it wasn't. He was disposing of the body, and who knew how long that took or what it entailed. Charlie's unhelpful brain supplied images from movies—concrete blocks tied to feet, acid baths, wood chippers.

As she got out of her car, stiff-limbed and shaking, she was reminded of how it had felt to come home from a job. She'd return from some carefully planned and frenetically executed heist to a world which she no longer seemed to belong. Like then, it felt surreal to walk through the same tiny front yard in need of mowing, across the same porch with an unplugged and dirty ghost lantern from Target lying on its side.

As she opened the door, exhaustion settled over her as adrenaline ebbed away.

Posey was standing at the stove, frying chopped meat and onions. She looked over as the screen door banged behind Charlie and gasped. "What happened to you?"

"Someone came into Rapture looking for a guy. The one I told you about, with the shredded shadow. I got knocked around a little."

Posey put her hand on her hip. "A little?"

Charlie made herself shrug. "Could have been worse. What are you making?"

"Spaghetti Bolognese. Who cares? You want to tell me what's really going on?"

She had to say something. And she needed a minute or two to figure out how to jump-start her brain. "After a shower. I'm soaked with liquor; it's disgusting and stinging the hell out of the cuts."

Posey pushed the metal spatula violently through the meat. "Where's Vince? I thought he was going to get you."

"I sent him to pick something up. Band-Aids." A wobbly lie, given the hour, but they had become something of a nocturnal family. Bats, with their night work and their night feasts and their night-mart shopping. By the time he came back empty-handed, Posey would have the pressing matter of magic to worry about.

Posey was clearly restraining herself from another speech about how there was something wrong with Vince in the soul department when Charlie escaped into their bathroom.

Her sister knew about her past as a thief. Charlie had brought a few books home for her, digital copies that were slightly suspect but still interesting, and once, a slim volume of shadow magic notes of a basic sort from the beginning of the industrial age. What Charlie had avoided, though, was telling Posey about the scary stuff. The times she'd almost been caught. The cons that had gone pear-shaped. The ways magic had been used by gloamists against one another, and against people without quickened shadows.

It had been easier to portray her whole career as a lark. A series of adventures. And if Charlie could just get herself together, she was sure she could make this sound just as unserious.

Their small shared bathroom contained a single sink and a tub shower. A dollar-store curtain, waxy with dried soap, hung from plastic hooks around it. Charlie turned the tap as hot as it would go.

As the room began to fill with steam, Charlie carefully removed her clothes.

Even having done her best to dust off her hair and skirt, she found tiny shards of glass visible on her skin. Wadding up the fabric of her bike shorts and wetting it, she tried to blot off the last of the splinters. When she was done, she rolled up all her clothes and shoved them into the small metal trash can, mashing down a bunch of crumpled tissues. She never wanted to wear any of it again.

A powerful shudder rippled over her as the hot water hit her skin. The stink of alcohol wafted up in a cloud. Images of the night washed over her—the rain of bottles, the feeling of lightning crackling over her skin as the shade struck her, Vince reflected in the shining mirrors, holding the bearded man against his chest, the thick dark rolling toward her, the electric flavor of the shadow against her tongue. She thought of the constellation of names—Paul Ecco, the Hierophant, Hermes, Edmund Carver, Lionel Salt. Thought of ragged shadow and white jutting bones.

Charlie forced herself to squirt some Dr. Bronner's peppermint soap into her hands and scrub herself, rinsing her hair twice and rubbing a washcloth over her skin with such vigor that it turned pink and raw. The soap stung. A few of the bandages Vince had applied were already coming off, swirling through the tub water to be caught against the drain.

Vince, who had been hiding plenty. A spike of anger went through her at the thought that he'd been conning *her*, of all people.

She should have noticed. He'd been entirely too free of strings, even for someone who abandoned an old life. No one is a blank slate, a tabula rasa, without enemies or friends. No one meets you and likes you so much right off the bat that they're willing to move in with you and your kooky sister, willing to pay *half* the rent even though they take up a third of the space.

He'd said he wanted his name off the lease because of some bad credit. The same reason why he had a prepaid phone. He worked off the books for his employer. But wasn't it better that way, since he brought his whole paycheck home? All of it had made sense separately, but now it added up to a cold pit in her stomach.

He saved your life.

Whatever secrets he'd kept, she couldn't deny what he'd done. She was glad Hermes was dead and that she was alive.

Had Vince been a gloamist? There were two usual ways to tell. If you shone a light from two different directions at a regular person, their shadow split. But a quickened shadow remained whole. The second way was the split tongue that most glooms had.

Vince's tongue was whole, and there was no way to test if his shadow split now that it was gone. But if he wasn't a gloamist, then who was he? What had he left behind?

Wrapping a towel around herself, she padded out barefoot, dripping on the tiles.

As she was pulling on a robe, headlights splashed across the room and then away. Vince was pulling into the drive. But when she came back to the table, he wasn't there, although the food was, spaghetti steaming on the plate.

She filled a bowl and sat down, spinning her fork in the noodles and red sauce.

"Charlie," Posey said.

"Yeah?" There was something in her sister's voice that made her look up in alarm. Posey's gaze was on the linoleum.

"There's something wrong with your shadow," Posey said in a hushed voice.

Charlie looked down. There was no ripple, but it had acquired a slight delay between her actions and its response. In all other ways, her shadow followed her movements exactly, yet Charlie had the disturbing feeling it was mimicking them.

"Do you know what's going on with it?" Charlie asked, thinking of an article she'd seen. *Ten Ways to Wake Your Shadow*, according to BuzzFeed. Put a bag over your head. Hold your breath underwater. Hit your hand with a hammer. One thing that hadn't come up: being attacked by another shadow.

Posey frowned as though this was the beginning of a particularly unkind joke. And it would be, for Charlie to get what Posey most wanted. No one knew why some shadows quickened while others never would. Trauma seemed to be a component, but not a surefire method. But if Charlie had magic, well, it was hard to think past the idea that her sister would hate her.

"Are you going to tell me what happened?" Posey asked, effectively changing the subject.

Charlie sighed. "The guy made his shadow change shape. It became solid. Knocked things over. Knocked *me* over."

"From one of the gangs?" Posey asked.

Charlie thought of Salt and shook her head. "I think he was working for someone independent."

Her sister looked skeptical. "You take something from him?"

"Not yet." Charlie stood, walking her half-empty plate over to the sink. As she did, she saw that the white van was in the driveway, parked, lights off. No one seemed to be sitting inside. She remembered the splash of headlights. "Did Vince come back?"

Posey shrugged as though nothing could interest her less. "I don't know. Did he?"

"I'm going to go see if he's okay." Charlie stuck her bare feet into a pair of work boots that Vince had abandoned near the door, the soles encrusted with dirt. They were much too big and her feet slid around in them, but she thought she could manage a slow stagger.

"He's fine. Why wouldn't he be?" Posey asked, standing. "I'm going to go check in with some friends. We have a chat tonight."

"You can't tell *anyone* what I told you," Charlie cautioned.

"I don't need to say it happened to my sister," Posey said, exasperated, as though the idea of not telling people was ridiculous.

"*No one*," Charlie insisted.

"Whatever," Posey said, lifting her phone to take a video of Charlie's shadow. At Charlie's expression, she sighed dramatically. "I'm just trying to figure out what's wrong with your shadow."

Charlie had been waiting for Posey to at least float the possibility that it had quickened. That she hadn't was a relief, and if Charlie felt some small measure of disappointment, it was easily ignored.

Charlie headed outside, the slam of the screen cutting off her thoughts on the subject. Her feet sloshed around in Vince's too-large boots as she walked around to the side of the house, and she tightened her robe against the icy breeze.

She found Vince on the back steps, staring up at the stars.

He seemed to have lost his jacket. He had his arms folded over his knees, forehead resting on his wrists, t-shirt pulled tight across his shoulders. The motion-sensing lamp over the back door gave off a faint golden glow, gilding him. Moths circled, sending little shadows over his shadowless body. He must have been sitting there for a while.

When he turned, his face was carefully blank, as though he'd made it that way for her.

Charlie rested her hand on the chilled skin of his arm, and he sucked in his breath.

"You okay?" she asked, and he nodded.

It occurred to her with a sinking heart just how much she liked him. She should have realized at Barb's house, when she'd been so angry with Suzie. Or when she continued to check for the photo in his wallet. Or at any moment before this one, when she'd discovered how little she knew about him.

He tipped his head up. "Do you think that stars have shadows?"

She followed his gaze. They were close enough to Springfield for light pollution to dull the night skies, but galaxies still spangled above them. The moon had marched nearly to the end of her night, ready to stagger to her own bed at dawn.

"I guess if there's some brighter star," she said, thinking of lying on the couch months ago, a deep-voiced man explaining the universe on her television while she tried to convince herself to apply for a new job. "Like the kind that's about to become a black hole. Don't they flare first?"

Vince nodded. "Quasars. They flare as they're dying. I guess that would give any other star nearby a shadow."

She thought about the struggling, squirming thing attached to the bearded man. She thought about just how sideways Vince's night had gone—from attempted good deed to body disposal. Just because he'd lied to her, it didn't mean she wasn't sympathetic to how terrible the last few hours must have been. Even if he'd seemed calm, even if he'd killed before, that didn't mean he was okay. Maybe she wasn't the only person pretending to be fine. Reaching over, she took his hand.

He flinched a little, as though she'd surprised him.

"That guy could have killed me." It was hard for Charlie to judge how long she'd been unconscious, but it had been long enough. "So, if you're feeling guilty, you should stop."

"That's not what I'm feeling," Vince said.

She looked over, trying to read his expression. It bothered her that she couldn't.

"You should come inside," she said. "It's cold and Posey made spaghetti."

He gave her a sideways glance, and she was tempted to push for answers, to tell him she'd heard what he'd said to Hermes back in Rapture. To demand he tell her all his secrets.

You've let your shadow feed for too long tonight. There's not much of you left.

He turned his hollow gray eyes on her. "I'm angry," he said. "I am still so angry."

Surprised, Charlie started to open her mouth and then closed it again.

"Last night, after you fell asleep, I couldn't stop looking at the swell of your cheek. The snarl of your dark hair. The chipped black nail polish on your toes, curled up against whatever dream you were having. The way you pulled loose the bottom sheet with the violence of sleeping. I looked at you and had a feeling so intense that it made me dizzy and a little sick." His gaze was on the silvery grass of the lawn. "It's no good to feel that way."

Charlie's heart hammered. He had never spoken to her like that. She didn't think anyone had spoken to her like that. "Vince?"

"When I saw you tonight—what he'd done, what he was *doing*, I wanted to kill him. I was furious and I haven't stopped being furious. I don't feel guilty. I wish he was alive so I could kill him again."

Astonishment robbed her of breath. Vince didn't get angry. He didn't talk about his feelings. He didn't sit alone in the dark, talking about shadows and stars.

He turned to her. "Pretend I didn't say any of that. If you can, pretend to-night never happened, Charlie."

She smiled a little, trying to regain her equanimity. "Then what are we doing together out in the cold?"

"Whatever you want," he said, and kissed her. A desperate kiss, his mouth bruisingly hard. Nothing like the way he'd kissed her before. Charlie's body reacted, the sharp shock of her desire unexpected. His lips moved along her cheekbone to her throat and she swallowed a moan. Her nails sank into the muscle of his arms.

She wanted him, right then, against the concrete steps. Despite everything that had happened that night. Maybe, horribly, some part of her even wanted him because of it.

Nothing about him was careful as his body bent in a cage over hers. All she had on was a robe, easy to part.

"I need to . . ." he began, hesitating. "You must be . . ."

Hurt. Tired. Uncomfortable.

She kissed him before he could finish the thought.

One of his hands stroked along her rib cage, his finger skimming the edge of the old bullet wound before moving to her thigh. Parting her legs. His desire was raw-edged, vulnerable. As though he'd shown her something true about himself for the first time.

She dug her fingers into his hair. Bit his lip.

Anger confused her body, making her desire burn brighter, making every-thing faster and sharper and hotter. Better. His hunger answered her ferocity. Blotting out the night and the fear and the cold and everything.

As her thoughts spiraled away, her gaze fell on the aluminum siding of the house. She watched as her shadow-self arched her back and rose up off the stairs at an impossible angle. Without Vince's shadow, it was like being in the grips of a demon lover. Possessed. Reaching for someone who wasn't there.

12
THE PAST

Hall Pass, they called her in junior high, as in "Did you get your Hall Pass?" Asked to the boys by one another, snickered about by the girls. There was some glory in it, to be thought of as the girl with all the experience, especially when in fact Charlie had absolutely none. But it was mostly humili- ating, her body drawing boys to her and repulsing them at once. It made group assignments fraught. Push your desks together and Matt Panchak spent most of his time sliding one sneakered foot up your leg, taking your lack of complaint for desire.

Never mind that you'd gone to kindergarten with him.

Never mind that once, during PE, he'd gotten a soccer ball kicked into his stomach so hard that he threw up, and you were the one who walked him to the nurse's office.

No, now you were a pair of legs with boobs on top, with the ability to banish all his insecurities. Venus on the half shell.

In gym class, while she was changing, Doreen Kowalski asked Charlie all kinds of questions about when she'd gotten her period and whether she shaved her underarms and what size bra she wore. At first, she wondered if Doreen wanted to be friends, but once Charlie answered, Doreen rushed back to her knot of buddies, giggling.

They didn't understand how her bra straps cut into her shoulders and un- derwires cut into her ribs, and that the bras that fit looked like ones a matronly nurse would wear in an old war movie. There was no way to make them understand.

Charlie put on darker eyeliner and wore baggier clothes and stompier boots.

Rand didn't seem to know what to do with her either. When he'd recruited her at twelve, she'd already looked older than her age. By the time she was starting high school, her body let her pass for a grown woman.

It didn't help that Charlie got a little too good at all the wrong things. She had a nose for where an unlocked window or door might be when she approached houses. Her pickpocketing was deft enough that Rand didn't let her get close to him. And when she played a role, she disappeared into it.

He liked the idea of passing on his knowledge to a kid with some natural talent, but he didn't want her to be better than him. And he definitely didn't want her as competition.

"You and me, we're the same," he'd remind her again and again, in case she forgot. "We pretend, so that other people will like us. But they wouldn't like us if they knew us, would they? That's why we've got to stick together."

Sometimes after she'd done particularly well on a job, he'd be in a spiteful mood. He'd condescendingly call her "Little Miss Charlatan," go over every mistake she made, and give her less of the take than she deserved.

But if Charlie's growing skill frustrated him, he also clearly enjoyed having someone to whom he could complain, or brag, or rant. The natural consequence of criminality was that he had to be discreet about it, and Rand wasn't a discreet person by nature.

Sometimes he could be fun. He took her with him to the Moose Lodge in Chicopee, where a bunch of old racketeers drank, and let her sit around drinking burnt coffee with lots of cream while they regaled her with stories. She rubbed elbows with fences and forgers. Learned how to count cards from Willie Lead, who told her about Leticia, his late wife and, according to him, the greatest stickup artist ever to knock over a liquor store.

"It was the throat cancer that got her in the end," he said mournfully. "The cops never even came close."

The Moose Lodge was where Charlie got her start as a bartender, at fourteen, pouring shots when no one else wanted to do it, making cocktails according to highly idiosyncratic instructions.

"Just wave the vermouth bottle over the gin," Benny would say. "That's how to make a martini right." His game was angling after rich widows, and he always looked sharp doing it, even if his breath was often perfumed with booze.

Willie would disagree vehemently, shouting that vermouth ought to be a full fourth of the drink, and that Benny was a drunk who'd burned away his good taste, if he'd ever had any in the first place.

"So I'm a drunk!" Benny would shout back. "If you can't trust a drunk about liquor, who can you trust?"

Charlie liked them. She told them about her grandmother and the shotgun, and the detail that her grandfather was sitting in his BarcaLounger when he got executed made them howl with laughter. Willie promised they'd take Charlie up to the North Central Correctional Institute in Gardner to visit the grand dame one day, although they never did.

Hanging around them made Charlie feel like maybe there wasn't anything wrong with her. It didn't matter if she didn't fit in at school, or that her body kept changing on her. It was okay when her best friend's parents took one look at Charlie and clocked her for trouble. When even Laura herself, who'd known her since she was eight, started acting weird. It was fine that she'd given up hoping her mother would notice there was something strange about Rand taking her on trips all the time. All those people who judged her or couldn't be bothered with her were marks. She'd have the last laugh.

"You gotta be like a shark in this business," Benny told her, with his soft voice and his slicked-back hair. "Sniff around for the blood in the water. Greet life teeth first. And no matter what, never stop swimming."

Charlie took that advice and the money from her last job with Rand and got a tattoo. She'd wanted one, and she'd also wanted to know if she could con a shop into giving her the ink, even though she was three years away from eighteen.

It involved some fast talking and swiping a notary sigil, but she got it done. Her first tattoo. It was still a little bit sore when she moved. Along her inner arm was the word "fearless" in looping cursive letters, except the tattooist had spaced them oddly so that it looked as though it said "fear less."

It reminded her of what she wanted to be, and that her body belonged to her. She could write all over it if she wanted.

O ver the years, as gloaming emerged into the general consciousness of the world at large, Rand became increasingly fascinated with it. He'd been pulling cons based around the occult for years—like the one where Charlie had to pretend to be a ghost child. While he'd particularly liked how a little sleight of hand could really impress wealthy old ladies, with real magic, he sensed larger opportunities.

Willie wasn't impressed and let everyone at the Moose Lodge know. "When I was a kid, there was that guy, Uri Geller, who could bend spoons with his mind. Guess what came of that? Nothing. Who needs a bent spoon?"

Benny knew a guy, though. Rand returned from the meeting excited. He told Charlie that this person promised them big money if they'd acquire something for him. "The guy probably doesn't even know how valuable the book he's got is. He's a rich old coot, not a gloamist. We just need the right angle."

"If the guy who's hiring us is a real gloamist and the mark isn't, why doesn't the gloamist steal it himself?" Charlie asked. "Why doesn't he send his shadow to get it?"

"Because of the *onyx*," Rand said, as though that ought to have been obvious. "It makes the shadows solid, so they can't slip through cracks or whatever."

Charlie was skeptical. "If the old coot knows that, he probably knows his book is valuable."

"We can do this," Rand told her. "If we do, he says he's got more work for us. If we're bold, we're going to get rich, I know it."

Charlie rolled her eyes. Rand dreamed of the one big score the way that Charlie's mother dreamed of love. It was the thing that would allow him to live the life of ease to which he thought he was entitled, and of which he was always on the very cusp. Always a mirage, always just over the next dune.

"Our client's name is Knight, but that's all I'm going to tell you," Rand said. "And so long as we bring him his book, he says we're free to bilk Moneybags for anything else we can get."

Charlie didn't like it. They usually worked for themselves. A client could be trouble.

"I've finagled us into a meeting in the house of this guy, Lionel Salt. Family wealth in medical manufacturing. That's where the big money is—making the widgety doodad that fits into a surgical thingamajig. I've informed him that I and my young daughter are occultists who communicate with the unseen world, which includes demons. And those demons are going to help him quicken his shadow." Rand sounded calm, but he kept twisting the end of his mustache.

"Lionel Salt?" she asked. "The guy with the car?" Even then, she'd been aware of his matte black Phantom, discussed in loving detail by half the boys in her class.

"Yeah, him," Rand said dismissively.

Charlie frowned. "This guy is going to think we're ridiculous. Demons?"

But Rand wouldn't be swayed. "Believers want to believe. He wants to quicken his shadow, right? They all do. We can give him hope."

And that was how Charlie found herself in the passenger seat of his car, practicing rolling her eyes up hard enough that only the whites were showing. It wasn't an easy technique to do without closing your eyes first—but it was creepier.

If she'd known how to do this back when she was "channeling" Alonso, she was almost certain her mother would have left Travis after the first visitation. It looked that good.

Charlie was hoping the job would go well enough (or that while she was in the house she could grab something worth enough) to buy a leather coat she had her eye on. She'd seen it at a thrift store for a hundred seventy-five dollars, and while she thought she might be able to convince the owner to give it to her for less, it was still going to be a lot.

"You remember the plan?" Rand asked her for the millionth time on their drive over.

She did. Rand was going to pose as her father and explain that Charlie (who would, of course, be using a different name) had begun speaking to unseen beings a few years back. People wanted to treat her for mental illness, but he realized she had a talent to speak with the supernatural world, including the infernal one. And so he had cultivated her talents.

Rand wanted the man to be a little disgusted with him. People trust that when someone is doing something terrible, the reward must be real.

All Charlie had to do was provide the special effect. She just had to be an intimidated, quiet girl until her eyes rolled up and she vomited beet juice all over everything. Finally, she was going to give them "the gift of the devil."

The rich believed they were lucky, and that any good fortune they didn't already have could be bought. They had so much already, disappointment became inconceivable.

"You should teach me how to drive," she said, looking out at the highway and the lights glittering across the Connecticut River.

Rand snorted. "You're not old enough."

"You mean it's *illegal*?" She shrugged. "Oh no."

He made an annoyed, huffing noise. "I guess I could. I've got time next week. You never know when it might come in handy."

They pulled off the exit, heading from city into suburbs and then stretches of woods beyond, where mansions had been nestled back when Springfield was a production hub.

Charlie bit her nail, looking out the window. Feeling a little sick to her stomach from a combination of beet juice and nerves.

She saw the mansion coming into view as Rand took the turn onto the drive. She'd never seen a place like it. It was like a museum, or a place out of a fairy tale where cursed princesses slept.

"This is a bad idea," she muttered, but Rand ignored her.

He got out and opened the door for her. "Stage fright," he said. "You want a swig of whiskey?"

"I'm fifteen," she reminded him.

"Oh?" he said, mimicking her voice. "Is it illegal?"

The front door opened. A small red-haired man stood there, squinting at them. Charlie realized she had no idea what Lionel Salt looked like.

"Is there anything I can help you bring inside, sir?" he asked, making it clear he was a butler or something.

"We don't have *props*," Rand told him, as though the very idea offended.

Charlie had her game face on, and so didn't roll her eyes.

Inside, several old men were sitting around on green leather chairs in a large library. The real Lionel Salt was an old man with a shock of white hair. A silver-tipped cane rested beside him. One of his friends appeared to be close in age, while the other was maybe twenty years younger. Rand introduced himself to them all, and then indicated Charlie, as though she were some kind of trained lemur instead of a person. She tried to surreptitiously read off the titles of the books.

The one they were supposed to get had a red spine and was titled *The Book of Amor Pettit*. But from a glance at the shelves, she didn't see it. She did spot an interesting section that had a few books with "Grimoire" in the title. That seemed promising.

The plan was supposed to go like this: Rand set things up. Charlie gave her performance. If the book was in the room, Rand took it. If it wasn't, he used her to distract them and made some excuse to search the other rooms on the first level. The person who'd hired him had assured them that he'd seen it there.

Charlie acted her part. Shy. Reserved. When she got possessed, she planned to really let go.

They were invited to sit down. The red-haired man took drink orders. Rand talked over several different magical theories, a glass of whiskey in his hand, while Charlie sipped her water.

"Have you heard the saying 'no man can jump over his own shadow'?" Salt asked.

Rand had not.

"It's a German saying. It means everyone has their limits."

"But you don't believe that," Rand said.

"No," said Lionel. "I've always believed there was a secret to the universe. A path by which man can acquire godhood. And that path is through shadows. You claim you can wake mine."

Sensing this was the moment, Rand stood. "Shall we begin, then?"

"Ah, yes, indeed," said one of the other men. He smiled in a way that Charlie didn't like.

"As you gentlemen are aware," Rand began, "the world is full of nearly limit-less strangeness for the seeker. We are not just believers. We are not the *faithful*, taking the work for granted. We are adventurers, explorers of the darkness. And so, you will understand when I tell you how surprised I was to realize the talents of my own child. She can make herself an empty vessel and allow in all manner of beings of great wisdom and power to speak through her."

Two of the men exchanged a glance.

Charlie bit the inside of her cheek. There was an undercurrent to the conversation that gnawed at her instincts. She wished she could find some way to catch Rand's eye, but the whiskey and conversation seemed to have gone to his head.

"That's fascinating," said one of them, in a bored tone that belied his words. "What sort of thing does she usually reveal? The location of buried treasure? Stock trades?"

A few of them laughed. Rand frowned, finally noticing that he'd lost them. But he didn't seem alarmed, didn't seem to sense the same danger that Charlie felt. "I can never tell what will come through, but I assure you it will be to a higher purpose. If you seek a quickened shadow, then we will guide it toward revealing that. But perhaps I am mistaken in you. Perhaps you are mere dabblers after all."

"Bring forth a devil," said one. "How about that? I want to talk to a being from hell."

"Are you certain?" Rand asked.

The others went quiet, smiling at one another.

Charlie's gaze went to a corner of the room where a shadow lengthened across the carpet. She hadn't noticed it before, but now that she had, she couldn't seem to look away. There was nothing that could be casting it.

"My dear Lexi," Rand said. "Are you ready?"

Charlie dragged her gaze back to him and took a breath. "I don't like doing this." It was the truth, but it was also part of her role.

"I know, my dear," Rand said, patting the top of her head. Then he stopped and frowned, as though he'd lost his place in the speech.

Her palms were starting to sweat. Nerves, she thought.

"I—" he started. His face was flushed. "You—"

No, not nerves. Something was wrong. Her stomach hurt.

One of the men turned to Salt with a smirk. "It worked faster than I thought. I was so hoping to see their performance."

"Very naughty to try to trick me," said Salt, smiling as he shook his finger in her direction. Then he turned back to his friends.

The drinks. There'd been something in her water. Something in Rand's whiskey.

Charlie covered her mouth, dipping her head the way she had planned during her possession, and thrust her finger into the back of her mouth, pressing against her hard palate. Gagging once, she pushed herself out of the chair and made her body quake just as she would have done if she were pretending to be possessed. Then she vomited beet juice all over their expensive rug.

She heard shouts as the men jumped back, but she slumped forward, keeping her eyes closed and her body still. Didn't allow herself to move, despite her cheek being pressed into her own sick.

"Is she dying?" one of them asked.

"You gave her too much." Another man's voice. Faint distaste.

She heard the creak of hinges from the direction of the bookshelves. The scent of moldering paper. The spinning of a safe's dial. A confusion of men's voices.

Don't worry about her. Get the man.

There's an experiment I want to try. Let's see how his shadow reacts to exsanguination.

If the girl dies, we can still harvest hers.

And then her thoughts spiraled away to nothing.

C harlie came to lying on the rug. The fabric beneath her was still damp with bile and beet juice. Not much time could have passed.

"Someone's coming. Don't move." A voice from behind her, a boy's voice. She wondered if he was actually there, or if he was the echo of a dream she'd been having before she woke.

She fought down the temptation to turn around. After a moment, she heard footsteps in the hall, the tapping of hard soles on the stone floor. Trying to slow her breathing, Charlie remained still until they passed.

After they faded away, she scrambled to push herself up. Her head swam. Whatever she'd been dosed with, it wasn't out of her system yet.

"Don't look behind you," the voice said.

She stopped.

"If you don't look at me, I'll guide you out of this house."

"And if I do?" she whispered.

"Then you're on your own. They believe that you're lying in a pool of your own blood, so they're not concerned about you at the moment," he said. "You might make it."

"What about the guy I came in with? Can I get to him?"

There was a long pause. "He's beyond helping."

The meaning of that settled over her, but she wasn't thinking straight enough to accept it. Getting up slowly, she balanced herself by holding on to the bookshelf. One of the volumes, a slim book with a red spine embossed in golden flames, was shelved puzzlingly sideways. *Inferno*, the title read.

She stared until she realized it wasn't a book at all, but a lever.

On her feet, she could see that one wall of shelves had swung inward, a door to a hidden room left open. Even in her current state, she couldn't help peering inside. It was another library, but this one held distinctly older and more valuable looking books. A sinister oil painting was hung against the far wall—a trompe l'oeil featuring a black goat on a wooden table, stomach sliced, shining entrails hanging out, a goblet and an arrangement of pomegranates beside it. With so much red, the artist had been at pains to separate the gleaming seeds from the blood.

Charlie took it in, especially the odd way it was hung. Farther from the wall on one side than the other, as though it were a door. That's where the safe would be, behind the painting.

She took a step forward, over the threshold. She scanned the shelves. There it was, another volume with a red spine. *The Book of Amor Pettit.*

Her hand went to it, then she hesitated. "Do you mind?" Charlie felt as though she were in a fairy tale, with fairy-tale rules. *Don't look.* But did that also mean she shouldn't steal?

"It's not for me to mind or not mind," the voice said.

That was answer enough for her to slip it out from the shelf and into her bag, which she slung across her shoulders.

"Turn two steps to your left." The voice came from directly behind her, close enough for the hairs on the back of her neck to rise, though she didn't feel the heat of his breath. "You're going to walk through the doors to the dining room. No one goes in there, so you should be able to walk to the servants' stair in the pass-through area just outside the kitchen without anyone spotting you."

"And then?"

"Never look back."

It felt like still being in a dream, walking through the house with just the voice behind her. Into a hall where the shining glass eyes of mounted animal heads stared down at her. Gazelle. Ibex. Rhinoceros. Then past a parlor, where Charlie spotted a blond girl flipping through a magazine. The girl didn't look up as Charlie slunk past her in the dark. When she got to the pass-through, she heard one of the household staff on the phone, ordering artichokes and organic spinach. There was a radio on in there, with Nina Simone singing about running to the devil, all on that day.

"Now what?" she whispered.

For a long moment there was no reply. Charlie started to turn, thought of Orpheus leading his girlfriend out of the underworld. Fairy-tale rules. She stopped.

There or not, the boy had sent her this way for a reason. He couldn't have meant for her to go into the kitchen, since it was occupied. He specifically mentioned the stairs. She went up them, turning the corner into a long hall.

She remembered the last time she'd been in a big house like this, how there was a second, more elaborate stair in the main entrance. Maybe he'd intended for her to get to the front door that way, while the rest of the household moved underneath her.

Or maybe Charlie was so drugged that she'd imagined him entirely.

She padded across the hall, bag clutched to her chest. In the direction of the parlor below, she heard a girl's voice. "That's not fair! I want to borrow him."

And a boy's voice, maybe the one she'd heard before. "He doesn't like you."

The girl laughed. "That's not true. We have games we play that he would never play with you."

And then Charlie was going down the stairs. Her head swam again on the way down, but she made it. She turned the brass latch and pushed. The door opened and then slammed behind her.

Loud enough that it wasn't possible for it to go unnoticed.

Charlie started to run.

There were only woods surrounding the estate, so she plunged into them, not caring about the branches pulling at her clothing. Not caring that her head pounded and nausea turned her stomach.

She raced into the night, crashing through buckthorn bushes that tore at her skin, tripping over ferns. Behind her, she heard shouting, but it was far behind. Flashlights cut through the night. Charlie kept going, her head swimming.

On and on through the dark, the moon and stars spinning above her, until she came to a clearing. A middle-aged Black man in a cap and heavy coat looked startled to see her burst from the brush.

"You're going to scare off the owls," he told her sternly. Then his eyes widened as he took in her appearance.

She had twigs in her hair, scratches on her skin, and dried beet juice all over her mouth.

"Run. You have to run," she told him, breathing hard. "The people from the palace are hunting me."

He shook his head as he pulled a phone from his pocket. "Oh no, young lady, you are not the trouble I want today."

"The people from the palace. They're coming," she said again, before collapsing in the dirt at his feet.

T hree days later, Rand's car was discovered. His corpse was inside, and he appeared to have committed suicide by cutting his wrists, although forensics couldn't account for how little blood was present. Police discovered the decomposed body of a teenage girl in his trunk. The girl had been missing for the better part of three years.

A week after that Benny called her up at home. Did she get the book? Because the buyer was still interested.

"Like a shark," he told her admiringly when she said that she did. "Teeth first."

Knight Singh met her in the parking lot behind a Dunkin'. He had a sleek silver car, wore a stylish wool jacket with a standing band collar, and paid her two grand for the book. "I have more work if you want it," he said, eyeing her over the top of his sunglasses.

Charlie swore that one day she was going to go back to Salt's mansion and get revenge on those fuckers. But she only swore it to herself, so there would be no one else to let down when she didn't.

13

IMPOSSIBLE ANGELS

Charlie blinked in confusion at the late-morning light streaming into the room. Her cuts still stung, her hip was bruised from where she fell, and her hair was a Medusa-like tangle from being half frozen and then slept on wet.

She got up from the mattress. Against the wall, she saw her own shadow, exactly as it had ever been.

Pretend tonight never happened, Charlie.

Dark gold hair dusted Vince's arms, shone on the lashes of his closed eyes. She watched the rise and fall of his chest, the curl of his blunt fingers, as though she were under a spell.

He turned in his sleep.

"Adeline," he mumbled into the pillow. "Adeline, *don't.*"

Charlie stepped back, stung. Was that the girl whose photograph was in his wallet? And what was he trying to prevent?

Pretend tonight never happened. Charlie had been pretending since the beginning of their relationship, pretending that her past was in her past and that she didn't care about the future. And he'd let her, because he'd been pretending too.

She knelt by his side of the mattress and whispered, "*Voulez-vous plus de café?*" The same phrase she'd looked up on her phone two mornings ago.

Vince buried his face deeper in the pillow, as though her breath tickled his skin. Charlie felt foolish. She was almost to the door when he mumbled softly, still half in dreams, "*Je voudrais un café noir, merci.*"

She thought that probably meant he did want a coffee, thanks. And also it meant that she was screwed.

There are lots of different kinds of lies. Fibs to lubricate society. Deceptions, to avoid consequences. Misrepresentations to hide behind, because you're worried another person won't understand, or won't like you, or because what you've done is bad and you're ashamed of it. And then there are the lies you tell because everything about you is a lie.

Posey's accusation that he understood French had been funny, because not telling someone a thing wasn't the same as hiding it. Maybe he'd spent a year abroad, or had a French side to his family, or had downloaded Duolingo and really applied himself.

But when she'd spoken to him in French, he'd pretended he hadn't understood a word.

Hiding a facility with murder was troubling but understandable. Hiding a history with shadow magic could have a reasonable explanation.

But hiding something that shouldn't have mattered made Charlie wonder if anything she knew about him was real.

Charlie went into the bathroom, latched the door, and then sat on the edge of the tub. She put her head into her hands.

Vince being a liar and a murderer proved that her instincts were unerringly bad, just like her mother and grandmother. Sure, he'd started out as a one-night stand, but Vince had seemed like a solid, responsible guy. A little too good for her, maybe, and unlikely to stick around, but still evidence that she was making responsible choices. That there was hope for her to be part of the straight-and-narrow world.

But there she was, more bent than ever.

Charlie Hall, drawn to trouble like an ant to a glue trap. The worst part was that she was more fascinated by him now that she ought to walk away. Now that he was a puzzle of a man, just waiting to be solved.

But if it was impossible for *her* to pretend all the time, the same was true for *him*. He'd left clues. And if she didn't like what she found, well, she'd known he was going to break her heart. That was the Hall family legacy. It had always been a matter of when.

Put on some lipstick and shave your legs, she told herself. *Screw your head on straight.* Vince wasn't her only problem. If Hermes had told anyone where he was going the night before, he might not be the last person to come looking for her. And Balthazar had told him something, she was almost sure of it. She'd bet money there'd been a conversation between them, about her.

She got a washcloth and some soap, ran water into the tub. Washed her pits and her bits. Lathered up her legs. A few of her fresh scabs sloughed off on the dull blade, setting the scrapes to bleeding anew.

She thought about that line: *Shadows are like the shades of the dead in Homer, needing blood to quicken them.*

She thought about Hermes. *You know what I feed this thing? Blood. Maybe yours.*

What if . . . ?

Charlie daubed her first finger in the blood on her leg. There was enough welling up that she could flick it toward her shadow. As she watched, it seemed to ripple, as though shuddering. Nothing hit the floor tiles.

She blinked a few times, trying to focus her gaze on the ground. Maybe she just couldn't see the blood because it was such a fine spatter. Or maybe she'd actually fed her shadow.

But surely if it was quickened, something else would happen. There would be some unmistakable sign.

Putting off the question, she pulled on a shirt and sweats she found in the laundry. Tied her hair into a loose bun on top of her head. Went to make coffee.

There were three texts on her non-burner phone. One was from Doreen, demanding Charlie give her an update on what had been taking so long and threatening to change Posey's record for the worse instead of the better if she didn't bring Adam home. Another was from Odette, sent to all Rapture employees, informing them that the lounge was closed until an insurance adjustor could come in and survey the damage following an attempted robbery. Odette estimated that would take three to four days.

Then there was a private message from Odette:

Have you told anyone what we saw?

Charlie wasn't sure what that was about. She texted back:

no, you?

No reply came.

Charlie didn't like to be paranoid, but she wondered why Odette had asked her that. As Charlie added coffee grounds, cinnamon, and water to the pot, she wondered if Odette might know Salt.

If Balthazar had had a conversation with Hermes, it was time he had a conversation with Charlie too.

She'd been to his place once before, an old brick firehouse that overlooked the canal in Holyoke. At the time he'd been having a party and hadn't invited her inside.

Good luck with that this time.

Charlie put on her coat, got her keys, and went for a drive.

The day was overcast, heavy with the threat of rain. She could already smell it as she got out of her car and went around the side of the brick building, to the entrance. The place was nondescript to the point of looking abandoned, but she noted that at least one light was on inside.

This part of Holyoke still had some old abandoned factories, ones that hadn't been turned into cheapish industrial work spaces for artists and other folks with businesses that either needed a large, messy space or at least didn't mind one. There were apartment buildings a few blocks over, and a few houses with scrubby lawns.

She pounded on the painted black door, ignoring the stenciled words: "GO AWAY."

When no sound came from inside, she pounded some more.

"Can't you read the sign?" came a shout from within.

Charlie kicked the door with her foot. "You know what a snap gun is? I've got one in the trunk of my car and it will pick that lock in seconds. Might damage the mechanism, might not, but I will still be inside."

Balthazar jerked open the door. He was wearing a red dressing gown, his hair mussed, and he looked ready to go to war with the person responsible for waking him up. He blinked a few times, obviously stunned that it was her.

"You almost got me killed last night," Charlie said.

"Well, fuck a duck. Hello, darling."

She pushed past him into the fire station. "Surprised I'm still among the living?"

"Delighted. Come in, I was just going to make some coffee." His tone let her know he was annoyed at her barging in, but not enough for it to matter. He signaled her toward some stairs and then went up a floor and into a surprisingly sunny kitchen with a few plants wilting in pots. On one of the burners sat the largest Cuban-style stove-top espresso maker Charlie had ever seen. "I said to ole Aspirins, there's more to that girl than meets the eye. And then Joey, *he* said I was just being sentimental, that you were an empty-headed—"

"Save it," interrupted Charlie, before he really got going. "I want information."

"Have a seat," he said, indicating a café table that looked like one corner of it had been set on fire at some point in the past. Raynham Park racing forms from the week before served as a tablecloth.

"I want to know about the book that Paul Ecco tried to sell you."

"Eavesdropping, were you?" He took out a jar of Café Bustelo and rough measured the grounds into the metal cage, then filled the bottom with water. He set it down on the stove and turned on the gas so that blue flames licked the bottom. "You were good. Most people who think they can do this kind of work, can't. But you've made it very clear you're out of the game."

Rand had told her that the world of heists and lies and lifts were what certain people were born for, and that Charlie was one of them. Her hands became steady, her fingers quick, and her mouth ready to talk a raft of shit. She had been good. And she'd liked it. That was the problem.

"I saw Paul's body that night, on my way home," she said. "It looked as though it had been ripped open. So, okay, I wanted to know who could have done something like that. Then some heavy comes in and acts like I know where Paul got the page. So then I was *really* curious, especially about who snitched on me."

"You wrong me," Balthazar said, all mock-innocence. "It's not my fault if you're a truffle pig for trouble. All I did was answer a few questions for an interested party."

Balthazar turned away to get down a can of condensed milk, but not before she saw the way his mouth had gone pinched. Among criminals, and the crime-adjacent, there might be a flexible sense of morality, but there was one thing every ne'er-do-well was firm on: no rats.

"Omitting the part where Paul tried to sell *you* the page?" Charlie reminded him. She wondered how long it was going to be before word got around that Hermes was missing. It was worth reminding him that if she went down, she could take him with her. "What is so important about this particular book?"

"It's called the *Liber Noctem*," he told her in a bored voice. "Colloquially, *The Book of Blights* because it's supposed to contain rituals specifically to do with them. Some gloamists think that's the key to immortality, to be able to live on as your Blight. But whatever's in there, it's a truly magnificent object. Metal pages, stamped instead of printed on. Bought at auction by that particularly wicked old gentleman, Lionel Salt. Rich as a Medici, and with the same set of interests."

Charlie's lip curled.

"Do you know him?" Balthazar asked.

"Of course not," said Charlie. "But he's the one who sent Hermes."

Balthazar set down two large mugs, generously filling the bottoms of each with gooey condensed milk. He poured coffee on top of both and brought one to her, then sat, smoothing out his dressing gown. "Salt's grandson is supposed to have stolen the *Liber Noctem* and run off. Ed Carter, I think his name was.

Carver? Anyway, the grandson gets involved in some kind of murder-suicide, but must have sold the book on beforehand, because it doesn't turn up with the rest of his stuff. Salt's so keen on getting the book back that he has a standing offer of fifty grand to anyone who returns it, no questions asked."

Edmund Carver. That was the name Hermes had asked her about. But he hadn't sounded as though the kid was dead.

"Sold it on to Paul Ecco?" Charlie asked.

Balthazar shook his head. "More likely to someone else, who then sold a single page to Paul Ecco."

"Why not the whole thing, then?" Charlie asked. "Fifty grand's nothing to sneeze at."

Balthazar opened his expressive hands, granting her point. "Maybe someone who wanted to get Salt's attention. Chum the water."

Charlie sipped the coffee. It was sweet enough to make her wince and strong enough that she was glad it was so sweet. "To make him pay more?"

"When the *Liber Noctem* first went missing," Balthazar said, "he hired one of my people. The new guy."

Charlie raised both eyebrows. "Adam?"

"Yeah, him. But my guy didn't work out. Found nothing. The old man didn't seem too surprised, either." Balthazar shrugged and took a long drink from his mug.

"Huh." It bothered her that anyone knew Paul Ecco was trying to fence the page so soon after he'd been thrown out of Rapture; that seemed too fast for a rumor to spread. And not only the presence of the Hierophant, but the brutality of the murder made her think it was something other than a human who'd done it. A Blight would have reason to tear a shadow to tatters when it killed. The strength to rip open a rib cage.

Why would a Blight be looking for the *Liber Noctem*?

And who the hell had it?

If Salt had hired Adam to look for the book, was it possible he'd found Edmund Carver's hiding spot and had been sitting on the thing?

Of course, it was asking questions like those that got Odette's place trashed and herself almost killed. She thought she'd let the dream of revenge against Salt go years before, and she ought to let it go now. It was impossible, and childish.

"*You* could take the job," Balthazar said. "You want to quit the game for good? Go out in style. Come on, Charlatan, you could steal breath from a body, hate from a heart, the moon from the sky."

"Flattery is so unlike you." Fifty thousand dollars was a lot of money, but it wasn't a fraction of what Salt deserved to pay. "I'll think about it."

Balthazar smiled, as though she'd already agreed. "There we are. I knew you'd come around."

As Charlie crossed the asphalt to her car, she noticed a man on the other side of the street. She might not have taken a second look if he were moving, or even had a phone out, like anyone would. But this guy was standing stock-still, staring at the firehouse with his hands—arms, even—tucked deep into the pockets of his coat.

In the daylight, she could see that the Hierophant was a young man, and yet his eyes burned with something ancient.

If he was hunting Blights, then what was he doing at Balthazar's place? She couldn't forget the way he'd walked toward her in the alley, with what had seemed like sinister purpose.

Charlie shuddered, got in the Corolla, and hit the gas. As she pulled out, she saw his head turn slowly and his gaze follow her car. Then his shadow became vast wings behind him, lifting him up into the air. He hovered against the blue sky, an impossible angel, coat flapping around him.

She almost veered into a ditch, heart hammering. At the first stop sign, she looked back again; he didn't appear to have followed her.

Back home, Charlie was full of nervous energy, and a lot of caffeine. She washed the dishes in the sink left over from the Bolognese. Wiped down the counters. And when that wasn't enough, she started to clean out the whole refrigerator. Not just her usual sweep, dumping out the most offensive things—a forgotten cucumber that had caved in on one side and become colonized with mold, a tiny piece of cheese that had turned white and hard and no one was going to eat, a sealed container full of grayish noodles that bulged alarmingly. This time she took out everything, condiments included, and wiped the shelves down with towels soaked in diluted bleach.

"You need help?" Vince asked, coming in from the bedroom and reaching for the coffeepot.

She startled at his voice.

He appeared to be the same man she'd lived with for months. Blond hair mussed from sleep. Stubble along his jaw. As he moved around the kitchen with no mention of the night before, it seemed impossible to believe he'd snapped a guy's neck and then fucked her on some broken steps in the moonlight.

And lied.

And lied and lied and lied—

"Can I borrow some cleaning stuff from your van?" Charlie asked.

He hesitated. "Let me get it for—"

"Great," she said, cutting him off cheerfully. If he didn't want her rooting around in his van herself, it was probably because he had something else to hide. Maybe she'd find a head rolling around in the back.

Or maybe he was just being nice, offering to get the stuff for her.

Or maybe Hermes's body was in plastic-wrapped pieces and he wanted to spare her the sight.

Charlie turned back to the fridge with renewed vigor. She scrubbed it as though she could scrub away all her desire for him, all her foolishness.

Vince brought in cleaning stuff and went out to clean the gutters, mug in hand. *And hide the head,* Charlie's mind unhelpfully supplied.

Posey got up even later than usual, around four. She looked ragged as she staggered into the kitchen and filled a cereal bowl with all the remaining coffee, then stuck it in the microwave.

Charlie had dated a fellow burglar for a couple of months, before he skipped town with a pair of earrings she'd managed to convince him were set with diamonds. He'd told her that when he'd first started breaking into houses, he'd thought rich people would keep their really expensive stuff in safes, but it turned out that people mostly kept things where they could see them. Wealthy people kept a key under the mat like everyone else, because they misplaced their keys too. They wound up locking away birth certificates, marriage licenses, and legal paperwork instead of valuables. Jewelry was in the primary bedroom closet, even the really good stuff, because people wanted to wear it. Laptops were on desks or sofas. TV on the wall. Expensive liquor on the bar cart. Guns in the first drawer of the nightstand.

People like their stuff close by, including their secrets. What makes you feel safe when you go to sleep at night? Being able to check and see that your secrets are still hidden.

If there was something for Charlie to find, there was a good chance Vince kept it in their bedroom.

Once she had the thought, it caught like a burr.

She needed to get him out of the house—and soon, before temptation overwhelmed her common sense and she went through his stuff while he was likely to walk in on her.

An hour later, Vince came inside, his hands sooty. By then, she had her story ready.

"Katelynn wants me to meet her for coffee tonight," Charlie said, trying to sound offhanded.

He washed his hands in the sink, soap all the way to his elbows. "The tattooist. With the moth-eating cousin."

"Right," she said, unnerved. She hadn't noticed them talking at the party. "I'm thinking about getting something new."

"Oh yeah?" he asked, wiping his wet hands on his black jeans.

The expression on his face—slight smile, seemingly honest interest, no judgment for the trouble of the previous night—unnerved her as well. He really seemed to care for her. He'd killed someone to save her.

She wanted to trust him.

"Vince?" She took his hand and looked up into his pale gray eyes. "How did you lose your shadow? For real this time."

His gaze slid away from her. "I didn't. I—" He stopped, then started again. "I didn't understand the danger we were in."

He wasn't necessarily lying. The truth was often complicated and hard to explain. "What danger?"

He shook his head and picked up their compost bucket—bought by Posey, online, in an effort for them to be better environmentalists, now filled with slimy cucumber remains and other fridge remnants, plus a lot of coffee grounds.

"That's not an answer," she called after him.

But whatever she'd been looking for, she didn't get it. He only went outside to dump the compost into a weird worm bin that none of them was sure was working. With all the coffee grounds they added, the only thing Charlie was certain of was that those worms were *wired*. If a bird ate one, it was going to fly directly into the sun.

By the time he came back in, he had his phone to his ear. He'd been called in for a job. A residential double homicide.

"I can stay if you want," he said to her, turning the phone away from his mouth. Faintly, she could hear his boss yelling at someone. Before that moment, she hadn't been sure if Vince had faked the call, just to avoid talking.

She shook her head. "I'm going out anyhow. Katelynn, remember?"

He got his coat. Kissed her on the mouth and then at the edge of her jaw. A kiss that obviously meant *something*, but whether it was apology or promise, she wasn't sure.

After he left, she stared at her bedroom door. If he hadn't gotten called in to work, he might have given her answers. And she knew that any newspaper advice columnist would tell her that she should wait, respect his privacy, and ask him more when he returned.

She made it fifteen minutes before she got up and made a show of stretching. "Well, I'm going to take a quick nap before I go out."

"Hold on," Posey said. "I was waiting for him to leave. There's something I need to talk to you about."

Charlie did not want to hear more about DMT and how it was absolutely necessary to steal some for Posey's let's-experiment-on-ourselves-in-the-woods retreat. "I won't be long."

In the bedroom, with the door firmly closed, Charlie looked around. Tangled sheets. Clothes and shoes scattered on the floor. A dresser cluttered with yellowed paperback books and pots of makeup and a vase stuffed with receipts.

When she looked down at her hands, she was surprised to find them shaking.

Charlie ripped the bedding all the way off, then pushed the mattress up against the wall. It was heavy and wobbled, but she got it up. Things got hidden under beds in movies. Which meant that people who watched movies hid things under beds.

But beneath the mattress, all she found was a pair of underwear she'd lost, a crumpled tissue, plus something gross and fuzzy and flat that might have once been one of Lucipurrr's hairballs.

She thought of her mother, looking for evidence of another woman, in drawers, in pockets. Impossibly trying to prove a negative. Hoping for nothing, and knowing that nothing only meant you weren't looking hard enough. Charlie swore that she would never wind up like that.

Yet here she was.

Charlie moved on to Vince's half of the dresser, shoving her hands all the way to the back, then taking everything out and turning over the drawers. Vince was tidy—never left his clothes on the floor, never left his hair in the sink—so it was a surprise to find shirts and jeans thrown together haphazardly. She hoped there was no system to the chaos, because she'd never be able to re-create it. If he left five balls of socks in a particular order to detect snooping, she was screwed.

But she found nothing of interest. Nothing incriminating.

She went to the closet next. Most of the stuff in there was hers, but he had a winter coat and a pair of boots shoved deep in on the left side. She wriggled her hands into the pockets and took out two receipts. One for gas, another for milk, bread, and eggs. Both paid in cash.

Peering into the darkness, she noticed an empty-looking black duffel bag on the floor, past the boots. She dragged it out and unzipped it.

At the bottom she found a metal disc about the size of a nickel, and a driver's license. She turned the bag over and shook everything onto the floor, but nothing else fell out.

She picked up the small metal disc. It was thick and heavier than she expected, almost like a watch battery, but without any markings. A part to something electronic? A piece in a game? She tucked it into her pocket.

Then she looked at the driver's license. The picture was of a younger Vincent, smiling wide, with neatly barbered hair that someone had used product on, a collared shirt just visible along the bottom of the image. An address in Springfield, with an apartment number. And over the state capital, an entirely different name.

Edmund Vincent Carver.

For a dizzying moment, she thought she was looking at a fake ID. But the card had uniform edges and bended right, and when she held it to the light, the telltale metallized kinegram shone over his picture.

Lionel Salt's grandson. The one who'd stolen the *Liber Noctem*. The one who was supposed to be dead.

Lionel Salt's heir, lying beside her in the dark.

Charlie found it hard to catch her breath. She was pretty sure this was a full-blown panic attack, and that if she kept inhaling so quickly and shallowly, she'd bruise her lungs.

She took out her phone and snapped a picture of his license, amazed to find that she could manage it. Everything seemed to be happening too fast. But she still made herself go to her laptop and open her search engine. She typed "Edmund Carver" and "Springfield."

The first hit was an article that came up from last summer, printed in *The Republican*:

> SPRINGFIELD—The burnt remains of two bodies were discovered in a car two blocks from the MGM casino in the downtown area in the early-morning hours of Monday.
>
> Police have identified one as belonging to Edmund "Remy" Carver, 27, socialite and grandson of Lionel Salt. The other was Rose Allaband, 23, who had been reported missing after disappearing from her apartment in Worcester four months ago. Early forensics suggest a murder-suicide.
>
> The sheriff's office is not looking for additional suspects at this time.

Charlie's heart sped.

A few more clicks and she found Vince's picture with a dozen other young, broad-shouldered men on the New York University fencing team. He wore a collared white bodysuit, arms folded across his chest, hair shorter than on the license, faded close to his scalp on the sides. He looked like he was in a costume, except for the way he was smiling at the camera, as though he believed the world was made for people like him.

Vince didn't smile like that.

Of course, back then he'd called himself *Remy* and been wealthy and happy. He hadn't killed somebody or faked his own death. He wasn't working an under-the-table job cleaning up corpses or shacking up with some broke girl to have a place to sleep.

She remembered the sweat trickling between her shoulder blades in the crowded bar the night they met, the taste of gin and tonic made with well liquor because she'd wanted to get drunk on the cheap, her friend dipping out early, how Vince had stood like a wall between her and getting shoved into the fire door.

If she'd known he was filthy fucking rich, would she have taken him home when she was feeling self-destructive and foolish? No way. Of course, she'd never have believed him either. She'd have thought it was the world's worst line. *Oh, the grandson of a billionaire, you say? Well, I only get down with bajillionaires. Just your luck.*

If he'd convinced her, though? Never. Not a guy who'd graduated from a prestigious university, a guy with a trust fund and a future ahead of him. No chance she would have brought him back to her rental house, so he could sneer at how she lived, so he could look down on her for her job, her lack of education, and all her choices.

And if she'd known he was related to Salt, she would have broken a bottle over his head.

Charlie tried to focus, to imagine what *he'd* been thinking that night. Probably worried that he *didn't* have a future, right? He'd stolen the *Liber Noctem,* and then something had gone wrong. Something to do with the girl? Something that had resulted in two dead bodies and a need to fake his own death?

He'd gotten that fake Minnesota driver's license somehow, one good enough for Charlie not to question it. Of course, she'd never seen a real Minnesota license, or taken his out of the plastic sleeve to inspect it, and she supposed very few other people had either. But he had no credit card and no credit. No social security number. Just a gruesome job cleaning hotel rooms under the table.

Enter Charlie. Probably saw her drinking alone and figured her for an easy mark. A sad girl, ready to take him straight to bed. Desperate enough not to ask too many questions. That's what good con artists did. They didn't need to convince you of anything, because you were too busy convincing yourself.

Then nearly a year later, Vince walks into Rapture and finds his grandfather's hired gun standing there. If Hermes spots him, he'll be in more trouble than ever. So Hermes has to go. He hadn't done it to save Charlie.

She felt a little light-headed, a little dizzy.

"Did you mean to leave—" Posey leaned against the doorframe, hand still on the knob. Her eyes widened slightly at the mattress shoved up against the wall, the dumped-out drawers, then her gaze went to Charlie sitting on the floor. "Did you know you left thirty bucks in singles in those clothes you tossed in the trash?"

"Shit," Charlie said. Her tips for the night. She was losing it. Seriously losing it.

Posey came into the room to hand her the money, then looked around again. "What's going on? Because you do not look like you're napping."

"No, not napping," Charlie admitted.

Posey gave a big sigh. "I am going to make some ramen and another pot of coffee. You have ten minutes to finish up whatever you're doing, and then we're going to have a conversation."

As soon as her sister was gone, Charlie went back to the internet. She typed "Edmund Carver" in again. Photographs came up in society blogs, him standing around at parties. None from the last four years, but before that, notices of his attending openings and balls.

She found an article about a French Heritage Society gala that showed a picture of him with a blond woman identified in the caption as Adeline Salt. She wore a white silk shift that looked particularly expensive on her tanned and toned and probably microsculpted body.

In the photo, Vince—*Edmund*—had an arm thrown over her shoulder and a champagne coupe in his hand. He was in mid-laugh, the light catching him so that his shadow loomed over them both.

Charlie knew the girl. She was the one in the photo in Vince's wallet. Salt's daughter, which would make her Edmund's aunt, even though they appeared to be around the same age.

Adeline. The girl he called out for in his sleep.

Several people had posted in the comment section of the newspaper article.

> This is the problem with celebrating the parasitic one percent. It's okay if he's a murderer so long as he knows all the right people.

> I don't believe the accusations against Remy and anyone who knows him wouldn't either. He was always willing to go out of his way for people, from getting soaked helping staff put up a tent after a rainstorm threatened to torpedo a party in the Hamptons, to lying down on the filthy sidewalk to retrieve a stranger's purse that had fallen through a grate. I will never forget sneaking out of the Central Park Conservatory's luncheon to walk through the park with him. That's the Edmund I choose to remember.

Maybe I'm a bad person, but I'm glad he's dead. I wish he'd died before
he could have taken the life of an innocent girl with him. It's disgusting
that anyone would defend him, no less "choose to remember" him as
anything but what he was—a sociopath.

Charlie heard her sister put something in the sink and knew she had only a
few more moments before she was going to have to talk to Posey. But there was
one more thing she wanted to do. She put the name Lionel Salt into Google,
something she hadn't done in years.

There was a profile on his estate in West Springfield, apparently bought for
$8.9 million in 2001, along with some links to his name associated with ongo-
ing legal cases. As soon as she saw a photograph of the house, Charlie's palms
started to sweat.

It looked just like the palace she remembered.

14

A SWARM OF
BLACK FLIES

Posey was slurping up ramen doctored with a ton of chili garlic sauce when Charlie emerged from the bedroom.

Dressed in leggings and an oversized shirt, Posey had pulled her brown hair into a single braid. Normal, except she was also wearing eyeliner, lip gloss, and calf-high zip-up boots. She was planning on going somewhere. Charlie just hoped it wasn't a lab.

"Okay, so you wanted to talk to me without Vince around," Charlie said, forcing herself to concentrate on this conversation and not everything she'd learned. "What for?"

Posey poked at her bowl. "You're not going to tell me why you trashed your bedroom?"

Maybe she should get a tarot reading, like saps everywhere. Maybe she needed to hear someone else say it: *He's no good.* "You go ahead with your thing first."

"Fine. So last night, I was talking to this guy . . ."

Charlie abruptly wished she'd said a lot less the night before. "You told me you wouldn't."

"I stopped arguing with you," Posey said. "I never actually agreed to do what you said."

With one stupid phone call, Charlie had almost gotten herself killed. What would happen if Salt somehow heard Posey's story and linked it to Hermes?

"I was careful," Posey insisted.

"Take it down. Whatever you put out there—*take it down*." Charlie looked around for Posey's laptop as though she could toss it into Nashawannuck Pond and somehow that would remove what she'd posted from the internet.

"It wasn't online," Posey insisted. "It was an encrypted chat that deletes everything after it's read."

Charlie sat down at the table. Her head was throbbing. The events of the last twenty-four hours were too much. She wanted to curl up in a dark hole and maybe engage in some screaming therapy.

"Forget about all that for a minute," Posey said. "Because that's not the part I want to talk to you about."

"*Fuck*," Charlie said, lacking any more coherent response.

"There's a graduate student over at UMass. Madurai Malhar Iyer. He's been working on a doctoral dissertation on quickening shadows. The guy who told me about him had been trying to get Malhar to talk to him for ages, but Malhar kept blowing him off."

Charlie had a feeling she knew what was coming next, and that she was going to hate it.

"I knew you weren't going to agree to meet him, so I wrote to him and said all that stuff that happened to you happened to me. Only . . ."

Charlie stared at her unhelpfully.

"Only I can't go alone," Posey finished.

"Why not?"

"Because it didn't happen to me," Posey said, as though that should be obvious.

Charlie stuck a fork into her sister's ramen and let the hot chili sear her mouth as she ate it. "That sounds like a big problem *for you*."

"I told him we could meet him at the UMass library tonight to talk," Posey finished, voice lilting up in the manner of someone who wants to ask something without asking it. "Tonight."

"No—*no*," Charlie said, holding up her hands. "No way am I going. That's not happening."

Posey narrowed her eyes. "Busy with something? Planning on ransacking the living room?"

Charlie got up. "Last night was real bad and I definitely don't want to discuss it with a stranger today."

"You lied about meeting Katelynn. I know you did. You were looking for something and you didn't want Vince to be here when you did it." Her threat was implied, but effective nonetheless.

They stood staring at one another. Charlie's hands had unconsciously curled into fists so tightly that her nails were pressing into her palms. "Don't do this."

"I don't have a car. At least drive me," Posey said. *"Please."*

Charlie groaned and headed for her room.

"Where are you going?" Posey called after her.

"To get my coat."

She passed Lucipurrr, tail lashing, staring at one of the walls near the bathroom. Sometimes you could hear mice scrabbling in there, and it set the cat on edge. She supposed they were all on edge, these days.

Back in the bedroom, Charlie tried to put it into a semblance of order—making up the mattress with new sheets to give her the alibi of cleaning if anything was out of place.

As they pulled out of the driveway, Charlie's thoughts were a jumble of memories of Salt's murder of Rand and the ease with which Vince had covered up a murder the night before. Had he killed for his grandfather? Had he killed that girl they found dead in his car for Salt? Had he killed her for himself?

Vince had been careful, and thorough, and unnervingly competent—but he hadn't seemed as though he'd liked murder or was eager to do it again. She had a hard time imagining him hurting someone for fun.

Of course, it's not as though she would have easily imagined him standing in the middle of the sort of gala that she'd only seen on television, wearing an outfit likely to cost more than her car, and guzzling Champagne that was allowed to use the capital *C* because it came from the right region of France. It was possible that Charlie had a severely stunted imagination.

"So tell me about this guy, Malhar," Charlie said, to distract herself.

She shrugged. "I don't know that much. He seemed nice over chat."

"No offense, Posey, but there are a lot of graduate students in the Valley, and they're just that, *students*. What makes you think this guy has that much more information than you do? I mean, you spend every night online doing research. You've probably read a million accounts of quickened shadows."

Posey's frown deepened. "I don't *do* research, though. People can make up stories, or exaggerate for attention. Videos can be faked. I might know a lot, but so many things I've thought were real turned out not to work. Meanwhile, he's authenticating the information he gets. He has proof." Posey shifted uncomfortably in her seat. Possibly because the seats were, like everything else in the Corolla, kind of busted. "Speaking of which . . ."

"What?" Charlie said.

Posey made a face. "I might have exaggerated some things too—"

"For his attention." Charlie looked out the window at the darkening sky. "I guess you got it."

After that, Posey was silent all the way until they crossed the Calvin Coolidge Memorial Bridge.

The University of Massachusetts rose like a surprise city in the middle of nowhere, complete with a football stadium, tall buildings, traffic jams, and a miniature Stonehenge. If you took a wrong turn at a farmers market you got surrounded by a swarm of students, arriving every year like locusts, thirsty for beer and boba tea. Students were the lifeblood of the Valley, and if Charlie resented them, she knew she needed them as much as anyone if she wanted to keep slinging drinks.

And soon Posey would be one of them, and go on with them to a future full of possibilities. At least, that was the hope.

Charlie parked in an enormous lot, one that was marked with some letters that might or might not mean she was in the right place.

As they got out, Charlie once again regretted her leather coat's lack of warmth. The sun slipped low and red in the distance. They could see the lightning farm over in Sunderland, harvesting energy with ominous crackles and strikes.

"You okay?" Charlie asked.

"I just can't imagine coming here every day," Posey said.

They stood there for a few seconds until Charlie reminded Posey that she was the one with the directions. She frowned at her phone for a while. "I think we're supposed to go toward that pond."

They got lost twice, wandering through the campus, passing clumps of students in UGGs and pajama pants. A Black woman with an on-point eyeliner game sat outside the student center, reading a feminist translation of *Beowulf*. A white boy tried to hand Charlie a flyer for an anime festival. Three guys in team sweats jogged by.

Vince had gone to a school like this, sitting in lectures, learning to fence. A more expensive university, one that was supposed to spit him out ready to rule over the less fortunate.

He'd had everything. Money. Privilege. Power.

For the first time, Charlie wondered what could have possibly made him run away.

Madurai Malhar Iyer was waiting for them in the lobby of the library. He was a tall guy, young, with brown skin, wearing wire-rimmed glasses and a flannel over a t-shirt, slender in a way that spoke of spending so much time studying that he forgot to eat.

"I'm Posey," Posey said. "And this is my sister, Charlie."

Malhar signed them in as his guests and led them into a study room in the back. "Thanks for agreeing to meet me so quickly," he said as they walked through the stacks.

Posey nodded, obviously a little embarrassed. She wanted to impress him, Charlie realized.

Malhar swung his bag over his shoulder and set it down on the table, removing his laptop and a notebook. Several pens fell out, an apple rolling behind them. "Do you want anything? There's a coffee machine, but it's not very good. The hot chocolate is okay, but someone told me they got a boiled roach in their cup."

Posey wrinkled her nose. "I'm going to pass."

"I'll take the roach coffee," said Charlie. The buzz of Balthazar's candy coffee was starting to wear off, and she needed something to keep going.

"I'll grab you some," he said, and then hesitated. "I'm sure it's fine. I mean, lots of people drink it."

He came back with three cups. Two coffees and a hot chocolate. She supposed he felt obligated to have one himself, like a host taking the first sip of wine to show they aren't poisoning their guests.

"So," he said, clearing his throat. "Posey, I'd like you to tell your story again, and I'd like to record it. Does that sound okay?"

Posey pushed back her shoulders. "It was my sister, really. I told you it happened to me, because she wasn't sure she wanted to talk about it. But I convinced her that it was important."

His gaze went to Charlie. She shrugged.

"So you're the one with the quickened shadow?" Malhar looked flummoxed.

Charlie didn't blame him. She turned to Posey. "The *what*?"

Posey looked sheepish. "It *is*. Or at least, it's something. You know how weird it was acting last night."

"I'm going to kill you," Charlie said, standing. "Straight-up murder. No one would blame me. I can't believe I let you drag me over here—"

Malhar held up his hands, forestalling violence. "We could do a few tests."

Posey had told her in the car that she'd exaggerated the story, but Charlie still hadn't seen this coming. "No way. We're out of here. She's wasting your time. All she wants is for you to tell her how to wake up her shadow. She'd say anything if she thought it would convince you to do that."

"Wait," Posey said, grabbing for her arm. "Let him look at it. Tell him the story."

Charlie shook her off. She wanted to knock over her coffee. She wanted to throw a chair.

And yet, another part of her wondered—could her shadow be magic? Wasn't it worth letting her sister get away with an extremely annoying scam, if some of the information they got was actually helpful?

"Fine," Charlie said, and threw herself back into the chair. "Go ahead. Test my shadow. Whatever. But when all this turns out to be bullshit, don't say I didn't warn you."

Malhar held up his phone. "So it's okay if I record this?"

"Nope. It sure isn't," Charlie said.

"Come *on*," Posey said.

"You won't have to give your names on the recording," Malhar said. "I'll keep your identities secret in my notes. This is just for me to go back over, so I'm sure I have everything right. No one else is going to hear this."

Charlie looked between him and Posey. "Okay. No names."

Pressing a button, he put the cell down between them. "Okay, well, we're rolling. We'll figure this out. First, tell me a little bit about yourself. Age. Any other details that seem important."

"I'm twenty-eight." None of the rest was anything Charlie was going to put on a recording. "Not much more to know."

"How about you?" He turned to Posey.

"Me?" She had been nervously picking the skin around her thumbnail. She bit the edge of it and then seemed to notice what she was doing. She folded her hands on the table.

"You're going to be speaking on the recording." He smiled in a reassuring way.

Posey raised her voice a little, as though afraid the recording wouldn't pick her up. "I'm twenty-five. I'm her sister and I read tarot cards for people over the internet."

"Really?" Malhar asked.

She nodded, tilting her head. "I could do a spread for you."

"Yeah, maybe I could use one." He looked as though he was regretting everything about tonight. "Let me explain a little bit about the project you're going to be a part of. It started as an ethnography—a cultural study of gloamists. You know, a deep dive into that community. It seemed important when there were still people around with living memory of it being secret and others who only knew it primarily through seeing altered shadows in magazines.

"But the more people I talked to, the more I became interested in quickened shadows, and their own ethnography. I was surprised by how differently shades were viewed in different eras, and among different groups. Which didn't fit the original concept of the thesis. So, uh, my thesis ballooned. I started collecting historical references and comparing them with modern accounts. And then I needed more interviews. I've been spending a lot of time defending my work to my professors. And my classmates. And my parents."

"They should be glad you're doing it," Charlie said. "Isn't the University of Massachusetts interested in, like, founding a school for witchcraft and wizardry someday?"

Malhar snorted. "There are physicists experimenting with aphotic shadows. And folklorists collating stories. Biologists sewing cat shadows onto mice. But I am supposed to be an ethnographer, and everyone seems to think that I am in too deep."

"Ah," Charlie said. "*You're* the one interested in founding the school of witchcraft and wizardry."

He shook his head, but he was smiling. "You know I am going to edit anything embarrassing that I say out of the transcript, right?"

"What if I say something *I* want off the record?" Charlie asked.

"I'll stop the tape for the duration of any comment you want to make and restart when we're done," he said. "Is there something you want to say that you don't want on the tape?"

"Maybe," she said.

Malhar waited for her to say more, and when she didn't, nodded encouragingly, as though he was used to interviewing paranoid weirdos. Finally, he cleared his throat. "Can you give me an account of what led to the change in your shadow?"

Charlie took a sip of the coffee, trying to figure out how to tell this story in a way that wouldn't come back to bite her in the ass. "A man came into my job and used his shadow to rough me up. His shadow was like a fog one minute, and then something that was sorta like a paper doll cutout of a person crossed with a black hole. A shape made from a lack of light. It could become solid enough to knock over some bottles of liquor. And it—"

Charlie stopped at the memory of the thing flooding her lungs, the helplessness of that moment. She drank the rest of the coffee in a gulp, hoping the bite of bitterness would help. Unfortunately, it was bland and watery all the way to the bottom.

"Then the shadow went down my throat. It felt thick and heavy, like I had swallowed a storm cloud. I couldn't breathe." She looked down at the chipped nail polish on her thumb so she didn't have to look at either of them. "I was unconscious, although not for long."

She thought of hearing Vince's voice when she woke. The softness in it when he'd spoken to Hermes. The softness in his voice when he spoke to her on the steps. *I wish he was alive so I could kill him again.*

"Just some clarifications," Malhar said. "Can you tell me how far the shadow was able to move from the person's body?"

"Probably about twenty-five feet," Charlie told him, glad to focus on the technical details instead of how she'd felt. "But usually less than ten."

He went through a series of questions like that. How often had it become solid, how solid had it become. Had it seemed connected to the gloamist. Had the gloamist seemed strained in any way or stopped to provide it blood. Had Charlie bled, and if she had, did the shadow seem distracted or interested in the blood.

He made a note. "And did the shadow speak at any time?"

Charlie shook her head, surprised by the question. *Blights* spoke, or at least some of them did. The very powerful ones, like Rowdy Joss, who'd been responsible for the Boxford Massacre, or Xiang Zheng, who dictated many observations about the world to scholars around 220 A.D. and had been thought of as a ghost. Most Blights were less clever than animals—a little low cunning borrowed from their human memories, mixed with the madness that afflicted most of them.

But *shadows* were still tethered. They couldn't speak, at least not on their own. Well, she'd thought they couldn't.

Posey must have been wondering the same thing. "They can talk?"

Malhar hesitated, not like he was trying to decide to answer, but like he was trying to decide how to put what he was about to say. "I don't know what you know about the mechanics of energy exchange that exists between gloamist and shadow."

Posey frowned. She didn't like to admit what she didn't know, but Charlie figured this was one of the things she'd want some definitive answers about.

"Tell us," Charlie said.

"The average human, at rest, produces enough energy to power a lightbulb. To charge a phone. And if we run, we produce enough to power an electric stove." He shook his head. "I am being inexact. According to the first law of thermodynamics, energy can neither be created nor destroyed. So we don't *make* the energy. We convert it from food and water."

Posey nodded along with his explanation.

"That's the energy that's passed along to shadows. They're a little like a parasite. The body produces excess energy anyway, and the magical parasite drains it off. The more energy it stores, the more powerful it becomes."

"And that's how you make it do things," Posey said.

"I noticed that you had your tongue split," Malhar said, "so I'm sure you've heard of the bifurcated consciousness. Gloamists train their brains to be able to control their shadows simultaneously with controlling their own bodies.

Ambidextrous people have an advantage. If you see a gloamist without a split tongue, odds are that they're ambidextrous."

"Sure," Posey said impatiently. To her, this was basic stuff.

"The problem is that a quickened shadow, on its own, doesn't store much energy. So, say a gloamist wants to do something that requires more energy than their shadow has—they can open a tap to their shadow, letting it pull energy from the gloamist. But leave the tap open too long and the gloamist will die. That's where the bifurcated soul comes in.

"If a gloamist puts some of *themselves* into their shadow, they can create a separate entity which holds energy. The shadow becomes a mirror self, reflected self, second self, upside-down self. But the more powerful your shadow grows, the more it controls you."

"Blights," Charlie said.

Malhar nodded. "When the gloamist dies, yes. But I believe they are conscious long before that."

It occurred to Charlie that Malhar said he was studying the ethnography of *shadows,* and suddenly understood why his advisors might have thought he was in too deep. Was he hoping to interview one? Had he interviewed one?

"Uh, well, we should get to the testing part," he said, perhaps seeing the expression on her face. "There are three things I'd like to try, but I am going to have to set up something first."

"You're filming video?" Charlie asked.

"It's part of the test," he said warily.

Charlie frowned as he got out a stand and plugged a cord from his laptop into his phone. "Don't even think about showing our faces."

He nodded distractedly as he got out the ring lights. Then he took out a finger-stick lancet in plastic packaging.

"Charlie, do you mind standing?" he asked, after he'd gotten his equipment where he wanted it to be.

She got up.

"Now, can either of you tell me what you observed that made you believe your shadow might have been affected by the experience?"

"It moved weirdly," Posey said. "Not like she was controlling it or anything, but weird."

He turned to Charlie. "Did you feed it blood?"

"I was cut up that night," she said. "And then, in the bathroom today I picked off a scab. So I don't know. Maybe."

Posey looked betrayed to be hearing this for the first time, but considering that none of this would be happening if she hadn't betrayed Charlie's confidence, Charlie refused to feel bad about it.

"Would you be willing to prick your finger now?" Malhar asked. "In front of the camera."

"Sure." Charlie picked up the lancet and opened the package. She jabbed the tip into her finger and watched a sudden bead of red appear.

All of them watched in silence. Nothing happened. Finally Charlie licked her finger. "Okay, that didn't work. Are we done?"

She wasn't sure how to feel. She didn't think she'd like to be a gloamist, but it still felt like failing a test.

"Can you try to make it move?" Malhar asked, although he must have known it was useless.

Charlie concentrated. She was at least a little bit ambidextrous, but her brain didn't feel particularly bifurcated.

"Are you trying?" Posey asked.

Charlie gave her sister a look.

"Okay, last one," Malhar said. He turned on the lights.

The first sent her shadow towering against the wall to her left.

Then the second came on. That ought to have doubled it, and yet it did nothing at all.

Charlie stared, unwilling to believe what she was seeing. "Is it . . . ?"

Malhar nodded, and when he spoke, his voice was hushed. "You have a quickening shadow. It's not fully there yet, but a day or two more of feeding it blood and it will be. I don't think I've ever seen one at this stage."

Charlie stared at her own shadow towering over her, her heart speeding. It was a part of her, she knew, but she couldn't help being a little afraid of it. "What do I do?"

"You could stop feeding it," Malhar said. "It would settle."

She nodded.

"But you wouldn't do that," said Posey, as though the option itself was an insult.

Charlie took the neglected third cup and drank some more lukewarm watery coffee.

"Or you could become a gloamist." Malhar started breaking down the lights with a grin. "Some people are uncomfortable with the idea of quickened shadows. There are even fringe groups that believe we're being deceived as to their nature."

Posey snorted. "He's talking about the people who think the shadows are *demons*."

He nodded. "Or aliens. They think our minds are misinterpreting what our eyes are seeing, because the truth is too horrible for the human mind to comprehend."

"But Charlie's not crazy," Posey said.

Charlie wasn't too sure about that. "Okay, so what *are* quickened shadows?"

"Theoretically?" Malhar cautioned. "You've probably heard of dark *matter*: the stuff that's keeping gravity from ripping our galaxy apart. It has to be there, or all the other mathematical calculations fall apart, but no one can prove it. And, well, dark *energy* is even more theoretical than that.

"Dark energy was used to explain ghosts, but is better suited to shadows. In some way, you could consider them ghosts of the living. And just like ghosts seem to be echoes of traumatic events, aphotic shadows are said to be formed out of trauma. Some professors here believe that aphotic shadows, like ghosts, reenact memories rather than have true life. Which is bullshit, by the way."

"Aphotic?" Charlie said.

"Growing in the absence of light," Malhar said apologetically. "The term caught on in academia."

"So trauma *is* what quickens shadows?" Posey's voice was a little breathless now that they'd come to the part of the conversation she was most interested in.

Malhar frowned. "It seems to be, but trauma is highly individual. There are some very disturbing videos of people doing extreme and irresponsible things to wake their shadows. But they're unlikely to work because they don't carry emotional weight. Trauma is more than pain."

Charlie gave her sister a look. "So, no ayahuasca?"

Malhar burst out laughing.

Posey, caught between embarrassment and anger, went silent.

"We should go," Charlie said, standing up, trying not to take too much satisfaction in the moment.

Malhar picked up his cell off the table. "I'd like you to talk to me again, so I can monitor your shadow's progress. I hope you know you can trust me."

"Can I ask you a question off the record?" Charlie asked.

He stopped the recording, frowning. "Sure."

"Have you heard of a book called the *Liber Noctem*?"

His eyebrows went up. "*The Book of Blights*?"

She nodded.

"I heard about the auction," he said. "There were a lot of wild claims—that it was written by a Blight, one that 'captured the breath of life.' I'd love to get a look at it. One of the books everyone wants to study, like *The Luctifer Treatise* or *Codex Antumbra*, or *Fushi-no-Kage*."

"You think any of the claims are true?"

He shrugged. "Like that it was written by a Blight? That would be fascinating. Almost all of the books on shadow magic are from the point of view of the gloamist, but what would it look like from the point of view of a shadow, one that was becoming conscious and learning how to follow its own desires?"

Charlie wasn't entirely sure she wanted to know, but she was getting an idea why another Blight might want to read it.

Minutes later, Charlie and Posey walked across the lawn to the parking lot. Knots of students passed them.

"Did you actually think my shadow was quickening?" Charlie asked her.

Posey shook her head. "Did you?"

"Of course not." Charlie stuck her hands deep in the pockets of her leather coat. "I would have told you."

Posey snorted, as though she wasn't so sure.

"You fit in here," Charlie said, looking around.

Her sister didn't reply.

"I'm serious," she said. "You're like these people."

Posey kicked a few wet leaves. "We're behind on the bills, and as you remind me, we can only afford the house because Vince is paying a chunk of the rent. School is a stupid expense. And besides, everything is going to be different now. You're one of them. In a year, when you're a gloom, we can do whatever we want. Even if what you want is for me to have a useless degree."

Charlie scowled at the ground, at her shadow. She'd never considered a future where she was one of the people with power. It would be nice to believe that meant she could give Posey something that would make her happy. But ever since they were kids, Charlie seemed to get things Posey wanted. Their mother's attention. Money in her pockets. And now, real magic.

But even if good things might be coming, first she was going to have to deal with Vince, who'd betrayed her, who was a liar with a hidden book, a connection to Salt and to violence. Knowing Vince's secrets felt like having a belly full of flies. Open her mouth, and she didn't think she could stop them from flooding out in a disgusting swarm.

15
THE PAST

With Rand gone, Charlie spent a few weeks kicking around. At school, she hung out with her friends. She had more time to go over to their houses and to party on the weekends.

For years she'd told herself that he was the one forcing her to participate in his schemes. But without them, Charlie found herself fidgety. She seemed to need more intensity than the people around her, required a higher dose of adrenaline before she felt anything.

Six months after Rand was buried, Charlie found herself back at the Moose Lodge. Benny laughed when he saw her walk through the door.

"Oh, come on, honey," he said. "You don't belong around here. Don't want to get the truant officer after us."

She dumped her backpack on one of the tables and walked around to the back of the bar. Checked the ice machine, which produced pellets that fused together and required vigorous use of the pick. She made him a martini just the way he liked it, cold vodka in a glass with the garnish of several olives to take the sting out.

"I want to do a job on my own," she told him as she pushed his drink toward him. "And I don't want to work for Knight."

He frowned at her. "The glooms are the ones that are hiring, these days."

"Okay," she said, although her palms had started to sweat. "Just not him."

He shrugged. "Willie's nephew, Stephen, got into stealing shadows. Says it's easy money. Says he can slash off a shadow the way you'd slash the strap of a purse; all you need is one of them onyx knives."

"So, what, you mug people?" She made a face, having picked up from Rand a dislike of crimes that didn't require any real talent.

"He's getting two hundred fifty a pop," he said. "Twenty times that if it's one of those magic ones, but that's dangerous."

She nodded thoughtfully.

He looked at her skeptically. "But you want a real job."

She straightened her shoulders. "What is it?"

"The kind of thing one of us might have attempted in our heyday, you know? You know the Arthur Thompson House?"

"Sure," Charlie told him. She'd gone there with her class, freshman year.

"There's this group of young gloamists who threw together some money and want someone to break in and steal a single page from one of the notebooks in a locked cabinet. It's supposed to have something to do with the use of shadows as absorbable energy to alter other shadows blah blah magical crap. You think you can do that?"

Arthur Thompson had invented harvesting electricity from storms and founded the first lightning farm around thirty years ago. That's what he'd been famous for, before the Boxford Massacre. That's what he ought to be best remembered for, according to Charlie's teachers, who wanted to preserve the legacy of a local legend in the face of kids' interest in the gruesome.

In addition to his interest in lightning, Arthur Thompson was interested in shadow magic. Being a man of science, when he discovered a booth at the county fair run by a group of fundamentalists who believed that gloaming was the work of the devil, he and two of his friends stopped to argue.

Long story short, they all got shot, Arthur died, and his shadow became a Blight who killed over a hundred people. But his house was preserved just the way he left it, including his workshop with all his notes.

"What does it pay?" Charlie asked.

Benny snorted. "Five hundred."

She eyed him, trying to figure how much his cut was. "That doesn't sound like much. That's the price of two stolen shadows."

He shrugged. "Yeah, you should probably stick to something easier."

She took the job.

Charlie had always considered herself prickly as a sea urchin, but if she wanted to be the kind of con artist that Rand had been, she was going to have to get better at charm. It was one thing following his cues, and another being responsible for the whole thing.

She practiced with the basics. The short-change con, where you buy a pack of gum with a twenty, then mess around trying to get the cashier to give you a ten for nine dollars while pocketing your change, then "correct" yourself by turning over a ten and getting your twenty back. It was some bullshit, but it required smooth talking and the appearance of honesty.

Then the pig-in-poke, which was particularly effective for a teenager. Charlie pretended to find a ring on a street that looked like gold, or something similarly valuable, then asked a passerby if it was theirs. Lots of times she didn't even have to suggest they give her a twenty and take the ring off her hands; they were so sure they were scamming her that they'd do it themselves.

It helped her figure out how much to smile, how shy to be, how eager. And she made sixty bucks, which wasn't nothing.

That Saturday, she got ready to pull her first job without Rand.

A call to the Arthur Thompson House got her the first bit of information that she needed. She discovered which groups were touring the house Monday, then went to the thrift store closest to the Catholic school the museum staffer mentioned. There, she was able to find herself a school uniform. It looked slightly moth-eaten and the skirt had been hemmed extra short by its last owner, but it cost only twelve dollars for the whole thing, including the white shirt.

At home, she experimented with her hair. Pigtails made her feel as though she was wearing a costume, but when she pulled her hair back into a high ponytail, put on black stockings and lip gloss and popped a piece of bubble gum in her mouth, it looked perfect.

It would be easy to get in—it was a museum, after all, and welcomed visitors—but much harder to get into a locked study and then a locked cabinet without anyone noticing. And much harder to cut a page out of a book and leave with it before getting stopped.

On Monday, she put her plan into swing. She told her mother she was sleeping over at Laura's house, then forged a doctor's note for school. Then she took the bus to Northampton. From a discreet distance, she watched the kids troop inside, gave them fifteen minutes, and showed up.

"I'm late," she told the woman at the front desk, looking as panicked as she was able. "I am so sorry. My mom had to drop me off and I am going to be in so much trouble. They're here, right? Can I go in?"

The woman hesitated, but only for a moment. "Go in. Hurry."

Charlie dashed past and joined up with them, relieved that the first part was over. She found the class but stayed clear of them until they went into Arthur Thompson's study. Then she moved into the flood of students and slid inside. This was the important part, because the door was alarmed and only one group was let in at a time.

Their teacher—a rather young-looking priest with an Eastern European accent—cleared his throat. "Now, we're going to listen with our ears, not with our mouths."

Charlie slid behind a bookshelf.

A museum staffer began to go into Arthur Thompson's childhood, the challenges of Harvard in the eighties, how the prototype of the lightning harvesting mechanism shocked him badly enough that he spent six weeks in a hospital.

"Is that when his shadow became magic?" asked one of the girls.

The priest gave her a speaking look, but the museum staffer nodded. "That's generally thought to be the case, since he pursued shadow magic after that. He joined some of the early message boards and even originated calculations about the energy exchange between the gloamist and their shadow."

"So what happened to him?" asked a boy in the back.

"Did you not do the reading, Tobias?" the priest demanded.

"No, I mean the shadow," the kid said. "Rowdy Joss, he called himself once he was a Blight, right? Like, did they hunt him down?"

"Nothing about that was in the reading," said the priest. "And we don't need to waste the time of the staff."

"I saw the video," the kid said. "Online."

The staffer smiled, although the smile had become slightly strained. "No one knows what happened to Arthur's shadow after the Boxford Massacre. There was some speculation that the transfer of energy created memory loss, or that it was confused. But remember that Rowdy Joss wasn't Arthur. Arthur died at the Boxford Massacre, a victim like everyone else that day."

Charlie listened to the conversation follow the familiar pattern, as the teacher and staffer valiantly struggled to get it back on track. Fifteen minutes later, the class filed out, leaving Charlie hidden behind the bookshelf. She waited until the room was empty to scoot out and crawl beneath Arthur Thompson's enormous desk.

She watched feet move back and forth, realizing she should have come in with the last group and not the third-from-last group. But it wasn't like she had to worry too much about not making noise or moving or something. Sound was all around her, a cacophony of giggling and gum chewing and lectures.

And then the final group filed out. From the other room, she heard the museum staffers—all two of them—talking together. One of them laughed. Then, distressingly, the hum of a vacuum began.

But it wasn't brought into the study and faded away after a few minutes.

Charlie breathed a sigh of relief.

She listened as the locks were engaged and the alarms set. Outside, night had fallen. Charlie crawled out, more nervous than she thought she'd be.

Despite all the houses she'd walked through, this felt different. The slightest sound made her start.

Taking a few steadying breaths, she used her phone to give her enough light that she could pick the lock of the cabinet. It took her three tries before her fingers were finally steady enough to open the door.

Behind it, she found the notebook they wanted—it was one of the ones on display. She flipped through until she found a page marked "Shadow Energy Exchange," then took a razor out of her backpack.

But as she got ready to slice, she felt guilty. It seemed wrong to hack up a book. When it was Rand doing stuff, she never had to think about *morals*. He was a bad guy, and they were doing bad stuff, and that was that.

Charlie ate a granola bar from her backpack, looking at the cabinet.

She walked around the room, looking at the photos. Arthur Thompson's original sketches of the lightning farm. A congratulatory letter from the governor. And in one corner, a letter from someone claiming to be a Blight in a looping, spidery hand.

To A. Thompson in the City of Northampton.

You have been trying to contact me and I urge you to desist. Yes, there are ancient beings in the shadows, but you are better off letting us stay that way.

I have no interest in being studied. My origin may have been with your kind, but I am of you no longer.

Written on the 23rd day of April by Cleophes of York

She frowned at it, wondering if Arthur Thompson's Blight was still hanging around, writing letters.

Finally, Charlie took out her phone and took a photo of the page from the notebook. It had the same information, and if that's what they wanted, this ought to be enough. Even as she did it, she had the sinking feeling that she was screwing up, but she couldn't bring herself to slice out the page.

Then she went to the windows, hoping there was a way out, but they were alarmed. Charlie sat down in the chair, spun it a bit. Played a game on her phone. Crawled back under the desk and napped.

And then she saw something in the window. A shadow in the corner of the room, sliding away from the wall. Charlie curled up more tightly and tried not to breathe.

It moved across the room, pausing at a strip of black tile that crisscrossed the floor. Then the shadow stepped over, becoming more solid as it did. For a moment, it took on features, as though of the gloom controlling it. Then it was past the onyx tiles and to the cabinet. It flooded through the keyhole and the cabinet door swung open.

Then the shadow became solid again, as though someone shaped the night into a human form. It must have to be like that to carry the book. Charlie's heart thundered and she held her breath again as it passed her by. It left the book tucked into a corner of the room, in a basket of rolled-up architectural plans that might have been reproductions.

As it flooded out the window, Charlie realized why it hadn't taken the book with it. It couldn't get it out the window or the door any better than Charlie could. But it could relocate the book so that the gloamist could come in tomorrow and slide it into his bag and leave without anyone the wiser.

It was almost dawn when she decided the shadow wasn't waiting outside and went over to the basket to look at the book.

And scowled. It was the exact volume she'd been sent to slice the page from. And belatedly, with a sense of wicked glee, she opened the book and took out her razor.

Whoever the gloamist was who was attempting to take the book was going to be very surprised when he got it. She hoped he was furious. She had the sudden, wild urge to sign her work and fought it down.

By the time the first class filed in the next day, Charlie was feeling giddy with victory and desperately in need of a toilet to pee in. As they left, Charlie scrambled out from under the desk and behind the bookshelves. One more class. One more lecture. And then she was out of there.

The next group filed into the study. Charlie smiled at a boy who moved to stand near her. She wiped the edge of her mouth and then frowned at him.

"You have something—" she said.

He knuckled where she'd pointed and she reached out to fix it for him. "There," she said. "Got it."

Charlie managed to stay out of sight of the teachers until it was time to leave. Then she tried to file out with the others, head down. Just at the door, she heard a voice.

"Hey," one of the teachers said. "You're not with this class."

She turned around guiltily, lipstick smudged. Watched the teacher's eye go to the boy, whose mouth she'd smeared with her lipstick.

"Keith!" she said. And then Charlie was out the door, and out of the museum, with what she hoped was a believable excuse for hightailing it out of there.

Benny set up her meeting for later in the day, at the parking lot behind a coffeeshop in the middle of town.

Three twentysomething glooms showed up. One of them had a vape pen in her mouth. Another was carrying a skateboard. They looked at her as though they would never have hired her if they'd realized how young she was.

"Here's your three hundred," the gloom with the vape pen said, gesturing airily.

Charlie opened her mouth to object and one of the others interrupted, smirking. "Take it or leave it."

"Leave it," Charlie said.

"Where are you going to sell the page, if not to us?" said the boy. "You think anyone else is going to give you a better deal?"

Charlie wondered if it was one of them who'd sent their shadow into the Arthur Thompson House, cutting out the others. Or if it was someone one of them had talked to, trying to snake it out from under them.

She could tell them, she supposed. But she didn't like them enough. "Six hundred, or I set it on fire. And the price is going up every time you negotiate."

They looked at one another. "No way."

"Seven hundred," Charlie said.

One of them laughed, and she fished a lighter out of the bottom of her bag. Flicked the flint wheel.

"Fuck off," said the one with the skateboard.

Charlie set the page on fire. It caught fast, burning to cinder in moments as they screamed. The ashes blew around, black shapes circling in the wind like shadows.

She sneered at the glooms, fighting down a wave of exhaustion at the lost night, the frustration at losing when she'd been so sure she'd won, and the certainty that this would have never happened to Rand.

"Do you know what you did?" the one with the vape pen demanded.

"I made sure no one would ever stiff me again," Charlie said, and walked off, keeping her head high and her shoulders squared.

That night she uploaded the photo she'd taken online. Sometimes she still saw it passed around. She could always tell it was hers because a corner of her finger was visible at the edge.

16

LICK YOUR WOUNDS

By the time Vince got home, Charlie pretended to be asleep, evening out her breaths, tucking her cheek against the pillow, pressing her nose to the cloth. He stood in the doorway, looking at her long enough for the hairs to rise along the back of her neck.

She knew she would have to confront him, but not now. Not when she was exhausted and the anger she should be feeling had somehow drained away, leaving her heavy with sadness. She didn't want Vince to be Lionel Salt's grandson, didn't want to have to wonder how far he'd go to protect his identity. If he'd murdered Hermes for recognizing him as Edmund Carver, did that mean he'd murder her too?

He can't realize I know, she reminded herself. *At least not yet.* But she still imagined Vince lying beside her, taking her pillow, and smothering her with it.

Imagined him holding a knife from her own kitchen behind his back as he got closer to the bed. Got distracted by remembering that she'd bought those knives at a TJ Maxx and they always needed sharpening. The last time she cut open a butternut squash, she'd really had to saw her way through. That would be a terrible way to go.

And given how fast he got rid of the last body, he wouldn't have any trouble getting rid of hers too. She didn't doubt that he had all the right solvents to clean things up so well that a forensic team would be hard-pressed to find evidence.

A shudder went across her shoulders and she bit her cheek to keep herself still.

That old chestnut about killers occurred to her—*a quiet guy, kept to himself.* That did describe Vincent.

She stayed still as he folded his pants and put his shirt in the laundry basket. Didn't move as he set his watch on the dresser, plugged his phone in to the charger.

Maybe she should get out ahead of this. When you lived with someone it ought to be easy enough to incapacitate them. Horse tranquilizers. Food poisoning. Offering to tie him to the bedposts for sex. Then she could interrogate him. Force him to admit everything. Ask him all the questions she'd always wanted to know.

And yet, what she longed for was for him to slide into bed and put his hand on her shoulder, to tell her he knew she was awake. To say that he loved her desperately and wanted to confess all the things he'd kept from her, and all the reasons for them. It was a childish desire, a wish for the world not to be as it was, for people to act in ways they just didn't. It was the wish of a sucker, ready to be fleeced for everything she had.

Vincent Damiano isn't a real person. She'd been so busy trying to make sure Vince didn't see behind her masks that she didn't notice that he was *all* mask.

Hole in the head, hole in the heart, or hole in the pocket. The Hall family curse.

Eventually, he left the room, flicking off the overhead light. She lay alone in the dark, eyes open. Outside, the streetlights shone. Behind her neighbors' houses, the old mill building rose, dark too, with the bright silver coin of the moon above.

It wasn't until the red light of dawn bled onto the horizon that she finally slept.

C harlie woke in the early afternoon, alone.

She stumbled out of bed, then poked her head into her sister's room to make sure that Vince hadn't gone crazy and chopped her in half or something. Posey was sleeping, one arm flung over her ancient MacBook.

Charlie put on a robe, went to the kitchen, and poured herself a mug of bitter, lukewarm coffee. She slid a steak knife into the pocket of the robe. Then she waited, stomach churning.

It was time to have the real talk.

Twenty minutes later, Vince came back in with two bags of groceries. Charlie couldn't help seeing the space through his rich-boy eyes. All the worn things. The grease stains. The shabbiness.

He took a look at her expression and set the bags on the counter, making no movement to unpack. "Did something happen?"

"You lied," Charlie said, meeting his pale eyes.

He didn't look defensive yet, but he did look wary. "I—"

"Trying to figure out which lie I'm talking about? It must be hard when there are so many," she snapped. *"Edmund Carver."*

"Don't call me that," he said.

"Because you prefer *Remy*? Or because you're afraid someone will hear?" She'd thought it would feel terrible to confront him, but it felt *great* to have the nastiness inside her finally spilling out. "Was it hard, to sleep on a mattress on the floor and not between your one-billion-thread-count sheets?"

He shook his head. "I swear to you, it wasn't like that."

But when she looked at him, all she saw was the Edmund Vincent Carver of the society pages, disdain in his smoke-colored eyes. Just a little pomade, the tilt of his jaw, and he'd be a stranger. If only she'd observed him more closely, she'd have seen it—picking out that Vacheron Constantin watch at twenty paces, knowing about the vacation homes of the upper class, the fucking love of gossip for fuck's sake. Not to mention the ability to murder people and believe there would be no consequences.

"Oh, you *swear* it. Well then, it *must* be true," she said, a snarl in her voice.

"I wanted to start over." Vince's voice stayed soft. "With no part of my old life. I didn't want you to see me the way I used to be."

"That's a good line. But it doesn't explain how you're supposed to be dead," Charlie told him. "Or how everyone's looking for a book you stole, including the guy who tried to kill me. Too bad you didn't keep that in the duffel in the back of our bedroom closet, along with your real license."

"You went through my things?" The sudden flatness of his voice was unnerving.

But Charlie rushed on, all her hurt finally alchemizing into anger. "That's right. I found the license. And then I found the newspaper story about how you murdered a girl, and then yourself," she said. "You want me to feel bad about invading your privacy?"

"Yes," he said, rubbing his hand over his face. "A little. I don't know."

"You know what else? I heard everything you said to Hermes. All of it. That's when I knew you were lying. And now I know why you killed him—because he recognized you."

Vince shook his head again, as though he could shake off her words.

"Go on," she said. "Deny it. Tell me you're not a pretend person in a pretend relationship."

"Is that what you really think?" His eyes were bright with a fury she'd never seen before. Shining with rage.

It made her hesitate. "What am I supposed to think? How many people did you kill for Lionel Salt?"

"Lots," he said, and closed his eyes.

She stared at him in horror. "The girl?"

He shook his head. "No, not Rose."

"How about the man they found in the car? The body you let everyone think was yours?" Her voice was as cold as she could have hoped, and as relentless.

"I couldn't make myself stop—" he began.

"—killing?" she finished for him. "My hand slipped and it happened to have an axe in it! Again. Whoops!"

"I'll go," he said abruptly, and turned toward the hall to their bedroom.

"You'd rather leave than answer?" she shouted after him.

He kept walking, his hand going to the wall at one point, as though he needed to catch himself. Of course he was going to go. Of course he was only there when she was easy, when everything was easy.

The cat followed him, tail lashing in an accusatory manner.

Charlie followed him. "Okay, where's the *Liber Noctem*? How about that? Everyone wants to know. Hermes did."

"What, so you can steal the book from me?" he asked, yanking open a drawer.

"Ideally," Charlie told him from the doorway, watching him start to stuff clothes in a bag. "It would sure make me a lot of money."

He stopped packing. "Salt is playing a game, and someone is playing a game with him. They want to make pawns out of all of us. The worst thing anyone could do is find that book."

"Okay, explain," she said. "Tell me what's going on."

"I can't," he told her.

"You don't want to," she said. "You never wanted me, did you? You only wanted somewhere to hide out and lick your wounds. You never loved me."

He looked as though she'd slapped him. Then something in his expression shifted, became a locked house at night, alarms set. "What do you know about love?" he said, hefting his duffel onto his shoulder. "I wasn't the only one who lied."

Charlie opened her mouth, but of all the things she had been ready to answer for, that hadn't been one of them. "Maybe I didn't tell you everything about me, but that's not the same as pretending to be someone—"

"*You're right*," he shouted, interrupting her. It was frightening to see him let go after so many months of restraint, and there was something in his eyes that made her wonder if he was afraid too. "I couldn't give you what you needed. I kept things from you. Even if you didn't know what was wrong, you could tell there wasn't enough of me. I wish I could say I was sorry, that I wanted to be honest the whole time, but I didn't. I *never* wanted to be honest. I just wanted what I told you to be the truth."

"Tell me anyway," she yelled back, unwilling to back down. "Be honest now. At least you owe me that."

"I don't," he said. "I won't."

"Fine, then fuck you. Run away. That's what you do, right? Go find another stupid girl to con."

The cat lunged and climbed halfway up Charlie's ankle and bit down on her calf three times in succession.

"Ow! Shit!" she shouted as Lucipurrr leaped away, racing into the other room. "The fuck is your problem, cat?"

Vince smiled, eyebrows going up, and Charlie laughed. A moment later, she was furious with herself for laughing, and with the cat, for being a demonic asshole, but she couldn't help it. And in that moment, she wondered if maybe she was wrong in thinking she didn't know Vince, that maybe there was some truer truth beneath the lies.

There was still a trace of a grin on his face when he turned away from her, duffel over his shoulder.

"It's not what you think," Vince said, from the mouth of the hall. He didn't turn, so she couldn't even try to interpret his expression. The humor had left his voice, though.

"Oh yeah?" she called after him. "Then why are you leaving?"

"Because it's worse."

A few minutes later she heard the screen door bang.

Charlie had to press her nails into her palm to force herself not to chase after him. Then the engine of the van started. Then the sound of tires on the crumbling asphalt of the driveway.

Charlie kicked the dresser. It hurt her bare feet more than she hurt the chipboard. She kicked it again.

Not only was there something so deeply wrong with her that the guy she'd been sure was a good person turned out to be a murderer who faked his own death and also the grandson of a person she hated, but *even that guy* left her.

She was a poisoned well of a girl.

Charlie kicked the dresser a third time for good measure.

And yet she wouldn't unknow any of it. She would have still stolen the receipt. Called the bookstore. Whispered mangled French. Gone through his stuff. That was her problem. Charlie Hall, never satisfied unless every last carcass was turned over and every last maggot revealed.

No, she was going to not think about the last forty-eight hours. She was going to rob Adam and then turn him over to Doreen, just like she'd planned. At least Charlie could torment someone else's terrible boyfriend, since she no longer had one of her own.

Charlie vaguely remembered that she wasn't supposed to want to do things like that, but that was back when she was trying to be good.

Trouble had found her once again, and she was ready to welcome it back. And if Adam happened to have the *Liber Noctem*, if by some chance he'd lifted it off Vince, so much the better.

Revenge on *everybody*. That would fill her time. That would keep her busy. Keep her from feeling her feelings.

If she couldn't be responsible or careful or good or loved, if she was doomed to be a lit match, then Charlie might as well go back to finding stuff to burn.

17

DO NOT DISTURB

O ne wonderful thing about heists was all the attention they absorbed.

When you were going to steal something or con someone, you couldn't think about your quickening shadow and whether to feed it blood or starve it back to sleep. Couldn't think about Vince's last words, or the way he'd looked at you when he'd come in from the store, grocery bags still in his arms.

What do you know about love?

Couldn't think about how she'd left the food on the counter and it was probably rotting.

No, she had to put aside whatever pain or trouble or sorrow she had. Table all her feelings until the work was done.

It stung to admit how right Rand had been about her, all those years ago. She'd taken to the hustle like a tiger takes to water, finding in it a respite from the heat.

Balthazar was right too. This was the only thing she'd ever been good at.

I n the parking lot outside the MGM hotel, Charlie got ready as quickly as she could. Primer over the lid, a smoky dark brown shadow in the crease. She drew liquid liner over the lash line on top, pressed white pencil to the tear line on the bottom, and black pencil lining the rest of her eye. She finished off with mascara—gobs of it, going over the lashes three times, four times. Then fake ones glued on top.

Blinking at herself in the rearview mirror, she smeared on foundation two shades lighter than her skin, blending it out with her fingers, added contouring under her cheekbones and along the sides of her nose with a brush, followed by more blending, blush, and highlighter. When she was done, her nose looked narrower and her cheeks fuller, changing her face. Finally, she put on her wig, pinned it, and brushed her red hair around a bit with her fingers until it looked as natural as she could get it.

When she looked in the mirror, Charlie Hall was gone. It was more of a relief than she liked to admit.

The hotel at the MGM Springfield was about twenty minutes from Easthampton. The casino had opened a handful of years ago, on the theory it would bring money into a city sorely lacking for it. Despite endless editorials in the local paper on how it was likely to make things worse for residents instead of better, nothing could stop the wheels of industry once they had whirred into motion.

The result was a football stadium–sized warehouse of slots, complete with flashing lights, multicolored carpet, and almost-all-night cocktails. But as Charlie walked into the hotel, she was surprised to find it to be both industrial and cozy.

Bookshelves covered the brick walls, with a balcony library suspended over the front desk. Oversized printer blocks hung behind the receptionists, and the couches were of brown leather, the kind you'd expect to nap on in a professor's study. The whole place had a Vegas-meets-train-station feel that Charlie didn't mind at all.

One look around, though, and she could tell it was populated the same way as any other casino hotel, people there to party with friends or to step away from their lives for a few hours, surrounded by grifters hoping to leech off any winnings. Charlie didn't mind that either.

An afternoon wedding must have just concluded in one of the ballrooms, because kids were running around in white dresses, their hair in puffs and their braids dressed with flowers. A few elegant sequined and suited individuals— including two women in magnificent hats—stood at the edge of the bar, talking.

Charlie sat in one of the library chairs, far enough from people so as not to be heard, and called Adam's room. It rang five times before it went to messages. He wasn't there.

Then she checked discreetly for the positions of the security cameras and got on the elevator. As she did, Vince's words came back to her.

I wish I could say I was sorry, that I wanted to be honest the whole time, but I didn't. I never wanted to be honest. I just wanted what I told you to be the truth.

She'd thought some variation of that before herself, and never admitted it to anyone.

In the elevator, Charlie was carefully not meeting the eyes of the other passengers—a pizza delivery guy and two girls with wet hair and towels, coming from the pool—while cultivating a demeanor of boring and slightly dissipated benevolence. On the eighth floor, she stepped out and followed the signs until she counted her way down to room 455.

A "Do Not Disturb" card hung from the handle of the door. Charlie pulled it off and stuck it in the pocket of her coat. For good measure, she knocked. There was no sound from within.

Better and better.

Charlie was well aware she'd missed her chance for the quick in-and-out of two nights before. This was going to be a bit trickier. Still, it was one door between her and success.

She knew a woman who'd stumbled into a lobby in lingerie, with an ice bucket, stinking of liquor, claiming to have locked herself out of her room. It had gotten her a "replacement key," but Charlie wasn't sure she could pull that off, nor was she sure she wanted to be quite that memorable. Her current scheme was less flashy but had a lot less potential for humiliation.

In all but the fanciest hotels in the biggest cities, there's a room with an ice dispenser and, if you're lucky, a soda machine. They never have cameras in them. She slipped into the one on the eighth floor, and from there, called the front desk.

"Hello," she said. "Could you transfer me to housekeeping?"

"Just a second," said a man's voice.

The phone rang twice and picked up. A woman this time, who grunted out a greeting.

"This is Shirley in 450," Charlie said, affecting a thick Long Island accent. "Can you send someone up to clean the room?"

The woman said she would. By the time Charlie disconnected the call, an anticipatory thrill sped her pulse, not unlike that from a downed shot of espresso. It was the worst cure for a bruised self-esteem, to test your mettle and wit against the universe.

The universe was always going to win, but maybe not today.

At her most depressed, Charlie had seen a therapist to whom she'd admitted a very abbreviated list of problems. She'd been told to practice "mindfulness," which involved "being present in the moment" and "not dwelling on all your past mistakes," as well as "all the mistakes you plan to make in the future." Charlie had not been very good at doing that in the therapist's office, nor had she been good at the mindfulness app she'd downloaded, but in the middle of a con, she felt as though she might understand what mindfulness actually felt like.

She was fully present in this moment.

A tense twenty minutes later, a young woman with purple hair pushed a cart full of towels out of the elevator and down the hall.

Charlie took a breath, stepped out, and passed her. As she did, she made herself stumble. One bump with her elbow as her fingers snatched the universal key card from the pocket of the woman's housekeeping shirt. Dropped it into her own pocket and took out a cinnamon hard candy, just like Ms. Presto had taught her.

It was possible that when the young woman noticed her key card missing she'd connect it to Charlie, but by the time a security team decided to knock, she planned on being long gone.

"You okay?" the woman asked.

Charlie laughed. "Got a little tipsy at the wedding," she said, and then she was three doors down and into Adam's room.

It was clear that the "Do Not Disturb" sign had been hanging on the door for some time. Clothes covered the wooden floor and a large plastic bottle of cheap vodka, half-empty, cap off, sat beside the sleek television in its modern frame. The air smelled of stale cigarettes, and wires hung from the smoke detector Adam had disabled.

Now she just had to find the book.

The side table next to the bed was empty, save for a box of condoms. In the bathroom, she found an array of hair products, aftershave, and cologne. The drawer held a gold vape pen and nothing else.

As she moved around the room, she was uncomfortably reminded of going through her own bedroom just a day before.

That memory brought her to the closet. She opened it to find only a coat hanging inside. She shoved her fingers into the pockets. Just some paper.

She unfolded that and found herself looking at the receipt for a ring, from Murray's pawnshop. Adam had gotten seven hundred for it. Huh. The description read: *Woman's cocktail ring, antique red gold, replacement stone.* Doreen had a ring like that, passed down to her from her grandmother.

Charlie shouldn't have been surprised that Adam was stealing from Doreen. Once you started light-fingering things, once you realized you could get what you wanted by saying what other people liked to hear, it was easy to make excuses and hard to stop.

Rand used to say that con artists lived on the edges of society, smiles firmly in place no matter how bad things got. It had seemed romantic.

But now Charlie saw the vast insecurity that fed it. The constant need to be the cleverest. The knowledge that no one wins every time becoming more dare than warning.

She wondered what Adam had gotten into, and how bad it had gone, that despite having a book to move, he needed money on top of it.

For regular people, pawnshops were used for a quick infusion of cash to get them through a tough time, hoping that the due date on the payback for their grandmother's porcelain, or their wedding ring, or whatever, didn't come before they managed to be able to put together the funds to retrieve it. For criminals, they were a decent way to move items. Murray's pawnshop was one that Charlie knew. She'd sold things there herself.

Since she had the receipt, Charlie could get the ring back, if she had seven hundred dollars. Which she didn't. And even if she had, she wouldn't have spent it on this.

Charlie shoved the paper in her pocket. It was possible that Doreen could take it to the police. Stolen items weren't supposed to be sold in pawnshops, and getting busted occasionally was just the price of doing most of your business looking the other way.

At least she had something to hand over to her client.

She was about to turn away when the coat snagged her attention. It was hanging oddly, as though a weight pulled down the back. Charlie pressed against the length of the lining until she felt something solid.

Solid and rectangular and . . . *fuck*.

Charlie took out her knife and carefully cut open the lining until the contents fell into her hand: an A5-sized leather notebook. This was no ancient *Book of Blights*. This was a modern notebook, the kind you could buy in any stationery store. The writing inside was done in ballpoint pen.

The first page was labeled *The Myriad Observations of Knight Singh*. For a moment, Charlie just stared at it.

This was the book Balthazar had tried to get her to find, and steal, on the same night Doreen came into Rapture. The night that Paul Ecco was murdered.

She was too puzzled to be disappointed.

What was in Knight's papers that was so important Adam would need to hide behind Amber with the long hair? Who was it that he wanted to sell it to that he didn't think Balthazar would work with?

Charlie had a sinking feeling.

Well, Adam might have been clever enough to get Knight's papers, but he wasn't going to be clever enough to keep them. Charlie shoved the book up under her dress, so the underwire of her bra pressed it against her skin.

Time to go. Halfway to the door, she heard the unmistakable mechanical click of a key card unlocking the door.

She veered into the bathroom, stepping into the tub just as the door opened.

Crouching down, she tried to soundlessly adjust the shower curtain so it hid her as completely as was possible. Not her finest moment.

Adam's voice came from the other room. "Yeah, I bet six hundred. You swear this thing's fixed?"

She heard the click and flare of a lighter. Scented the catch of the cigarette. Felt the strain of crouching like she was already, her fingers on the edge of the tub to steady herself, a corner of Knight Singh's book jabbing her in the stomach.

"Yeah, box exacta on Vantablack and Wild Mars Rover." His voice changed, suddenly deferential. "No, I'm not doubting you. Of course not."

Charlie tried to stop breathing so she could be sure to hear what he was saying.

"When I make fourteen grand, the book's yours. Going to go home to my girl a hero."

That would have been a much sweeter sentiment if he hadn't ditched Doreen and their kid for days, and stolen her ring to boot. At least now Charlie understood what he needed it for. Someone had offered him a gambling tip for the book.

Knight had been a member of the Cabal, a local governing body for gloamists. On his own, he had a small organization with its hands in a lot of things, including art theft and political manipulation. He mainly employed puppeteers.

With him gone, there might be a power vacuum at the top. Knight's accumulated knowledge would help anyone make a play for the leadership role. Another puppeteer, using their shadow to mess with the world. Slow a punch in boxing. Jerk a hand on a wheel while coming around a turn. Or trip a horse on a track. Another puppeteer, with a lot of ambition and not a lot of cash.

She supposed it could be a decent deal, but it was definitely a *bootleg* deal. Adam really must have wanted to move the book fast.

"I got it off Raven," he said from the other room. She heard the springs of the bed groan. "I don't know if she read it."

Charlie's legs shook from holding her position. She could risk sitting, which would be bad if she had to get up quickly. Or she could stay like she was and hope that her muscles didn't cramp, which would make her even slower and less able to run, if it came to that.

She frowned at her shadow, dark against the white tile, another thing that might give her away.

The cat had bitten her that afternoon. Could that have been enough blood to finish its quickening? A shadowy form coming toward Adam could chase him straight into the hall. He'd probably continue on to the lobby, shouting at the top of his lungs, imagining it was an angry gloamist after him.

Move, she told her shadow. *Do something.*

Her shadow remained just where it was.

Oh, come on, she thought. *Be magic.*

Inert.

You'd do it for blood, wouldn't you? If I tossed a napkin soaked with it, like a stick for a dog.

Or like a napkin soaked with blood for a dog, she supposed.

Please. But nothing happened. And her legs only hurt worse. *What good are you then?*

Taking a chance, putting her hand on the tile, she slowly pushed herself to her feet. She could stand for a lot longer, but if he came into the bathroom, he'd be sure to see her.

She hadn't heard him throw the dead bolt. If she could hop out of the shower, get across the room fast enough, she could be out the door before he got up off the bed. Except that it would be almost impossible to get out of the shower without making some sound. If he just turned on the television, she might be tempted to try.

In the other room, Adam was on a second call. "Yeah, I'm just going to take a quick shower and then I'll meet you at the bar."

She had to get out of the room, *immediately.*

Slowly and carefully, she pulled her cell from her pocket.

He'd already found a way to move the book, so Amber would hold no appeal, even if he hadn't blocked her. Charlie could use her regular phone—send him a text, pretending to be a stolen credit card alert, or the hotel manager. But if he called back, it wasn't like she could answer from his bathtub.

Charlie flipped a mental list of people she knew, plus the things she might be able to convince them to say. Maybe she could convince Barb to call and tell him there was a delivery for Adam that he needed to go down and sign for. Maybe she could get Posey to call and tell him that his car was on fire.

Then she thought of the one person who could definitely get him up and out of the room. *Doreen.*

From the other room, she could hear him rummaging through his drawers.

Fucker sold your gram's ring, Charlie wrote.

For a moment there was no response and Charlie started to sweat.

Then Doreen's text came: *Asshole. I'm going to kill him. Where is he?*

Charlie smiled. She typed as fast as she could. *MGM hotel, Room 455. He's there right now, if you want to give him a piece of your mind.*

There was a long pause. Charlie put one hand against the wall.

The response came back: *Are you with him?*

One thing Charlie could rely on was how much Doreen hated to wait. She'd been restless at Rapture, impatient in every text. Back in high school she would tap her foot against the back rung of Charlie's chair and futz with a pen all through class.

Charlie simply didn't answer. In less than thirty seconds, the landline hotel phone started to ring.

He picked up, and there was a long pause. "How did you find me?

"You're coming *here*?" he said. "Baby, wait a second. How do you have my room number?"

Charlie heard steps coming toward the bathroom and she went back into a crouch. Listened as he pissed in the toilet. He swore twice, kicked the wall, then walked out of the room. She heard the door close and the electric lock engage.

Legs stiff and shaking, Charlie climbed out of the bathtub, using the towel rack to help her. She hobbled to the door. She wanted to yank it open and run, but forced herself to count to fifty. Then she walked into the hall and headed for the stairs. Taking the steps two at a time, she headed down. On the fifth floor, she had to stop and take a few deep breaths. Panic had made her breathe too shallowly and she was dizzy from it.

In the lobby, she kept her head high and her gaze on the exit. She reminded herself that even if Adam knew what Charlie looked like, she was in a wig. She could probably walk right past Doreen without being spotted.

As she hit the doors, fresh, cold autumn air broke over her. She inhaled and felt the pure hit of adrenaline that came when a job was almost over. And now, with Knight Singh's book tucked under her bra, she had the promise of a new job ahead of her.

Ten minutes later she was parking too close to the curb on Meadow Road, in front of Murray's Fine Jewelry. If she got Doreen's ring, then she'd have something to turn over in exchange for fixing things at Posey's school. And to make up for having boosted the book from Adam.

"Charlie Hall," Murray said as the bell clanged behind her and she looked around at the familiar, dusty shelves. "What did you bring me?"

He was a small man, red-haired and wearing wire-framed glasses that magnified his eyes uncannily. She'd been selling him stolen goods since she was fifteen and Rand decided it was important for her to learn "the back end" of the business.

Charlie walked to the counter. She looked down at the rings. "Can I see that one?"

Murray's eyes narrowed slightly, but he took out the tray.

She put her finger on Doreen's ring. "This ring was stolen, you know."

He raised both eyebrows. "That's a real shame."

She sighed, because while it was true that Doreen could call the cops, they didn't usually get involved in domestic disputes about communal property. "I'll trade you for a tip on a fixed horse race."

He laughed. "You want me to play the ponies? And if I lose, what, come collect the ring from you? You know I like you, kid, but I deal in sure things."

"It's a box exacta on Vantablack and Mars something," she said, turning the ring over in her fingers, admiring the flash of the stone and the richness of the gold. "Oh, come on, you can't tell me that a pawnshop isn't a little like gambling."

"If you're good at it, it's not," he grumbled. "That stone's fake, you know."

"Huh," she said, bringing it closer to her face and giving it a more thorough inspection. The tines holding what she'd supposed to be a diamond were a different shade from the rest. A bright, yellow gold.

"Does Adam know?" Charlie asked.

Murray shook his head. "Him? He sold it to me years ago."

"Then how come you paid him so much for what's left?" Charlie asked, wondering whether, in the end, Doreen would consider the ring recovered if she found out her diamond was gone.

"So you know the price I gave him too?" Murray snorted. "For your information, I paid for the *gold*. Twenty-two carats. That's why the band is so scratched. Too soft for regular wear not to damage it."

Charlie gave Murray her best good-pupil smile. "Come on, this tip's good. And it sounds like the ring is only so-so."

Murray grunted. Then he opened his laptop and started typing something into it. Charlie slid the ring onto the knuckle of her middle finger. Looked around the store.

In one of the other cabinets, she noticed a display of onyx. Rings, earrings, pendants, a net of polished onyx beads, and handcuffs lined with strips of onyx rested in the case. Beside those were gloves like the ones that Odette had, but instead of shining nails, they were black stone. Then there were powders to add to nail polish or press into lipstick, a few fake teeth, and a large array of carved onyx knives. A big one hung behind the register. Murray's other business. Selling protection from shadows.

"I see your race here. *Wild* Mars *Rover*. How sure are you about this?" Murray asked.

A good question. Adam had seemed certain, but Adam was an idiot. "Totally sure." After all, equivocating wouldn't make him blame her less if he lost the money.

"All right," he said. "Take the ring back to your little friend. But if this doesn't come through, you're going to be getting me twice the value of what I lost—and you're going to get it in something easy to move, like uncut gems. Or stolen shadows. Agreed?"

"Yeah," Charlie said, slipping the ring all the way onto her finger and then pointing down at the black knives. "You sell a lot of these?"

"More all the time. You can't be too careful," he said. "People say onyx can cut through the night."

"How much?" she asked.

Murray smiled a kind, grandfatherly smile. "I'll add it to your tab. Better get it from someone you trust. Too much shined-up resin out there, looking like stone."

"Appreciated," she told him.

He chose one of the knives from the case, wrapped it in a cloth, and slid it into a bag. "Hope the horses come through."

"You and me both," she said, and headed out the door. As she did, she noticed one of the bricks on the threshold was a polished black. No puppeteer was sending a shadow in there.

In the car, sitting behind the wheel, she opened the pouch and took out the knife. Pressed her finger against the side. It wasn't particularly sharp—stones didn't hold an edge like metal did.

Onyx can cut through the night.

She hadn't carried an onyx knife with her since she stopped stealing from gloamists—and her old one had a big chunk broken off it. Despite not being sharp, an onyx knife was an excellent weapon against a shadow. The onyx forced it solid, so it could be hit, and weakened it.

She'd need the knife, now that Vince wasn't around to break people's necks.

With the job over, there was no way to prevent herself from thinking of him. No way to avoid the gut punch of him being gone. No way to avoid the sadness that was coming to smother her.

But at least he understood that Charlie Hall was no sucker. She wasn't a mark.

Edmund Vincent Carver. She took out her phone to stare at the picture of his license again, to study it as though she could know him from that picture. Her gaze slid to the address, right there in Springfield.

Might as well swing by.

The apartment building was on the smaller side, with four high-ceilinged stories. Old brick covered the exterior. If she hadn't been able to guess the age of the building from the patina, the nonstandard-sized windows would have given it away. Every air conditioner jutting out from one had to be braced at an odd angle to fit.

Charlie went up the steps. There were ten buttons on the buzzer. The first three didn't get a response. The fourth and fifth had no idea who she was asking about. The sixth got a grumbled hello.

"I have a package here for Edmund Carver," she said. "Needs a signature."

"He doesn't live here." A guy, from the sound of the voice.

"Well, maybe you could forward it to him," Charlie suggested. If he would open the door, she believed she could weasel her way inside and refuse to leave until he told her *something*. "I just need someone to sign."

"I told you, he's not here. He's dead."

It was not particularly convincing that he started out with "not here" and ended with "dead." She decided to take a gamble. "Look, I lied. I'm a friend and I really am trying to find him—"

There was a quaver in the voice. "Go away. I don't want any of this at my door. I've told all of you—I don't know anything. Most nights he didn't even sleep here, and he didn't leave anything behind. Now, *go away*." The intercom stopped crackling.

Charlie pressed the buzzer again, and again, but he didn't return.

She looked over at her car but walked around the back of the building instead, where the trash cans were kept. It didn't take her long to find one that had junk mail addressed to apartment 2B among the coffee grounds and eggshells and takeout containers. A glossy catalog of scrubs, only slightly smeared with old soup, had the name Liam Clovin, MD, printed on the back.

18

THE PAST

Born as a wisp of a thing, ephemeral as smoke from a cigarette. Succored with blood, with scraps of horror and self-disgust. Embarrassing desires. I want her. I want him. I want that.

Catch the ball, he says, and I catch it. Are they my hands or his?

Chase me, he says. *Find me.* It's too easy. To lose him, I'd have to lose myself.

He wants me to laugh. Shows me how. Shows me funny things. Cats that fall off tables. Teenagers skateboarding into lakes.

You're my only friend, he tells me sometimes. But that's only true because his mother keeps him home from school. Because he has dirty clothes. Because he can't invite anyone over.

I'm scared she'll die. I want her to hold me when I am crying, when I am feverish, when I am afraid. Want her to smooth back my hair. Kiss my forehead. I hate her. Maybe I'd be better off if she were dead. None of those feelings are mine, but they become mine. They become me.

Sometimes she takes us to the supermarket and only puts the cheap, heavy stuff in her cart. Sugar. Flour. Milk. She tells him to shove packages of chicken breasts and pork chops into his backpack.

No candy, she says. They expect kids to steal candy. That's how they catch you.

There are mirrored pieces of the ceiling that let people watch. There are security cameras.

But none of them are watching me. We take what she wants. We take candy. We take everything.

Then his grandfather takes us to his big house, where there is a girl to play with and enough food for everyone. If Remy is hungry, someone makes him food. If Remy cries, someone will come. But Remy doesn't cry anymore. He gives all his tears to me.

The arrangement is simple. We can stay here so long as I do bad things. People have a spark inside of them, and what I have to do is put it out. Every time I do, some of the spark gets on me, in me like the smear left behind from crushing a lightning bug. Killing is easier than stealing, but I don't like the way that Remy looks at me when we're done.

I am changing. The sparks are doing something.

I am having trouble going back to sleep when Remy doesn't need me.

I am restless. Something is wrong with me. Something is right with me. I can do things that Remy doesn't know about. When he's asleep, I wander the house, the thin tether never growing taut. I can juggle oranges, and turn on the radio like a poltergeist. Read books, draw a picture in the condensation on the windows.

It's my idea, the first time. I want to see what will happen. Cut the cord. And then when it happens, I am scared. There is an emptiness where Remy was, and it feels like falling through the night. I have never been alone. There isn't enough of me to be alone.

Each time it happens, I forget things. Little things. Where I was. How long I was gone.

Adeline tells me things, but they're not all true. I don't want to listen to her anymore.

Sometimes, the air around me feels charged, like a storm coming on. I think I might be angry. I think I might be furious. I think I might be about to do something I am going to regret.

Remy makes me a promise. Shhhhh. We're going to run away. Then it will be just me and not me and not him. He's going to fix me. He's going to help me.

But first, blot out a few more sparks. Drown a few more stars.

19
CANDY CRACKS TEETH

Charlie texted Doreen that she'd gotten the ring and then took herself to Blue Ruin to wait and think through what she was going to do with Knight Singh's book.

The bar was in a tiny, grotty brick building, far from the downtown. On the outside, a faded sign proclaimed it "The Bluebird." No one ever called it that, though. It was a third-shift bar, opening at five a.m. and announcing last call at two a.m. Between two and five, it became a restaurant with an extremely limited menu. If you ordered enough cocktails to get you through the three-hour lull in service, you could drink for twenty-four hours straight.

The five a.m. crowd were usually nurses and doctors from Cooley Dickinson Hospital, mixed in with maintenance workers, hospital concierges, and second-shift restaurant workers looking for a place to go after exhausting all other venues.

Blue Ruin wasn't pretty. The scarred bar and tables in it had been purchased during the liquidation sale of an old tavern and didn't fit well into the space. The floor was sticky all the way to the door, the liquor was served in plastic cups, and the only thing they had for garnish were sad-looking limes.

If ever there was a bar that perfectly captured how Charlie felt that afternoon, it was Blue Ruin. She sat down on a stool, reassured to know she could stay all night.

An hour later, she was three Maker's Marks in, with no desire to slow down.

Doreen had texted to say that she was on her way over and a lot of other things that Charlie hadn't bothered to read. Charlie had another text from her high school friend Laura about missing her barbecue, plus one from her mother about her new boyfriend's birthday and how she was hoping they could all get together. Maybe the girls would like to host, since their place was bigger?

There were two voice mails from work, asking about her coming in on Monday night. She tried to imagine being back there behind the bar, making drinks. Trying not to think of the glass and the blood and choking on shadow. Trying not to think about the sound Hermes's neck made when it broke.

She ignored the messages and went into the bathroom to wipe off her makeup. She managed only to turn it into a glittering charcoal smear that covered her eyes and part of her cheeks. Exhaustion and irritability were creeping in on her faster than the alcohol could stave off.

There was always a dizzying high immediately after a job, followed by an adrenaline drop. Then everything felt a little too dull and you became a little too sensitive. Like right then, when she looked at herself in the mirror, staring into her own dark eyes and drawing a finger over her own scarred lip, she felt unexpectedly and humiliatingly like crying.

It wasn't because of Vince. It had nothing to do with him.

She went back to the bar and ordered another drink. If you were going to drown your sorrows, you needed a lot of liquid.

The bartender was a friend of Don's and tried occasionally to make conversation, but Charlie wasn't doing a good job of keeping up her end. At some point she realized he might be flirting.

"Kyle," he told her with a grin, looking up from his phone. "That's my name. Maybe Don told you about me."

Charlie was suddenly sure that Don had told Kyle about *her*.

Kyle had a head full of thick, wavy brown hair. A tattoo of a rosary climbed his arm from the wrist. His shadow appeared utterly normal. He'd be better at erasing her dread and horror and sadness than all the whiskey in the world.

For fifteen to twenty minutes, at least.

She ought to call someone. Laura, so she could apologize for not showing up for the barbecue. Barb, who could make her laugh. José, who was sad too.

"Did you know," she told Kyle, trying to make conversation, "a few grains of salt are supposed to take out the bitter in coffee. Isn't that strange, to think it works better than sugar?"

"I don't think that's true."

Kyle was probably a terrible bartender. She shrugged. "I like things bitter anyway. Like me."

He gave her a look like he wasn't sure how to take that.

A warning, she ought to tell him. *Take it as a warning that I am in a very bad mood and happy to have an excuse to take it out on you.*

Charlie wanted everyone to think of her as hardheaded and hard-hearted. Hard as old petrified wood, as rocks, as candy that cracks your teeth. But she wasn't.

"There you are." Doreen sat down next to her at the bar, clearly seething. "The great Charlie Hall." She was wearing work clothes—white jeans and a collared blue shirt with the name of the dental place where she was a receptionist embroidered over her heart. She must have dashed out of work when she'd gotten the texts about Adam's whereabouts.

Charlie rolled her eyes. "What? I got your guy and your ring."

"Please tell me you didn't rob a pawnshop." Doreen's voice was loud enough to make the few other grizzled-looking patrons wasting their day look over at her.

Charlie shrugged.

"Adam was just borrowing the ring. He told me he was using the money to make a deal that was going to change our lives." Doreen obviously wanted to believe that. "He wasn't rolling bliss."

"Maybe he told you about the stone in the ring not being original too," Charlie said. "Because he sold it years ago."

Doreen flushed. "You really are like the devil, you know that? Knowing all our sins."

Charlie felt as though she was observing the conversation from very far away. "That's ridiculous. I'm a fuck-up, Doreen. But I found your guy and even got your ring, so if you learned something you didn't want to know about Adam, too bad."

They stared at one another for a long moment.

Charlie took off the ring and put it down on the bar top. When Doreen reached for it, though, Charlie covered it with her hand. "You made some threats about what your brother could do to Posey's account at UMass. I want a confirmation that the deadline for paying has been pushed back. Three months at least. I need to see the notice on my phone when I sign in to my account."

"You can't expect him to risk—"

"I one thousand percent do." One of the more frustrating things about trading her work for other work was that people put a high value on her trade until a thing was done, then became convinced it must have been easy. Renegotiation was never in her favor.

Doreen looked at the ring under the cage of her hand. "That's mine."

"It will be," Charlie said. "As soon as you call your brother and I get that email."

Doreen made a show of taking her phone out of her pocket as she walked to the door. A few minutes later she came back in, mouth pinched.

"You know, Adam said he was going to get my ring back. He used it as collateral for a loan."

"That's interesting," Charlie said, in a way that let Doreen know how uninteresting she found it.

Doreen sighed. "I talked to my brother. He says he can't access your bill. It's not working."

"You've got to be kidding me," Charlie said. "What does that mean?"

"He doesn't know." Doreen looked worried, which was the only reason that Charlie didn't accuse her of making this whole thing up. "It could come from a different department that doesn't run their billing through his office. Or your account could have been flagged. But he *tried*."

For a moment, Charlie felt a white-hot flush of anger, most of it at herself.

She took her hand away from the ring. It occurred to her, not for the first time, that if she had been half as interested in making money from her schemes as she was in the schemes themselves, she'd be better off.

Doreen hesitated. "Now what?"

"Go on," Charlie said. "Take it. Fuck it. Fuck you. Fuck me. Fuck *everything*."

"What is wrong with you anyway?" Doreen gestured around, as though to indicate that Blue Ruin wasn't a very nice place, it was late afternoon, and Charlie was well on her way to wasted.

"I'm celebrating," Charlie said. "Being single."

Doreen gave a bitter little laugh. "Well, look at you. Brought down by love. Suffering just like everybody else."

"Have a drink with me," Charlie said, raising her plastic cup. "To suffering."

"I've got to get back to work," Doreen said, disgusted. "I have responsibilities. And I guess you do too, so don't suck down so much whiskey that you forget yours. Oh, and if you did knock over a pawnshop, don't implicate me when the police come after you."

"If I'm lucky, I'll suck down so much whiskey I forget we had this conversation." Charlie threw back the Maker's in a single gluttonous gulp. "Bring me the bottle, Kyle."

"You know," said Doreen, halfway to the door, "I saw your guy once, and the minute I saw him I knew he was going to cheat on you. Guys who look like that—"

"Nobody knew him," Charlie told her.

"Except for you?" Doreen snorted.

Charlie shook her head. "Nobody. He didn't exist. Never did."

Making a noise of frustration at the incomprehensibility of drunks, Doreen left.

"You didn't really knock over a store, right?" Kyle asked her as he brought over the bottle of Maker's.

She gave him her toothiest smile. "Definitely didn't."

"You actually want to buy this?" He set it down next to her.

"Definitely do." She poured her own drink out of her own bottle. It was like being in one of those fancy places with bottle service, except for the fancy part.

It didn't matter if she couldn't afford it. Her future was clear. She was going back to work for the gloamists. Paying for Posey's school the way she should have from the start. Making a clean break from her friends. If she was going to blow up everything around her, then she needed to keep everyone she cared about far away.

Fuck everything.

Charlie stayed at Blue Ruin into the evening, messing with the jukebox in the corner, going in with two elderly alcoholics on a pizza they got delivered, and dancing around with one of them to an old song from the eighties. Things started to blur together. The room began filling up. She remembered sitting on the toilet in the bathroom, sticking the back of a pin she found in her bag into her skin over and over. She remembered falling down on and lying on the floor and Kyle saying something about how he wasn't supposed to serve her if she couldn't stand, which made her laugh and laugh.

She didn't need him. She had her own bottle.

As she climbed back up on her stool, holding on to the edge of the bar to steady herself, her former boss from Top Hat walked into Blue Ruin with three of his friends.

"Well, well," he said, giving her a once-over. "Look at what the cat dragged in."

"Richie, never met a cliché you didn't like," she said, trying to disguise the slur in her voice. He was in his early fifties, with hair that was thinning on top and eyes like a raptor. He owned property all over the Valley, including two bars and three restaurants. When he'd fired her, it was with the expectation that it meant she wouldn't be able to work anywhere else, and he took it as a personal affront that she had.

"Over at Rapture, I hear."

"Yeah . . ." The Valley was small, but she didn't like the idea of it being *that* small.

He mimed the lashing of a whip and waggled his eyebrows. "You tying people up now? I bet you like that." His friends chuckled.

"Rot in hell," she said, without any heat.

"Oooh, don't get out the thumbscrews."

Charlie threw the mostly empty bottle of Maker's at him. He dodged in time so that it smashed against the wall behind him. Liquor ran down the dingy paint.

"Crazy bitch!" But he was no longer smug, no longer sure that he could say whatever he wanted and the people around him were going to take it. He even looked a little bit scared. She liked scared.

A smile pulled at the corners of Charlie's mouth.

"You've got to go," Kyle told her, then leaned forward and lowered his voice. "You probably shouldn't come back for a while, either."

"Been kicked out of better places." Charlie got up and carefully put on her coat while Richie glared. She counted the cash for her tab and tip and placed it on the wet counter. Then she blew a kiss to the old man she'd danced with and was immensely gratified when he mimed catching it.

She only stumbled twice on her way out the door.

C harlie woke in the back seat of her car with a dry mouth and a pounding head that felt as though it were stuffed with insulation foam. Her limbs were stiff with cold. Rain pattered against the roof, and the sky outside was dark and heavy with the promise of more.

Moving to sit up, she caught sight of her reflection in the glass of the window. Her mascara had run and, although she didn't remember crying, her cheeks were streaked with the tracks of tears. A familiar shame washed over her. She'd had so many nights like this, when she'd woken up with the knowledge that she'd done something for momentary satisfaction that would turn out to be in no way worth the cost.

But as she clambered down the hill into the stretch of woods to piss on some leaves, she was willing to embrace all her faults. She'd been lying to herself when she thought she could change.

She was the exact same Charlie Hall she'd always been. Messy. Impulsive. Alone.

Walking up to her car, Charlie saw that someone else was standing beside it. A man with white hair and a long black wool coat.

Her stomach churned.

"You must be Charlie Hall," he said. "I'm Lionel Salt. I believe I have a job for you."

20

TWO-PART POISON

The man leaned on a silver-tipped cane. Behind him was the matte black Rolls-Royce of legend. Even the windows of the car were tinted dark. A small elderly man stood beside him, holding an umbrella so that Lionel Salt would stay dry. Half the man's coat was already dark with rain.

Just looking at him filled her with a feeling of horror so strong that it locked up her muscles. She knew she had to get to her car, but her body urged her to run deeper into the woods and hide.

"A job?" she called up to him, her voice surprisingly steady.

"I hired a man, Hermes Fortune, who is in the same line of work as you. Unfortunately, he's gone missing. It seems I need a new thief. And I hear you're quite good?"

Charlie made it up the hill and gave him a wide berth as she headed for her car. The sparkly dress she'd worn to the MGM burned bright in the late-morning light. In the reflection of the car window, her smeared makeup, marred by tear tracks, made her feel entirely too vulnerable. Maybe the rain would wash her face for her, although she suspected it would only make things worse. "I'm out of the game," she said. "There's a guy named Adam that does a bunch of my old gigs. Balthazar can put the two of you in touch."

The corner of his mouth turned up. "Adam Lokken? I have him working on something else for me."

Balthazar had told her that Adam failed to find the *Liber Noctem*. She didn't think of Salt as someone who went back to people who'd disappointed him. Had Salt been the person on the other end of the phone call she'd over-heard?

"That's too bad," Charlie said. "I still can't help you."

"I spoke to an old acquaintance of mine, Odette Fevre. It seems you might have been the last person to see Hermes alive. Such a coincidence, don't you think? She called you *Charlie Hall*. Is that your real name? I've only ever heard you called the Charlatan."

It just figured that Odette knew him. She had enough wealthy clients to have had to cross paths with local billionaire Lionel Salt. And Odette had implied to Charlie that she'd talked to someone about Hermes. Charlie ought to have immediately jumped to the worst possible conclusion.

At least Salt hadn't recognized her. Of course, she'd been fifteen, just a kid. And it wasn't like there'd have been anything special about that night for him. He'd probably killed lots of people before and since.

But if he thought blackmailing Charlie by holding the disappearance of Hermes over her head would work, he was far off the mark. After Rand, Char-lie had learned that blackmail only gets worse with time. Also, she didn't think Odette gave a shit if Charlie was a stone-cold killer, so long as she showed up for her shifts on time and kept the till balanced.

After the silence stretched long enough that he realized she wasn't going to answer, he spoke again. "Speaking of coincidences, what are the chances that a well-known pilferer of magical books would find herself involved with a man who ran away with one of mine?"

"I do appreciate you calling me well-known," Charlie said.

"My grandson certainly knew you, didn't he?" Salt's voice stayed level, but he clearly didn't like her attitude. Probably he thought someone who'd peed in the woods, and who looked as though they'd had the kind of night peo-ple promise not to talk about outside of Vegas would have the grace to act ashamed.

"The late Edmund Carver," she said. "My condolences."

His eyes narrowed. "I believe you call him by his middle name. Odette de-scribed him in unmistakable detail, so let's drop the charade."

"Vince?" Charlie said, all innocence. "He dumped me yesterday afternoon. It looks like you just missed him."

"I think you better get in the car," Salt ground out, no longer trying to hide his anger. "We have a lot to discuss, and I don't think either of us want to do it out here in the rain."

So many young men of her acquaintance would be envious that she'd gotten an invitation to ride in the Rolls, but the idea chilled her blood. "I'm already wet, so no thanks. I'd only drip on your nice leather seat."

Lionel Salt reached into the inside pocket of his wool coat and took out a matte black Glock. It matched the car perfectly.

The elderly man holding the umbrella didn't so much as flinch.

"I'm afraid I am going to have to insist," Salt said, pointing the barrel of the gun casually. Waving it toward her. Not aiming. Not yet.

It was broad daylight and they were standing in the middle of a parking lot. Anyone could have walked out of Blue Ruin. There weren't many cars in the parking lot, but there weren't *none*. The road running past wasn't heavily trafficked, but vehicles passed every now and again. For Salt to be comfortable having his gun out reminded Charlie that he believed he could get away with anything.

It had been more than a decade since vomiting up beet juice and running had saved her life. The night had haunted her since, but drugs and time had blurred her memories into a kaleidoscopic nightmare instead of a recollection.

But the moment she'd seen Salt, that horror had surged back. She'd felt like a child again, running through the woods, monsters at her heels. She had no urge to go back to his big house and finish bleeding out on his library carpet.

"Under the circumstances, I really don't think I should go with you," she said, not moving.

"But you will," he told her, circling around the Corolla toward her. "You're a smart girl. You'll make the smart choice."

Charlie raised both her eyebrows. "Clearly you don't know anything about me."

As Lionel Salt glowered at her, she couldn't help seeing the familial resemblance between him and Vince. They were both tall and had the same hard jaw and angry eyebrows. But where Vince had no shadow, Salt's flickered behind him like a furious flame.

She noted its height, its profile when Salt turned, and wondered whose shadow he'd stolen, to finally be a gloamist himself.

"My daughter is waiting for us in the car," Salt said, pointing the gun at Charlie with real intent now. "I'd prefer not to upset her. I'll even pay you for your time. But this is your last opportunity to make the correct choice."

"So you're going to pay me if I go and shoot me if I stay?" Charlie asked.

His smile grew, appreciating her observation. "The world works by two principles, the carrot and the stick."

"If you know Odette, then you know sometimes the carrot *is* the stick." But despite the remark, and despite her certainty that going with him was stupid, she was aware of how few choices she had.

Getting shot the last time had sucked, and this time was likely to kill her.

"Come along," he said. "We'll have a little lunch. In public. Very civilized.

We can discuss what you're going to do for me, and how much time you'll have to accomplish the task."

Without quite agreeing, she moved in the direction of Salt's car. There might be no getting out of going for this ride, but she reminded herself that she'd gotten away from him once, and would again.

Oh, and this time she really would make him pay. For the past, for the gun he had on her, but most of all for sending in Hermes and wrecking a perfectly good relationship built on perfectly good lies.

The elderly man with the umbrella—small and wiry, built like a jockey— opened the door to the back seat.

I told you my grandfather was strict, right? He taught me lots of stuff. He believed in the improving power of work, no matter how old you were. He didn't believe in excuses. And he had a limo that broke down sometimes.

There was no way Salt had taught Vince to fix cars himself. But he could have insisted that someone else did.

"You liked Edmund, didn't you?" she asked the driver.

He didn't look particularly pleased to be spoken with. "Everyone liked Edmund, Ms. Hall," he answered, low-voiced.

She slid into the car.

Even with sunglasses on, the woman occupying the seat on the other side of a large center console was unmistakably the one from the photos of galas in New York. Salt's daughter and Edmund Vincent Carver's aunt, though so alike in age she looked more like a sister. She wore tight black pants tucked into suede boots, a patterned blue georgette blouse, and a shearling jacket. Her blond hair was much lighter than Edmund's, duckling gold. They must have cut a swathe through Manhattan's elite hearts—and beds.

"I'm Adeline," she said as Charlie slid in. "Sorry about Father. He can be a terrible bully."

Carrot and stick.

Salt said something to the driver in a low voice, then got in the front passenger seat.

The smell of leather and expensive air freshener made Charlie's head spin.

"Let's get some coffee," Salt said, turning to look back at her. "You look as though you could use some."

"And fresh clothes," Adeline said, wrinkling her nose, then smiled at Charlie. "No offense. I've woken up plenty of mornings in last night's party rags."

Party rags? It wasn't that she couldn't picture Vince spending time with her, because he had a deep well of patience. What she couldn't picture was Vince being *like* her.

The car pulled out onto the road, swinging away from the bar, Charlie's Corolla, and any hope of an easy escape.

A few minutes later the car stopped in front of The Roost, a coffeeshop at the edge of Northampton's downtown. An employee came out with a tray of coffees and a bag that the driver accepted through the front window.

Charlie wondered if there was a sign she could give that she was being kidnapped, like those clever women who manage to signal that they're in trouble during pizza deliveries.

If there was something, though, Charlie's hangover prevented her from thinking of it. The car pulled away from the curb, in the direction of I-91. The wipers swept across the windshield like a metronome.

She took a nervous sip of the coffee. Adeline had gotten some matcha concoction, which left a trace of green foam on her upper lip.

"I am a person who is used to getting what I want," Salt began, an understatement if ever she'd heard one. "And what I want is a book returned to me. *Liber Noctem, The Book of Night*. Look for a book that Edmund is keeping under lock and key, with a metal cover, and that will be it. There are no words on the cover. It may appear like a journal."

Charlie nodded, unwilling to agree to get it for him, and took another sip of coffee. She waited. Sometimes silence kept people talking. Sometimes if they talked enough, they wouldn't notice when you didn't.

In this case, it worked. Salt went on. "My grandson can be charming, but selfish. It's not his fault that he uses people; he grew up with an addict for a mother. She put him into situations and left him among people with whom no child should associate. They lived on the street, even slept in cars. From a young age, he had to learn to survive, and to shape-shift into whatever pleased the people he was around. By the time I got hold of him, he was thirteen and practically ruined."

Charlie cut a glance in Adeline's direction. The woman was frowning at her hands, as though she didn't like what her father was saying but was unwilling to openly disagree.

Although Charlie was loath to believe Salt about anything, a history like that would explain how Vince was able to behave like a normal person, even after more than a decade of being steeped in extreme wealth. A child who'd lived in poverty for thirteen years, one who'd been the responsible person in a household, might well know how to clean gutters. Might have learned how to make tacos and do laundry and all the stuff that would have come less easily to a rich layabout.

And as for using people, well, he'd used Charlie, hadn't he?

Salt went on. "When most people look up at the stars, they are frightened by the vastness of the universe, and their own lack of significance."

She heard the echo of Vince's voice: *Do you think that stars have shadows?*

"But I have always been comforted," he said. "And do you know why?"

Charlie shook her head, since that seemed like what she was supposed to do.

"Because they signified *possibility*. In all that vastness, it was impossible that the universe didn't have secrets left to be ferreted out. And when I took in my grandson, I saw that I was right. Because for all that was broken in him, he had one incredible talent."

"Magic," Charlie guessed.

Salt nodded. "When I saw him command it—which he did without a split tongue, having had no formal education with any gloamist—I felt as though I had found what I'd been looking for my whole life. A true secret of the universe, and a path to greater mysteries. But for Edmund, it was merely a crude little trick. He played with the thing like it was some imaginary friend and sent it off to steal candy and cigarettes."

The car pulled into a long drive marked with a carved and painted sign proclaiming they were entering the grounds of the Grand Berkshire Private Club. It seemed as though Salt intended to keep his word about taking her to lunch, in public.

"I will send you two girls to the spa. There are showers with which to refresh yourself, Ms. Hall. The staff can bring you clothing. We'll meet for lunch in a half hour. And then we can finish our business. Now, see, isn't that civilized?"

It was, except for the gun in his pocket.

The driver came around again and opened the door. Adeline allowed him to take her hand as though she were departing a carriage. Charlie followed, scooting out inelegantly, trying not to flash her panties.

The rain had turned into a light drizzle. She looked around, taking in the rolling green grounds, most of them golf course. The grass looked impossibly bright for this late in the fall. There was a large building in the distance that seemed to be the common space of the country club. The spa building was smaller, its wooden shingles painted the charmingly cottagecore color of a fern.

A sign set to one side of the door proclaimed that this was the relaxation and wellness center.

Inside, the air was warm, humid, and scented heavily with eucalyptus. A woman behind a desk took two towels from the shelves behind her and placed them on the counter. She smiled at them as though it was utterly normal to have a hungover client in a spangly dress with makeup all over her face. The steadiness of her gaze didn't so much as flicker.

"We'd like a private sauna room," Adeline said. "And we need some clothing in a size . . . twelve?"

"Fourteen," Charlie corrected.

The woman continued to smile. "There are towels and robes waiting for you. Would you like some cucumber water?"

"Absolutely." Charlie felt dehydrated enough to drink a *bathtub* of cucumber water. "Do you have aspirin?"

"Of course. Anything else?"

Charlie wondered if there was anything they could ask for that would dent her smile. A giraffe? A hot-air balloon? The loan of a crossbow so she could shoot Salt in the back?

Still making that mental list, Charlie followed Adeline into the sauna room. White lockers lined the left wall, robes hanging on attached hooks. The door to the sauna itself was shut, with a lot of dials on the door meant to, she supposed, optimize the heat and moisture levels, as though she and Adeline were lizards in an extremely fancy tank.

And there was a shower room.

Charlie grabbed a robe. "Back in a minute," she called to Adeline.

Under the steady heat and excellent water pressure, Charlie scrubbed her face with body wash, ignoring the way it stung her eyes. She shampooed her hair twice, then shrugged on the robe.

Adeline stood waiting for her, hair twisted up in a tortoiseshell clip. "The sauna really is the best thing for a hangover. You sweat out the liquor."

Charlie spotted a pitcher of cucumber water and a bottle of aspirin sitting on a silver tray. She took a generous helping of both before following Adeline into the steam.

The air inside the little room was scented even more strongly of eucalyptus than the front desk, and so thick she seemed to be drinking it as much as breathing it in. Charlie hadn't been in a sauna before, so she wasn't sure if that was normal. The combination of heat and moisture created a claustrophobic but not entirely unpleasurable sensation. She sat on a bamboo bench and stretched out her bare toes.

"You've got a bruise," Adeline said, pointing to where Charlie's calf had come up black and blue after being knocked around by Hermes's shadow only three days before.

Charlie decided the best thing she could do was ignore that and redirect the conversation. "You and Edmund are almost the same age, right?"

Adeline hesitated, as though the question bothered her. "We were close from the time he first came to live with us. My half sister was so much older than I was that I never knew her well, so it was easier to think of Remy as a brother, more than anything else."

Her half sister. Right. Edmund's mother. "What about your mom? Did she mind having another kid in the house?"

"She was a model from the Netherlands. Used to children behaving differently than American kids. She thought there was something wrong with him." Adeline smiled as though recalling a fond memory. "Edmund cursed. *A lot.*"

"What about now?"

Adeline sighed. "She lives in New York since the divorce. My mother found Father's obsession with gloaming . . . distasteful."

The painkillers must have kicked in, because Charlie's head hurt less. It was a little easier to think and it bothered her even more that this whole situation didn't add up. "Why did Edmund decide to take off?"

"He didn't want to do what Father said anymore." Something in Adeline's face made Charlie wonder if Adeline wasn't feeling a little rebellious herself. "Father asked a lot from Edmund."

She could imagine. His grandson was the one with the magic, after all. Even once Salt got himself a quickened shadow, he still wouldn't have the years of experience his grandson had. That was impossible to buy, and Charlie could only imagine how much that would grind Salt's gears. A man who was used to buying anything, unable to buy the power a kid had.

"What was he like with you?" Adeline asked. The question was inflected oddly, as if one of the words meant something else.

Perhaps Adeline thought of Edmund as a shape-shifter, the way his grandfather had described him, changing to suit the person he was with. It was hard to argue with that. After all, if he was different with everyone, then how could she know?

But Charlie did have one way to describe him. "You ever been to the Quabbin?"

"The reservoir?" Adeline looked slightly horrified.

"You know there's a whole town down there," Charlie said. "Buried under the waves. That's what Vince was like. A drowned town. Still along the surface. Everything's hidden underneath."

"You can't know—" Adeline started, then cut herself off. Looking down at the slim gold watch with the diamond case on her wrist, still miraculously running despite the heat and the moisture of the room, she cleared her throat. "It's almost time to meet Father for lunch. We ought to go."

She stood. Charlie followed her lead, rising and stretching until she got a satisfyingly audible crack from her shoulder blades.

In the changing room, Adeline regarded her speculatively. "I know you're not going to think this is nice of me to say, but I'm glad you're not with Edmund anymore."

She was right. It wasn't nice. But it was interesting.

The spa had left an outfit for Charlie hanging from one of the lockers. It had the look of coming from a golf shop, one that she imagined was probably in the main building. Pants in a stretchy navy material, a white collared shirt, and a navy chevron zip-up jacket. They'd brought her white tennis shoes and socks, but her flats were fine, with just a little dried mud at the edges. She got dressed and braided her hair, but without a clip, it immediately began to unravel.

Charlie's gaze fell on her shadow.

In all this talk, no one had quite explained how Vince lost his—or when.

"Charlie?" Adeline called.

She blinked, coming out of her thoughts.

A golf cart idled in front of the spa, the driver waiting to take them to the main building. Charlie didn't have to go to lunch. She could head back inside, insist that someone call her a cab. Put on her own clothes back at home.

But if Salt wanted to find her again, he had the resources to do it. He could tail her to and from work in his Rolls. For all she knew, he might be able to send a cop to her house to pick her up for him.

Maybe that nice Detective Juarez.

Enough money bought anything.

The grass was wet against her ankles as she walked to the golf cart. Then she hung on as they crossed the parking lot, past Bentleys and Lexuses. Charlie wondered how many of Odette's clients were members here.

Inside the main building, Charlie followed Adeline across a gleaming stone floor to the restaurant. The host didn't ask their names, just led them to a private room where the walls were covered in yellow silk, and paintings of horses, coats gleaming like polished mahogany, hung atop the cloth.

Lionel Salt was already waiting for them at the table, nursing a lowball glass of whiskey with an ice globe sitting in it. She took in his wrinkles, his faded age spots and too-pale skin, as though he'd tried to bleach them away. The smoothness of his forehead from injections. He wore a black turtleneck and dark gray pants. On his finger, a gold ring marked with an unfamiliar arcane symbol gleamed. Charlie noted that neither he nor Adeline wore any onyx.

"This is a lot of trouble to go to for a conversation," Charlie said as the host hastened to pull out her seat for her.

"You look refreshed." Salt exchanged a look with Adeline, who nodded. Maybe there had been some kind of two-part poison in her cucumber water. If she started to feel woozy, she was going to stab Salt in the chest with whatever knife there was, even if it was a butter knife.

He leaned over to a waiter. "We will have the smoked pheasant confit salad, the Kanzan cherry blossom tea–cured salmon, and the grilled lamb loin." He looked at Charlie. "I assume you're not a vegetarian?"

She shook her head. After a night of drinking what she really wanted was a greasy egg-and-bacon sandwich, but he was the guy with the Glock.

"And a bottle of Château d'Esclans 2018 Garrus rosé," he concluded. The waiter nodded.

"I'll just take an iced tea," Charlie said.

After the waiter departed, Salt put his hands on the table. His nails were clean and buffed. If she were conning Salt, she'd note the veneer of perfection. The need for control.

It manifested in the way Adeline was quiet unless invited to speak. The way he'd immediately taken the gun from his pocket when Charlie refused to go with him. He expected automatic obedience and acknowledgment of his superiority from people like Charlie. And like Vince.

The best way to con Salt would be to let him dominate. Let him win. He'd believe that and he'd never look deeper.

"So," Salt said, putting his elbows on the table and peering across at her. "We have something in common. My darling grandson wronged us both. He took something from me and broke your heart. Isn't that right?"

Adeline frowned at her plate. Either she was more on Vince's side than she wanted her father to know, or Charlie being with Vince had really bothered her. Maybe she hated all of his girlfriends.

"I suppose so," Charlie said.

"Then let us be allies. You won't just be helping me by getting back my book. You will be stopping Edmund from committing a great wrong. You see, as I told you before, my grandson, in his idiosyncratic way, treated his shadow like some cross between a pet and a friend.

"To command a shade, one must be a good custodian. Provide blood and energy from our own bodies. We gift unto them life, and in return they give us utter obedience. They *are* us, after all. Formed from us, as we were once made of sculpted clay and the Lord's breath."

Charlie was surprised by the religiosity of his description. She had spent a few Sundays at Laura's church, trying to con Laura's parents into believing that she wasn't a terrible influence. The only parts she remembered in detail were the songs, the free doughnuts in the basement, and a lot of language like this.

Salt went on. "But the sacrament is an unholy one. We give our shadows the parts of us that we want to shove down into the dark. Our anger, our jealousy, our gluttony, our most shameful desires. Imagine a hate-filled creature, made of everything monstrous about a person, a thing that feeds on energy and blood. Now imagine coddling *that*, Ms. Hall."

Charlie tried to picture Vince with a shadow like that and found it easy to see why he'd been willing to overlook so many of Charlie's faults.

"He named it Red," Salt said. "Red and Remy, isn't that sweet? Maybe that's what it calls itself now."

"What do you mean?" Charlie asked.

"Once Edmund's shadow was cut free, it became a Blight."

"A Blight of a *living person*?" Charlie objected.

"Formed in childhood, with a child's foolish allowance for gluttony. He over-fed the thing. Gave it too much blood, and not just his own. By the time Edmund was an adult, his shadow was very powerful. Powerful enough to have desires of its own. It was for that reason Edmund stole the *Liber Noctem* from me—to bring his Blight to full life, a shadow no more."

"That can't be true," Charlie said, not even sure to what part she objected.

"The *Liber Noctem* details the method by which a Blight can acquire and maintain enough substance to pass for human." He looked across the table at her, as though willing her to understand. "The author presented this as the secret to immortality. But what no gloamist attempting to re-create the ritual realized was that it wouldn't be their consciousness that survived. And so, they were deceived unto their own deaths, and their shadows, swollen with stolen energy, walk among us. To all appearances, human. Perhaps to this day."

That sounded like internet creepypasta.

Impossible. Ridiculous.

But Charlie couldn't help remembering how Vince had told her that what he'd done was worse than her accusations. Something so bad he refused to explain it.

"You don't want to believe me," Salt said. "But you do."

The waiter came in, interrupting them to bring in the wine. He filled all three glasses with the deep pink rosé, then wrapped a towel around the neck of the bottle and rested it in a silver ice bucket. Finally, he set Charlie's tea in front of her, a thick lemon wedge decorating the side and a sprig of mint in with the cubes.

Lionel waved him away when he began to ask if they needed anything.

"What did you do to Vincent, Mr. Salt?" Charlie asked.

Adeline gave her a sharp, surprised look.

"What did *I* do?" he asked, as though trying out being offended.

"Something caused him to leave when he did. Do you really expect me to believe it was because you had a crisis of conscience over him experimenting with his shadow?"

Adeline took her wineglass and drained it in one long swallow. "This is awful. Just tell her—"

"I *am*, my dear," he said, with slightly too firm an emphasis for the words to be true. He turned to Charlie. "Edmund was unreasonable about Red. You know enough of Blights to know how horrifying they are. They're made from the worst parts of us. They can be enormously powerful. And they are invariably insane. That's why some Blights are disposed of, and others are caught and tethered to new wearers. Controlling them is the only thing that keeps humanity safe."

Charlie knew a few gloamists wore Blights instead of their own quickened shadows, although it had never seemed like the wisest idea. Gloaming was too young an art for its practitioners not to attempt dangerous paths to power, though. Posey might be willing to do it.

Who was she kidding? Posey would jump at the chance.

But it didn't seem like Vince not to be aware of the danger in letting a Blight roam free. And it didn't seem like Salt to worry about the safety of humanity.

Charlie was glad when the waiter came back with the food, forcing the conversation to a stop.

Salt directed him to set the lamb loin in front of her. Charlie took an absent bite and chewed mechanically, barely tasting what she was eating.

"It's true I had a hand in what happened next," Salt said, once the waiter had refilled their wineglasses and departed. "I tried to save Edmund from Red, but my grandson released his shadow before I could destroy it. Now it's loose in the world. You see why I must have my book before he manages to complete the method outlined in it. What Edmund intends cannot happen. A Blight who could pass for human, with an endless hunger . . . would you want that walking our streets, doing to others what it did to Paul Ecco and Knight Singh?"

"Vince wouldn't do that," Charlie said.

"He *won't*," Salt said. "Because you're going to bring *The Book of Night* to a gathering this Saturday, and we are going to keep it safe. Do we understand each other?"

Charlie was still stuck on his accusation. "Why would Vince's shadow— *Red*—have killed those people?"

"One of them got a piece of the book, which it wouldn't like," Salt said, with a twist of his mouth and a glare. "The other knew too much about the contents of the *Liber Noctem*. But Red needs to kill. The more blood and shadow energy it consumes, the more powerful it becomes—and the more ready for the ritual."

By the time Charlie looked down at her plate, the only thing that remained were smears of red from the rare meat. She wiped the edges of her mouth with her napkin. She didn't recall eating any of it.

"This book has been missing for a year or more. What makes you think I can get it by Saturday?" Charlie asked.

"You *know* Edmund. You can do what no one else can—determine where he could have put a book he didn't want anyone to find. I am having a little soiree for the gloamist community in celebration of my elevation to the Cabal.

Having the book would be a worthy proof of how successful I will be in my new position."

Charlie stared at him in horror. Sure, the Cabal was a bootleg governing body, but it served to identify threats to the community—like loose Blights, or laws meant to regulate gloaming—and employ a Hierophant. It also kept the local gloamists in check. Someone as monstrous as Salt on there, to be one of the five people making decisions, was going to be bad for everyone.

No, one of *four* people, Charlie realized. Because Knight Singh was dead.

"I appreciate the offer of work, but the job's not for me," Charlie said. "I have no idea where Vince is or what he did with your book. For all I know, he got rid of it. And besides, I don't like you. You kidnapped me at gunpoint. And you're kind of a dick."

Telling him that wasn't revenge, but it wasn't nothing.

Adeline sucked in her breath.

Salt looked at Charlie across the table, and there was something in his face as though in anticipation of some great pleasure. That's all the warning she got before his shadow flowed toward her and sank into her skin. Before she understood what was happening, her hand lifted the steak knife just as the waiter returned to the room.

She could sense the shadow inside her, a separate consciousness. She could hear its thoughts and sense the enormity of its hatred.

Her mouth opened and she could feel her tongue begin to form words, her voice rough with resistance. "I wi-ll mur-der—"

Then she was free, and shaking with horror. Uncertain if she cast the shadow off with her will, or if Salt let her go.

He laughed at the waiter's startled face. "She becomes heated when we discuss politics, but there's no harm in her. Isn't that true, my dear?"

Charlie bit her tongue and didn't answer, too afraid that it wouldn't be her own words coming out of her mouth.

Salt leaned in close, dropping his voice to a whisper. "You have a week to steal the *Liber Noctem* for me. Given your reputation, I am certain of your success. But if you fail, we'll see what else I can make you do, and to whom. You have a sister, isn't that right? Now, would you like coffee before you go? A cordial?"

Anger and fear and fury rose in Charlie like a wave, sweeping every other thought away. She hadn't thought it was possible to despise him more than she did, but now her hands were shaking with a desire for violence. She wanted to break a glass and use it to slice open his face. She wanted to watch him squirming on the carpet as poison stole his consciousness.

Salt's smile grew as he studied her expression. She had the sinking suspicion that he enjoyed her hating him. It was another kind of power.

He wiped the edges of his mouth with a cloth napkin. "I need to hear you say that you understand. That you will be at my estate on Saturday, book in hand."

Charlie pushed back her chair and got up, biting the inside of her cheek. "You have my word."

He nodded. "Good day to you, Charlatan."

As she turned to go, though, Adeline grabbed her hand. "I know you saw the news stories. Before you judge my father, remember what Red is capable of doing."

Was Vince's shadow really out there, murdering people in anticipation of some transformation? Was that what had happened to Rose Allaband? How responsible had Vince been for all of this?

And yet, Rand's body had also been found in a car, along with a dead girl that Charlie was fairly certain he'd never even met while alive. All staged by Salt.

Maybe Vince *hadn't* faked his own death. What if he'd just taken the book and run? If Salt had set up the burned husk of the car, with charred bodies inside, Vince would have been pronounced dead, making it impossible for him to get far, or to go to the authorities. If anyone thought he was alive, he'd be wanted for murder.

Of course, that didn't explain Red.

"Let go of me," Charlie told her.

Adeline's fingers dug into Charlie's skin. "You think you know Remy, but you're wrong."

Charlie pulled her hand out of the woman's grip and walked from the room as fast as she could. She wasn't even sure where she was going, as long as it was away from the Salt family and their horrifying desires and demands. As she crossed the smooth tiles of the reception hall, she spotted a man leaning against the wall.

Charlie's heart sped.

He was younger than most people walking through the country club, dark-haired with deep-set eyes and bruised skin underneath. Bullet holes, she'd thought of them that night when she first saw him in the alley. But up close, his eyes just seemed tired.

Then her gaze fell to the area between the edge of his gloves and the cuffs of his shirt. It didn't show much, but she could see there was shadow where the skin of his wrist should have been.

"You're the Hierophant," she forced herself to say.

He smiled, but it was all wrong. Too many facial muscles were engaged. His mouth was pulled in too many directions.

"Yes," he said, as though forcing the words out. "I am hun-ting a Blight."

Charlie took an involuntary step back, alarmed more by the way he spoke than what he said. It reminded her, suddenly and horribly, of how she had sounded when Salt controlled her.

"Red?" she asked him.

A gleam appeared in his eye. "You've seen him, haven't you?"

She shook her head.

The Hierophant gave her one of those strange smiles. "I was a thief once. Like you."

If she'd gotten caught in the wrong place, at the wrong moment, she could have wound up like him. Hands cut off, sent out to kill Blights. Had he been a gloamist before? Most thieves weren't, if for no other reason than it was hard for a shadow to cross the onyx protections most gloamists put in place.

"Your shadow—" Charlie began, wanting to ask if it had quickened on its own, or if they'd bound him to something.

His eyes narrowed and he pushed off the wall, taking a step toward her. "Once they get their claws into you, they never let go."

She scuttled back.

The Hierophant cocked his head to the side and began to speak, at first in a monotone, then in a rising shout. "Tell Red I want the book. Tell Red we can share. *Tell Red that I will rip him to pieces.*"

As he continued to advance toward her, Charlie turned and ran. Her flats slapped against the polished floor.

"No one can fight their own shadow," he shouted after her.

She hit the doors with her shoulder, throwing them open. The matte black car was waiting for her, and she didn't stop running until she was inside.

21
THE PAST

Remy Carver stood on a cobbled street in Boston's Beacon Hill neighborhood, trying to appear like a normal teenager instead of the conductor of a murder. He felt the pull of his shadow, as though there was a rope between them, thinning as Red floated up the stairs of the rowhouse.

Across the street, an elderly woman in a fur-collared coat walked a fat Chihuahua. She glanced toward Remy, and he turned away, moving deeper into the shadows, his heart hammering.

Maybe he should have come at two in the morning, instead of just past eleven at night. His grandfather argued for this hour, saying that he would be less conspicuous when there were other people on the street, but there was no time when it didn't look a little suspicious for a fourteen-year-old boy to be hanging around with a couple of trash cans, waiting for his invisible friend to finish killing somebody.

Remy didn't belong in a place like this, no matter who his grandfather was. The window boxes full of spring flowers and gleaming brass door knockers made him uncomfortable.

He tried to concentrate on something other than what was happening upstairs, even though part of him could see out of Red's eyes. His shadow had made it to the man's bedroom. The door was slightly ajar, no barrier at all. The man was asleep, wife beside him. She had one of those cannulas in her nose, the ones that supplied extra oxygen—

Remy shook his head, pressed his eyes shut as though that would stop the images from coming. *No. No.* Think about the last time he saw his mother and how much better she was doing. But that memory wasn't so good, either, because she'd wanted him to come live with her and he couldn't.

Think about the fancy private school he was attending and how Adeline had introduced him to her friends. They'd thought he was cool. He knew how to score drugs and how to spot a guy heading into a liquor store who'd buy them a bottle of Grey Goose for an extra twenty. They wanted him to come to their ski lodges this winter. They wanted him to come to their islands for spring break.

And wasn't that a hell of a lot better than what he'd been doing last year, wrapping duct tape around his sneakers so his feet wouldn't get wet, trudging through the gray snow?

It was worth it. This was worth it.

That's what he concentrated on as Red flowed down the man's throat, as Remy's head echoed with awful sounds. As the wife woke up and started screaming. Think of having a home. Think of Mom going to the kind of rehabs that celebrities hung out at. Think of a future. Think of Adeline, who wanted to be his sister.

Don't think about Red.

Ever since his grandfather had discovered how useful Remy could be, he'd wanted him to use his shadow. And his grandfather started collecting books on gloamists, spouting off about how Remy was doing it wrong. How Remy needed to understand that Red was just an extension of him, like a hand, something he had total control over.

That acting like Red could make his own decisions was dangerous.

But Remy didn't want to kill anyone. It was bad enough he had to be a participant in it. He couldn't imagine being wholly aware of what he was doing, pushing himself down the man's throat, watching his eyes bulge and his tongue loll. Listening to the frantic howls of the wife close enough that his ears would feel like they were bleeding.

When it was done, Remy wiped tears from the sides of his eyes.

He hated knowing the man was dying, and he hated the dying man too. If only he'd just gone along with Remy's grandfather's business stuff, then they'd all be less miserable.

It didn't take long for Red to return, sliding across the cobblestones toward him. But his shadow stopped before returning to his dormant place. Instead Red stood black against the brick wall, as upright as Remy was, in defiance of the streetlights and any natural law.

"You're unhappy," Red said, although the words could only be heard in Remy's mind.

Adeline had explained to him that Red was the part of Edmund that Edmund didn't know about. Like his subconscious.

But Red didn't feel like his subconscious. He felt like an attic. A place to shove things Remy didn't want to deal with. At the new fancy private school that his grandfather insisted he attend, they didn't like people getting into fights. So Remy didn't get into them anymore, even though at his old school he had to get up in people's faces if he wanted to be respected. But that anger had to go somewhere.

And when Remy felt sad at times like this or when he was missing his mother, he put that sadness into Red too. His pity for the people his grandfather wanted dead. Which wasn't fair, because Red shouldn't have to kill people and feel sorry for them.

But Red wasn't real. He was Remy's subconscious. Or an attic.

He used to be a friend.

"So what? It's over," Remy said, thrusting all the sadness away from him. He wondered if Red would complain, but it was energy, right? Like the blood that fed him.

"Next time cut me free," Red said. "And when the thing is done, I will return."

Remy hated it when his shadow said stuff that didn't seem to come from his thoughts at all, things that surprised him. He'd used to like it, back when it was moves in a game, or sprinting ahead in a race.

"We need to go," he muttered, and set off, stalking down the sidewalk with his hands in his pockets. The police would be coming soon, and an ambulance.

Let his shadow follow. That's what shadows were supposed to do.

He felt better once he turned the first corner. There was nothing to tie him to the murder.

And the more he thought about it, what Red wanted was what he wanted too, wasn't it? Even if it was impossible. So it shouldn't have been that surprising, what Red had suggested. Remy was just being weird about things, on account of what his grandfather had told him.

"I promise I'll come back," Red whispered. "Cross my heart and hope to die. Stick a needle in my eye."

"You don't have a heart," Remy thought at him. "Or an eye."

"On my life then. I promise on my life."

"You're just me," Remy said.

"I'm just you," Red echoed, but Remy wasn't sure what it meant now that the words were coming from his shadow.

When they were younger, he always knew what Red meant.

"I'll think about it," Remy said.

But he already knew he'd do anything if it meant he didn't have to have a night like this one again.

22

THE SCHOLAR AND THE SHADOW

O nce they hit the highway, the elderly chauffeur cleared his throat. "There's something in the back seat for you, Ms. Hall."

On the floor mat, where it must have slid, she found a book with a red leatherette cover, stamped in gold. After stealing so many old, crumbling volumes, there was something odd about holding a modern book crafted to seem to come from another time.

The title read *Complete Works of Hans Christian Andersen*. A hundred-dollar bill was tucked into a page, acting as a bookmark. The story was called simply "The Shadow."

With little else to do on the ride home, she read.

It featured a scholar from the cold north who traveled to a marvelous city in the south but was unable to bear the heat of its days. He shrank beneath the hot sun, growing thin and exhausted. Even his shadow seemed to fade. Only in the evenings, as the cool breezes came, did he begin to feel like himself again. He would sit out on his balcony with a candle and watch his shadow stretch and lengthen in the night air.

Charlie felt a little shiver go through her. She read on.

Beneath the scholar and his shadow, the city appeared magnificent by moonlight. Rattling carriages passed musicians playing mandolins. Church bells rang. Donkeys carried carts of ripe fruit back from the markets. The scholar drank in scents of spices and smoke and lush flowers. He was particularly struck by those blooming on the balcony opposite his, from where the sound of singing came.

Each night, the scholar would sit on his balcony and look across. Once, he thought he spotted a beautiful maiden among the flowers. When he looked again, she was gone. But in the candlelight, his shadow became long enough to stretch across the street, to the girl's window.

Make yourself useful, the scholar told his shadow, laughing. *Go look inside and tell me what you see. But be sure to come back.*

And with that, the scholar went to bed. But his shadow did not. It scampered away to look, and, despite his command, never returned.

The scholar found this very vexing. Soon, however, he found a new little shadow beginning to grow from the very tips of his feet. By the time he returned from the hot country, he had a freshly grown shadow that was perfectly sufficient, and decided to be content with that.

One night many years later, there was a tapping on his door. On the other side was a very thin person, immaculately dressed. Looking at him made the scholar feel odd, but he ushered the stranger inside despite his misgivings.

The stranger introduced himself as the man's shadow. Astonished, the scholar was nonetheless a little amused to see him again. The shadow told him many tales of his adventures and how, since he was able to slip in anywhere and see all those things that the powerful wanted to keep hidden, he had done very well for himself. He had become quite wealthy.

The scholar marveled at this, for he had remained poor. The shadow invited the scholar to travel with him, and offered to pay his way. This was a bit too much for the scholar's pride, but in the end, he relented.

Away they traveled to a place where they could take the waters, with the shadow claiming he hoped it might heal his lack of a beard. As they went, the shadow made all the decisions and paid for all that they ate and drank. Soon, the shadow began to treat the scholar more like a servant.

Many people from all over came to the healing waters, and the shadow met a princess who had come to cure a condition she had—one which allowed her to see things too clearly. She took a look at the shadow and told him that he had come to the waters in the hopes he might grow a new shadow. He laughed and said that she must be cured already, because his shadow was right there. And he indicated the scholar.

The idea that his shadow was so much finer than anyone else's intrigued her. That night they danced together and she told him of her country. He had been there, and had such a breadth of knowledge that she quickly fell in love with him.

She wanted to marry him but needed to assure herself of his wisdom, since a ruler ought to be wise as well as knowledgeable. She tested him by asking him a series of difficult philosophical questions. The shadow laughed, saying they were so simple that even his shadow could answer them. And when she put the same questions to the scholar, he answered them so handsomely that she agreed to marry the shadow immediately.

That evening, the shadow made the scholar an offer. He could live with them and be wealthy all his days if he would tell everyone that he was the shadow, and the shadow was the man.

The scholar refused. He said he would go to the princess and tell her everything. But the shadow told him that if he tried, the shadow would tell the princess and her guards that the scholar was a liar.

Be reasonable, he said. *I am the one who is going to marry her, and they will listen to me instead of you.*

But the scholar insisted. And all was as the shadow predicted. The shadow told the princess's guards to seize the scholar and they did. By the time the shadow and the princess were married, the scholar had been put to death and was no more.

C harlie closed the book and saw that they had left I-91 and were weaving through back roads toward Blue Ruin. Putting her hand on the leatherette cover, she tried to put aside the story itself and focus on why Salt had given it to her.

He wanted her to believe that Red wasn't just a threat to the world, but to Vince. She shouldn't care, but she had to admit that she did.

Hatred of Salt burned in her gut, but no matter how much she despised him, no matter how sure she was that he was deceiving her, she was equally certain that he hadn't lied about *everything.*

The chauffeur pulled into the lot and parked beside her Corolla. She got out, taking the book and the hundred-dollar bookmark with her. Salt had promised to pay, after all.

The matte black Rolls-Royce was back on the road, speeding away into the late afternoon, as Charlie opened the door to her car. She held her breath until the engine started its usual miserable sputtering. Her purse was where she'd left it, in the back seat. Her phone was there too, with a missed call from Posey and another from work.

She ignored those and called UMass's bursar's office to try to straighten out whatever was wrong with Posey's account. She got a busy signal. When she tried again, the call went to voice mail. Between one call and the next, the office had closed and was going to stay that way through Veterans Day.

Frustrated, she drove home. It was just after four in the afternoon, and the house was quiet. Her sister either hadn't risen from bed, or had shut herself up in her room. Exhausted, Charlie went straight to her mattress and face-planted on it. When she woke, the house smelled like something was burning. She found that she'd been clutching the red book to her chest, as though it were a stuffed bear.

In the kitchen, Posey glared at a sheet pan of blackened cookies. "You didn't come home last night," she said. "Neither did Vince. And . . . what are you *wearing*?"

Charlie looked down at the athleisure the spa had picked out for her. With a shrug, she sat on a chair and tried to pry up a cookie. She could use some sugar. "Vince left. Packed up his stuff. He's gone."

She'd expected Posey to be thrilled, or at least smug, but she appeared shocked instead. "You dumped him?"

Charlie shook her head. "No. I told you. He left."

"But *why*?"

"Because his name isn't really Vincent Damiano. He's Edmund Carver, and he's filthy rich, and he's supposed to be dead." Charlie sighed, gave up on the cookies, and went to pour herself some cereal.

All they had were bran flakes, boring, and purchased by Vince at her request. She poured them into a bowl.

"Seriously?" Posey said.

"I think he's in trouble," Charlie said. "I mean, obviously he's in trouble. But he's in *more* trouble, and it's got to do with his missing shadow."

Vince had been thirteen when Salt took him in, troubled and probably desperate for stability. What might he have been willing to do for that?

She bet the answer was absolutely anything.

Posey poked at the burnt cookies with a slightly melted plastic spatula that was probably leaching toxins into their baked goods. A chunk of one came off. "Who's after him?"

"It's a little bit of a complicated story. Do you remember Mom's old hocus-pocus friend Rand?"

Posey wrinkled her nose. "That old guy that was always hanging around with you. Didn't he die in some really weird way?"

"He was murdered," Charlie said.

Posey shook her head. "No, that's not it. They found him with another body in his car. Suicide. Or murder-suicide. I remember now. Dad blamed Mom for letting you go off with him all those times. He was worried that guy had done stuff to you like everyone figured he did to that girl before he killed her."

Her father had, of course, said absolutely *nothing* to her. Until this moment,

Charlie hadn't known he'd been aware of Rand's existence. It was hard to balance her surprise with annoyance at Posey, who apparently thought that Charlie just misremembered one of the most horrific events of her life.

"*Rand was murdered,*" she said. "I know, because I was there."

Posey began to open her mouth, possibly to object, and then abruptly closed it.

"Vince's grandfather killed him. Lionel Salt."

"Why were you there?" Posey asked, her voice much quieter and less sure.

"Because Rand was a con artist," Charlie said. "And I was his helper. Like a magician's assistant, but for crime."

"So *nothing* like a magician's assistant," Posey said.

Charlie ran her finger through the blackened crumbs. "Look, Rand wasn't the best guy. He was vain, and irritable, and conned me into working for him in the first place. But he taught me a lot. And he didn't deserve to die, and definitely not like he did. No one deserves to die like that."

"You always told Mom you *wanted* to go with him." Posey bit a cookie, then made a face and put it back. "I thought that he was buying you stuff, and back then I was envious, but then later I didn't know what to think. You always had money. And, well, he was a creep."

When she put it like that, it did sound bad. Charlie wondered more than ever what their mother had thought she was doing with Rand, and why she'd been okay with it.

Charlie chewed her good-for-you cereal, frowning.

Her past problems might be unsolvable, but Vince was the key to fixing her current problems. He either had the *Liber Noctem,* or could tell her its whereabouts. And if he was really attempting to make his evil shadow into an evil person, maybe he'd be done by Saturday and she could take the book back to Salt.

And if it felt like a relief to have a reason to contact him, she refused to dwell on that. Pulling out her phone, she sucked in a breath as she tapped his name, waiting for it to ring.

A moment later an automated voice told her that the number had been disconnected. Of course it had.

Well, she'd spent the better part of a decade finding things. She could find one tall guy with no working credit cards and a fake ID.

Charlie looked across the kitchen to her sister. "Do you think you could be *friends* with your shadow?" she asked. "Like, come to really care about it?"

Posey frowned consideringly for a moment. "There's a lady who married the Berlin Wall. She was super devastated when they knocked him down. Carried around a brick for a while."

Posey had a point, but that wasn't what Charlie had meant. "Yeah, okay, but could you *reasonably* be friends with it?"

"I don't know."

"Yeah," Charlie said. "Me neither."

"If it could talk, maybe," Posey said, still chewing over the question. "But then aren't you just talking to yourself?"

Charlie frowned at the floor. She hadn't been talking about her own shadow, but perhaps she should have been. It was as unresponsive as ever. Definitely not friendly. "You hate me a little, don't you?"

Posey gave her a look. "You mean because it's unfair that it's your shadow that's quickening when becoming a gloamist is the thing I want most in the world?"

Charlie nodded.

"I'm angry," Posey said. "At the universe. And at you, I guess, even though I know it's not your fault. I'll get over it. But if you fuck this up, I *will* hate you."

Charlie sighed, half sure she was fucking it up already, and entirely sure she'd fuck it up somewhere down the line. That was just her nature. Charlie Hall, Maker of Mistakes. Patron Saint of Disaster.

The only things she'd ever been good at were trickery and deception, so she better stick to those. Paul Ecco had gotten a page of the *Liber Noctem* somehow. If Vince sold it to him, there'd be some record of the transaction. Maybe Vince had left Ecco with a phone number that worked, or even better, an address.

Curiosity Books, that was the name of Ecco's shop. Well, Charlie was feeling curiouser and curiouser.

"I'm going back out," she said, heading to her bedroom for a change of clothes.

Posey gave her a sideways look. "You coming home tonight? I'm going to order lo mein."

"Get me some," Charlie called back. "I can always eat it for breakfast."

Curiosity Books was on the third floor of a slightly shabby converted mill building, just above a concrete artisan and across the hall from a circus school where small children were taught how to juggle and spin plates. The locks on the doors were a joke. Charlie didn't even need to pick it; she just slid her Big Y points card into the gap between the frame and the door, then brought it up hard enough to depress the latch bolt. Turning the knob, she nudged the door with her hip. It opened.

The walls were lined with bookshelves that seemed to have been scavenged from every library closeout sale and Craigslist giveaway in the neighboring towns. The volumes were so tightly packed that Charlie wondered how any of them could possibly be removed. Cardboard boxes had been stacked in small towers, some with their sides ripped, others containing more folded boxes inside, presumably for shipping. High on the back wall, above a bank of windows, an unattributed quote had been painted: "The universe belongs to the curious."

An old 1950s-style metal desk rested in middle of the floor, with a computer humming away on top, an ancient-looking landline phone, and a label printer. Loose paper carpeted the floor, as though recently pawed through.

Charlie walked from one end to the other, inhaling the powdery dust of old books. A locked glass cabinet had been smashed and the shelves inside emptied. A single bookshelf rested on the floor, books seeping out from underneath.

She went back to the desk, sat down, and moved around the mouse in a circle. After a moment, the computer monitor sprang to life, showing a ridiculously cluttered screen. She opened a search window and typed in "name:Noctem." Nothing came up. She replaced it with "name:Blight," and that got nothing too.

Then she tried "inventory" and got an .xl file. When she opened it, she found a list of books Paul Ecco had in the store, with short summaries, the price Paul paid for them, and the price he'd sold them for.

She typed "Noctem" into the search area of the file. No results.

Frustrated, Charlie took out her cell phone and called Balthazar. He answered on the third ring.

"Darling," he said, drawing out the vowel. "To what do I owe the pleasure?"

"What if I want to take the Knight Singh job?" she asked, kicking the file drawer and making the chair spin.

"Too late, alas. I hear someone got the folio already. Regretting it? Don't worry. I have a half dozen other jobs. A few out of state, if you're willing to travel. A few impossible, if you're looking for a thrill."

"Always," Charlie said. "But who wanted them?"

"Wanted which?"

"Knight Singh's papers." Idly, Charlie began to open the drawers of the desk. They made a grating metallic sound.

Balthazar hesitated before answering. "Is there something you ought to tell me?"

"I don't think so." In the files drawer she found dozens of manila folders, all labeled with the dull needs of business: bills, rent, takeout menus, insurance, bookseller organizations with acronyms: ABA, IOBA, NEIBA. "It was a puppeteer, wasn't it?"

"There were several underlings from carapace who wanted the folio, and yes, a puppeteer. A very wealthy puppeteer." He paused, as though troubled. "Now do you want to tell me how you knew that?"

She fought down the urge to show off, to mention that she was aware Raven was the one they'd been taken from.

"It's my job to know stuff," Charlie said innocently. She ought to thank Balthazar, hang up, and leave things at that, but she owed him something in the way of information. "Remember that job you said I should do, finding the *Liber Noctem*? Salt basically told me he'd kill me and everyone I love if I don't."

"Good thing I'm not likely to find myself in that category," said Balthazar.

"Oh, I don't know. You're growing on me," she told him as her fingers went to the far back of the files in the bottom drawer, stopping on a thin folder marked "Porn." It was empty.

"You're trouble, Charlatan," he said, but with fondness.

"Goodbye, Balthazar," she told him, and hung up.

Turning to the computer, she typed "Porn" into the search bar. A folder came up. Inside, were a half dozen .jpgs, three .mov files, and another folder marked "Geriatric Porn." That contained a single .xl file. When she clicked it, a new inventory opened, listing a collection of occult books that might be of interest to gloamists. This spreadsheet included the year created, the specialty of the gloamist, whether it was a one-off or mass printed, whether there were other editions, what shelf it was on, and how Paul had acquired it.

Then there was a list of gloamist ephemera. To hide knowledge from one another, gloamists had taken to writing out their secrets in nontraditional ways. Stitched into the lining of a leather coat. Written in tiny letters inside of artwork. Objects whose real value was disguised so thoroughly that they might be thrown out or sold for pennies at a flea market.

And then there were NFTs. Popular among the wealthy, and still far from commonplace among most gloamists. Paul had one in his inventory, and seemed to have listed it for a hundred grand two weeks ago.

Charlie scanned down the list of sellers, looking for Remy, Edmund, Vincent, Red, even Salt. But the only name she recognized was Liam Clovin.

Liam Clovin, MD. Vince's old school chum.

It looked as though he'd sold Paul Ecco three books within a week of the time that Edmund was supposed to have died. According to the entries, two were memoirs from the eighteenth century, worth five hundred bucks a piece, which had been kept in the shattered glass cabinet—clearly, those were gone. The third was *Umbramagists Through History*, self-published through Lulu in 2011. Instead of a shelf, the book was marked as being in a cardboard box on the other end of the room marked with a "7-A."

Charlie went to retrieve it. As she did, a knock on the door startled her.

"Paul?" A gruff voice came from the hall.

Book in hand, Charlie went still. The door was slightly ajar and she saw the moment that it began to swing inward. She ducked down behind some boxes.

Someone in heavy work boots crossed the floor toward the desk. "Come on, man," the person said in exasperation. "Paul! You owe me the goddamn rent. You can't hide from me forever."

He exited the room with a slammed door.

Charlie liked to think of herself as light-footed when she wanted to be, but in an old building, it was almost impossible to tell which floorboards were likely to creak and groan. She figured it would be the better part of valor to stay where she was for fifteen minutes, until she was sure Paul Ecco's landlord had gone.

With nothing else to do, she opened up *Umbramagists Through History* and read it by the light of her cell phone.

It contained a collection of curated excerpts taken from other books. And although the introduction of misinformation was often a concern with reprints, there was an air of authenticity in the sheer neglect with which the author had put it together. Each page was clearly just scans of the original material, in the original font.

Charlie scanned through the excerpts from newspapers, histories, and other documents. Whatever she'd thought of how it had been put together, the actual information in the book was compelling.

A warrior in Thebes fell in a field of blood, but his shadow fought on until his killer died.

A member of a shadowy secret society operating around the time of the Order of the Golden Dawn claimed she was able to send her consciousness out of her body at night and discover her enemies in their most private moments. That same account suggested that while her shadow was on a mission, she was vulnerable to other shadows taking control of her body.

A mystic attempted to feed his shadow all of his blood and live on through it.

A woman had woken on a hillside to three elderly folks trying to cut off her shadow at her feet. She shouted and they ran. She never found out exactly what they'd been doing, but she had a sense that if they had succeeded, something terrible would have happened.

A man had nearly choked to death when a dark figure had turned to smoke and gone down his throat. A servant carrying a candle and entering the room by chance caused it to flee before its dread mission was accomplished.

By the time Charlie looked up from the book, the building was quiet. Tucking the book into her bag, she slipped out the door and down the stairs.

She'd have to talk to Liam Clovin, but there was someone she wanted to talk to first. If Red had really murdered Knight Singh, then what was Raven doing with his papers? And if Salt was the very wealthy puppeteer looking for them, why would he be scrambling to get the notes of someone from carapace when he was supposed to be obsessed with the return of the *Liber Noctem*?

In the car, Charlie turned to the empty seat beside her where her own shadow fell.

"Okay, kid," she told it. "The universe belongs to the curious."

23
BEAR CLAWS

Charlie pulled into the parking lot in front of Eclipse Piercing & Shadow Modifications in Amherst around ten that night. It was in a strip mall, positioned between a Korean chicken place and a laundromat. Charlie parked in the back, against a thin copse of trees. The chilly night air carried the scent of beer and fried things from a bar one lot over.

Grabbing a Dunkin' Donuts bag from the back seat, she went to the door near the dumpster, a red bulb burning above it. She knocked, knuckles hard on the wood. A sliver of light peeked out the edge of blackout curtains hanging inside the window.

Moments later, a Black woman opened the door. She wore a tank top and ripped jean shorts. Her curls were dyed the color of flames, with yellow at the root, red for most of the way, and little licks of blue at the tips. Tattoos covered her arms, from a dark-skinned moon goddess new enough to be shiny with moisturizer to older and less well-rendered spiderwebs, roses, and a skull with a serpent snaking through its eyes.

Folding her arms across her chest, Raven regarded Charlie suspiciously. "I don't take walk-in clients, especially at this hour."

"You had something stolen from you recently," Charlie said. "I want to talk to you about Knight Singh, and his book of observations. Tell me what I want to know, and you can have it back when I'm done with them—less than a week, I promise."

Raven narrowed her eyes, then stepped back so that Charlie could come inside. As Raven closed the door, Charlie saw the words "El arte es largo y la vida breve" ran down the inside of her left arm in large gothic script.

Scabs dotted her legs, as from fleabites. Marks made by feeding her shadow.

Charlie held up the Dunkin' Donuts bag. "I brought coffee, if it's any consolation."

"Okay, thief, let's hear what you want." Raven poked around in the bag, then looked up. "Fuck yeah. You got bear claws."

The first part of any con was winning someone's trust, and every conversation was a little like a con. Coffee and pastries couldn't hurt.

"How did you wind up with his papers?" Charlie asked. "From what I heard, his death was unexpected."

"You could say that." Raven raised her eyebrows and took a sip of coffee. "They found him in his home, on the rug near his desk. The walls were painted with gore. The Cabal didn't want anyone to know details, but I found out." Raven went on, not leaving space for comforting words or horrified astonishment. "Another gloamist said they heard a man's voice screaming, someone other than Knight. To do what was done to him required a kind of strength that could only come from a shadow—a very powerful one, glutted on energy and blood."

"That's awful," Charlie said.

Raven nodded. "Knight was the first gloamist I ever met, the one that taught me how to use my magic properly. Got pissed when I decided I wanted to focus on alteration. Said I was chasing money. Maybe he was right.

"The thing was, though, he gave me that book, a week before he was murdered. Told me to keep it safe. He had information that could bring down someone important. Holding it over that person's head kept him safe, and not just him. I guess he was wrong about that."

"Lionel Salt?" Charlie asked.

Raven gave her an odd look. "Maybe. That old man is a freak. Stole the shadow he's wearing. Lots of people are supposed to have disappeared into his house."

"If that's common knowledge, how come the Cabal never did anything? How come Knight Singh never used what he had?" Charlie asked.

Raven went to a cabinet near a kitchenette and took down a metal dog dish. "I've got a couple of things to do. Do you mind if I work while I talk?"

"Go ahead," said Charlie.

Raven opened a mini fridge jammed into a corner behind the counter and took out a plastic bag of blood. She ripped open the edge with her teeth.

"Hand me one of those coffee mugs?" she asked, nodding toward a sink where a few clean forks and cups rested on a scratched plastic drying rack.

Charlie stared at her incredulously. "You want me to do what now?"

Raven smiled. "Mugs. By the sink. Get one."

Charlie chose one at random. It read: "KICK TODAY IN THE DICK."

Raven poured the blood into the cup and then stuck it in the microwave, setting the timer for a minute and a half.

"To get the chill off it," she said, as though that explained anything.

As the mug went around in circles, Raven turned to her. "Nobody has any real proof. And Salt's rich. That's why the Cabal won't do anything. As for why Knight didn't use what he had, I don't know. Depends on what he had."

"You can't expect me to believe you didn't read through Knight's book while you had it," Charlie said.

Raven smiled. "Oh, I did. Lots of information, most more relevant to shadow-wearers than alterationists, but absolutely nothing that seemed like it could take down anyone."

Charlie frowned. "Other than whatever Knight had, would Salt have any reason to want him out of the way?"

"Knight was against his being a Cabal member, and now that Knight's gone they're bending the rules and letting Salt join, even though Malik's already representing the puppeteers."

"So they're not going to have anyone from carapace?"

Raven's gaze went to the mug, turning on the plate, her expression remote. "It's not fair. Knight helped build the Cabal. He was one of the early gloamists to be open about shadow magic."

Charlie opened her coffee and took a sip, thinking about Red, and what Salt had said about Vince. "What was Knight's connection to the *Liber Noctem*?" He might not have one, but she hoped that by putting it like that, Raven would believe she knew more than she did.

"*The Book of Blights?*" The microwave beeped and Raven dumped the contents of the mug into the stainless dog dish. "He thought it was hilarious that Salt got scammed into paying so much for it, I guess.

"That's the problem with rich gloamists. They buy up all the magical books, because they can, and then use that knowledge to tie other gloamists to them. Salt wouldn't follow anyone's rules, and now he's going to be the one making the rules."

There were stories of cults formed by gloamists in the early days of shadow magic becoming public. Lots of bloodletting to juice up their shadows. Lots of creepy robes and creepy sex. And in the end, lots and lots of death.

When Charlie thought of what a gloamist organization run by Salt would look like, she imagined the high-class, corporate version of those cults. But people would join. He had the books and the money. And the bigger his organization became, the more influence he'd have with the other gloamists. His seat on the Cabal would mean no one could stop him.

Shoving the empty, bloodstained mug back into Charlie's hands, Raven went to the door and set the dog dish down on the step.

"Do I want to know?" Charlie asked, eyebrows raised.

"You will in a minute, whether you want to or not." Raven appeared immensely amused. "Why do you want to know about the *Liber Noctem*—didn't Salt's grandson make off with that before he kicked the bucket? Why do you want to know *any* of this?"

Charlie flopped down on a bench, near a stack of flash magazines. "Something's gone wrong, and I guess I'm caught up in it. I can't walk away now, even if I wanted to—and I don't. What I really want is to figure out who's been lying, and about what."

Raven snorted. "Probably all of them, about everything."

Outside, a passing cloud changed the way the moonlight fell. Charlie saw a few shadows slipping toward the bowl.

They were faint, indistinct things even as they moved into the strong light of the bulb over the door. Barely noticeable. But the area around the bowl grew ever darker as more congregated.

The surface of the blood rippled, as though disturbed by some phantom cat tongue. Then it was all ripples.

"There is one thing about the *Liber Noctem*," Raven said softly. "Knight knew a guy at an auction house and they let him put on white gloves and take a look before Salt bought it. He copied out some notes on the binding of Blights, but nothing else."

Could he have overlooked the ritual to give Blights weight and form, or had it seemed so terrible that he simply didn't want to know it?

Charlie sat there, more frustrated than ever, watching blood drain from the bowl. The shadows thickened around it, dense and dark. "How about the Hierophant? He's supposed to be hunting down Blights, and you said it must be a powerful shadow that killed Knight Singh. It could be a Blight, couldn't it?"

Raven sighed and looked out toward the edge of the parking lot, near the trees. "That guy, Stephen. I knew him a little before he was the Hierophant. It wasn't even that he was a bad thief, it was that he stole the wrong thing from the wrong person. The gloamist who'd hired him hung him out to dry. Then they punished him by stitching that old Blight to him and, well, I don't think things are going well. A shadow like that—conscious and whispering in your ear? Creepy as fuck. I doubt he's going to catch anything."

Charlie recalled Salt's comment about powerful Blights being tethered to new wearers.

She recalled the Hierophant's words too. *Tell Red I want the book. Tell Red we can share. Tell Red that I will rip him to pieces.*

"Why would a Blight agree to be tethered?" Charlie asked.

Raven shrugged. "Most don't."

Charlie gestured toward the bowl. "Those are Blights, right? But giving them blood, that gives them power, right?"

"A little," Raven agreed. "You're wondering why I'd want to do that."

Charlie eyed them, thinking about Red, and the Hierophant, and the feeling of a shadow making her mouth move. "I was actually wondering how much blood it would take to make a shadow powerful enough to be a Blight, without its gloamist dying."

"I'll tell you what," said Raven, standing. "I'll give you a demonstration of both."

Her shadow shrouded her hand in what appeared to be a glove of fog. She reached out and plucked one shade up from where it licked at the bowl. It wriggled in her hand, but the other was holding what appeared to be a needle and thread, all formed from shadow.

It continued to twist, like an eel, or jellyfish, or some internal organ dragged outside of the body. And also like none of those things. If you looked fast, it might seem that Raven was miming holding something. That she stabbed an imaginary needle into an imaginary thing.

Charlie couldn't decide if she was more disgusted or fascinated.

Raven saw her expression and smiled. "Every time an alterationist changes someone, we have to use some of our own shadow to do it. If we're not careful, we'll give ourselves away, piece by piece, until there's nothing left. But I'm careful.

"These little shadows—they're nothing. No cleverness in them, barely any consciousness. Might not even survive being stitched to a person. But you're right that, strictly speaking, they're Blights. Shadows that have survived being apart from their wearer."

On the steps, Charlie could see a few slinking off now that their feast was over, but some still remained, a translucent darkness, like a film in the air.

"This part might freak you out," Raven said. "You can close your eyes if you want."

There was absolutely no way she was going to look away, like a coward. "I'm good."

Raven took the shadow and dropped it into her open mouth.

Charlie bit her lip to keep from making an astonished sound. That hadn't been at all what she was expecting.

Raven continued with a smile. "When a gloamist puts a piece of their consciousness into their shadow, they grow a kind of homunculus. Power is only part of what makes a Blight. If you don't want your shadow to be separate from you, don't *consider* it as separate. Never name it. And never feed it blood that's not yours, because that's giving it energy that also isn't yours."

Charlie nodded.

"But most Blights are formed on the deathbed. Gloamists often push parts of themselves into their shadow in those last moments—often all of their fear and pain. Scary things get made like that. But powerful things. To create a Blight without that would probably require *stealing* energy, maybe through someone else's deathbed and someone else's blood."

Charlie thought of Salt and what he'd done to her, of her fingers around a knife. "If it was powerful enough, could it control you? Could it puppet you?"

Raven studied her for a long moment. "I've never heard of a shadow being able to control the person to whom it's attached, but there's only one way to be entirely safe. To have no shadow at all. The shadowless can't be controlled. There's a door shut inside of them."

The shadowless can't be controlled. Could that be why Vince cut his shadow loose? To avoid being puppeted by his grandfather the way she had been? To avoid being controlled by Red?

Raven turned to Charlie. "I think that's enough answers for you. And so help me, if you fuck me over, I'll make sure you wind up the next Hierophant, with something ancient whispering in your ear while you chase down Blights until one of them catches you and devours you whole."

"I'll bring you Knight's papers," Charlie promised.

"Bring more bear claws when you do," Raven said, sending Charlie back into a night that felt more full of shadows than before.

T he next afternoon, Charlie sat at the kitchen table with pens in either hand and two sheets of notebook paper with tattered edges beneath them. In synchronized movements, she wrote the same words over and over, on both pages.

HEY DUMMY IS YOUR BRAIN SPLIT YET?

"I didn't know you were ambidextrous," Posey said, frowning at her.

"Not sure I am," said Charlie. "But maybe good enough is good enough."

Posey got a seltzer out of the fridge and popped the tab. She leaned against the counter and watched Charlie write. "Do you feel like your consciousness is bifurcating?"

Charlie sighed and stopped writing. "I don't know. If it was, what could I do?"

Posey pointed to her shadow. "Try moving your fingers. Those fingers, I mean."

Charlie frowned in concentration, focusing on attempting to feel a hand that wasn't attached to her. But no matter how hard she stared or tried to shift her consciousness or tried to think in two places at once, there was no perceptible change.

Posey shook her head. "Okay, what about lengthening it?"

That seemed even harder to Charlie, but she complied, attempting to imagine her shadow spreading, like it was melting. She tried to make it ooze, even just to blur a bit at the edges. Again, nothing. "I'm trying," she told her sister, forestalling any criticism.

"Maybe you could try to *inhabit* your shadow," Posey said.

Charlie threw up her hands in frustration. "What's that supposed to mean?"

Posey shrugged.

They went on like that, with Posey looking up exercises online, and Charlie becoming increasingly frustrated.

Eventually, Posey had a Zoom call with a client, bringing their session to an end. Charlie was relieved to give up. She pulled out her own laptop and stared at the screen.

With a sigh, she pulled up the article about Edmund Carver's death, copying over the name of the girl whose body was found in the car with his and putting it into the search engine.

Rose Allaband.

There weren't many mentions of her, the longest being from a week after she went missing:

> Family and friends of Rose Allaband are asking the public to share any information that could lead investigators to her location.

> Allaband, 23, went missing a week ago, after what was described by witnesses as a heated argument with a friend. According to investigators, she'd been spending time with some new people. Her cell phone was found by the side of Interstate 91, just past exit 19B, with the SIM card removed.

> Allaband's mother extends this plea: "Rose was a nice girl who trusted people too easily. She thought magic was all fun, and didn't understand how people would use her for what she could do. I am terrified to think

what might have happened to her. If anyone has seen my daughter or has
any information about her whereabouts, please, we're begging you to call
911 and report anything, no matter how small."

Vince *could* have had something to do with Rose Allaband's disappearance.
He'd convinced Charlie to trust him, after all. She'd gotten in his van lots of
times. A nice girl wouldn't have stood a chance.

But to be that person, he would have to be what Salt had called him—a
shape-shifter. Because the Vince she'd known was the kind of person who'd
go to the store and get those stupid bran flakes because they were healthy, and
Charlie had been wanting to eat healthier. Who'd patched up Charlie's cuts just
because she'd been bleeding.

But if Red had committed the murders, Vince would feel responsible. Red
had been part of him, after all.

Lucipurrr came over and butted her head against the edge of the laptop.
Absently, she scratched under the cat's chin.

Lionel Salt wanted Charlie to believe that Vince was planning to use the *Liber
Noctem* to make his shadow into some kind of immortal monster. According
to Knight Singh, it wasn't worth what Salt paid for it. But the Hierophant sure
acted like the book did *something*.

If Salt were right, and Vince intended to do this ritual with Red, what was he
waiting for? He'd had the book for a year, and it wasn't like he was a procrasti-
nator. He didn't put off stuff. He was the only person in her household who had
ever taken lint out of the dryer.

Impulsively, she typed "Edmund Carver + Adeline Salt" into the browser window. Scrolled through articles with more photos of them—Vince with a scarf
around his throat, Adeline hanging off his shoulder as though trying to appear far
more sober than she was, a small smear of lipstick at the very corner of her mouth.

Then a gossip blog article, with aerial photos of some people on a yacht.

Charlie squinted. On the prow, two bodies were entangled with one another,
half hidden by a shade sail. The woman's blond hair was tossed to one side, and
her bikini top was pushed up. The man was bent over her, but she knew him
even without seeing his face. She knew them both. Adeline and Vince.

IS HEIRESS CHEATING ON SHIPPING TYCOON?

Charlie couldn't help remembering how Adeline had outright said she was
glad he and Charlie weren't together anymore. And all those photos of Adeline
and Edmund together at all those fundraisers, balls, and parties in New York.
Never anyone else by his side, or hers.

Couldn't help thinking of the photo in his wallet.

Posey came in, leaning against the doorframe. She was holding a pack of worn tarot cards in her hand. "What are you looking at?"

"Proof the Hall family curse is real," Charlie said, and closed her laptop.

"How about you shuffle the deck and pick three cards."

Charlie gave her a look. "Oh, come on."

"Think of tarot as a psychological tool," Posey told her. "Accessing the unconscious. Jung was all for it. And you need to get at the part of your mind that's holding you back from being a gloamist."

"Fine," Charlie said, accepting the stack. She shuffled them as though she was about to play poker.

"Concentrate on your question," Posey told her. "It helps if you close your eyes. Ask the cards what's blocking your magic."

But what Charlie wanted to know about was Red.

She flipped over the top three cards without looking and handed them to Posey. Maybe this is why people went to psychics, in the end. Because they needed help and stopped caring how they got it. Any port in this motherfucking storm.

"These are all major arcana," her sister said, frowning at them. "Interesting."

"What does that mean?"

Posey didn't look happy. "That something big is going on."

"Okay," Charlie said uncertainly. "What else?"

Posey set down the first card. "The Magician. The conversion of the spiritual into material. It's a card of new beginnings, so I am guessing this is about you being a gloamist."

"Nothing we don't know," Charlie said, although she was a bit impressed.

Posey set down the second. "The Fool."

Charlie rolled her eyes.

"See how he's about to step off that cliff? And is oblivious to the danger."

"I see."

Charlie's sister looked at the final card, raised an eyebrow, and grinned. "Ooooh. Looks like there's a taboo that you're in danger of breaking."

Charlie frowned. "Which card is that?"

Posey showed it to her. A religious figure sat on a throne in red robes holding up his hands as two monks knelt before him. The Hierophant.

T hat night, Charlie went down to the basement and took out the aerial silk that she hadn't practiced on for months, the one that was supposed to keep her limber enough to slither through windows like the Grinch. She strung the cloth up on a hook, shook off the dust and at least one annoyed spider. Then she climbed in and went through the old exercises. The ones she used to do every morning, before pickpocketing practice. She was stiffer than she used to be, but as her muscles warmed, she found herself relaxing into the rhythm of it.

On the wall, her shadow followed every pose.

24
SAD SONGS ON REPEAT

The next morning, Charlie brought a cup of coffee back to her mattress on the floor and finally returned the call from Rapture. They wanted her to come in the following night and then go back to working regular hours for the rest of the week.

Charlie was fine with that, so long as she could take off Saturday, for Salt's party. Book or not, she was going to have to attend.

Then, after taking a huge sip of coffee, as the lazy golden light spilled over her worn sheets, she called the bursar's office at UMass. A grouchy-sounding woman picked up.

"Can you look up my outstanding bill?" Charlie asked. "It's under Posey Hall."

"Hold on," the woman said with a long-suffering sigh.

Charlie bit the skin around the edge of her thumb, trying not to play out the worst possible scenarios.

"It looks like you missed a deadline," the woman said. "There's a hold on your account."

Charlie's heart kicked up. "No, I had until the end of the month. I have the letter around here somewhere."

"End of *last* month," the woman said.

For a moment, all Charlie could do was stare at the wall. It was possible that Doreen had gotten her brother to do this, but it was equally possible that Charlie had made a mistake.

"I can get it to you," she said. "Monday."

"Monday, or you wash out and have to reapply for next semester," the woman said impatiently, and hung up.

Charlie flopped back on her bed, looking up at the ceiling, trying to convince herself to keep going. If she stopped, she might not get out of that bed for weeks.

She dialed Vince's boss, a story ready. But as soon as he picked up the phone, he launched into a tirade. "Tell that son of a bitch that he's dead to me! You hear that? You tell him that he can't just go on a bender and expect to have a job when he sobers up."

"He's not—" Charlie started, but he'd already hung up. And even if he hadn't, he obviously had no idea where Vince was.

Three calls. Two hang-ups. Maybe she'd lost her touch.

Charlie sighed, letting her head fall back to her pillow. She missed him, and wasn't sure she'd ever known him. She might be able to guess where Vince would go, but Remy Carver was an utter mystery.

But maybe not to Dr. Liam Clovin, who'd sold three valuable books to Paul Ecco. Who'd obviously known a lot more than he'd let on.

Charlie got up and started pulling off the sweatpants she'd slept in, her shadow following her motions. She watched it against the wall, stepping into panties, tugging its bra over its head, tying back its hair with an elastic band.

"We're magic," she whispered to her shadow, to herself.

There was no response.

"Are you hungry?" she asked.

As she moved her hand to her leg, the hairs stood up on the back of her neck and prickled all along her arms. She hooked a nail under the hard edge of a scab and pulled at it, like she was ripping off a Band-Aid. Blood came sluggishly, beading up and running off her ankle.

It never hit the floor.

After a breakup, it was normal to listen to sad songs on repeat. It was normal to spend hours staring at old photos and letters, or burning them on the grill, or even drawing devil horns on every picture you could find of your ex. Normal to eat an entire carton of ice cream on the couch and wash it down with a bottle of chardonnay. Normal to talk about the guy incessantly to your friends, to call his number just to hear his voice on the answering machine and then hang up without leaving a message.

But just because people did those things didn't mean they were *good ideas*. More like pressing a bruise to check if it still hurt.

Going to bother your ex-boyfriend's roommate felt a lot like one of those things people did but shouldn't.

It took a few more calls, but Charlie discovered that Liam Clovin was a resident at Baystate Medical Center. That made getting to him more difficult in some ways and simpler in others. Charlie couldn't just make an appointment and confront him when he came in to treat her for her bunions, or whatever.

But medical residents are famously exhausted, and exhaustion means limited attention. Liam was going to be concentrating on his job, which meant that he'd have nothing left over to detect a trap before it sprang.

Not only that, but Liam Clovin was on the cusp of all his hard work paying off. He'd sacrificed a lot of wild nights to get where he was, put in the time studying, took out loans. As a medical resident, he was so close to six figures that he must be able to taste them. He had plenty to lose.

Charlie had practically nothing.

There were several ways to waylay medical students, but the simplest was to hang out in the cafeteria around lunchtime. They might have lectures, or other duties keeping them from a particular hour, but if she waited, he'd get hungry eventually.

But to spot him, she was going to have to figure out what he looked like. Her initial searches online were fruitless. No photos of him with other medical residents at Baystate, although she scrolled through official images for the better part of an hour. He didn't seem to even have a Facebook. Finally, she discovered a picture of him in Remy's graduating class at NYU. There he was, Liam Clovin, red-haired, squinting against the sun. And not far off, Edmund Vincent Carver, looking straight into the camera.

Charlie pulled out clothes she used for this kind of role. A pale blue turtleneck to cover her tattoos. Her regular jeans. A brown bobbed wig that she could shove her hair under. Neutral makeup.

By the time she'd driven to Baystate Medical Center and parked as far out into the visitor lot as was possible, she'd slid into character.

Inside, she gave her driver's license to the bored woman at the desk, and when asked, claimed to be meeting a cousin in the cafeteria. That part of the hospital was open to the public, so no one had any follow-up questions.

She asked for directions at the gift shop, her gaze checking for cameras as she went. There were plenty.

The Baystate cafeteria reminded her of the one at the community college where she'd taken two classes in psychology before dropping out and taking a six-week bartending course instead. It had steel counters, no surface that couldn't be quickly wiped clean. The smells were familiar too—reheated frozen things in gravies thickened with cornstarch, milky chowder, onions, and hazel-nut coffee.

Charlie found a table in a corner and waited. After the first half hour went by without incident, she got up and found herself a prepackaged ham with swiss on rye, a coffee, and a water. By the time Charlie returned, someone had snagged her table. She found a new spot, chewed, and checked her phone.

She had an angry—and possibly booze-soaked—message from Adam on her real phone:

> *you bitch you should have just left us alone. You think that _oreen is I to leave me bacuase of what you said to her then you ha ve another thing comgin. she is as angry at you as I am and amybe more now that I told her the wayt hat you tricked me and stoe what was mine. She tld me ev-erything/ bitch bitch bitch I hoper you die.*

She set the cell down on the table, feeling as though it had bitten her. She ought to have seen that the situation was going to go bad once she'd lifted the book. Hell, Suzie Lambton had told her it was going to blow up in her face way before that.

I hoper you die too, fuckknuckle, Charlie thought, and deleted the message.

She was trying to calculate just how much she'd screwed up, when Liam Clovin walked into the cafeteria. He was pale and skinny, with a reddish beard. Since he was a classmate of Edmund's, she knew he had to be around her age, but the scrubs and facial hair made him seem older.

Because he'd done something with his life. Not like her. Charlie Hall, spending half her time trying to blunt her fangs and the rest of it hunting.

She waited until he'd gotten his food and found a table.

"Hello," she said, sitting down next to him. "Mind if I sit here?"

Now, some guys think that women con artists have it easy. That all they have to do is show some leg, like Bugs Bunny hitchhiking in drag, and the mark screeches to a halt, tongue lolling.

First of all, that's not even a little bit true.

And second of all, if a woman decides a low-cut top is necessary, that's be-cause cons work differently for her. Offer a man a business opportunity and he's suspicious, not that it's a con, but that because she's a woman she doesn't know what she's talking about. It's a delicate business, to act clever enough to be taken seriously and still make him feel like he can screw her over.

And if he wants to screw her too, well that's an even more delicate business.

But while the disadvantages that a woman con artist had were manifold, there were advantages. For instance, women seemed less threatening. If a man had sat down across from Liam, he would have reacted differently. He might not want Charlie there, but he didn't seem worried she was dangerous.

"No," he said, annoyed. "I mean, yes, I do mind. I really don't want compa—"

She reached over and took his hand. He jerked it away from her. Which made sense. Who wanted a total stranger grabbing you?

Charlie let her eyes fill with tears. She pressed her fingers to her mouth in horror. "But it's the truth!" she sobbed, loud enough for people—including nurses and doctors—to hear her.

He started to stand. No doubt he wanted to get away from her as quickly as possible. A totally reasonable reaction. The problem with reasonable reactions, though, was that they were easy to predict.

She grabbed his wrist, and this time she spoke low enough that only he could hear. "Sit the fuck down, Liam Clovin, or I am going to make such a scene that everyone in this room is going to believe that when you treated my dying father, I smelled alcohol on your breath. I am going to be loud, and I am going to be convincing. Or you can tell me what I want to know, and I will act like you're a sympathetic doctor comforting a patient through a tragedy. You can even pick the tragedy, if you like."

That was the other advantage women con artists had, the flip side of not being taken seriously. To the public, they looked like marks.

"Who are you?" He was obviously furious, but he sat in the chair across from her. "What do you want?"

"This won't take long," she said. "I just have a few questions about Edmund Carver."

His frown deepened. "You were at my door the other day."

She probably had only a few minutes before he managed to shake her. "Where is he?"

"Dead," he said.

"Try again," she told him.

He started to stand. "I don't need to tell you anything."

"Maybe you also got me pregnant," she mused.

"This isn't a soap opera!" he hissed.

"Not yet, it isn't," she told him, eyebrows raised.

He glared, but he sat. Put his head in his hand. Then he grabbed his sandwich and started taking it out of the plastic. "Look, he paid me to let him keep some stuff at my apartment and to use the address for mail he didn't want his grandfather to see. That's it."

"What did he keep there?" Charlie asked, wondering if it could be this easy.

"He had a closet with a padlock on it. It wasn't any of my business what he kept in there."

"But you knew," Charlie said, hoping that if she sounded sure, he'd believe she was sure.

"Some." Liam looked across the cafeteria, as though hoping to spot someone who could save him. "A spare phone. Books from his father's collection. Clothes. His driver's license. A fucking krugerrand, if you can believe it. He was planning on leaving, I know that."

"Then you—what? Broke in there and sold his books to Paul Ecco."

"He *asked* me to sell them!" Liam said, a little too loudly.

She smiled to let him know that he'd screwed up, because the sale of those books occurred after Remy was supposed to be dead. "And when was that?"

Liam sighed. "Okay, I saw him that night, okay? He showed up absolutely out of his mind. He was practically naked, wearing a woman's robe he told me he swiped out of a laundromat. Bare feet. Wasn't himself. Said he needed me to sell some books for him. I did it. I didn't know about the girl. I didn't know about any of it."

"And then you helped him fake his death," Charlie said. "You got a body out of the hospital, is that it?"

"No!" Liam half stood before realizing how many people had turned to look at him. He sat back down, even angrier. "No, of course not. I had nothing to do with that. Any of it."

"What did he say happened to him?"

He shrugged. "He didn't. What I worry is that he came from killing someone and got rid of his clothes because they were covered in blood. But back then, I figured his grandfather had thrown him out after he discovered Remy had a plane ticket booked for Atlanta."

Something drove Vince away from that house, after years of going along with whatever monstrous business his grandfather was engaged in. On his own, he'd be broke, after more than a decade of living like a prince. And he'd been poor enough that he wouldn't have had any illusions about what that would be like—or how quickly a couple of grand of stolen money could get spent. "What was in Georgia?"

Liam nodded, rubbed his face. "His mother. She was the one whose letters he was trying to hide from his grandfather. She died of an overdose the night before he showed up at the apartment. It must have pushed him over the edge."

"Did he seem like the kind of person who could kill someone?" Charlie knew the way she was asking was wrong, that it was giving him cover to deny it. She wanted him to deny it.

Liam considered the question. "Remy had a morbid sense of humor, but I've heard worse. I'm a doctor. Gallows humor is our thing."

She smiled encouragingly.

"Anyone can do anything under the right circumstances," he went on. "And look—one of the doctors that works here is known for being generous with prescriptions. I saw Remy's cousin Adeline buy some ketamine off him. Rich partiers like prescription drugs. They're more expensive than street drugs but come in safer formulations, and you're dealing with people unlikely to roll you. Who knows what Remy was into when he wasn't around me."

"Ketamine?" Charlie's friends were more a weed-and-oxy crowd.

"It makes you dissociative," Liam said. "In lower doses, it confers feelings of euphoria. In higher doses, people enter a state not unlike a coma, except they're partially conscious. Sometimes unable to speak, they can have hallucinations, and memory loss."

Charlie wondered what had been in her drink, all that time ago.

"And that's enough from me," Liam said, moving to stand. "I don't know where he is, and I don't know where the book is either. Okay?"

"The book?" Charlie echoed.

Liam snorted. "You think you're the first person to come around looking for it, or him? Two months after Remy showed up half naked, this young guy comes by, muttering to himself. Never taking his hands out of his pockets. Threatening me. There have been other visits since too. If I knew where Remy was, I would tell the police, not any of you."

Charlie took out her phone and flipped to a photo of her with Vince. They were at the Loews in Hadley on Throwback Friday, waiting to see *The Bride of Frankenstein*. It wasn't a great picture; he was a little blurry, but it was still obviously him. "I was his friend. See?"

Liam appeared visibly relieved. "I still don't know anything. Remy's gone."

"He mailed me something." Charlie reached into her pocket and took out a tiny key. It was actually to a music box their mother had given Posey, but it was small and silver and might have gone to anything. "And said that if anything happened to him, I'd know where to look. But I have no idea where to even start. He insisted it was important, that it had something important in it. I was hoping it would prove he was innocent. If you can't help me find him, you can help me find that."

It wasn't the worst story Charlie had ever come up with.

Liam frowned, considering. "Back in college, Remy's grandfather would yank him out for weeks at a time, on a whim. And when Remy came back, he'd be a mess."

"What kind of mess?" Charlie asked.

"Angry," Liam said. "But because he didn't know when it was going to happen, he hid stuff, even back then. He used to talk about how there are places rich people will never see, even if they're staring right at them. If he really hid something, he would hide it in a place like that."

Charlie wondered if, when Liam was a surgeon, and rich, he would look past those places too. Wondered if that was the dream.

She reached across the table to put her hand on his arm, trying to radiate sincerity. "Thanks for talking with me, even though I pressured you into it. Remy always said you were a good guy."

Liam gave her a sad smile. "I thought he was too."

Out in the parking lot, the sun had sunk low and red behind the buildings. Charlie checked the time on her phone. One more night before she had to be back at Rapture. Four more days before Salt wanted his book.

Liam's description of the person who'd been looking for Vince had matched the Hierophant. She knew he wanted the book and had apparently been wanting it for a while. But what she still couldn't figure was, lies aside, what all these people actually wanted the thing for.

The sound of footsteps interrupted her thoughts. A man was behind her, his footfalls faster the closer he got.

25

BLACK CAT.
TOAD. CROW.

There's a moment of dissonance when people break the social contract. A moment when the civilized mind searches for some reason why a person might be running toward you that doesn't mean they're out to get you.

Luckily, Charlie's mind wasn't particularly civilized. She raced for her car.

He chased after, boots thudding dully on the asphalt.

She ran, full-out. Eight hours on her feet most nights meant her leg muscles were no joke.

But he was already too close and had momentum on his side. He caught her arm, spinning her around. She stumbled against her car and looked up into his face.

"Adam?" His eyes were bloodshot and his breath could peel paint, but it was him nonetheless.

He grabbed hold of her wig and tugged hard. It ripped loose, pulling pins and hair with it. "Charlie Hall. You miserable, monstrous bitch. Thought you were going to con me, and then rob me?"

"Yeah, something like that," Charlie said evenly, meeting his gaze. No point in denying it.

He hit her, knuckles hard against her cheek. The back of her head hit the window of her car. She would have fallen except her fingers caught the handle of the door and she was able to hold on and stay mostly upright.

He punched her in the stomach.

All the air went out of her. She curled around the pain like a pill bug.

Charlie might talk tough, but she had never been in a real fistfight. Even with her sister, they'd mostly resorted to hair pulling and the occasional mean scratch.

Think, Charlie, she told herself, but shock and pain dulled her thoughts.

"Where's the book?" he shouted. "Give it to me!"

"Gone," she managed.

"I am going to break your face," he told her. "Your ugly fucking face. I am so sick of hearing about you. Everyone thinks you were so great, but I'm better. You hear that? I was always the best."

She spat at him. Saliva sprayed his cheek. He flinched in surprise, closing his eyes, giving her a moment to tear out of his arms.

Racing around to the other side of her car, she jerked open the door. He grabbed her throat.

And then she was in two places, as though there were more than three dimensions to the world. Her consciousness split. She was both the person screaming and trying to claw at his hand and she was something else, which rammed into him from the side.

Her shadow. She felt a pull somewhere in the center of her. And she saw it, a figure all of darkness, as though someone cut a hole in the universe. Her and not her. A mirror that reflected back no light.

He stumbled, and her butt hit the seat before he got hold of her again.

Animal instinct took over. Her body went wild, kicking and screaming. One kick landed against his upper arm, another scraped his knuckles. He howled in pain and let go of her. Charlie yanked the door shut. She slammed her hand down on the lock button.

The clicking sound from all four doors felt deafening.

Adam pulled on the door handle and Charlie had a horrible moment of being sure that it would open.

He beat his fists against the glass window.

She just sat there, her fingers running over the steering wheel. He was shouting at her, but her mind felt far away, numb with shock.

Even though she'd *known* Adam was terrible and that she'd robbed him—she'd underestimated the danger. A year out of the game, and she was fucking up left and right.

Though it was dormant, there was something new between Charlie and her shadow, a buzzing of sensation, an almost umbilical connection. A phantom limb. A homunculus.

With shaking hands, Charlie rooted out the key from her bag. Thankfully, the car roared to life. Adam pounded on the hood, and Charlie gave him a momentary warning of revving the engine, before hitting the gas. He reeled back just in time to avoid being hit. Heart thundering, Charlie steered herself out of the parking lot.

At the first red light, everything looked a little hazy, as though she was seeing it through a Vaselined lens. She realized her eye was starting to swell.

Also, she thought she might be having a slight panic attack.

She pulled over at a gas station about a mile away and checked her face in the mirror. Her left eye was purpling. Her mouth was cut, upper lip swollen like an aesthetician had gone ham with a needle full of filler.

Charlie was a mess. There were enough people wanting to knock her around that they were going to have to take a number, like at a deli counter.

And what it had taken out of her shadow. She remembered Vince's words about *unspooling*. Remembered that it was freshly quickened, with no reserves of energy.

She had to feed it.

Charlie couldn't remember where she'd first seen an image of a witch feeding her familiar from a third nipple. She recalled a woodcut, or an illustration meant to look like one. It must have been in the research she did for the Inquisition, back when she was Alonso.

As a kid, Charlie hadn't believed third nipples could be real until she looked them up. It turned out they could show up anywhere on the body. Imagine having a nipple on the back of your calf. Or on the knuckle of your finger.

It made her think of a pronouncement some misogynist barstool scholar once made with great seriousness: *Martinis are like breasts; one is too few, and three are too many.*

Which was bullshit. Ask anyone who'd been through surgery to remove a tumor. Or any fan of science fiction. Or anyone who liked martinis.

Ask her shadow, which was curled around her, nursing as tightly on her skin as any familiar. Black cat. Toad. Crow. Spirits sent from the devil to make mischief in the world. One wound was fine for it, although even a few drops of blood are hard to squeeze out when your scabs were shallow and are healing.

"You're okay," she soothed, as though to a child after a fall. "You're okay now, right?" So hard not to think of it as a separate thing. So hard not to treat it like one.

So hard not to love it. Or not feel responsible for it.

It settled back into place, a cloak on her back, a carpet at her feet, a veil. Real magic. Her magic.

It was never great to get punched in the face, but Charlie found herself smiling through her split lip. Until she realized that to have followed her from the hospital, Adam must have tailed her *to* the hospital. Which meant that he knew where she lived. And as angry as he was, he might drive straight there.

She picked up her cell and, cradling it painfully against her cheek, called Posey.

It rang. And rang.

"I know you're awake," she muttered.

Posey's voice mail started up. She must be Zooming with a client. Charlie tried her again, letting it ring, hanging up and calling right back.

Finally, Posey picked up. "Charlie, I'm—"

"You've got to get out of the house. *Now.*"

"Why do you sound so weird?"

Charlie didn't have time to explain about her swollen lip. "Seriously. Now. A coffeeshop. The drugstore. Doesn't matter where. Just pick up your laptop and your wallet, go out the back door, and hop the low fence into our neighbor's yard. The one with the trampoline."

"What's—"

"I am going to stay on the line while you do it."

"I'm in the middle of a card reading," Posey protested.

"It's got to be *right now*," Charlie said.

"Gimme a sec." Charlie could hear her talking to someone in a conciliatory way, although she couldn't make out the words. Hopefully explaining to her client that she had to go.

She came back a moment later. "You know I can't drive."

"I will be with you the whole way," Charlie said, keeping her voice calm and low. Radio voice. Hostage negotiator voice. "I promise. I'm coming to pick you up."

There was a long silence on the other end of the phone.

"*Please*, Posey." So much for staying calm. "Hurry."

"Fine. The backyard?"

"So you're not visible from the street." Charlie wanted to get on the highway and race toward home, trying to beat Adam, but she knew it was better to focus on getting her sister out of the house. "Just. You know. Quick."

As Posey moved through the house, grabbing some things she said she needed and herding Lucipurrr into a cat carrier, Charlie dug her fingernails into the mound of her thumb. She wanted to scream at Posey to move faster. She wanted to do anything but sit there in the parking lot, hurt and powerless.

Some huffing and rustling later, Posey said, "Okay, I'm outside with the cat. I'm heading toward the back."

"Go over the fence," Charlie said. "You're almost gone."

"You've got to explain—"

"I will, I promise. And I'm sorry."

"What if the neighbors—"

"Just keep going. Don't look back. Go, go, go."

"Okay," Posey said, sounding fragile. "I'm over the fence. You know I hate walking through someone else's property. What if Elias comes outside and yells at me for cutting through his yard?"

"You're doing great, all you have to do is keep going. Avoid the main roads, and cut through to . . ." Charlie tried to think. There were a lot of streets criss-crossing around there. It would be easy to choose the wrong one. She didn't think Adam knew what Posey looked like, but a woman with a cat carrier was hard to miss.

There was the Williston Library one way, attached to a private high school for rich kids that had perks like riding horses. Posey might be able to talk her way inside, but she'd have to deliver her story with conviction. In the other direction was a Dunkin', a lunch place that would already be closed, a tattoo studio called Needle Inc., Union Package liquor store, and Glory of India, which mostly did takeout.

"You should have come out on Clark, so cut through the parking lot on School Street. You're going into Union Package. Browse the wines until I get there."

"What if they don't allow pets?" Posey asked.

"Then we'll figure out something else. There's a Walgreens that's not far."

Charlie waited, listening to the sound of Posey's breath, until she heard the jangle of the bell on the shop door.

"You're coming right away?" Posey asked in a hushed voice.

"Right away," Charlie confirmed, and hung up.

This was why she'd stayed away from gloamists, away from cons and heists of magic. How had she not yet learned the lesson of juggling knives? Even when you kept them all in the air, you still cut yourself on the blades.

She glanced at her shadow one more time, trying to shift her perception toward it. It flickered in response.

"Okay," she said, and pulled out of the gas station.

Her car sped down the highway, the rattling of the engine barely noticeable. Whatever Vince had done held even as she pressed down on the gas and wove around delivery trucks and commuters. Her swollen eye made it hard to switch lanes to the left, and a pickaxe of a headache cleaved through her thoughts, which were mostly a litany of what-else-could-go-wrong—*What if Adam decides he needs a shot of courage before he busts into my house and goes into the nearby liquor store, what if he is following my car right now, what if he has an accomplice, what if Lucipurrr pees in the cage and gets Posey kicked out at just the moment when—*

Charlie pulled up to the curb and fought down a wild urge to jump out of the car. Keeping the engine running, she called Posey.

Her sister picked up on the second ring.

"I'm out front," Charlie said, feeling out of breath despite having done nothing more than drive. Maybe she'd cracked a rib.

A few minutes later, Posey emerged with a bottle wrapped in a paper bag, an overstuffed backpack on her shoulder, and the cat crate swinging from her hand. She climbed into the back. Lucipurrr let out a miserable yowl as her cage was unceremoniously dumped into the seat well. "I got both our laptops and some wine for Mom."

"Mom?" Charlie echoed.

But Posey had lost interest in that line of conversation. She was gaping at Charlie in the rearview mirror. "What happened to your face? And who are you afraid is coming to our house? Is it Vince? Did he threaten you?"

"*Vince?*" Charlie gave her sister an exasperated look.

Posey frowned. "I don't know! Was it the gloamist from Rapture?"

Charlie shook her head, pulling away from the street. She needed to put some distance between them and anywhere close to her house. "That guy's dead."

"What?" Posey's eyes widened. "What do you mean dead?"

"Check behind us. See if anyone's following," Charlie told her.

Posey shrugged off her backpack and turned around, kneeling up on the seat. She looked pale and a little sweaty. "How am I supposed to tell?"

"You keep watching. Not just the cars behind us, but the cars behind them. I don't know. I've only seen it done in movies." Charlie took a turn. "No one follows the exact same route, especially the one I am going to take, doubling back on the same roads. So if they stay with us too long, we worry."

"Okay," Posey said, staring.

"*Are* you okay?" Charlie asked, her gaze on the road.

"Of course I am," Posey said. "You're the one with the face that's swelling like a balloon. Now will you explain?"

"Doreen has this on-again-off-again boyfriend named Adam," Charlie started.

"The guy you were texting," Posey said.

Charlie nodded, remembering her sister grabbing her phone on Wednesday, back when it had seemed as though she wasn't going to blow up her life again.

"So *Doreen* beat you up? For messing around with her boyfriend?"

"No! Are you serious? Adam was pissed because I ratted him out and stole something from him." Put like that, it did sound bad. "Which he deserved. And that thing I stole, he stole first."

"I don't think anyone's following us," Posey told her, slumping down and returning to a normal, legal seated position. "Can we go home?"

Charlie shook her head. "Let's give Adam a night to cool off, where he doesn't know where I am. I'll talk to Doreen. She'll calm him down."

Posey frowned at the window, clearly unhappy.

Charlie sighed. "Sorry about your client."

"You know that Vince knew about Adam, right?" Posey said.

"That I was conning him?" Charlie cut her gaze to her sister in the mirror. "How could he—"

"Okay, *knew* was the wrong way to put it. He *thought* he knew about Adam."

"Just come on out with it," Charlie said.

"He heard me reading off your phone. You know, about meeting Adam in private."

Charlie felt sick. "Did he say something?"

"He asked me if I saw *when* you were going to have the meeting." Posey looked deeply uncomfortable. "And said that I was right about him. That I'd been right all along."

"And what did you say?"

"Nothing," Posey told her. "I was too surprised. I really didn't think he noticed what I said or what I thought. And I guess maybe I wasn't fair to him."

"*Now* you think that?" Charlie had to force her foot away from the gas, so strong was her impulse to take out her feelings on the road.

Posey shrugged. "He was too calm. I was always waiting for the other shoe to drop, for him to hurt you. I mean, hot, built guys are supposed to be assholes. I figured he was probably bad news. But in the end, even though he was a huge liar, I think he might have been your most successful relationship."

Charlie briefly contemplated driving them both off the road and straight into a tree.

I wasn't the only one who lied. He'd said that when they were fighting.

Now, much too late, she understood what he'd meant. *I couldn't give you what you needed. I kept things from you. Even if you didn't know what was wrong, you could tell there wasn't enough of me.*

On Friday morning, when he'd gone to Rapture to pick her up, had he known she was supposed to meet Adam? She'd thought he was there because he'd been worried her car wouldn't start, but what if he'd been there expecting to find her with someone else?

I wish I could say I was sorry, that I wanted to be honest the whole time, but I didn't. I never wanted to be honest. I just wanted what I told you to be the truth.

Charlie had always believed that nothing really touched Vince, because everything he really cared about had been left behind in his old life, the one he was exiled from. The one to which he longed to return.

But it was entirely possible that he'd hated his old life.

And that she'd lost more than she ever realized she had.

26

THE PAST

The glass of champagne in Remy's hand was warming too fast. Too many bodies pressed together. All around him, delicate laughter floated through the stifling air. Adeline was talking to a viscount or a baronet or someone with one of those titles that didn't come with any money but did come with invitations to parties.

It bothered Remy a little that he could tell that without trying, that his eye automatically picked out the lack of tailoring in the man's suit and the worn leather strap of a third-generation Rolex. He tried to convince himself that it was mere cleverness and not snobbery, but knew it wasn't entirely true. He'd gotten used to having money he didn't earn, and feeling smug about it.

The fundraiser was being hosted in the home of one of Remy's ridiculously wealthy school chums. It was to benefit children of some kind. Maybe they'd been sick. Maybe they were going to be given art therapy. Or ponies. Or their ponies would be given art therapy. It didn't matter. There was a theme too— old Hollywood, which basically meant wear something fancy or ridiculous or both. That didn't matter either.

The important thing was for the young people to get their parents to shell out a donation of fifty grand. Ten would go into their youthful pockets, with forty left for the charity. Later, he and his friends would take their ill-gotten gains and go to a club where they'd get bottle service and drink enough to forget the whole night.

Remy would dance and howl at the moon and stagger back to his grandfather's pied-à-terre with his arm around Adeline, every choice he'd ever made seeming worth it in those giddy predawn hours.

His phone pinged, bringing him back to the present. His grandmother again, suggesting they meet for brunch the following day. Terrible idea. Not only was he planning on being *extraordinarily* hungover, but he didn't want to talk about the only subject they had in common—his mother, who hadn't been doing so well at the new rehab.

Being with his grandmother made him feel a rush of longing mixed with resentment, and that was the other reason he didn't want to see her—he didn't like feeling things.

He'd lived with her when he was small, he and his mom. He'd had a bed all to himself, and they'd eaten dinner together every night. But Mom wound up stomping out, dragging him with her, and that had been that.

Remy felt exhausted by the thought of brunch. But he felt guilty about making an excuse and not going.

Maybe he felt something other than guilty, but he didn't want to dwell on it.

You're ashamed, Red whispered to him, always there in the back of his head, like a fucking evil cricket masquerading as a conscience. *You don't have to feel that way. I can be ashamed for both of us.*

Remy glanced at his shadow, thrown on the floor, larger than he was in the light. Maybe *Red* could have brunch, and he could lie in bed. He might be able to hold Remy's shape for long enough. Between the murders and the energy Remy was feeding him, he was becoming alarmingly stronger. Each time he became a Blight, he seemed to be able to do much more than before.

"What's the matter?" Adeline asked. She was wearing a stiff vintage McQueen dress covered in shining beads that gave the impression of slashes. She carried two old-fashioneds, holding one out as though it was for him.

"Nothing," he said, tucking his phone back into his pocket.

She grinned. "Bored?" she asked. "I hear there's a pool in the basement. Come on. Let's go skinny-dipping."

Remy snorted. Then he stashed his champagne flute behind a plant and took a slug of whiskey fragrant with orange peel. He loved Adeline's cheerful sociopathy. It reminded him of her father sometimes, but where his was bent toward conquering the universe, hers was bent toward fun.

The fundraiser was being held in an Upper West Side town house, the kind that went for fifty million, easy. The kitchen was done up in brass and marble with a fancy Italian stove. The walls were papered in bright, modern designs, hung with amusing art. Even the carpets were clever; one was in the pattern of a maze and another had a wash of turquoise color over a traditional design. The place made Remy's head swim as they made their way to the stairs. It was so far from his grandfather's grim, fusty house, with its dark wood and heavy drapes.

He caught sight of himself in the mirrored bar. Black suit, white scarf around his neck. Covetous eyes.

"Let's go," he said, pasting on his usual amiable smile. He had nothing to be unhappy about. He was having a wonderful night.

The stairs spiraled down into a lower-level lounge full of scarlet and pink and pillows. The air was faintly perfumed with chlorine and the windows glowed with subaquatic blue light. A chandelier projected shadows that dappled the ceiling with the shapes of goats and wolves.

"Unzip me," Adeline said, laughing as she turned around.

Remy tossed back the rest of his drink. The world had blurred a little at the edges, and he had the beginning of a pleasant buzz.

A woman in black pants and shirt came down the stairs at a run. "Excuse me," she said, looking slightly panicked. "You're not allowed here."

"Who are you?" Adeline asked, sounding impressively haughty.

"I'm part of the staff. We've been asked to keep people out of the private parts of the house." Her tone was apologetic but firm.

"This is Jefferson's place," Remy told her. "My *friend*. He doesn't care if we're down here."

"Well, his parents do." She nodded toward the glass in his hand. "You've been drinking. It's an insurance thing."

"Red could make her change her tune," Adeline said to Remy.

He rolled his eyes. "Overkill."

The woman took a step in the direction of the stairs. Probably the word "kill" in any context made her nervous.

"Let Red play," Adeline insisted, a cruel little smile on her mouth. Maybe it was because she'd been embarrassed, her zipper half down her back. Maybe it was the flip side of cheerful sociopathy, but when she was like this, she wouldn't back down. "Come on. It'll be funny."

"Use your own shadow then," Remy told her. "Or better yet, let's just go upstairs."

This was the second quickened shadow to which she'd been tethered. The first one withered away, the graft failing. The second one took, but she seldom practiced with it. He thought it made her uncomfortable, but she didn't like admitting it.

Adeline gave him a look. "We're not going anywhere."

What is it I am supposed to do? He heard the question in his mind, felt his shadow's annoyance and wasn't sure if it was his as well.

Puppet her, Remy thought back. *Make her go upstairs or say something stupid. Scare her. Don't hurt her.*

You don't want me to make her drown herself? He was almost sure Red was joking.

There was a time that he would have had to maintain a bifurcated consciousness, but not anymore. Red just *did* things. Ideally, what you told him, but occasionally something else entirely. Remy could probably stop him if he tried. Probably.

The woman gave a shudder and a gasp as Remy's shadow shifted to overlap hers.

Adeline clapped her hands in delight.

The woman's mouth moved, grating out words. "I'm not getting paid enough for this shit. Go ahead. Use the pool, assholes."

Remy laughed. He found it a little disturbing how much Red would have to know about people to come up with something so entirely realistic, but it was still funny.

Adeline gave a sigh of annoyance. "No, make her say something *embarrassing.*"

The woman's body moved jerkily, her eyes wild with panic. "Stop ordering me around, Adeline," she said. "I don't like it."

Adeline turned to Remy, astonished and offended. "Did you—"

"Oh, come on," Remy said. "He's just having a laugh."

Then the woman gasped, hand going to her mouth as Red let her go. She looked at them both, tears starting in her eyes, then ran up the stairs.

Adeline turned to Remy, eyes blazing. She was furious. Remy didn't think she'd have been so angry if *he'd* said that, but she thought of Red as a toy, and toys weren't supposed to answer back. Especially not in *public.*

Before she could lecture Remy on controlling his shadow, Madison, Topher, and Brooks thundered down the stairs. Topher had gone to the same prep school as Remy, and he and Adeline knew the others from running in the same circles.

"My man," Brooks said, going in for the one-armed guy hug. "Heard there was a pool. Should have known you would get here first."

Maddy had swiped a bottle of Don Julio 1942 from the mirrored bar. "Oh, I should have gotten glasses," she said.

"I can pour a shot straight into your mouth," offered Remy, relaxing in their company.

The five of them skinny-dipped in the pool together, drinking tequila and laughing. Adeline seemed to forget about what had happened, and everything was normal again. Then they put back on their clothes, got hold of Jefferson, his girlfriend, and someone else's cousin and went out to The Box, where acrobats were flying through the air, along with a single shadow. At various points, it held them suspended above the crowd, making them appear to be hanging on to absolutely nothing.

Topher wanted to roll bliss, and Adeline showed off her gloaming ability by sending him off. When she was done with him, he was in such a state that he could only loll in a corner of their private booth, murmuring to himself and twitching. Remy hoped that she'd given him the promised good time. She'd sent people off into weeklong bouts of terror before, and by then it was clear her foul mood had returned.

Brooks and Jefferson, impressed, asked her a lot of questions in a way that made it clear they were interested in more than the answers.

Maddy and the cousin had begun making out, both their skirts pushed up so high that it was clear only one of them was wearing underwear.

Remy tried to avoid Adeline's wrath by talking to the girls at the next booth, who recruited him to play a drinking game. You were supposed to all stare at one other person, and if you locked eyes, shout "Medusa!" before the other did.

He'd had at least three more shots of tequila when Adeline put her hand on his shoulder.

She appeared to be quite drunk. "Tell Red to kiss me."

Remy was far from sober himself, but even he knew that was a bad idea. "Come on, Adeline. Sit down and play with us."

Her shadow whipped toward one of the girls, smacking her in the head hard enough that she bit through the glass she was about to take a sip from.

He stood as the girl's friends tried to use napkins to stop the bleeding.

Remy didn't want to think about the girl's pink teeth. The way the chunk of glass had fallen onto the table, glossy with spit. "Come on, let's go home. It's late."

"Don't you want Red to?" she shouted as he dragged her through the club.

Remy didn't answer.

"Tell him he has to do what I say." They were out on the street. "Or I'll tell my father that he's a Blight half the time."

Remy groaned. "Stop with the threats. It's exhausting. You're exhausting tonight."

"*Tell him,*" she insisted.

"Fine," he lied. "I just did." It wasn't like Red hadn't heard everything anyway.

"I think *you're* the one that made him be awful to me," she said.

Remy didn't bother to deny it. They were both wasted, and likely to get into a stupid argument. They'd been together too much these past few months, living in each other's pockets. It wasn't normal. They shared too many awful secrets. It was making them snipe at one another.

Adeline was still sulking as they staggered into the pied-à-terre. Remy didn't care. He was planning on going to bed and sleeping through brunch.

He sobered up fast when he saw his grandfather waiting for them. He sat on the couch, a single light on, giving his face an eerie illumination.

"Have you ever heard of Cleophes of York?" he asked them, as though continuing a conversation they'd been having.

"No?" replied Remy hesitantly. This was the price of Salt's money, living on his terms and his time.

"A very old Blight," Salt said. "Tethered five years ago. I think I figured out a way to talk to him without the person who's been wearing him knowing. We're going to try an experiment."

Adeline frowned. "What kind?"

"Good old ketamine." He picked up a vial of liquid from the coffee table and shook it. "I am going to inject Edmund and we'll see if that allows Red to puppet him."

"I'm too drunk," Remy protested. "Mixing booze and drugs is how rock stars die."

Salt snorted. "Don't flatter yourself. Now sit on the couch and roll up your sleeve."

"Seriously," Remy said. "Tomorrow."

"Now," Salt corrected. "You will find that I am very serious."

Remy gave Adeline a beseeching look, but she didn't meet his gaze. She was looking out the window, her face carefully blank as though her thoughts were far away. She'd stopped fighting her father years ago. The price of disobedience was too high.

I could possess you without any needle, Red whispered. *If you let me.*

But his grandfather didn't want to know what Red could do, he wanted to know what ketamine could do.

Then let me kill him.

No more murders, Remy thought automatically. All he needed to do was get through this unpleasant thing and then forget it. Shove more fear and anger into Red. And if sometimes Remy felt as though he'd given so much of himself away that there wasn't much left, he was unwilling to contemplate any of the alternatives.

Remy flopped on the couch, shook off his jacket, and began unbuttoning his shirtsleeve.

Remy's grandfather took a needle out of plastic packaging and removed the safety thing. Then he stuck it into the top of the vial and sucked up the clear fluid. He was having a hard time telling the difference between his and Red's thoughts. They were running together in panic.

If Remy stopped breathing, no one would believe that he hadn't taken ketamine at the club. That was the real genius of his grandfather, to set up things so that no matter what happened, he would never be accountable.

Then there was a sharp prick on the skin of his arm. He glanced at Adeline. She was watching him, her expression soft. And then he felt a sensation like falling.

He tasted blood, as though he'd bit his tongue.

The last thing he remembered was the sound of his own voice, turned unfamiliar in his ears. "No more Remy now. Only Red."

27
THAT AWFUL THING I LIKE

W hen Charlie had moved out from her mother's apartment, she figured that she'd finally be free of the fear and guilt that followed her through adolescence. But seeing her mother always brought its return, ready to fill the air to choking with everything unsaid between them.

She hated the feeling. Hated the long-stay motel where her mom lived because her credit was bad and her job history patchy. Charlie hated the better-than-average chance she was going to wind up living in a place just like it one day.

Lots of people lied to their mothers; there was nothing special about Charlie having lied. The problem was that her mother would never forgive her if she found out. Charlie had made her mom believe that the universe cared about her, that spirits had arrived to protect her in her time of need. If someone took that from her, she'd hate them. Even if it was the person who'd given it to her in the first place. Especially when those lies had made her mother susceptible to more lies from more liars.

As Charlie pulled the Corolla into the parking lot of Residence Suites and around to the side where her mom's room was, her chest felt tight. This late in November, leaf peepers had stopped coming through the Valley, and no one was driving up from Connecticut to pick apples, so the hotels were mostly empty. There were plenty of places to park and no excuses to delay.

As she took the key from the ignition, Charlie noticed that there was some kind of small metal thing stuck to her keys. It took her a moment to remember that she'd taken it from the bottom of Vince's duffel, thinking it looked like a watch battery. Apparently, it was magnetic.

Frowning, she tossed the keys back into her purse, magnet still attached.

Posey knocked. Bob, Mom's current boyfriend, opened the door, took one look at Charlie's swelling face, and yelled, "Jess!"

Their mother came to the door. She had been in high school in the eighties and still used a crimping iron faithfully. Her long, dry hair fell over her shoulders, rippled with ridges from the hot ceramic, and bottle-black. Her fingers were covered in silver rings and her eyes were thick with liner. "Oh no, what happened? And why do you have the cat?"

Charlie gave an abbreviated version of the story, omitting the theft. Mom was sympathetic, but it wasn't lost on Charlie that, once again, she'd won that sympathy with lies.

"You should call the police," Mom said. "Have them escort you home and arrest Adam. He assaulted you!"

Charlie didn't plan on doing that, but she wasn't above suggesting to Doreen that she would. Adam wouldn't want them nosing around, what with his illegal dealings. Maybe it would get him to back off.

Once ushered into the motel room, Charlie let her mother steer her to the couch, while Posey found a perch on a barstool beside the kitchenette counter where she could plug in both her phone and her laptop. The place was essentially three rooms—a bedroom with a door, a bathroom that you had to go through the bedroom to get to, a kitchenette, a little bar-height table with two chairs, and a couch in front of a television. Cable came included in the week-to-week price, no extra charge.

Mom and Bob had brought in some furniture from previous residences. Two lamps Charlie remembered from her childhood, an unfamiliar but obviously not hotel-originated rug, some bookshelves, and stacks of Bob's cardboard boxes of individually plastic-sleeved Magic: The Gathering cards, of which he had *a lot*.

He claimed that they were valuable enough that when he was ready, he was going to sell the whole collection and buy a house, but he couldn't until he finished his legal battle with his old employer. Mission Trucking was the unambiguous cause of his back problems and had been court-ordered to pay for his insurance. They wanted to settle so they could wriggle free from their obligation, but Bob wasn't taking less than a million.

He kept promising her mom that once he got it, they'd live in style.

It was his version of the big score. And about as likely.

"We need to put something on your eye," Mom said. "Oh, honey, that doesn't look good now, but it's going to look even worse tomorrow."

"I'll get her some ice," Bob said. "You get in a few good hits?"

Charlie laughed. "You bet."

"Hope you kicked him where it counts." He brought her a package of frozen peas, and she pressed them to her eye. Bob had a balding head and a paunch and wore a t-shirt proclaiming his love for the Ramones.

Having plugged in all her devices, Posey hopped down off the stool to get the cat some water in a plastic takeout soup container.

"So you two are going to spend the night," their mother said. "I insist."

With only days until Salt's party, Charlie didn't have time for a black eye or being stuck at her mother's place. And yet the pain in her face was yielding to exhaustion. Besides, there was something she'd come here to find.

"You want me to get the blow-up mattress out of the station wagon?" Charlie asked.

Her mother shook her head. "No, you stay put. Your sister can go. Or Bob."

Charlie got up, glad to have an easy excuse for her search. "I got it."

A constellation of magnets covered the refrigerator. A few were from local businesses, and others were emblazoned with sayings like "All I Need Is Coffee and Wine" or "So Punk Rock I'm Out of Safety Pins." Charlie grabbed the car key from where it was suspended and headed back out into the cold.

At almost sixty, Charlie's mother had collected more stuff than was going to fit comfortably into the hotel, especially given Bob's cards, which required a "climate-controlled environment" and were too important to him not to be kept nearby. And so, the back of Mom's wagon was full of her clothes for the off-season, decorations, taxes, and, apparently, an air mattress. The bins were crammed in tight. One of them was marked "CHRISTMAS," another "FAMILY PHOTOS." Charlie found the stale-smelling plastic mattress under a tub marked "VITAL DOCUMENTS."

That was what she'd come for.

After she'd escaped from Salt's house, the guy who'd found her had called an ambulance. She didn't remember much after that, but they must have done a tox screen at the hospital. The results ought to be with the rest of her medical paperwork.

Charlie pulled the lid off the bin. And there, under birth certificates and her mother's divorce proceedings, she found a folder with her name on it. Inside was a copy of the police report, hospital release, and the bill sent to the insurance. She skimmed over the details. *Scratches on arms and face consistent with branches. Mild dehydration.* One stood out: *traces of ketamine in system.*

She closed the folder, Liam's words echoing in her head: *One of the doctors that works here is known for being generous with prescriptions. I saw Remy's cousin Adeline buy some ketamine off him.*

It seemed that stealing a quickened shadow hadn't slowed down Salt's experiments, and that he'd gotten the rest of the family involved.

"Did you find it?" her mother called across the lot.

Charlie stuffed the folder under her shirt so her jeans held it in place. "Yeah, Mom," she called back, and dragged the mattress inside.

Her mother had made feverfew tea, which she said was good for pain. Bob slipped her some ibuprofen, which worked much better.

Charlie went back to the couch and the frozen peas. After a few moments, when she was pretty sure no one was looking, she eased the folder out from under her shirt and into the seam on the side of the couch, where the cushion would cover it.

Lucipurrr patrolled the new space, meowing as Mom took out some chopped meat and started making something for dinner. Bob put on that show where people bring in old stuff and experts tell them whether the item is worth money.

A long-haul trucker had brought in a cuckoo clock of his grandmother's that turned out to be a real antique, from the Edwardian period. When it struck midnight, a man appeared, running from his own shadow. "This was a time of great spirituality," said the elderly appraiser, stroking his beard thoughtfully. "Gloamists performed elaborate shadowplays against the walls of ballrooms. Magic was right in front of people, and yet few looked closely enough to discover it."

"Don't let the front desk know you've got a cat in here," Mom told Posey. "There's a hundred-and-fifty-dollar cleaning fee for bringing a pet into the room."

"I wasn't going to tell anyone," Posey complained, an adolescent whine creeping into her voice. "And I don't know where I am supposed to talk to clients. It's so loud in here."

"Try the bathtub," Mom said unhelpfully.

An hour later, they ate goulash sitting on folding chairs around a café table that couldn't hold all their plates at once. They drank Posey's wine. They were following the Hall family tradition of pretending everything was okay, and Charlie was glad. Nothing was okay and she had no idea what to do about it.

"Posey tells me that Vincent moved out. I'm so sorry," Mom said.

Charlie nodded. The less said about that, the better. One more thing that was definitely not okay. "Yeah, well. You know my luck." She didn't say *our* luck, because she liked Bob. Of course, it was possible that she would have liked anyone who'd brought her ibuprofen. If he'd brought her coffee too, she might have married him herself.

Her mother waited, as though hoping she might say more. Might *share*. When Charlie didn't, her mother deflated a little. Charlie felt guilty all over again, in a new way.

After dinner, Mom turned to Bob. "I want to show them where we sit outside."

"Outside?" Charlie asked. "It's cold."

"Under the stars. You get the blankets and I'll get the folding chairs."

A few minutes later, they were in the parking lot, looking at the lights of Springfield in the distance and the stars above.

"Not bad, right?" Mom said. "Like a porch."

Bob stood by the car and looked up obligingly. "Rain cleared out the clouds."

"I am not staying out here, freezing," Posey said. "I have a chat with some friends. We're revising plans."

Hopefully, that meant ayahuasca was off the table.

"Be careful," Charlie reminded her.

Posey gave her a sharp look and went inside.

After a while, Bob left too, saying something about making himself some tea. Charlie stayed wrapped up in her blanket. She didn't want to go back to that claustrophobic room, air thick with her own mistakes. And she worried that Posey was desperate enough to be a gloamist that she'd allow herself to be tricked, and that all the promised sweetness would be there to drown in.

"I'm glad you came to us," Mom said.

"Me too," Charlie replied automatically, alert to the dangers of this conversation.

"I've got a lot of regrets about decisions I made as your mother. When I was younger, I wasn't always paying attention to the right things. I wish you felt like you could come to me when you were in trouble years ago."

Charlie had a sinking feeling that this was about Rand, that Posey had said something during their daily tarot chats. "When was I in trouble?"

"I know you don't like talking about it—"

"There's obviously something you think you know, so go ahead and say it." Charlie needed to stop talking. Instead of splitting her tongue into two parts, she needed to bite the whole thing off. She should be trying to avoid this conversation, not indulging it.

"I saw you take your old medical file out of the car," she said. "And I'll never forget how I felt when I got that call from the police. And then, when they found Rand's body, with that dead girl in the trunk. That girl could have been you."

That was true, but not for any of the reasons that her mother was imagining. "It wasn't me, though. I'm fine."

"Are you?" her mother asked. "I know you were with him that night you wound up in the hospital. If you never deal with what happened, you'll never heal from it. You'll stay in that hurt, angry place."

Charlie Hall, with a furnace inside her that was always burning.

Of course she was angry.

She wanted her mother to have believed her when Travis smacked them around, to have loved her better than Alonso, who wasn't even real.

She wanted her mother to have protected her from Rand, who was bad enough, and still so much better than he could have been.

She wanted her mother to believe her now, even though Charlie had lied before.

"I'm fine. Sound as a bell," Charlie said. "Right as rain."

"I wanted you and your sister to have the freedom to express yourselves, to make mistakes, to discover yourselves. I didn't want to hold you back." Mom was playing with one of her chunky silver rings, rolling it around her first finger. "I didn't have that as a kid. And you had a *gift*. I thought Rand would show you how to use it."

Guilt came over Charlie in a swell. She had to change the subject. She couldn't stand feeling this way anymore, torn between a desire to scream and a desire to confess. "Maybe when I stopped using it, the gift moved on to Posey."

Her mother gave her an impatient look.

Charlie sighed. "You want me to talk to you? Okay, here's what I want to know. Have you ever met Lionel Salt's daughter?" They were around the same age, and the area had been even smaller back then. If her mother knew Vince's, maybe she'd know what happened to her.

"Kiara?" Her mother looked up, blinking like she was trying to refocus her thoughts. "We didn't run in the same circles."

"But you know her name," Charlie insisted. "So you must know something about her."

Mom shrugged. "She used to buy shrooms off a friend of mine. Partied hard. Told disturbing stories about her father, but people want to believe that the rich are keeping their fingernails in jars like Howard Hughes, and she seemed like the kind of person who'd say whatever got her attention. Fell in with some ex-cons up in Boston, got knocked up. Eventually her father put her in rehab, and that's the last I heard. She didn't talk to any of the old crew after that. Why?"

"I heard she died, that's all," Charlie said.

"Sad," said her mother.

Charlie stretched, rolling her shoulders. "I think I am going to go inside and see about the air mattress."

"Think about what I said," her mother told her as she stood.

As Charlie walked away, a memory came to her of when she was very little and her parents were still together. She was sitting in the back seat of the car, the window down. Wind whipped her hair. The radio was on, Charlie's little legs swinging along with the music, and Mom and Dad were laughing together. Golden sunlight had turned the world dazzlingly bright, and it seemed as though night would never come.

As she and Posey took turns pumping up their bed, Bob and Mom moved comfortably around the room. They seemed contented. It was weird, but nice. Like there was no curse, just a casual family inheritance of bad relationships, in a cycle that no one was doomed to repeat.

Charlie and Posey lay down next to one another, trying not to bounce the mattress. Charlie remembered a whole childhood of sharing beds with Posey, whispering to one another, back when they had the same secrets.

Back when they had the same gifts.

Charlie thought of the moment when her consciousness split, when she understood how to be in two places at once. Even now when she closed her eyes, she could feel her shadow. If she concentrated hard enough, she could see herself from its vantage.

As soon as she did, though, panic sent her spiraling back to her own body.

Charlie didn't have a goldfish or a turtle, because she worried she'd forget to feed anything that couldn't yowl for its dinner. She forgot to take her birth control pills at least twice every month, sometimes for two days at a time. When she'd downloaded an app to help her remember to drink water, it had come with a pixelated plant you were supposed to tap when you drank a glass. She killed the plant over and over—sometimes she'd drink the water but forget to tap the plant, and sometimes she'd just forget to drink the water. How was she going to remember to give blood to a shadow every day?

How was she going to keep from accidentally letting it drink up all her energy until she withered away? How was she going to keep it from becoming her own personal monster?

Lying on the mattress, the soft susurrations of breath surrounded her as the others succumbed to sleep. But Charlie's mind couldn't stop racing, couldn't stop worrying, wouldn't stop assembling and reassembling the information she had.

Once Salt realized his grandson had magic, he would have wanted to control him. Kiara's situation was rife with opportunities for exploitation. Salt could easily get custody of Vince in court. He had the money to feed Kiara's habit; she might not even contest it.

And for Vince, the promise that his mother would be sent to rehab, that she might get better. And then doling out access to her as a reward for good behavior, the promise of reuniting hanging forever over his head. And the fear of her being punished for his missteps motivating him further.

If Charlie could come up with that plan, she had no doubt that Salt had concocted a worse version.

And so Vince does what Salt tells him, and Red, whatever he was before, becomes a reflection of those things they do together. But controlling an adult is much harder than controlling a child. Especially one with a long education in manipulation and cruelty.

So Vince plans to leave and join his mother, but something goes horribly wrong. Possibly Salt realized that he didn't need Vince if he had Red, and cut off his grandson's shadow.

But if he planned to have it sewn to him, that didn't happen. It became a Blight, the talking kind, so he had to make a deal. He could have been the one who offered the ritual from the *Liber Noctem,* and Vince the one who stole the book to keep Red from walking the world.

There was no way Salt would mind making a monster, so long as it served his interests. And in the meantime, Red keeps on killing for him. Keeps on doing his bidding. Together, they get him accepted into the Cabal.

But if he'd promised Red his reward by the time of the announcement, then she could see why he needed the book. The problem with monsters is that you need to keep them leashed, or they turn on you.

The Hierophant wanted the book as much as Salt did. Had the Blight tied to him made him some kind of promise, some arrangement to get the same ritual? Or was he working on behalf of the Cabal, trying to keep Red from becoming a new and more terrible form of Blight?

And, more importantly, what was Charlie going to do? Salt expected her to bring him the *Liber Noctem* by the weekend, and the weekend was coming up fast.

Charlie's head hurt and her eye hurt and her ribs hurt.

Her gaze rested on the refrigerator, with its dozens of magnets. And as she looked at them, a thought came to her, about the little magnetic silver thingy dangling off her keys. The one she'd found among Vince's belongings.

Maybe that's all it was, a magnet. A magnet for holding a metal-covered book.

She got up as quietly as she could and, clad in a borrowed shirt of Bob's, slid on her shoes. Put on one of her mother's coats. Slipped out the door as quietly as she'd slid into plenty of other homes.

In the parking lot, the angle of the streetlight gave everything long shadows. The hiss of cars on the highway was distant, the streaks of the lightning farm barely visible.

She popped the hood of her Corolla and looked at the puzzle of the engine and spark plugs and other things she didn't really understand. Rich people never performed their own oil changes, or rotated their tires. They never even vacuumed their own seats. And Vince had spent a lot of time working on her car.

But the *Liber Noctem* wasn't stuck in the guts of the Corolla, and though she crawled underneath, the only thing she discovered was an oil leak.

I n the morning, Charlie's neck felt hot against the press of her fingers. She went into the bathroom and splashed cold water in her face, combing it back through her hair. Her mother's dire predictions hadn't proved accurate. The swelling had gone down around her eye. It had, however, turned a magnificently dark purple, with plenty of yellow and green bruising at the edges.

"I'm heading out to Rite Aid," she announced over breakfast, drinking down the sweet milk in her cereal bowl.

"You can't go to work like that," their mother said.

"I know," Charlie told her. "That's why I need to go to the drugstore first."

Posey snorted indelicately.

A few minutes later, Charlie was out the door.

According to the YouTube tutorials she'd watched while the air mattress slowly deflated beneath her, Halloween makeup was her best chance to fix her face. Luckily, some remained in the clearance section. She got herself a cheap palette that consisted of white, lime green, royal blue, bright yellow, and cherry red. Charlie was concerned she was going to look like a clown.

She added to that some regular stuff—a full-coverage concealer, liquid eyeliner, distractingly red lipstick, new deodorant, a three-pack of panties, and the only black t-shirt in her size. Unfortunately, it was emblazoned with a red-nosed reindeer below IT'S BEGINNING TO LOOK A LOT LIKE FUCK THIS in puffy letters. Still, it was a fine opportunity to break Salt's hundred-dollar bill.

Back at the motel room, Charlie poured the stuff out on her mother's bed and sprawled on the comforter to put it on.

After a lot of googling of color wheels and watching that video again, she mixed bright yellow with a little red and dabbed it on the purpling parts. Then she waited for it to dry.

Surprisingly, by the time she applied the concealer in careful dabs, the only thing that showed she'd been hit was the swelling—and even that was less obvious next to a red lip and a little bit of gold dusted on her eyelids.

"You look good," her mother said with a frown. "But I still think you should call out sick and go talk to the police."

"I'll think about it," Charlie lied.

"Are you ready to go?" Posey asked. "And can I use some of that?"

Charlie ducked into the bathroom to fix her hair and turn the disturbing reindeer shirt inside out. When she returned, Posey was wearing eyeliner and some sparkly shadow.

They split the pack of underwear.

That night, being back at Rapture was strange. The mess had been cleaned up, the broken glass was gone. New bottles rested on the shelves. Although the bar wasn't as well stocked as it had been—the unusual whiskeys and gins that Odette liked (rose and rhubarb were favorites) would take time to replace—it was functional.

Normally, Wednesdays were slow, but since the bar had been closed for the better part of a week, there was a lineup of performers. As Charlie came in, a body modification artist was up on the stage doing public piercings and tongue splittings.

By the time she was pouring her first drink, an acrobat with labrets through fresh holes in the dimples of her cheeks was performing a set that was half sleight of hand and half burlesque.

An hour in, Charlie was sweaty and footsore. She had to make a conscious effort not to touch her face and wipe away her careful makeup. Even with it, customers had to notice the swelling.

Balthazar gave her an odd, guilty look the one time she saw him out of his shadow parlor.

"Make me that awful thing I like," Odette said, sitting herself down at the bar. She was in a red vintage Vivienne Westwood sweater set printed with black barbed wire.

Charlie turned away to spray a coupe glass with absinthe from a spritzer.

"How are you holding up?" Odette asked.

"I'm fine." Charlie shook up Odette's burnt martini and pushed it over to her, along with a twist of lemon peel for garnish. "Glad to be back."

"You're a darling for saying so, anyway," Odette told her.

"I met a friend of yours," Charlie said, keeping her voice low. "Is it true you have a client who's an actual billionaire?"

Odette took a sip of her drink and grimaced a little at the bite of the alcohol. "Lionel? A client? Goodness no. He'd rather be on the other end of the whip."

Charlie pretended to be surprised.

"Have you ever been to his house?"

"I certainly have. It's a grim old place, plush carpets, lots of incense, and horrible art. But his liquor is top-notch and he knows a lot of interesting people." She paused. "He called me the morning after that man came in. Asked me a great many questions about your Vincent. What do you think he wants with him?"

Charlie looked at Odette as steadily as she could. "No idea. Maybe he's got an odd job he wants done."

"Ah, yes," Odette said. "It must be something like that."

"You remember that thing you said about pasts being the only thing that matter?" Charlie said. "What did you mean?"

"Did I say that?" Odette looked surprised. "Well, if I did, I suppose I must have meant it exactly as it sounds."

"Isn't who we are today what counts?" Charlie didn't know why she was pressing this point, since she wasn't particularly happy with the person she was today. And Odette had been talking about Vince when she'd said it, not Charlie.

Odette laughed. "Sure, honey."

"Isn't that the point of reinventing ourselves?" Charlie asked.

Odette took a second sip of her drink and closed her eyes in pleasure. "Ah, yes, that's good." Then she fixed Charlie with a look that made her remember that Odette had lived longer than she had and maybe lived harder too. "Who we were and what we did and what was done to us—we don't get to shrug that stuff off and become some new shiny person."

Charlie raised her eyebrows. "We can *try*."

"Take fetish. No one is into sucking on someone else's feet or worshipping their shoes or rubbing a balloon all over themselves for no reason. I know a boy who used to sit under the kitchen table and draw while his mother and her friends talked. He would look at their shoes, and know that if he touched one, he would be discovered and then he'd have to leave. You can guess what he likes. But if he didn't admit it to himself, what then? It takes bravery to be an adventurer," Odette said, lifting her drink and walking away. "And what better adventure than the discovery of our true selves?"

As Charlie worked, she let the physicality of the tasks take over, let herself fall into the rhythm of the work. Fill this, shake that, swipe a card, start a tab, pocket the change. Hold the pilsner glass at the exact right angle for the exact right head on the beer, do a boss pour for the hipster requesting one, dole out Fireball to a trio steering straight for regrets.

As she wiped down the bar top and collected wet napkins and wooden stirrers, her thoughts turned to her last days with Vince. The day before he'd left, he'd gone outside with the excuse of cleaning the gutters. He must have known that it was only a matter of time before Salt connected the dots and discovered him. Maybe he'd taken that opportunity to move the *Liber Noctem* to his van. She'd tossed the room only hours later. She could have been that close to finding it.

Hiding the book in his van was a short-term strategy at best, though. Since Vince had no legitimate ID, he couldn't have a vehicle registered to him. If he was ever pulled over, the van would be impounded.

And if Lionel found his grandson at any point, it would be an obvious place to look.

Now that she thought of it, her car would have been an equally bad hiding spot. Someone like Hermes might have taken it apart that night he came to Rapture. Salt had been standing right next to it not four days ago.

But that left the whole rest of everywhere to have put *The Book of Night*.

Liam said that when Vince would hide something, he'd pick one of the places rich people don't see. Perhaps he'd hidden it in one of the areas of Salt's own house he'd never gone. The laundry room. The pantry. Behind the television. That would be something, for Salt to be walking past it the entire time and never noticing. But it was risky too. It would be hard to reobtain the book, and there was no guarantee it wouldn't be disturbed by someone else. Even if he taped it to the chimney, slate repair people might stumble on it.

Even on a roof—

Charlie stopped, nearly overpouring soda in the scotch and soda she was making.

Who cleans the gutters the day after they murder someone and the day before they leave their girlfriend? A ridiculously considerate person, she supposed. Someone who'd been meaning to get to the task and wanted to get it done before they were gone.

Or someone who was moving something to a new hiding spot, one that no one was likely to stumble on, and which wasn't the sort of place that someone like Salt would even remember existed. Their rental house had a chimney, connected to the furnace and water heater rather than a fireplace.

And it had a metal top on it. One that magnets might grip.

Of course, there were lots of things that were made of metal in a house. But *outside* of the house made sense if he wanted to protect the people inside. And if Vince wanted to be able to retrieve it without having to face Charlie.

She could look, anyway.

It would give her a chance to check and see if Adam had busted up their place. If it didn't seem like he'd been there, Charlie would call Posey and they could move their stuff and themselves back in the morning. Put a baseball bat by the door. See if their landlord would mind if Charlie installed a couple of better locks.

If she did find the *Liber Noctem,* she had a different problem. No one blackmailed you into one job. Do that job, and there'd always be another. Carrot and stick, back and forth, until you forgot you ever had a choice in the first place. And then what? There wasn't a reward at the end, just a knife in the back.

Charlie might not agree with Odette that the past was the only thing that mattered, but it had taught her something.

Besides, she'd be damned before she rolled over for Lionel Salt.

She was going to have to con him. She wasn't sure how, but she would have to beat him at his own manipulative game. Realizing she had to manage that or die trying brought her a great calm, like letting a riptide drag you away with it.

As she waved good night to Odette and got in her car, Charlie had the bittersweet feeling one gets just before leaving town. Bidding farewell to everything, because you're not sure you're going to see it again.

Charlie parked a block down from her house and walked over. As she got close, she saw lights moving on a screen inside. The television was on.

She slowed her step. Had Posey forgotten to turn it off before leaving? Was Adam so arrogant that he'd broken in to the house and then kicked up his heels?

Quietly she took the ladder from where it was leaned against the side of the house and set it against the gutters.

As she climbed up the rungs, she could see inside more easily.

Someone was in the house. In the shifting light of the television, she was able to make out a figure slumped to one side of the couch, as though he'd fallen asleep while waiting for someone to return home.

28

ABANDON ALL HOPE

U p on the roof, Charlie crawled over the asphalt shingles. The pitch wasn't particularly steep and the moon was bright enough for her to see her way to the short faux chimney, with a metal grating covering the top. She pulled herself upright, looking out over the neighborhood for a moment, then, satisfied that no one was out on the street watching, she checked for bolts screwing down the cover. To her surprise, the whole thing lifted off. It was flimsy, like tin or aluminum. Looking down the chimney, she saw that the inside edges were lined in heavier metal strips.

And there, attached to one side, was a steel box with a lock on it.

Her heart stuttered. Stealing had often been a game to Charlie, one where her cleverness was pitted against that of the person who'd hidden the prize. Solving their puzzle was the goal, and the thrill. But as her hands reached for the box, what she felt was uneasiness. She couldn't shake the feeling that the darkness itself was watching her, waiting to strike.

Charlie pulled the box free, sending two of the magnets falling down the flue. They made a clanging sound that she hoped wasn't amplified inside.

For a moment, she went still, listening.

No sound from inside. Was it Adam? Certainly, he'd been angry enough to break in and trash her place, looking for Knight Singh's book. But she didn't think he had the patience to wait more than twenty-four hours for her to return.

Vince, however, had fallen asleep in front of the television like that loads of times.

Maybe he was ready to tell her the truth. Or maybe he'd come up with a fresh bouquet of lies. He wouldn't know what Salt told her, or what she'd ferreted out on her own. He certainly wouldn't know that she'd already stolen his prize. It'd be satisfying to explain how wrong he'd been about her and Adam.

It made her a little giddy to think of having another fight with him. It made her want to put on lipstick.

Carefully, she crawled back to the ladder and slid down, box cradled against her, wincing at the sound of the wood creaking.

Quietly, she eased to the ground and padded through her neighbor's yard, staying away from the light. At her car, she stuffed the metal box under the front seat.

What she ought to do was leave. Go back to her mother's motel room and try to jimmy the lock on the box. But the combination of hoping for Vince and hating Adam lured her.

She crept back to the house. It was odd to evaluate her own place like a burglar. But the first thing she tried was the first thing she always tried—the front door. She turned the knob and found that it was unlocked.

Posey might have left it open when she ran out. And Adam could have broken in another way and then used the front door if he'd left and come back. But the simplest explanation was that Vince had used his key to let himself in and hadn't locked up after since he expected Charlie home later that night, after she'd finished work.

She reached up to smother the sound of the bell on the screen door as she eased it open. She slid through the kitchen, pausing to pick up a heavy pan with little pieces of burnt noodle attached to it, just in case.

A few steps more, and she stopped in the doorway to the living room. It was the smell that hit her first, the odor of decaying flesh that made her gag. There was something dark smeared on the walls.

The body on the couch was too still. Dread turned her limbs to lead.

Vince.

Her trembling hand went to the light switch and everything became obscenely clear.

Writing in blood, thick and clotted, covered the walls. In some places caught with hair. The words continued high up on the walls, where a human hand couldn't reach.

On the couch, Adam's body lay cracked open, ribs exposed. Charlie stared at the open cave of his chest and the too-dry mess of his insides. At the tattered sail of his shadow, flying off the mast of his feet.

Her gaze went back to the walls. Over and over. The same word in finger-painted letters: *RED. RED. RED. RED.*

C harlie was still in that doorway when the police arrived. She wasn't sure she remembered calling them. She didn't remember how long she'd been standing there.

"You," one of them said, hand on his gun. "Drop what you're holding. Hands in the air."

She discovered she was still gripping the pan from the kitchen. She let go. Distantly, she heard it clang as it hit the floor, but that felt very far away. Outside, the strobe of blue and red lights added another layer to the surrealness of the moment. She raised her hands.

It wasn't that Charlie hadn't seen a corpse before. She'd seen two in the last week. But this belonged to someone she knew. Someone who'd been murdered in her living room. His blood soaking her secondhand couch, which they were going to have to throw out. The rug would have to go too. Maybe she should just burn the whole place to the ground and let her landlord get the insurance money.

Another cop—a woman—crossed to Charlie and patted her down. The buzz of radios in the background and muttered conversation made it hard to focus.

"This is your place?" the cop demanded, obviously having asked the question twice. "Are you the one that called this in?"

"Yeah, I think so," Charlie said. "Yes."

"Did you kill him?" one of the others asked her.

Charlie laughed, which wasn't a great look. "You think I could do all this?"

They exchanged glances.

"Did you?" the woman asked.

"No. I just got off work. My sister and I were at our mom's place all yesterday." She kept her hands up and open.

A photographer from forensics came in. At least Charlie thought they were from forensics. She wondered if someone would have to climb up the walls and get those invisible hairs. She wondered if the police would recommend someone from Vince's company to clean this all up once the body was gone.

"Did you know the deceased?"

She nodded. "Adam Lokken."

"He live here? Your neighbor said a man shared the place with two young women."

Charlie considered what she could say. No matter what name she gave, his prints were all over the house. The minute they ran them, they'd discover Edmund Carver wasn't dead. And they would believe he was the killer. "That was my boyfriend, Vincent. But he moved out."

"Last name?"

"Damiano," she told them, wondering if such a person even existed.

"What's with the message?" one of them asked. "Do you know what it means?"

RED.

The color of blood. The name a boy gave his shadow.

Never name it. Raven's words echoed in her head. But children named everything. They named teddy bears and goldfish in duck ponds and pieces of gum on the sidewalk. Of course Vince was going to name his shadow.

Perhaps it had come looking for him, like the shadow in the fairy tale. Perhaps it had mistaken Adam for Vince and then became enraged when it realized it had the wrong person. Or it killed Adam *for* Vince since he had a grievance. Or it had come looking for her, and saw an opportunity for some fresh blood.

And then it signed its work.

"I don't know," Charlie told them.

One of them walked behind her, jerking one of her hands behind her back. She felt the cold metal of cuffs. "I think you better come with us. We'll go down to the station and you can make your statement."

"Am I under arrest?" Charlie asked.

"I'm giving you a ride." He was a short guy with broad shoulders and dark, curly hair. His badge was shiny. He told her his name was Officer Lupo as he led her out to the car and pushed her head down as he got her into the back seat. Neighbors had come out of their houses in bathrobes to check out the drama. Charlie wanted to wave, but she was cuffed.

The big brick building housing both the police station and the fire department was only a few blocks away. It wasn't long before she was being led into the station and put in a back room with a big table. They asked her for her fingerprints for "elimination purposes" and she let them press each finger into a pad and then onto a paper. They asked for her license and she handed it over. They wanted her to unlock her cell phone, and she did that too. Mostly, they left her alone in the room, coming in once or twice to check on her.

After about forty-five minutes, Detective Juarez rolled in, looking as though he'd just been roused from bed, and not happy about it.

"You again?" he said when he saw her.

She didn't say anything. What was there to say?

"Does this have something to do with what happened in Rapture?" he asked.

Charlie shrugged. "If it doesn't, I guess I've got the devil's own luck."

"What was this Adam guy doing in your house?" He looked at his notes. "You knew him, right?"

If you want a lie to pass the sniff test, it helps to put your worst foot forward. "He was cheating on his girlfriend with me. After he broke it off, I told her. Day before yesterday, he came after me in a hospital parking lot and beat me up pretty bad."

"Did you make a police report?" he asked, studying her face.

"I guess I should have." She didn't doubt he believed her about getting knocked around, though. The makeup she'd done was okay, but she'd been wearing it for hours and she was sure that her bruises were showing through. And nothing could disguise the swelling.

After that, someone brought her a coffee, but that was the only consideration they gave her. The questions went on and on, doubling in on themselves. Most of them were about Vince, but she was asked about Doreen too, Charlie's hours at work, when she'd come home, what she'd touched. Over and over, Charlie asked if she was under arrest.

Finally, they said she could go. Told her to stay away from the house, since it was an active crime scene. Cautioned her to stay by her phone, that they would contact her again.

"There's too much weird shit in the world," Officer Lupo said to one of the other cops, under his breath. "Not all of it needs to be washing up around here."

Charlie was on her way out when she passed Doreen, wearing pajamas, a trench coat, and UGG boots. Her face was blotchy and tearstained. When she saw Charlie, her eyes seemed to roll back in her head.

"*You*," she said, her voice so guttural that it seemed like she was making sounds more than words. "*You did this.*"

Charlie wanted to snap back at her, but it wasn't fair. Doreen had loved Adam, and even if he had been terrible, he was dead. "Look, I'm sorry that he—"

Before she could finish her sentence, Doreen lunged. Nails raked across Charlie's cheek.

A cop grabbed Doreen and hauled her back, although she kicked like she thought she could get free. "Calm down," he said. "Jesus, lady."

"Ow," Charlie said, putting her hand to her face. "*Fuck.*"

"This is because of *you*," Doreen shouted. "You were supposed to help him. You were supposed to bring him home."

Hard to be too sympathetic when he'd been hanging around waiting to hurt her, but she saw Doreen's point. Adam might have screwed over Balthazar and Doreen both, but Charlie had certainly screwed him.

"You *are* the devil, corrupting everything you touch," Doreen shouted. "Remember that favor my brother was supposed to do for you? Well, it's undone. You're in default."

Charlie shrugged, turning to head toward the doors. "You can't threaten me with what's already happened. You got him to do that the minute I gave you the ring."

Doreen, held back by two policemen, still managed to spit in Charlie's direction.

Exhausted, Charlie walked back from the station to her car just as dawn was breaking on the horizon. The Corolla was where she'd parked it, metal box tucked under the seat. She slid in and looked at her face in the mirror, studied the fresh red marks, which stung like hell.

Abruptly, she tasted salt in the back of her mouth and her eyes stung. She blinked back tears.

"Pull yourself together, Charlie Hall," she told herself in the mirror.

It was Thursday morning, which meant she had two more days before Salt's event. Two more days to discover what Vince's shadow wanted, where Vince was, and who was lying. Two more days to know what she was going to do with the book in the lockbox.

But what she needed right then was sleep. She couldn't go inside her house, since it was an active crime scene, cordoned off with tape. And she wasn't sure she could bear going back to Mom's place. The thought of sleeping on the air mattress while they moved around the room, of fending off questions, of telling more lies, made her feel claustrophobic and panicky.

Not to mention the threat of a Blight out there, one looking for a book she might have in her possession. Maybe looking for her. So, she couldn't go to Barb's either. Not to any of her friends.

You are *the devil, corrupting everything you touch.*

The devil, like Suzie Lambton said. With the devil's own luck.

But maybe her luck was changing, because Charlie remembered something. Suzie Lambton had gone on a yoga retreat, leaving behind an empty condo for Charlie to break into.

S uzie's place was within walking distance of the center of downtown Northampton. When Charlie pulled up, she realized right away that getting in was going to suck. The units were newly built, with large windows, and no trees or overgrown bushes to hide her from Suzie's neighbors while jimmying the door. The last time she'd been there, she'd admired the place but hadn't done nearly enough casing.

Charlie parked three streets over, tucked the lockbox into her bag, got supplies from the trunk, and walked. It was just after six in the morning and she was sure people inside the units were just getting up, getting ready to send their kids to school and take themselves to work.

Cutting behind the units, Charlie noted they had patios in the back. That was promising. People were more likely to give someone hanging out in a backyard the benefit of the doubt, and sliding glass doors were incredibly easy to open.

People put dead bolts on their front entrances, with keypads and steel doors, and then neglected the back. Charlie positioned a screwdriver under the bottom of the patio sliders, then pushed up hard at the same time she turned the handle. Ten seconds later, she was inside, and the doors, no worse for wear.

As she walked through the modern white kitchen with thick marble counters and pristine subway tile, Charlie's steps echoed. She had a moment of feeling entirely out of place, as though she wasn't just an intruder, but a traveler from another world.

She made herself climb the stairs. Suzie's bedroom was wallpapered in a cheerful pattern of tropical leaves. The door to the walk-in closet was open, and clothes were scattered on the floor, as though Suzie had packed in a hurry.

Charlie staggered to the bed. She fell asleep on top of the coverlet, with early-morning sunlight flooding in through the picture window, still in her clothes.

She woke to the red and golds of sunset. Her head felt cottony and her mouth was dry. For a disoriented moment, she didn't know where she was. Then everything came flooding back, and along with it, a stab of panic.

This is a job, she told herself. A job, even though she wasn't sure she had a client. When working, you couldn't afford to let yourself get freaked out.

Forcing herself up, she handled the practical things. She plugged her phone into her charger and sent her sister and mother a text, saying she was okay and giving them a brief outline of what happened to Adam. Then she got into the shower.

One of the things Charlie had always loved about breaking into houses was the pretending part. Here she was, trying on Suzie's life, like the fresh tee and hoodie Charlie found in the closet. Suzie had body wash that smelled like vetiver and shampoo that smelled like hemp. In the medicine cabinet, an assortment of half-used bottles of painkillers greeted her. A book on her bedside table promised the eight secrets of being an effective communicator.

All the lights were so bright that there were barely any shadows.

As her jeans went around and around in the washer, Charlie made a pot of coffee. In Suzie's fridge, she found a can of Diet Coke and a jar of peanut butter. Charlie stuck a spoon into the peanut butter and took a bite of it while she poured the contents of the soda can down the sink. Then she picked up some kitchen shears, took out Vince's metal box, and got to work on the padlock.

First, she had to cut the can so that it became a large rectangle of aluminum. Then she cut out two shims, each with a long wedge. Since he'd used a spring-loaded double-lock padlock, she knew she was going to need to hit the two tabs on the inside to wedge them open.

Carefully, she pressed the first of the metal shims around the shackles, adjusted it a little with her fingers, and took it out again. Then, positioning the long wedge on the outside, she pushed it down into the gap between the shackle and the body of the lock. With enough slight back-and-forth twisting, she got it to slide in deeply enough that she was ready to rotate it. No audible noise came from it, but there was a feeling of resistance. When she couldn't turn it any farther, she found pliers under the sink and used those to get it the rest of the way. Then she worked the other side. When both were done, and the shims turned, she gave a firm pull.

The lock opened.

She sucked in her breath and opened the box.

No *Liber Noctem* rested there. Only a slim piece of paper, the edge tattered from being ripped out of a notebook.

Charlie slammed her open palm against the marble counter. Fuck fuck fuckity *fuck*.

What was she going to do now?

She supposed the box was a decoy. A piece of misdirection. Vince had left it to slow down anyone looking for *The Book of Blights*. Which meant that wherever he was, the book was with him.

Unfolding the paper, she was surprised to find it addressed to her.

To the Charlatan,
If you found this, things have gone all the way wrong.
The key is abandon all hope.

V

Charlie poured coffee into a mug and took the letter over to the couch. Her heart was speeding. The sight of Vince's handwriting, blocky letters written in a rush, brought back an intense longing to speak with him. To yell at him. To make him believe that so long as he wanted to be known, she wanted to know him.

The key is abandon all hope. Maybe she should. Maybe she was being a fool.

But her gaze strayed back to the words.

The key is abandon all hope. Not *to* abandon all hope, the way you'd write it if you were suggesting it literally. The words had the feel of a riddle, but she didn't understand it.

Staring at the wall, she sipped her coffee.

She had no better idea of where to find him than before. Her mind traveled down predictable paths to the same dead ends. She'd already tried his cell phone. She'd gone to the address on his license and talked to Liam. She'd called his boss and found out he hadn't shown up for work and was pretty much fired.

What had he wanted with grotty hotel rooms and cleaning blood off ceilings anyway, being the grandson of a billionaire? But maybe he'd gotten used to that, tidying up after his shadow's messes.

Maybe he liked it, being in all those empty hotel rooms, the way she'd liked breaking into houses.

But then she had a very different thought.

There was a story that Vince told, about how his boss's wife was furious because her husband brought her to a fancy hotel for the weekend, not revealing that he had the key because the room was the newly cleaned scene of a murder. *Probably cleaner than any other room in the hotel,* his boss had told everyone at work. *Nothing for her to complain about.* The wife hadn't agreed, and made him spend a week on the couch.

If there was an unoccupied hotel room, Vince could have gone there. He wouldn't have needed any identification. He wouldn't have even needed to break in.

Charlie took out her phone and poked around a bit until she found the number of Craig, one of Vince's coworkers. The young guy who'd taken a job cleaning up bodies so he could one day do super authentic special effects makeup for movies.

The last text she had from him was from four months ago: *Vince's cell died & he wants me to tell you he'll be home in 1hr w veg lo mein.*

It was such a normal message that she couldn't stop looking at it.

Charlie thought about the horrible moment when she'd been sure it was Vince's body on the couch, Vince's blood on the walls. She had to find him before Red did.

She called the number. Craig picked up.

"This is Vince's girlfriend," Charlie said. "I know he's in the doghouse at work, which is why I'm calling you."

"Is he okay?" Craig asked, sounding like his usual friendly self. "Winnie and me were saying it wasn't like him to just drop off the face of the earth." She always found it a little funny how upbeat Craig and Winnie were, considering what they did.

Their boss, not so much.

"He got really sick," Charlie said, thinking that covered a host of possibilities. "When he's feeling better he'll give you a call, but he wanted me to ask about a place he cleaned. It's the room that wasn't going to be able to have guests for a week or two? He thinks he left his watch there."

"In Chicopee?" He sounded a little wary, but not yet suspicious.

"Yeah," she agreed. "But he totally spaced on the room number and he doesn't want to ask at the desk."

"Gimme a sec." The tension had gone from his voice. She hadn't asked for the name of the hotel, after all, or an address. He believed that she knew the place. "Says here it was 14B."

"Thanks," she said. "Vince'll give you a call when he's feeling better."

"Tell him to hang in there," Craig said, and disconnected the call.

Charlie typed in "murder" and "Chicopee" into her phone's search engine and sorted the results by most recent. It appeared that there'd been a stabbing at the East Star Motel, on Armory Drive, eight days before.

She gave herself a victory spoonful of peanut butter and went to get her jeans out of the dryer.

T he East Star Motel hunched on the corner of two streets, a one-story building with exterior entrances to the rooms, not unlike where her mother lived. But if that place was intended for long stays, this was the opposite. It rented by the hour, its sign promising vacancies, Wi-Fi, color television, and discretion.

Charlie pulled into the lot. The Corolla made a strange sound as she did, a sputtering sort of cough. And then the engine died.

"No," she told the car, in what she hoped was a stern manner. "This cannot happen. Not right now. Come on. *Come on.*"

But all it did was drift a short ways forward and then stop, halfway in and halfway out of a parking spot.

She slammed both hands down on the steering wheel, but that did nothing. Turning the key in the ignition did even less.

Finally she got out, slung her bag over her shoulder, and pushed the car so the back of it wasn't sticking out. It was on a weird angle and taking up more than one parking space because of it, but there wasn't much she could do.

At least her car had gotten her to the motel before it died.

There was no white van in sight, which wasn't a great sign. But then, Vince might have gone out—or even stolen himself a new vehicle. She could hear a television on in room 12B and some moaning from 15B. Her gaze went to the locks on the rooms with a professional eye.

They were digital, but not expensive and not all that secure. Unless someone had done up the dead bolt, it was possible that she could force it with a well-aimed kick.

The blinds on 14B were drawn and shut. She hesitated, hand on knob, thinking of walking into another darkened room just hours before. Thinking of the husk of Adam's body and a single dripping word written all over the walls.

The idea that Vince might actually be on the other side of the door gave her pause too, as much as she hoped for it.

She needed to be ready for the possibility that Remy Carver wasn't much like Vince. He could have played her. He could have been acting. He might even be in a relationship with Adeline, which was deeply messed up, but people in messed-up families did messed-up things.

If Vince didn't exist, then better she observed it for herself. Like going to an open casket funeral: sometimes that was the only way you could accept someone you loved was truly gone.

She tried her Big-Y-card-in-the-seam trick, but the lock resisted. In her car, she had a wire bent into an under-the-door-device. These didn't look great to use, since you had to squat down and shove a wire into the seam between the door and ground. Once inside, the wire bent up, and if you angled it right, the loop at the end grabbed the lever. You tugged, and the knob turned.

Glancing around the parking lot, she was ready to go back for the wire when a woman came out of one of the rooms, holding an ice bucket.

While she waited for the woman to get her ice, then mess around with the vending machine, Charlie wondered if there was a simpler way to get inside the room.

Her shadow. She sent it out deliberately for the first time. Pushed it through the open spaces between door and frame. Her vision split, and a headache started between her eyes.

She tried to concentrate on her shadow hand becoming solid enough to turn the lever, but it felt like grasping at nothing. Part of her was conscious of the woman moving back toward her room, of a light drizzle starting up. The rest of her was fumbling in the dark.

She tried to push energy *into* her shadow. She wasn't sure if she was doing it correctly, until her hand became briefly solid, and the lever turned.

Her shadow flowed back to her in a rush, and the sensation was so intense and strange that Charlie had to lean against the wall, shudders running through her. It was as though moths alighted everywhere on her skin and then were somehow absorbed into her.

And even more overwhelming—the possibilities that opened up, the vast expanse of things she would be able to do, the places she'd be able to worm her way into, unfurling in front of her.

Taking a deep breath to steady herself, Charlie pushed the door the rest of the way open.

She flipped the lights and had to smother a scream. A massive bloodstain covered the gray patterned rug. It took her a few moments of standing there, light-headed, fighting down panic, to absorb that it was only a stain, and an old one at that. There were smears at the edges, where scrubbing had made the blood blur.

That was why the room couldn't be rented. It needed a new carpet.

Charlie closed the door slowly behind her, making sure it didn't slam.

Photographs had been taped up along the wall, above a cheap-looking press-board cabinet. A bed resting in the middle of the floor had a stripped-down mattress covered in clothes. The blinds on the window had been taped over from the inside with garbage bags, and a rolled-up towel rested near the door, probably used to hide any light from peeking out while Vince was inside.

Torn packaging from Williamson's Clothier was scattered over the chair near the bathroom—a shoebox, a heavy wooden hanger, and one of those zip-up body bags fancy suits came in.

As she stepped into the room, she realized the lamp on the bedside table had been knocked over and smashed. The bed itself was pushed a bit diagonal, as though something heavy had shoved it. And on the other side, she found a chair, turned on its side.

There'd been some kind of struggle. Was the absence of the van in the parking lot evidence that Vince had escaped his assailants? Or had Salt taken him and the van both?

Charlie forced herself over to the wall. Photos of the Hierophant had been taped there—standing on a street corner, meeting with Malik from the Cabal. A shot of him covered in what looked like shadowy armor, as though he were some kind of knight.

And beneath them, a printout of an article from two years before: *Suspect in Shadow Theft Case Has All Charges Dropped, Victims Outraged.* The photo of him was small and blurry from being printed off the internet, but she recognized him right away. The Hierophant's name was Stephen Vorman.

But she still didn't understand the connection between him and Red, unless the Blight to whom Stephen had been tethered *was* Red. But he'd wanted *her* to give Red a message, so that couldn't be right. It bothered her, the idea that she wouldn't be able to tell. If she knew Vince, she ought to know his shadow.

On the nightstand, she found a notebook, rinds of paper stuck in the coils left over from pages that had been ripped out.

In the bathroom, she found a comb and pomade.

And in the trash can beside the toilet, she found a glued-together box with clay inside of it, a Styrofoam cup stained with black paint, a bottle of clear nail polish, and two empty plastic containers that had a two-part resin in them.

He'd obviously been molding something, but what? Turning over the box, she noted the squarish-shaped depressions.

Charlie went back to the bed, with the notebook. Fishing around in her bag, she came out with a pencil and did the old trick of running the graphite lightly down the page so the marks of previous writing would be revealed.

Char,
   I don't know how to say goodbye to you.

Charlie sat there for a long time, staring at the ghost of a letter.

While she didn't understand what it was, Vince was out there executing a plan of his own. And given what he'd written, he didn't seem optimistic about how it was going to turn out. She needed to *think*.

Paul Ecco had a page of the book. He'd gotten it from *someone*.

And Knight had *seen* the book, although he hadn't found the ritual that made *The Book of Blights* famous. The ritual that Red was hoping to enact.

Maybe Knight had missed that part. After all, a quick flip-through in an auction house wasn't enough time to be certain there was nothing important inside. Charlie had seen plenty of secrets that weren't readily apparent. Tiny words written in artwork. Lemon-juice print revealed by heat. Ciphers that were all but impossible to decipher without an equally well-hidden key. Any of the puzzles that gloamists created for one another.

But Knight had said he had the means to bring someone down, and she had every reason to believe that person was Salt. So there had to be something.

Fetching Knight Singh's book, she smoothed out its leather cover and thumbed through the pages, skimming for Salt's name. For anything to do with Blights, or immortality, or the breath of life.

Nothing. And Raven, who'd read it, claimed not to have found anything either.

Charlie went through the book again, more carefully. She felt each page's thickness, to see if any had been glued together. She checked the spine, to see if anything had been inserted into it. Then she checked the endpapers, running the pads of her fingers over them to check for any unevenness. On the back inside cover, she found light glue marks along one edge, as though perhaps the paper had been removed and replaced. Getting the knife attached to her keys, she tried scraping at the edge. Sliding it into the seam, she pried up the edge, loosening the leather. And there, underneath, were papers written in an unfamiliar hand:

There seem to be various ways to cut a dormant shadow away from a living person. Remy is able to make Red pick up the shadow of a knife and wield it. (Interestingly, the knife does permanently lose its shadow, and the next morning, I perceived spots of rust on the blade, which warrants further investigation.) Remy, as a gloamist, can use his fingers and, while making a snipping motion, use those "scissors" to sever the bond between person and shadow. It was also possible for me to cut away a shadow using an onyx knife.

All those means can also be used to remove a shadow from a corpse, but this shadow has a discernable difference in texture and weight. This also warrants further investigation.

That had to have been written by Salt. It wasn't quite a confession, but it was damning nonetheless.

The next page was worse.

I cut her wrist several times, thinking that perhaps that would be enough trauma to quicken her shadow, but she died like all the rest, despite the alterations done to her.

Yeah, that was bad. Charlie wasn't sure if any of this would be admissible in court, but it would lead investigators to look for evidence, which was almost certainly out there.

And it would ruin him in the court of public opinion. Not to mention what the Cabal would be forced to do, since it was other gloamists he'd been targeting.

The third page was about Red.

Remy has been doing experiments of his own, ones he's been hiding from me. He has been setting his shadow free. I have no idea how he's managed this, and have it return to him, but it does.

Does he feed it excess blood? And if so, how much? How long has he been doing this? Now I will be paying close attention.

Another thing I must know—is he controlling it? And if not, does that mean Red is self-aware? Cogito, ergo sum? And if so, what has it stolen from Remy to become that way?

And then a final page.

I have made a mistake, one I hope I will be able to correct.
If I can't have Red, then I will have to kill him.

If Salt knew that Knight Singh had those papers, then he would certainly have wanted Knight dead. Salt had to have been the client paying Adam, the one he'd hidden from Balthazar.

Now she had the leverage, if she could figure out what to do with it. If she could solve the puzzle in time.

A con, after all, was about uncovering the truth. Warping it, sure, but uncovering it first. It was the closest thing Charlie had to Posey's tarot, a belief in something larger than herself. Just like Posey could put down cards in neat little rows, Charlie could plan out her schemes. But eventually she had to surrender to improvisation and trust her instincts.

Charlie recalled lying on the rug of Salt's house, with a hidden room and a safe only steps away. Where all his most valuable possessions would be kept, including ones that were never supposed to be found. That was what she needed to get into.

Just in case Vince came back, Charlie ripped a piece of paper from the back of his notebook and used her pencil to write him a message.

> i found the letter you didn't send me. Call me if you find this. And don't do anything stupid.
>
> Love, char

She left the note on the mattress. Then she flipped off the lights and carefully closed the hotel room door, keeping her head down as she crossed the parking lot.

29
THE PAST

Vince sat at the bar, every part of him alert to the crush of people around him, to the smell of sweat and the sweet rot of syrupy drinks sunk down into the grooves of the floor. The music was turned up loud enough to discourage much in the way of conversation, but to the right of him, a guy was trying, shouting at another guy about a video game where you built a house underwater.

That's the whole point, the guy was yelling. *To survive. Build your base. You've got to get ready for when they launch the update and the sharks come.*

It had been a month and a half since he'd left Salt's house, and every day he was away from the place he simultaneously hated it more and missed it. He felt homesick for what had never been his home. And for the one person who had mattered to him most, and was gone.

The hardest part was having so much time to think. To have to make his own decisions. To wrestle with the guilt of being alive when by all rights he shouldn't have been. Vince was used to measuring out his life in small moments, never letting himself look much ahead, and never daring to look behind.

Here we are, on a boat.

Here we are, with a knife.

Here we are, in the bedroom of a CFO in the middle of the night.

And now Vince had to make plans if he was going to survive. He had something he could use to bring down the old man, but he couldn't use it on his own. Better to pass it off to Knight Singh, with his web of connections and his dislike of Salt. The item was in the messenger bag slung across Vince's shoulder, and he wanted nothing more than to be rid of it.

Maybe Vince could have a future where he wasn't constantly looking over his shoulder. That thought brought a rush of guilt with it.

The problem was that Vince wasn't used to the setting-things-up part. He'd been all about the execution.

"Another?" the bartender asked.

Vince had allowed himself to be talked into a pumpkin beer, having no idea what to order in a place like this. Adeline would have had champagne with vodka to "wake it up." Salt would have had a single malt from a place that Vince was certain he'd butcher the pronunciation of, and which was likely to dig deeply into his cash reserves.

Remy had always had whatever everyone else was having. But Vince didn't have to act like Remy anymore.

The pumpkin beer had the virtue of being cheap. Unfortunately, in Vince's opinion, that was its singular virtue. "I think I'll try something else."

While the bartender went through what they had on tap and Vince chose something at random, he noticed two gloamists walking in. Out of the corner of his eye, he saw them spread out, their gaze sweeping the room, trying to spot someone with the description Vince had given. He supposed that they were attempting to be subtle, allowing their shadows to seem dormant, but Vince clocked them immediately. There was an energy to them, a dark swirling at the edges, like smoke trickling out from hidden hot embers beneath char.

Knight Singh had promised to meet him alone. He'd lied. Which meant that Vince had very probably walked into a trap.

He'd chosen this place because it was crowded, and was glad of it now. There couldn't be many other people in the room—if any—without shadows. But so long as he stayed part of the crush at the bar, what he was lacking wouldn't be apparent.

Vince was glad he'd only described himself to Knight as "wearing a red scarf"—one which was still resting in his bag, waiting to be put on.

He turned to the woman standing beside him. If he was part of a conversation, he'd give the gloamists another reason to overlook him. Around his age, her cheeks were flushed from the warmth of the room. She signaled to the bartender, who seemed to be aggressively ignoring her. Her licorice-black hair hung down her back and a tattoo of scarab beetles formed a collar just beneath her throat.

Across the room, one gloamist had positioned himself near the entrance, and another was standing in front of an empty booth. Knight must be on his way.

Vince raised his hand and somehow caught the bartender's attention.

"I think she'd like a drink," he said.

The woman flashed him a look he found hard to read.

"A gin and tonic," she said. "The cheapest gin you have, with three limes."

The bartender turned to Vince, and he realized that his second beer was half gone. He didn't remember drinking it. He didn't even remember if he'd liked it.

"Bourbon. Neat," he said, dredging that up from a movie or something. When it came, he learned that "neat" meant without ice.

"I don't usually order godawful drinks," she told him, squeezing the first of the desiccated and slightly brown limes perched on the side of her glass.

"So tonight's special," he said.

That got him a quick smile. There and gone. And suddenly, Vince had the terrible certainty that he knew her. He couldn't remember where, or under what circumstances, but they'd met before.

The crowd surged in and he put one hand against the bar to brace himself. "You grow up around here?" It was not a particularly clever question, but maybe her answer would help him place her.

The woman pushed back her mane of black hair and took a deep swallow of her drink, trying to avoid being shoved off the barstool by a guy on the other side of her. "Yeah, I'm a local. But I bet you're not."

He nodded, tailoring his story to her lead. "Only been in town a few months."

She raised her eyebrows. "School?"

He shifted position so that he was standing between her and the press of people. Got an elbow in the back for his trouble. Shook his head. "Looking to make a change."

"We've got a lot of asparagus." She laughed at his puzzlement. "So much that they call it Hadley grass. There's even a festival. And three different asparagus ice creams. That the kind of excitement you're into?"

"Sounds about the level I can handle." The funny thing was, it might as well have been true that he wasn't local, for all he'd seen of the towns.

"I guess there's an archery school. And a place where you can learn how to swing a broadsword." There was a slight slur to her voice that made him wonder if the flush in her cheeks was as much from liquor as warmth.

"In case I want to slay a dragon."

Her nails were ragged at the edges, the nail polish chipped from her biting them. "Do you?"

A quick glance showed him that Knight Singh had arrived. He sat in a booth at the far end of the room. Knight's people had positioned themselves in strategic locations so that once they spotted Vince, they could close in and cut him off from the exits. He counted five.

Definitely a setup. Vince eyed the nearby fire door the crowd was trying to press him into.

"Want to slay dragons?" he echoed. "I don't want to slay anything."

The bartender walked by and dropped a receipt in front of her, and seemed about ready to ask Vince if he wanted another round.

She lifted it and eyed the guy. "What's this?"

He shrugged. "Your bill."

"Maybe I wanted another drink," she said, ground glass in her voice.

"So pay for the last one." He wore an arrogant little smile, aware he ruled the bar.

She leaned toward him, her voice loud enough that people waiting for their drinks could hear her. "I've been sitting here watching you short pour the guests, give people the wrong change, use sour mix instead of lime juice, and wipe down the counters straight into the ice bin," she told him, reaching into her bag and pulling out a handful of coins. "You're going to burn in bartender hell."

"You're drunk," he said defensively.

"If I am, it's despite you." She counted out what she owed in quarters and dimes, leaving him as many pennies as she could find at the bottom of her purse.

She turned to Vince, and the fire hadn't gone out of her eyes. "You think I'm petty, right?"

He thought she was everything Remy had been afraid to be. "I think you're a vigilante," he said, smiling.

She contemplated him for a long moment. "Come outside with me," she said. "It's too hot in here."

Vince was torn. If he left with her, Knight and his people would be less likely to spot him. Walking beside her, his missing shadow could be easily overlooked.

But part of him wondered if Knight had come there expecting to be set up himself. If the gloamist was taking precautions instead of making a move against Vince, then the situation was still salvageable.

What he *wanted*, though, was to go outside with the woman.

He got out his wallet and threw down a couple of bills.

She took his hand and led him toward the door.

He watched the confident sway of her hips. She walked through the bar as though she expected everyone to get the hell out of her way. And, amazingly, they did. "I'm Vince," he told her.

But her gaze was on Knight Singh, recognition in her expression. Then her gaze slid back to Vince. "Charlie," she said, pointing to herself. "Charlie Hall."

Vince had counted five gloamists, but that didn't mean Knight hadn't hired people who weren't gloamists.

People like Charlie.

She might lead him around the back of the bar and sink a knife in his side. And if he was lucky, that was when Knight Singh's people would restrain him and sell him back to Salt. If he wasn't lucky, she'd have orders to finish him off.

The cold air of the alley hit his face and he felt a rush of indifference toward risks. He *liked* her. He liked that she was mean and funny and willing to make a scene.

He liked that she was nothing like him, or anyone from his old life.

He liked her enough to follow her deeper into the alley, despite his suspicions. When she turned against the brick facade of the building and threw him a look that felt like a dare, he pressed her back against the wall and kissed her.

Her lips were chapped. He could smell her perfume, something with smoke and roses in it. Her mouth tasted like gin.

Knight Singh could go hang. Vince could make the exchange some other time.

Drawing away, he looked down at her. Traced the line of scarabs across her collarbone. "Do you want to go somewhere?" he whispered against her hair, although he wasn't sure where that would be. He'd spent the last night in a van. All he knew was that he wanted her.

"Here," she said softly, reaching for his belt.

He wasn't sure if she actually liked him. Maybe she just wanted to forget whatever sadness she'd come to the bar to drink away. He could make her forget.

He concentrated on the hot rush of her breath.

The softness of her hip when he lifted her.

The scratch of the brick against his palm.

He didn't dare think about the past, and he wouldn't let himself think about the future. All he let himself think of was her.

30
YE WHO ENTER HERE

On Saturday night, Charlie pulled her mother's station wagon to the curb far enough from Salt's house that she didn't think anyone would notice their arrival. Pressing her forehead to the steering wheel, she took a deep breath.

Then she turned to her sister in the passenger seat. "You don't have to do this."

Posey made a face. "You don't either. At least I'm getting something out of it. I don't know what you're getting."

"A preemptive strike," Charlie informed her.

She knew Salt was perfectly capable of fulfilling all the worst of his promises. If she didn't get this right, she might not have another chance.

Charlie got out of the car. "See you later, alligator," she said, leaning on the door.

Posey grinned. "After a while, crocodile."

Charlie made her way along the side of the road, backpack slung over one shoulder. The closer she got to Salt's fairy-tale castle of a house, the more clearly she remembered the last time she'd been there, the panic she'd felt running through those woods. The cockiness Rand had as they went inside. The churn of her guts.

And there she was, years later, about to con her way into a party. Dressed in a scratchy white shirt, cheap black pants, and a vest, looking the picture of a cater waiter. She liked to think Rand would be proud.

She'd spent all of Friday getting ready. Abandoning her collection of wigs, she'd gone to the mall and had a recent beauty school graduate give her a pixie cut. It made the back of her neck itch, but she definitely looked different. With that, she added a fresh round of Halloween makeup to cover her bruises and tucked all the supplies she thought she would need into her backpack. The swelling in her face had gone down a bit, and she was almost entirely sure that her rib was okay.

She was doing great.

Charlie tried to sink into character—resentful and underpaid employee arriving late to a gig to which she already regretted agreeing. It wasn't that hard.

As she swung through the open gates—which, she couldn't help notice, were connected to a fence topped with what appeared to be an electric wire—she had almost convinced herself that it wouldn't bother her to see the estate. Then it came into view and her stomach tried to crawl out of her mouth.

Constructed of some gray stone and crawling with Boston ivy turned bright red and gold in the late-autumn air, it loomed in the distance. Gargoyles made of bronze and streaked with verdigris squatted above the roof, watching her approach. The more she looked, the sharper her memories became, so she turned her gaze to the grass and kept going.

Run. You have to run. The people from the palace are hunting me.

Charlie had worked enough jobs that she ought to trust the tug of intuition, that antenna inside her attuned to wrongness. There was something she was missing, as though she was looking at dots up close, but if only she could step back she'd see another pattern. That feeling had kept her from getting caught before. Sometimes you felt the air change and knew to abandon a con.

But no matter how wrong this already felt, she was going to see tonight through.

A valet watched Charlie in a considering manner as she approached the house. She gave him the long-suffering nod of one person working on a Saturday to another. That seemed good enough to convince him she was staff, and he lost interest.

Around the back, Charlie found the kitchen. She'd called around until she discovered someone involved in the party. It turned out that José was part of the on-site catering.

He'd left the door propped open for her.

Inside, cold shrimp were being tweezered onto silver platters topped with lettuce leaves and some kind of creamy sauce. Risotto balls were being lowered into a portable fryer set up on a large marble island big enough to lay out a dead body on.

She turned her thoughts away from that.

It was easy to be overlooked at a party like this, with multiple vendors and freelance waitstaff. José's catering would be supplemented by specialty offerings, like a caviar station, or a sushi station, or a human sacrifice station. Hopefully, she could get lost among them.

She was just stepping into the hall when someone called after her.

"You're late," said a harried-looking woman with a clipboard and a lot of curly blond hair. Probably the event coordinator.

With what Charlie hoped was a sufficiently blank look, she turned. "Sorry. I was looking for a bathroom to use before I started."

"There isn't time. Put your things down and take these hors d'oeuvres." Charlie shoved her backpack under a table where she could grab it easily later and took the metal tray.

Across the room, she saw José, rolling prosciutto roses. He winked.

Cheeks prickly with warmth after going from the cold autumn air into rooms full of bodies, Charlie moved through Lionel Salt's mansion. Passing leaves smeared with blue cheese and candied walnuts to anyone with empty hands was a good cover for reacquainting herself with the house and trying to spot Vince.

Charlie gritted her teeth against the uncomfortable mix of familiarity and dread she felt as she walked through the rooms. She kept a little smile on her face and didn't meet anyone's eyes. Balthazar had shielded her from direct contact with clients, but stealing things occasionally meant conning people, so it wasn't like no gloom had met her before. She just hoped no one would recognize her.

Passing through a gallery-like hall near the entrance, she covertly observed a display of antiquarian books under glass. Beside that was an etched plate that said "The Lionel Salt Library will be open to all gloamists, and cultivate a space where arcane knowledge can be shared." The taxidermied animal heads Charlie remembered looked down from where they hung, their shining glass eyes, polished antlers, and sharp horns catching the light.

Usually collections like Salt's were hoarded, so the idea of getting a look must have gotten the glooms, especially the younger ones, salivating.

As a thief of magical secrets, Charlie was not unlike a bee, pollinating many flowers. Once gloamists digested an old book, copying down the experiments or techniques they thought might be useful into their own notes, the only reason they hung onto the original copy was to guarantee that what they learned stayed exclusive to them. Charlie had once failed to steal a volume from a guy, because when she arrived, she discovered that he burned every single book he'd acquired as soon as he copied down the parts in which he was interested. She still got angry sometimes, thinking about him.

If Salt wanted to found a library, that would make him very popular. It showed a willingness to share his secrets. A generosity of spirit.

Or that his secrets were so much greater and more terrible that he could afford to have a collection like this mean nothing to him. Either way, he ought to have no problem convincing the local gloamists that his elevation to the Cabal had been long overdue. His influence would grow, and so would the horror that followed in his wake.

Charlie's gaze went to her own shadow, then away.

At the end of the hall hung an oil painting of a dark-haired woman, lying on a couch, wearing a diamond-encrusted crown. Her dress was parted, showing her naked body from the waist down. And suspended over her by straps was a stallion. Charlie frowned at it, then glanced around. It was far from the only piece of disturbing art. A painting of a Roman king being devoured by his horses hung by a door. Beneath a sconce, she spotted a sketch of a decomposing fawn.

As though Salt's house needed to be creepier.

Charlie walked by massive and magnificent stairs carved in the shapes of lions, through an arch into a sitting room. There, two bartenders poured drinks from behind a wooden bar topped in pewter. A small knot of people waited for their drinks. Gangsters stood shoulder to shoulder with academics, performers chatted with mystics. Gloaming was a new science, and its practitioners as hungry as the shadows that fluttered behind them in the shapes of capes, or wrapped around their bodies like snakes. Others drifted a bit behind their wearer, leashed by a single silver cord, moving to peer out the window, or fetch a drink.

One shadow even drifted up to her tray, plucking an endive off of it before she could pause. Startled into stopping, she swallowed a curse as she almost dropped the food.

She heard a bark of laughter from across the room.

A prank. It reminded her that no matter how tense she was, and no matter how terrible her suspicions were, to most of the glooms present, this was a party.

With effort, she swallowed her irritation and glanced into the great room with its towering two-story ceiling and its wall of windows.

She spotted Salt in a tuxedo, standing beside one of his four enormous couches, declaiming to a few older gloamists. Adeline, in an elegant black column of a dress, stood beside the limestone fireplace, in which green and blue flames burned. An enormous painting of a forest hung over the mantel. Only when you looked closely did you notice that it was full of shadows wearing deep red slashes for mouths and that gray body parts had been rendered among the ferns of the forest floor.

Two additional Cabal members were there as well. Bellamy stood in a corner, and Malik looked particularly regal. His locs had been pulled into flat twists on the sides and wrapped in gleaming gold thread, his shadow hanging across his body like a sash.

A trio of musicians in animal masks played classical music. An owl with a violin. A fox with a cello. A bear with a viola. Through the windows, an outdoor garden was lit with low lamps that showed off marble statues of shrouded figures.

What must it have been like to grow up in a place like this? Surrounded by this much wealth? Force-fed untold depravity?

Charlie finished her circuit and ate the remaining hors d'oeuvres so she had an excuse to go back to the kitchen. Setting the silver tray down on the marble island to be wiped and refilled, she took the opportunity to grab her backpack. Then she headed directly for the library.

Charlie's memories of the house were blurry and indistinct, more nightmare than recollection. A voice close enough for her to have felt breath on her neck. Cavernous rooms linked together in a puzzling maze.

The library, with a secret door leading to a room of treasures, including a safe. With the rug she vomited on, and where she might have died.

When she glanced in, she found two men in the leather chairs, talking in an intense way, one gesturing with a snifter of cognac. An empty glass and a napkin rested beside the other. They looked extremely settled.

Charlie needed to make them move, and quickly.

"Excuse me, sir," she said, squatting down in front of the one she thought seemed more self-important. "I'm sorry, but there was a woman asking for you in the other room. Tall, with red hair. Very pretty. She described you and told me that if I saw you, I should inform you of her interest."

He looked smug, and rose. "I'll just be a second," he said to his friend, but his friend was rising too.

"Going to refresh my drink," the man said with a little too obvious relief, and Charlie had the sudden thought that perhaps she'd saved him from being buttonholed for the entire evening.

Charlie picked up the crumpled napkin and began to sweep up imaginary crumbs until she was alone. Then she went to the light switch on the wall, throwing it so that the darkened room would seem off-limits to other guests.

She reached into her backpack and drew on gloves and glasses with tiny lights attached to both sides. Once she switched them on, they would make her face a confusing blur to cameras, as well as provide a way to work in the dark.

Finally, she went to the wall of books. Red and gold. Red and gold. Something with flames, something with a title that started with an *I*. She couldn't find the lever. Two pulls of books with red spines and gold type went nowhere. Then she spotted it, a shelf lower than where she'd been looking and a foot to the left. *Inferno.* She lifted it and the bookshelf door swung jerkily inward, revealing the smaller library, and the painting with the safe behind.

Charlie stepped through into the secret room, its walls covered in shelves packed with older books. Nausea abruptly constricted her throat. The memory of lying on the library carpet rushing back at her as though no time had passed between then and now, as though she were still a terrified kid. The rough texture of the merino wool against her cheek, the wetness from her vomit, the voice coming from the dark.

Don't look behind you.

The smell of beets still made her gag.

Charlie stepped through onto the onyx tiles of the smaller chamber. Shelves lined the walls there too, with older and more precious books filling them. Memoirs, notebooks, and scientific journals, a hundred at least, all worth stealing. *The Mystical Discoveries of Tovilda Gare* sat beside *Confessions of Nigel Lucy, Magus* and *Diarios de Juan Pedro Maria Ugarte.* There were other books, in Portuguese, Chinese, Arabic, Latin, and Greek, as well as a whole half wall in French. Her fingers itched to choose a few at random and stuff them into her bag.

Pushing the bookshelf door closed, she checked for any additional wiring that might indicate an unexpected surprise.

Charlie didn't find anything that seemed worrisome, and turned toward the back of the hidden room.

A trompe l'oeil of a dead goat, entrails spilling out and mingling with split pomegranates, hung above a club chair, the only piece of furniture.

Gingerly, she felt around the edge of the hideous painting. She found hinges, with no lock on the other side.

She swung it open to reveal the wall safe she remembered.

Made by Stockinger, who were known for offering solid, bespoke models with the bells and whistles of all the custom luxury safe makers like Buben & Zorweg or Agresti. There would be winders for watches, cloth-lined wooden drawers, but none of the ridiculous golden and bejeweled neo-Victorian extravagances of Boca do Lobo pieces. Stockinger made serious safes for serious people.

A dial rested on the front, beside a gleaming handle engraved with Lionel Salt's initials. And beside it, a keypad.

Most modern safes were digital, offering none of the romance of breaking into the old ones. None of the listening for when the spin changed, the infinitesimal slotting into place, the softer *click-click* as satisfying as the crack of knuckles. If she could ignore the keypad entirely, she would. Digital safes weren't just unromantic, they were nearly impossible to open without the code.

Taking a deep breath, she reset the lock by spinning clockwise, then started going counterclockwise. She heard the first notch at five. Then she reset and spun again and again until she had five numbers: 2–4–5–63–7. She was certain of them. She was as sure as sure could be.

But what there was no way to know was the order. And five numbers meant five tumblers, five interior wheels, and one-hundred-twenty possible combinations.

All she could do then was grind through them, while sweat beaded up at her forehead and in the hollow of her throat. She was conscious of the party going on, of time slipping away, of the possibility that someone might find her.

Charlie could hear the moment the fence fell and released the locking mechanism. She let out a long, unsteady breath and turned the lever.

It only moved halfway.

Then the digital keypad lit, green and bright and blinking.

Charlie stared at it in disbelief. This safe wasn't digital *or* dial; it was both. Her heart rate kicked up and her mouth tasted sour with panic. She had no way to know if there was a timer on entering the code, and she'd be limited in the number of tries. Safes like this offered three, usually, before locking up and setting off an alarm.

Fishing a UV penlight out of the bottom of her backpack, Charlie turned off the lights of her glasses, pushing them up onto her head. Then she shone the penlight onto the keypad.

Very few people wiped down their keys after use. The light revealed the grease of fingertips, limiting the number of options for the combination.

2–3–4–5–6–7.

The same numbers as the other side. Relieved, she moved to type in the order that had worked on the dial. She stopped herself a moment later, finger hovering over the keypad. There were more markings on the two and the six than on the other numbers, suggesting they repeated. If that was true, then this was a seven-digit code, at minimum.

If cracking a mechanical safe was about understanding the machine, cracking a digital safe was about understanding the person who set it. Would they choose a random number and then hide the combination somewhere they could find it? Or would they pick something less random and therefore more memorable?

Lionel Salt was the kind of person who needed to be better than everyone else. With his carved stairs, his awful paintings, and his willingness to murder for his own amusement.

Not his birthday, since it would be a reminder of his age and mortality. Not his name in numbers, because even he would know that was too obvious. Perhaps a word, then? *Blight? Shadow? Gloaming?*

She stopped.

The key is abandon all hope.

Abandon all hope. It used all of the numerically converted letters and used the six and two four times each. And Salt would like the idea of giving a clue in the form of the book that opened the secret door, referencing the most famous quote from Dante's *Inferno*, the one that even Charlie, who'd never read it, knew: "abandon all hope, ye who enter here." She bet he felt rather smug about his cleverness.

Charlie ignored her racing heart, her sweaty hands and panicked thoughts. She went over the word again, writing it out in numbers in the dust of the onyx floor: *22263662554673.*

Carefully, she punched the code into the still-blinking pad. There was a sharp beep, as though an alarm was about to sound. Then she heard the second locking mechanism opening.

She turned the lever again.

A soft glow came from inside, showing off felt-lined drawers and several shelves of items. Charlie opened one. A small bag of diamonds rested inside. In another, she found an antique pistol chased in gold. And at the bottom, wrapped in cloth, the thing she'd come looking for.

Quickly, she made the exchange, shoving the item deep into the bottom of her backpack, hoping like hell that she knew what she was doing.

Then, in the privacy of Salt's hidden room, she got out her party outfit. Suzie Lambton, the only person whose closet she had access to at the moment, wasn't even remotely her size. She still had her key to Rapture, though, and there was no better time to borrow that red satin suit abandoned in the back. With a little stretch to the fabric, it fit her like a second skin. Add to that some notice-me red lipstick, and Charlie would seem like she'd just arrived at the party, instead of robbing it for the better part of an hour.

Before she was ready to go out there, she pushed on a three-finger knuckle ring set with onyx and shoved the onyx dagger she'd gotten from Murray's into her bra. Holstered with a makeshift sheath of duct tape, it would be there if she needed it. She waited for the familiar rush, that pleasurable hit of adrenaline, but it wouldn't come.

Charlie turned back to the safe, intending to close it, when she noticed a black button in the upper corner, close to the back. Could there be something behind the safe? A compartment she hadn't opened yet?

Come on, Charlie Hall. You don't have to stick your finger in every socket.

But that cautious instinct seemed to belong to someone who hadn't already chosen the path of recklessness. She pressed the button.

A click came from the shelf to her left. Another bookshelf swung open, revealing a hall. A passageway that must run behind the walls of the house.

Taking out her phone, Charlie checked the time. She'd gotten to the house at half past six. José had told her that the party was supposed to go officially until ten, and that there was going to be a champagne toast at eight thirty. It was seven forty-five. Time was tight.

Still, Charlie stepped through, into the dark.

She switched back on the lights on her glasses. They illuminated something that mixed the architecture of a wine cellar with that of a mausoleum. More tiles of onyx ran across the floor. Two cells were ahead of her, with a door opposite them. A groove had been carved into the ground, running in front of the bars, the blue line of a gas flame outlining the edge. The air had a faint smell of rot, and of incense.

Sweat dampened her palms and brow. This was the bad kind of adrenaline. The kind that made her twitchy instead of careful, that made her stomach sour and her hands shaky.

This felt like a haunted place.

Still, she kept walking. The soft soles of her flats scratched against the floor. The cells were deep enough that Charlie's little lights couldn't pierce the darkness.

Along the wall were an assortment of restraints. A rope that had been threaded with onyx beads. A pair of shackles with blue silk padding on the inside, the cloth sewn tightly with rectangular onyx tiles. Above them, a shelf with onyx containment boxes.

The door on the opposite side was slightly ajar, flickering colors within. She pushed slowly with her foot and found herself staring at a bank of screens. Surveillance footage of the house.

Caterers in the kitchen. Partygoers moving through the rooms. The Hierophant, speaking with Vicereine, seeming completely composed. She peered at him more closely, hoping for some tell. The only thing notable was that he was thinner and more unhealthily pale than ever.

In another room, two men were making out, one a blurred outline. Was he kissing his own shadow? Someone else's? Charlie couldn't tell.

Outside in the garden, three men were arguing. One had the other by the shirt, their shadows looming large behind them like the spread plumes of fighting peacocks.

Salt was walking through the rooms with purpose, a drink in one hand, looking as though everything was going his way. He glanced up, for a heart-stopping moment, peering directly into the camera. The time in the upper right-hand corner read 7:52.

"Charlie?" Vince's voice came out of the darkness.

She whirled around.

He was in the cell, standing just behind the bars. Broad-shouldered, hair like old gold. A small smile turning up the corner of his mouth. As familiar as her own heart.

"What happened to your eye?" he asked.

"Hold on," she said, so relieved at the sight of him that her voice broke. "I can get you out of there."

Before Charlie could pick the lock, she had to disable whatever the gas line running along the seam beneath the bars was supposed to do. She guessed it was on some kind of trip wire that would send up a burst of flames when the cell door opened. There had to be a way to turn it off.

Charlie hesitated. The wrongness of the scene bothered her, like an itch in the mind.

Pale, hollow eyes followed her movements. She wanted to believe it was Vince in the cell, behind bars of onyx, with a gutter of fire between them. But those weren't restraints meant for a human.

"You're not Vince, are you?" she asked softly, walking to the bars.

The silence from the cell was her answer.

Charlie met the Blight's gaze. "You're his shadow. You're Red."

31

THE FOOL,
THE MAGICIAN,
AND THE HIEROPHANT

O nly when her back hit the wall did she realize how far she'd moved from the cell. "You found the *Liber Noctem*," she managed to choke out. "You did the ritual."

"Because I look like a person?" the shadow asked. "It was Edmund who made me like this."

"He wouldn't do that." Her voice came out too high. She didn't know how to comprehend the being in front of her. It was a doppelgänger. A mirror reflection come to life. A thing Frankensteined together from discarded parts of Vince: slime and snails and puppy dog tails. "Is he here? Is Vince all right?"

The shadow shrugged. Even its expression was one that Vince would make, slightly chagrined. The tailored suit it wore was the color of its eyes. "We met before. Do you remember?"

Don't look behind you.

Charlie didn't speak for a long moment. It wasn't as though the thought hadn't crossed her mind, but she'd had a hard time believing it. "In the library."

"I suppose you wanted it to be Remy who saved you," the shadow said, voice soft. "Not Red."

Charlie wasn't about to answer that. Yes, she had a naive desire for the sort of romance a palm reader would trace on the inside of a hand. A fated love, begun in childhood. Love was a family religion, passed down to her when she'd been too young to protect herself from belief. "Even back then, you were already a Blight?"

The shadow nodded, allowing her to turn the subject.

"And you killed people for Salt." She kept her voice stiff.

"Yes," it said.

She had to remind both of them that she wasn't some fool who was going to trust it just because they had a weird past together. "Tell me—the way you killed Adam, was that special? Cracking his ribs open like you were going to spatchcock a turkey, and painting the walls with his blood? Or is that how you did them all?"

It stepped closer to the bars. *"Adam?"*

"You've got to remember the guy you murdered on my couch. In a very gross way."

The shadow stared at her with what appeared to be real horror. "I'd never do that to you. Never."

Charlie hated how much it looked like Vince, and how much that made her want to trust it. "Okay, tell me about all the other people you didn't murder."

"You're clever," it said, with a small rueful smile. "And I'm not used to explaining things. I didn't do much talking, before. I don't think I'm very good at it."

"Try," Charlie said.

"You shouldn't have had to come back here." It seemed sad, and tired. She had no way to know if that was something it was putting on, or if flesh conferred weakness. "You should go and never come back, like I told you that night."

"So, what, I'm supposed to grab my sister and mother and blow town? Let Salt win? Do whatever he wants to Vince?"

"Yes," it said, with more heat than she expected. "He can handle himself."

"He shouldn't have to," Charlie said.

"He left you," the shadow said.

"And you as well, didn't he?" Charlie asked. "Must piss you off, to have him create you and then shed you like he was crawling out of a chrysalis. Leave you behind."

Red looked at her with Vince's eyes, but there was a little amusement in them. "I'm made of his anger. What do you think?"

"I don't know," Charlie said, refusing to be distracted. "I don't know anything about you."

The shadow turned its face from her, the amusement gone. "I was always the part of him that took care of things when he wasn't able to manage. I was given everything that made him uncomfortable—the desire to cause pain, the terror at what Salt made us do, the ability to intuit how other people felt when the bad stuff happened. I was made to be strong, so he didn't have to be. So yes, I was angry when he was gone, but I loved Remy, no matter what he did and no matter what he made me do."

A shiver went through Charlie's shoulders.

Red went on. "He wanted to block out what was happening when I was on his grandfather's missions, so I asked him to try untethering me. We didn't understand about Blights then; all we knew was that it worked. Each time I returned to him, I was stronger than before. More solid, and for longer. We hid it from Salt," he said. "Adeline knew, but she kept our secret."

"Because she and Vince were close," Charlie offered.

His lashes brushed his cheek as he looked down and away. "We all three were, once. Too close, maybe. We only had each other."

It came to her, one of the things she'd heard that night. The boy's voice. *He doesn't like you.*

And then the girl. *That's not true. We have games we play that he would never play with you.*

There was something bad there, lurking beneath the surface, but Charlie was too much a coward to ask.

She glanced into the room with the monitors. On the screens, Charlie could see that speeches were underway. She was running late.

"Where's Vince?" Charlie asked.

The shadow stared back at her with Vince's pale eyes and she could feel the hair on the back of her neck begin to stand. The itch of wrongness was back, worse than ever.

"I know this house," Red said. "I could help you get out without anyone knowing you were ever here."

"*Not without Vince,*" Charlie said. "You say you care about him. Help me save him. Help me *find* him."

"I'd do anything for you, Char," he told her. "But don't ask me for that."

There was only one person who called her Char. "No. You're not him. Stop acting like him."

"Char," he cautioned.

"*Where is he?*" she demanded, heart thundering.

"You already know," he said.

She didn't want to put the pieces together. Vince had snapped Hermes's neck and gotten rid of the body. He cleaned up crime scenes awash in blood for a living. None of that sounded like Remy. But it sounded a lot like Red.

"Vince faked his death," Charlie protested. "Or Salt faked it for him. He was on the run. And two days ago, he was in a hotel room . . ."

The shadow didn't speak.

It was hard to fake a death. There were dental records. There was evidence of past surgeries or fractures. Forensics could tell a lot from bones—sex, ancestry, age, height.

Salt could have paid someone, or several someones, to cover all that up. There was another answer, though: that the burnt body found in the car had belonged to Edmund Carver, and the person she had known wasn't him at all.

The shadow wasn't a malevolent entity taking the shape of Vince. It was Vince. *He* was Vince. And Vince had always only been the lost parts of Edmund Carver, the scraps from his table, his upside-down self, his mirror self, his night self.

He was right, part of her had known from the moment he'd been horrified about Adam. She hadn't wanted to admit it to herself. Charlie Hall, flinching, finally discovering the puzzle she hadn't wanted to solve.

"When Remy was dying," Vince said. "After his grandfather stabbed him. While Adeline screamed. Remy grabbed hold of me, and pulled me to him, so I would have all his blood, all his strength. As it left him, it became mine. He breathed his last breath into my mouth.

"For a moment, I didn't understand how I could be naked, how I could feel the cold floor under me. Then I ran. Hours later, I woke up beneath an underpass, lying on asphalt and broken glass, with no idea how I got there. And then I had to learn how to be a person all the time. I tried to be, for you."

Charlie recalled his words during their last fight, their only real fight: *I wish I could say I was sorry, that I wanted to be honest the whole time, but I didn't. I never wanted to be honest. I just wanted what I told you to be the truth.*

If this was what was behind the mask, she understood why he hadn't wanted to remove it.

"And called yourself Vincent," Charlie said.

"The one thing Remy didn't give me that I took anyway," the shadow said, lifting his chin, as if daring her to judge him for it.

Down the hall, gears shifted in the wall, making a soft but distinct noise. Someone had entered the secret room beyond the library. In moments, they'd enter the corridor where Charlie was standing.

"Vince," she said. Their eyes met.

"Hide," he told her.

Charlie made it to the shadows of the security room, crawling under the leather couch at the same time she heard steps in the hall. How many times had Salt sat on that couch, watching something awful on the screens? Rand might have died in one of these cells. Charlie herself could have died there.

Could still, if she wasn't careful.

"Red." A woman's voice, soft and worried. Adeline, Charlie realized. "He didn't tell me you were here until now. Did he hurt you?"

Only silence answered her.

"I know. I should have left when you did," she said, with a big huffing sigh. "You must be very angry with me."

Vince's voice had a veneer of calm, but beneath you could hear the vibration of some very different emotion. "Once his mother was dead, he wasn't going to rest until the world knew what your father had done. You should have warned him she was in danger."

"I didn't *know*. How could I have known she was going to overdose? I thought she was getting better. We all did."

"You know why she never got better," Vince said. "Your father needed her to be sick, and then he needed her to be dead."

Vince sounded as though he was talking about a family that wasn't also his. *His mother. Your father.* The only person he considered to be his family was Remy.

"I swear I didn't know about any of it," she protested.

The hall was dark, and Charlie thought it might be possible to slip out past Adeline while she was distracted. Quietly, she pulled herself out from under the couch. But as she edged closer to the door, Charlie's whole plan started to seem wobbly.

Maybe she should bonk Adeline over the head and try to get Vince out of the prison. But if Adeline didn't have the key—and neither Adeline nor Vince were behaving as though there was a possibility of her freeing him—then they were all screwed.

Carefully, Charlie slid behind Adeline's body, moving slowly and sticking to the shadows.

"You can still help me." Vince's voice was soft. He didn't look in Charlie's direction, but there was something so carefully blank in his stare that the effort showed.

Adeline put her hand on one of the onyx bars of his prison. "How?"

Charlie was far enough down the hall by then that she didn't hear Vince's request. Maybe it was unfair to think he couldn't trust Adeline as far as he could throw her.

If Charlie's plan worked, it wouldn't matter. She'd come back with a hammer and a flame-retardant blanket and get him out.

She would. Even if she was afraid of him.

Sliding the door open, Charlie slipped through. Then she climbed back through the second hidden bookcase, into the library. She needed to get outside and meet Posey, but she was distracted, thinking of how he'd guided her through the house that night.

Don't look.

What would she have seen if she had, back then? Perhaps a smudgy shape, like a ghost. Perhaps he would have been half boy and half shadow.

Don't look at me.

She snuck into a garden room. Ominously large plants with waxy leaves filled the spaces between pieces of white cast-iron furniture. Through the windows she could see the gardens. Charlie took out her phone and sent a text. The time on her screen read 8:16. Fourteen minutes to do what she needed to do, and no chance for errors.

But she had at least one answer she hadn't before. If Red wasn't the Blight that Salt had been using to do his dirty work, she knew who had been in his employ.

Opening a multipaned glass door halfway, she slipped through into the cold night air.

Posey met her on the side of the house, breathing hard.

"I made it." She looked wide-eyed with panic.

"You're still sure?" Charlie asked her sister.

"You're the one who has to be sure," Posey told her, although she was obviously nervous, and not just about getting caught. "We can still walk away."

Walk away. Wasn't that what she'd tried to do for years? Walked away from the death of Rand, pretended it hadn't scarred her. Pretended she didn't remember. That she didn't blame herself for surviving.

Walked away from being a thief and told herself it was because of the bullet in her side, that she'd lost her nerve, rather than admit she'd scared herself with how easily and brutally she'd turned the betrayal back on Mark. She'd never been all that afraid of getting hurt, or dying. It had always been her own abilities, her capacity for solving a puzzle, for getting a job done at any cost. She was terrified of what she could do if she tried.

From the time she'd pretended to channel Alonso and it had actually gotten rid of Travis, she'd been afraid of herself.

Somebody needed to keep her in check, and so that person became Charlie herself. Making sure she got knocked down every time things were going too well, picking the wrong people to love, getting fired from jobs, screwing up.

Charlie had been walking away from herself her whole life.

She sat down on the grass.

Posey sat down opposite her, their feet touching. Charlie took the onyx dagger from its sheath.

"Ready?" she asked.

Posey nodded.

Charlie wasn't sure what she expected, but the first cut didn't feel like anything. The real challenges were spotty moonlight and inexperience, and she was relieved when her part was done and Posey took over.

Inside the house, she watched Salt move to the front of the great room. He had a champagne flute in one hand. This must be the part where he thanked them all for coming and the Cabal for accepting him as a member.

Charlie staggered to her feet, not quite sure how she felt. Not lighter. Not less herself. But changed.

Maybe there really was such a thing as fate. Maybe people really did have destinies that could be deciphered through cards. Maybe Charlie needed to stop fighting hers.

With a last look back at Posey, she opened one of the glass doors to the great room. A great gust of cold wind whipped through the room behind her, filling the long white curtains like sails. Conversations went out like candles as the gloamists turned toward her.

She hadn't expected to make quite so dramatic an entrance.

Charlie stuck close to the doors, making sure the light was coming toward her.

"Hello," she said, her voice carrying in the high-ceilinged room and remaining steady, despite all the eyes on her. "Sorry I'm late."

"Charlie Hall," Lionel Salt said, furious at the interruption and doing a bad job of hiding it. "I didn't expect you'd make it."

Tension straightened her spine, drawing back her shoulders. She was certain he'd been counting on her not showing up. After all, he'd given her a terrifying threat and then set her a task at which she'd been guaranteed to fail. The last place she ought to be was at his party. The smart thing to do would be to leave town for a couple of weeks, until things cooled off. Maybe not come back.

But of course, whatever kind of smart Charlie was, it wasn't that kind. "You told me what would happen if I didn't."

A few hushed conversations became less hushed after that. Gossip was the lifeblood of any party.

A musician—the one in the owl mask—made for the exit, instrument in hand. A waiter whispered to José. The waiter pointed. José took a canapé off a silver tray and ate it. This was definitely not going to help her reputation back home.

Across the room, the Hierophant left where he'd been standing and began to move toward her. His eyes were more sunken than ever. His lips had a faintly blue cast.

"I would think that this was a piece of performance art for our entertainment, except that Lionel seems absolutely flummoxed," said Vicereine. The head of the alterationists was in a tuxedo, her shadow taking on the appearance of a large hunting cat pawing the ground beside her. "Maybe you missed your cue?"

Salt cleared his throat. "I hired her to steal back a book that I lost, the *Liber Noctem*. It is a jewel in my collection, and I had hoped to have it on display tonight. So, Ms. Hall, do you have my book?"

"I do," she said.

He smiled at that, with all the satisfaction of someone checkmating a rogue king. "Well then, come and give it to me."

He had, after all, arranged a situation where all her choices were bad. The only book she had was the one that had belonged to Knight Singh. She could bluff and give him that. He'd probably appreciate having it, since the cover was stuffed with pages full of heinous shit he'd done. But no matter if she gave him something valuable, he'd still accuse her of foul play. Of trying to pass off that book as his lost one.

Charlie took a deep breath, letting Salt really enjoy the moment. Then she reached into her backpack and took out what she'd brought from the safe in the library, where it had been locked up tight the whole time. The famed *Book of Night*. The genuine *Liber Noctem*. Light streaming through the crystals of the chandelier reflected off the polished metal cover, sending rainbows along the wall.

The smile left Salt's face so quickly that it seemed as though it had been slapped off. "Where did you find—"

"I stole it," Charlie said. "That's what I do. You told me to get it, so I got it."

The Hierophant reached for the book with pale, trembling fingers. "*Mine.* Those secrets belong to me."

32

THE CHARLATAN

This close, Charlie could smell the sour sweat of the Hierophant's body. She held tight to the book and turned her gaze to Salt. "Shall I give it to him?"

"No!" Salt barked, then saw the warning in the Hierophant's face and modulated his tone. "Bring it to me, so I can verify this is the authentic volume."

Charlie frowned. "So you *don't* want me to give it to him?"

"Do not make me repeat myself," Salt said. "*Bring the book to me.*"

Her heart pounded. There were so many chances to get things wrong here and only one chance to get them right. People were watching. Vicereine was close by, but so far with no reason to be anything but amused.

"I can promise you this copy of the *Liber Noctem* is authentic," Charlie said. "Since I got it from your safe, along with a certificate from Sotheby's and a receipt from the auction. The book never left the house. You just let everyone believe that it was stolen."

"Is that true?" the Hierophant croaked out.

Salt began walking toward Charlie, allowing him to lower his voice, making it harder for the rest of the crowd to listen in. "Let's discuss this further in private."

Charlie had puzzled over why Salt had set her an impossible task with an even more impossible deadline, unless he wanted her to fail. It was thinking about that which had made her remember Knight Singh's opinion on the *Liber Noctem*.

If there had been a ritual in the book to let a Blight take human form, then nothing made much sense.

But if there was *no* ritual, if the book was as useless as Knight had claimed, then Salt was free to employ the rumor to convince a Blight to help him. But that depended on keeping the book forever out of the Blight's hands—and yet seemingly obtainable enough to stay hooked. Hence the need for a thief of the original volume (Edmund Carver), a new possible lead (Paul Ecco), and the most recent red herring (Charlie Hall).

If she hadn't shown up, Salt could have convinced the Hierophant she had the book and was hiding it from him. And Charlie would wind up with her guts smeared on the ceiling, just like the others.

Or she could have shown up to the party to say she hadn't found the *Liber Noctem*. That might help some, but Salt would accuse her of holding out, and her guts would still wind up on the ceiling.

What Salt needed was someone for the Hierophant to blame. Anyone other than him. Which meant he knew where the book was, and the simplest answer for how he knew was that he still had it.

She'd had a bad moment when she saw Red in the cell, not just astonished by him, but abruptly sure she'd been wrong about everything. But then she realized he must have been the convincer. The reason the Hierophant believed Salt in the first place. If there wasn't a ritual, then how could he exist?

"Private? I don't think so," said Charlie, shaking her head. "You're responsible for a lot of murders. Knight Singh, for one. I'd rather not be next."

A wave of murmuring moved through the crowd. It was one thing to chuckle at a party's host bickering with a guest; an accusation like the one Charlie was making required a more serious response from the Cabal.

"Come along." Salt grabbed for her arm.

"What did that young woman say?" asked Malik. He stepped forward, several others with him. Charlie didn't think surrounding Salt was intentional, but it spoke to how the mood of the room had shifted.

Two things she'd known from the time Salt forced her into his car at gunpoint were that he wanted control more than anything, maybe even more than power. And that he expected absolute obedience from those he considered beneath him.

He sent his shadow toward her. They were close enough that it might not have been immediately noticeable to the crowd, but she felt it brushing against her shoulder and cheek, as though she'd been touched by a piece of muslin whipped by a breeze.

She only had time to gasp once before it flooded into her skin. She could feel it worming inside of her, trying to force her to speak. Trying to make her tongue form the words that would cause her to deny everything.

Long ago, when Charlie had come to Salt's house with Rand, she had practiced rolling up her eyes into her head to indicate that she was possessed. Had been ready to speak with another voice. Ever since Alonso, she'd found it disturbingly easy to be someone other than Charlie Hall. A relief, to give in to such an old urge.

"I'm drunk!" she shouted in a deeper voice than her natural one. "And a liar! A drunk liar! Also, I have a secret resentment toward the fantastic, handsome, totally-not-a-killer Lionel Salt! Who is most certainly not trying to puppet me!"

He stared at her, mouth agape. Everyone was looking at his shadow now, the way it had bent against the light to get to her.

"Get out of my head, Mr. Salt," she said in her normal voice.

Laughter bubbled up around them. Charlie allowed herself to step away from the door to the garden, the one whose proximity to the darkness had hidden what was changed in her, what she was lacking.

The shadowless can't be controlled. There's a door shut inside of them.

There would have been no way for Charlie to come here and confront Salt if it was possible for him to puppet her. It had been surprisingly hard to give up her shadow, but she'd sewn it to Posey's feet and trusted her sister to care for it. Charlie wasn't destined to be a gloamist. She was destined for this.

"Lionel," said Vicereine. "That was naughty of you."

"I wanted to force her to confess the truth," Salt said, a hectic flush on his cheeks. He managed to sound calm, however, as though this was all just a small and embarrassing disagreement. "I shouldn't have done that, but she has herself been deceived."

"Do you know something about the death of a Cabal member?" Malik asked Lionel. "Because that would have been a hell of a thing to keep to yourself, no matter what the truth is about your involvement."

"I did not think I would have to reveal this, certainly not here," Salt said, looking around, annoyed. "But you see, I have been working with the Hierophant to catch the murderer of Knight Singh. And we have succeeded."

"Oh, did he catch himself, then?" Charlie asked. "Because he's the one who killed Knight, on your orders."

"Be quiet!" the Hierophant ground out.

Salt turned toward Charlie with a sneer. "The Hierophant has served the Cabal faithfully," Salt said. "Who are you to question his loyalty, thief?"

"Stephen, what's this about?" Bellamy asked, peering at the Hierophant. The name of the human, the one who Charlie was almost sure wasn't in control of the body anymore. It wasn't just the way he spoke, but that he had the wan, sickly appearance of someone whose energy was being consumed.

"She's a liar," said the Hierophant.

Salt looked at Charlie and shook his head sadly. "Oh dear, yes, our boy tricked you, didn't he? The deceiver deceived. You're not the first." He turned back to the others, his confidence that he could get away with this growing. "Now, perhaps we can do this part in private? I have something to show you. Something I would prefer we kept between the four of us."

Vicereine and Malik shared a glance. Malik nodded to Bellamy.

"Yes, I think so," Vicereine said, with a look at Charlie. "I believe you said your name was . . ."

"Charlie," she said. "Charlie Hall."

"Ms. Hall, I promise you that we'll hear your accusations and pass judgment."

Malik nodded. Bellamy regarded her with interest. "We can be fair."

Charlie was certain they could, but less certain they would.

"Let us adjourn to the library," Salt said. "And I will tell you everything." He signaled to a young man in a suit and tie. "Get him for me. Bring him in the cuffs."

The other gloamists watched them leave, a few of them stopping one or the other Cabal members to ask them a question, or make some comment. A few laughed. The Hierophant walked behind them, his gaze returning over and over to the book in Charlie's hands.

"You," Salt said to her, under his breath. "Are nothing more than a piece of gristle between my teeth."

She tried to ignore him, tried to ignore the shudder that went through her. He was just picking at stitches, hoping she'd unravel.

It was uncomfortable to be back in the library, her gaze going automatically to the small stain on the rug. But only for a moment, because Vince was already there, standing against a shelf, his arms bound in the same onyx restraints that had been hanging on the wall in the hidden hallway.

She took in the despair in his gray eyes, his broad shoulders and the muscles beneath them. Took in the dark gold of his hair and the angry line of his mouth. Looking at him made her stomach hurt.

"Char," he said. "You should have gone when you had a chance."

She turned her face away, not sure if she was capable of doing what was necessary with him watching.

"And who is this?" Malik asked.

"That's Edmund, his grandson," Bellamy said, peering at Vince as though trying to convince himself of something. "I thought he was dead."

"Oh, we'll get to that," Salt said.

Adeline entered the room in her long black gown and perched on the arm of a chair. "Can I get any of you a drink?"

Charlie, having been drugged once in this room already, shook her head.

Vicereine settled herself into a chair opposite Adeline. "All right, Lionel. Now, explain yourself."

He looked relaxed, pleased. Charlie thought he might even be enjoying himself. "I became involved with the Hierophant because we had a common interest. The murderer of Knight Singh was also the murderer of my grandson. It stands before you, in his guise. But it isn't him. You're looking at his shadow."

"That is impossible," said Malik.

"Are you saying this *man* is a *Blight*?" asked Bellamy, walking up to Vince.

Vince glowered but made no move to step away.

Bellamy reached out a hand. Almost immediately upon touching Vince's upper arm, he pulled back in surprise. He turned toward Vicereine, who said nothing.

"My grandson had always taken a somewhat unorthodox approach to shadow magic. He treated his shadow like an entirely separate being, one he let make decisions for them both. Eventually, it became independent enough to trick him."

"Trick him?" Bellamy echoed, more intrigued than astonished. Masks were almost exclusively interested in mysteries, which led to lots of academics and even more mad scientists. Charlie had always figured they were a bit of a hodgepodge of the other specialties, and she could see why someone like Vince would be especially intriguing to them.

"He was deceived into conducting a ritual from the book, one that proved fatal—"

Charlie interrupted him. "That's not true. *You're* the one that killed Remy."

"Did it tell you that?" Salt asked, making his voice gentle. "It used Remy's life, and created this shell in which it's hiding. It then absconded with the book and began murdering anyone who knew about it. A rare book dealer. Knight, who'd had access to the *Liber Noctem* while it was at Sotheby's. And finally, a thief who I'd contracted to steal it back."

It all sounded reasonable when he said it, and Vince stood there, denying nothing. Charlie could feel her control of the situation slip away.

"Shadows lie, my dear," Salt went on. "If you have a Blight stitched to you, it will whisper in your ear, and every gloamist knows not to believe everything it says. That is why it is a heavy burden to drape yourself in another's shadow."

Charlie glanced at the Hierophant. As much as Salt might be enjoying this, the Hierophant was not.

"Both of you are claiming to have solved the murder. You're saying that's a Blight, and it's responsible for all those murders," Malik said to Salt, then turned to Charlie. "While you, for some reason, believe it was Lionel and Stephen?"

She nodded, glancing at Vince, who still didn't speak. "Knight's not the first gloamist Lionel Salt killed, either."

Salt smiled and stood, pacing the room, clearly believing he'd already won. "Allow me to order proof of my version of events. Adeline, my dear, what did Edmund call his shadow?"

Charlie was dressed in the color. Red, the scarlet of poppies and cutthroats. Adeline smiled at her. "Red."

"And what was on the walls where Adam Lokken—that thief I hired—was killed?" he asked Charlie.

"The word 'red,'" she told them reluctantly. "Painted in blood. But it was meant to threaten Vincent, since the Hierophant believed he had the book."

"Vincent?" Bellamy echoed.

"She means me," Vince said.

Adeline startled, and the others seemed surprised too, as though they'd forgotten he could speak.

"Isn't it more likely that the Blight wished everyone to know who had murdered Adam and that's why it covered the walls with its name?" Salt said. "The Hierophant has, again, I remind you, shown no inclination toward bloodshed."

"The fuck he hasn't," Charlie said.

Salt's hooded gaze was on her, unrelenting. "Now, how close to where Red was living was Paul Ecco murdered?"

"A few blocks, but I don't see what that has to do with—"

"And how close to where Red was living was Adam Lokken murdered?"

Charlie sighed, frustrated. "He lived in the house where the murder happened, but he'd left. He wasn't there. He hadn't been there in days."

"And who had he lived with in that house, prior to leaving?"

"Me," Charlie admitted.

"And isn't it likely that you got the book from Red, since you've been living with him—rather than that you broke through my extensive security."

"I could show everyone how I did it," Charlie offered sweetly.

"Yes," said Salt. "That brings us to one other thing. Do you think there's a reason he insinuated himself into your life, something about you he might have wanted?"

Charlie folded her arms over her chest, looking Salt in the face. "I don't know. My tits? Maybe my ass?"

It broke some of the tension in the room. Vicereine snorted. Bellamy smiled. But Salt was undeterred. "You don't suppose it's because you're a well-known thief? *The Charlatan*, who stopped taking freelance gigs, coincidentally of course, right around the time she met Red."

Charlie took a stuttering breath. It had been one thing for them to know she was a thief, but it was a little different for them to know she was someone they all had some experience with. Although she'd done a job or two for Vicereine, the others had only experienced her as a cause of misfortune.

You've lost them, Charlie Hall. They're never going to believe you now. You should have figured that a billionaire would make a pretty good con artist.

"Tell us, did it inform you it was a living shadow?" Salt asked. "Or did it give you a false name and a false history, along with its false face?"

Charlie couldn't help thinking of the fairy tale of the scholar's shadow, playing at love. Of Vince's hungry mouth on hers. Of him cooking her eggs.

"I know who Vince is," said Charlie. "And I know who you are. You poisoned me when I was fifteen. Your people chased me through the woods. Don't talk to me about false faces."

Bellamy raised his eyebrows. Adeline looked over at Vince, as though for confirmation. But it wasn't like Charlie thought any of the Cabal would care all that much about something that had happened over a decade ago, to someone who wasn't a gloom, even if they believed her.

But she wanted Salt to know.

"So you have a grudge against me," he said smoothly, which was ballsy but clever. Put your worst foot forward, admit to one bad thing so they think you're honest when you deny another.

His attempt to cast the blame on Vince was unnervingly convincing. Salt had strung together enough parts for it to make sense, especially since the proof could cut both ways. And he was rich, which always helped, while Vince was a terrifying monster, even without the question of the murders.

The knowledge that she might not be able to turn this thing around ramped her nerves up even higher.

"Well?" Malik asked Vince. "Did you kill those people? We know you can talk."

Vince looked at him expressionlessly. Charlie thought his assessment of the situation might be even more grim than hers. "I was Remy's shadow. I would never have hurt him. And I didn't touch Knight Singh."

"Do you have anything else to add, Stephen?" Vicereine asked. "You have been acting strangely lately."

"I haven't been sleeping well," Stephen said, looking at them. "I have a lot of nightmares."

Bellamy touched his shoulder and he flinched.

"I understand my punishment," Stephen told them. "All I want is to be done serving out my sentence."

"Did you murder a gloamist?"

He shook his head. "No. I hunt Blights. Which is why I've been seeking Red. Just Red." Halfway through that second sentence, Charlie thought she could tell that something else seemed to be speaking. It was a smooth transition, easy to miss if you hadn't been looking for it.

"What made you so interested in the *Liber Noctem*?" Vicereine asked.

The Hierophant shrugged. "Lionel promised that I could read it. To help with my work."

How long had this Blight been bound to a series of fuck-ups and ne'er-do-wells? Forced to hunt its own kind? Charlie would have felt sympathetic if she thought it was interested in something other than killing her.

Salt cleared his throat. "Red is a deceiver, a thing formed of envy and corruption and hatred that my grandson sought to slough off. It has poured honey in this poor girl's ears. Let us end this ridiculous conversation and go back to the party. I will keep the Blight restrained, and you can determine what to do with him tomorrow or the next day."

"Wait!" Charlie said. "I can prove I got the book from his safe. I can show you where it is, and I can open it."

"I'm not sure that's—" Malik began.

"I offered before," Charlie interrupted. "And he barely even acknowledged it. Right now, I am the only one with any proof. I have the *Liber Noctem*."

"Which could prove your point as well as mine," said Salt. "And you forget, I have Red."

"Let me show you," Charlie said. "Please."

Vicereine glanced at Salt. "Is it possible?"

"Absolutely not," he said with a small smile. "My security is impenetrable. She has that book because the Blight stole it."

Bellamy raised his eyebrows. "Then why not? A small demonstration and we can go back to the party."

Charlie's hands were sweating as she nodded to all of them. She set down the *Liber Noctem* on a table near where the Hierophant stood and ignored the way he moved automatically toward it.

"Very well," Salt said. "Go ahead, thief."

She walked to where Dante's *Inferno* sat and pulled it. One of the bookshelves swung open.

"Interesting," said Vicereine.

"Yes," said Salt. "I rather like that little room."

Charlie went to the painting and pushed it so that the safe was revealed. Then she went to work. She already knew the codes, but she needed to make something of a show of the first part, so she found the notches all over again for them. It was dramatic, and bought a little time. She could see they were impressed when the handle went down halfway.

"What are we going to find inside?" asked Malik.

"Gold, gems, the usual," Charlie said.

Salt just smiled. He'd taken a few steps back from the others, one hand going to the inside pocket of his coat.

When it came to the digital part, Charlie keyed in the code carefully. She looked back at the Cabal, at Vince, took a deep breath, and turned the lever.

The alarm went off, filling the room with a sound like a siren. Salt punched in another code and the sound stopped.

"You did that," she accused him.

He shook his head, eyes lit with the satisfaction of winning. "Don't be ridiculous. You failed, that's all."

"Okay, so open the safe," Charlie said, her heart speeding, a blur of hummingbird wings in her chest. "Prove you didn't."

"Very well, I will indulge you one last time," he said, enjoying the moment enough to draw it out. He punched in what she could see were the same set of numbers that she'd used. The lever turned and the door to the safe swung open.

His phone. He'd slipped it out while she was working and activated the alarm as she finished. While she'd been showing off, he'd been finding a way to stop her.

"We're sorry for doubting you," Malik said to Salt. "But you understand we had to—"

"Wait," Vicereine said, reaching past him. "I know that book."

And from the safe, she took out Knight Singh's notebook, papers detailing Salt's crimes in his own hand shoved hastily back into the leather cover, edges sticking out. Right where Charlie had left it when she'd taken the *Liber Noctem*.

"I—" Salt began, but no words came.

Charlie had known the way to trap Salt since the day she'd spent with him. She'd thought it then, idly, not realizing how much it would matter. Let him dominate. Let him win. He'd be so certain he belonged on top that he'd never guess he was being drawn into a trap.

He'd honestly believe that she gave him all that time while she futzed around with the first lock for no goddamn reason.

He'd honestly believe that she could crack a safe but not be able to guess he had a security app on his phone.

"Ms. Hall must have put it there, whatever it is," Salt said finally, recovering enough to realize he had to pin the appearance of Knight's book on someone else immediately.

Lionel Salt was a planner. Charlie was sure he'd planned for being confronted with any number of his crimes. He'd be able to explain lots of true things. But no one can plan for planted evidence.

"I thought that I couldn't get into your safe?" Charlie reminded him. "Isn't that what you were trying to prove? Which is it: Did you hide the *Liber Noctem* in there, and I stole it while putting something else in your safe? Or did I lie about the *Liber Noctem,* and you're lying now?"

Lionel Salt cut his gaze toward the Hierophant. Admitting to the first was less damning, but it meant admitting he'd been stringing along a very old and powerful Blight.

Vicereine was opening the papers stuffed into the top of Knight's book, smoothing them out. Charlie wasn't sure that Salt knew what they were, but she could tell by the way Vicereine's expression shifted that she realized who'd written them.

Malik frowned. "I think it's time the Cabal spoke with you and Stephen separately, Lionel."

Salt reached into his pocket and took out his matte black gun, pointing it directly at Charlie. "You have made a very bad mistake crossing me, Charlatan—"

Charlie froze. Vicereine's shadow cat roared as three shadows spread from Malik, their mouths full of teeth. Bellamy drew a sword of shadow.

"Lionel," Malik said. "There's no need for this."

Behind Salt, Vince lifted his wrists and the cuffs came away, falling to the ground. He stepped forward with inhuman swiftness, pressing the point of a letter opener to Salt's throat.

Adeline made a sharp sound that was almost a scream.

The sounds of the party seemed very far away.

"You said I was a creature of hate." Vince spoke into Salt's ear. "And I do hate you. For Remy, whose blood is my blood, whose flesh is my flesh, and whose hate is my hate. For Char, who will survive tonight. Aim that gun somewhere else, or I will hurt you and go on hurting you until there is nothing but pain."

"You can't—" Salt began, voice trembling.

"I'm sorry, Char." Vince wore a small, sad smile. "It was always going to happen like this. I knew he'd let me get close to him, and it'd give me a chance."

When they found Vince waiting in the library, alone, Charlie should have realized something was off. Should have seen what the disappearance of the man in the suit meant. Should have realized what Vince had been making in the hotel room—faux onyx tiles. Ones that made him seem safely cuffed when he was entirely able to pull his hands free.

He had known that, Charlie or not, Salt was going to show him off to the Cabal. And then he'd planned to slip his cuffs and kill Salt before anyone would be able to stop him.

And after that?

Vince pressed the knifepoint harder, and a bead of blood trickled down Salt's throat like the track of a single tear.

He made a choking sound, and his arm sagged, although he didn't drop his Glock.

Still, it wasn't pointed right at her face. Charlie let herself breathe.

"Drop the gun on the rug, Lionel," Vicereine said. "The Blight will remove the knife, won't you?"

"Will I?" Vince asked lightly. "I didn't come here planning on leaving."

Lionel Salt's face had paled and his eyes darted around. How odd the moment must be for him. Malhar had called shadows "ghosts of the living," but Vince was the shadow of a dead man.

Vince, who was almost Salt's grandson. Who was that grandson's avenging specter.

"You're going to leave," Charlie told Vince. "With me. Plans change. The Cabal knows what he's done. Surely they're not going to ignore the murder of one of their own."

Vince lifted the point of the knife infinitesimally away from Salt's artery.

"I have done nothing—" Salt's words came to an abrupt stop as the Hierophant stepped between him and Charlie. His back was to Salt and his eyes blazed.

The Blight looking down at her through Stephen's eyes was ancient. And wrathful. He held the *Liber Noctem* in his arms.

"Tell me," he said. "Tell me about this book. Tell me about his lies."

Charlie cleared her throat. "Vince could probably answer this better—"

"You," the Blight said.

She nodded. "Okay. When Remy died, he pushed all his energy, his last breath of life into his shadow. That's how Red became able to pass for human." She looked directly at the Hierophant, not allowing herself to flinch. "The ritual, the one that was supposed to have made Red like this? It doesn't exist. It's not in the *Liber Noctem*. It's not anywhere. That was the thing I couldn't figure, at first. Why would Mr. Salt tell me to find a book when it was locked away in his safe?"

She sucked in a breath and let it out slowly, forcing herself to pause for dramatic effect. "Because he'd promised you something he could never give."

The Hierophant's fingers closed over the metal, pressing hard enough to bend the edge.

"He convinced you to compromise yourself for him," Charlie said. "And you know that young man you've been possessing isn't doing well. There's not much more energy there to take. Killing Knight Singh was for nothing. Killing Paul Ecco was for nothing. Killing Adam Lokken was for nothing."

Salt laughed, although it sounded forced. "Is that what this is about? Of course I know how Red became the way he is now. It's all in *The Book of Blights*."

It was hard to argue convincingly against an old man with a knife to his throat. She decided to ignore him. "Red was already pretty solid because Remy had put so much of his own energy into him, and then cut him loose for short periods of time, over years. He started to appear like Remy, and to hold that shape. Isn't that right, Adeline?"

She gasped in surprise, as though Charlie had asked her something awful.

"You murdered your own grandson?" Vicereine asked. "And Knight?"

"You lied to me." The words boomed out of Stephen's mouth, but the voice was nothing like his. "Deceiver, I will strip the flesh from your bones. I will—"

The sound of the gun going off cracked through the air.

The Hierophant fell on the rug, blood seeping from the wound, fingers clutching at it. Mouth opening.

And behind the body, the shadow of the Hierophant rose larger and larger.

"Breath of life," it said.

The shadow swept over the body it had worn. Stephen gave a wordless howl as he withered, his skin shrinking in on itself, his body curling and then going limp. The blood around the bullet hole was dry, crystallized.

The shadow towered over them, crackling with fresh energy.

"Oh god," Vicereine said. "Oh shit."

Salt ducked away from Vince's hand, bringing his hand up to touch the shallow cut at his throat.

The Blight looked down at them, growing so that the library lights dimmed as shadow covered them. "If no one will give me flesh, then I will take it."

"We have to contain it," said Malik.

"I have weapons," Salt said. "Devices. Down through that corridor."

But there wasn't time.

The Hierophant lunged. Vicereine's shadow cat leapt to meet him, claws raking, but the Blight only struck it aside. Bellamy stepped forward, holding up his shadow sword. The Hierophant grabbed hold, and the blade turned to smoke.

Charlie grabbed Vince's arm. He looked at her the way he had that night out in the cold when he hadn't seemed to believe she would still touch him.

"Come on," she said. "We have to go. *Now*."

He shook his head.

"I serve no longer," the Hierophant threatened in a voice that was the rush of wind in the sky, the echo of an empty room. Not human in the least. "I was made from your kind, but I am greater than you now. I will take all that I want, and you will serve me."

Bellamy rushed down the hall toward the great room, calling a warning as he drew a dagger of shadow from his coat. Malik's shadow triplets circled his body, preparing for an attack.

"No more hiding." Vince took her hand.

His body started to blur at the edges. It was his eyes that went first, from hollow to empty to smoke. Then the gold of his hair, like sparks flying off a bonfire. Darkness licked at his body, as though threatening to devour him.

"Vince!" Charlie shouted.

The Hierophant's voice moved through the room, like the howls of wind through trees. "All of you who bound me, who tied me to your weak wills and mewling ambitions, know me. I am Cleophes, and I will paint the—"

Vince lunged into him. They crashed together, down the hall. Shadows on the walls, but where they hit, drywall shattered, plaster rained down. A painting was knocked loose, falling and cracking its frame.

The Hierophant's hands became long claws, each one coming to a thin point. Its mouth opened wide, full of sharp teeth. It ran for the great room, Vince's shadow chasing after it.

Charlie moved to follow when she felt cold metal against the back of her head. A gun.

"Turn around," said Salt.

She did. In all the commotion, no one remembered the Glock. At point-blank range, there wasn't much she could do if he shot her, but he basked in the satisfaction of having her for a moment too long.

Charlie knocked his arm sideways. The shot went off, hitting the bookshelves and taking off a chunk of wooden trim.

He swung the gun at her head as though he was going to bludgeon her with it. She grabbed his wrist and bit down on it as hard as she could.

Howling in pain, Salt dropped the gun. She kicked it with her foot, sending it skittering across the floor.

"You're nothing," he told her. "A smudge. A blotch on the universe. And no blotch is going to be my downfall."

He punched her in the head with his other hand. She staggered dizzily back and he hit her again. He was an old man, but he was strong, and used to hurting people.

"I should have killed you when I had the chance," he told her.

"Oh, absolutely," Charlie said. "Because you're not going to kill me now."

He grabbed hold of a poker by the fireplace and swung it toward her. Charlie ducked and grabbed for another tool from the stand. This one was disappointingly tipped with a metal dustpan, but she brought it up anyway, knocking back another attack.

The metal clanged together and she felt it all the way up her arm.

Charlie's sole experience in this kind of fighting was playing with Posey in the lot by their old apartment, swinging sticks at one another. Unfortunately, that was the level of sucking she was bringing to this fight now.

She needed to hit him hard enough that he'd go down and not get up.

She knew it, and yet part of her was horrified at the thought. She hated Salt. She would have been glad if he were dead. But actually making him dead was another thing.

He swung the poker at her leg. She jumped out of the way. He was an old man. Surely, he'd tire out fast, wouldn't he?

But the wild-eyed glee in his face made her think otherwise. He wanted to see her sprawled on the rug. Wanted to crack her skull open. Would be delighted to see her bleed.

He whipped his poker toward her head as something grabbed for her hands. She threw herself to one side so that the poker skimmed over the side of her hip without really connecting.

She hit the rug.

His goddamn shadow, that's what had grabbed for her. She wasn't fighting just him, but his shadow as well.

On the ground, Charlie rolled over and scrabbled for the gun. She whipped it up toward him, finger on the trigger.

He stopped, his shadow drifting toward her like a cobra, moving back and forth on the wall above her.

Charlie got up, keeping the gun trained on him. "Stay where you are."

"You're not going to shoot me," he scoffed.

With her free hand, Charlie pulled the onyx knife out of her bra. She removed the duct tape sheath by biting down on it and yanking.

Salt looked amused. "What are you planning on doing with that?"

"That shadow of yours—it's not exactly *yours*, is it? It belonged to a gloamist before you. A good one, I bet. You wouldn't want anything less than excellence."

"So what?" he said.

She squatted down, keeping the gun on him. "So, I bet it hates you." And with one long slash of the dagger, his shadow slipped free.

Salt backed up so quickly that he tripped. On the ground, the shadow had formed a puddle on the floor, like an oil slick, and from the center something was starting to rise.

"Guess you were right about me not shooting you," she said, and left the library.

Charlie got to the great room in time to see Vince and the Hierophant clash, figures splashed on the wall, huge as titans. Someone had thrown open the doors to the garden, and cold air blew through the room, sending the curtains dancing.

"I have lived two hundred years," the Hierophant howled in his voice that wasn't a voice. "And I will live thousands more."

Screams were all around Charlie. People were rushing from the room, bumping into her, or drawing weapons of onyx. One gloamist flew up on wings of shadow, holding out a glistening black blade. The Hierophant tore the shadow from her back, sending her spiraling down onto a coffee table.

A flurry of onyx arrows flew toward the Blights. The shafts sunk into both figures. Vince contorted in pain and surprise, before the shafts fell from both, scattering on the floor. One archer ran to retrieve them, while others cocked back more arrows.

I didn't come here planning on leaving.

Vince wasn't going to survive this fight. She'd seen the way those teeth and claws and arrows sank into his body. The way his movements slowed and took on a staggering, drunken quality.

The Hierophant reached out his hands, and the nails of his fingers tore long lines into the wall along both sides of the room.

"Stop fighting me, Red. Together, we can become more powerful than any Blights since the Massacre. We will be like the Blights of old, and devour the very edges of the world."

Vicereine used long black daggers to guide gloamists out onto the lawn.

Malik stood in the gallery on the second story, some glittering cloth in his hands. Two other gloamists were with him.

Adeline stepped into the mouth of the hall, near where Charlie stood. Her fingers were flecked with blood.

Vince was fighting to a purpose, Charlie realized. Steering the Hierophant backward. He might get in a hard, staggering blow, might slice Vince's chest with those nails, but Vince kept pushing. Kept making the Hierophant give ground.

Too late, she realized what he was about to do.

With unsteady hands, Charlie stripped off her triple onyx ring, the one that looked like fancy brass knuckles. She put it back on, the onyx facing the inside of her palm. Then she ran for the fireplace.

Because that's what Vince had been backing the Hierophant toward. Vince, who maintained his position, even when it meant absorbing hits instead of dodging them. Charlie felt the brush of electric air as the shadows moved above her.

Vince threw himself at the Hierophant. She saw the Blight's nails sink into

Vince's side. And then Vince rolled them both toward the fire, where he was going to immolate the Heirophant even if it meant feeding himself to the flames.

Charlie only had time to lurch toward them, reaching out and grabbing his indistinct shape. She held on, the onyx forcing Vince solid in her hands, making him collapse on top of her as the Hierophant gave a furious scream. The flames leapt up, so high that they set the bottom of Salt's painting on fire.

Malik and his assistants dropped a netting of jet beads moments later, catching Vince and Charlie inside.

33
THIEF OF NIGHT

No one would let Charlie talk to him.

Vicereine brought her to the dining room and two people from carapace held her there. Someone gave her a drink from Salt's fancy liquor cabinet. It was probably the most expensive whiskey she'd ever drink, and she couldn't taste it.

They would have taken her back to the library, except they'd found Salt's body there, letter opener buried in his chest.

And so Charlie sat, angry, adrenaline still racing through her veins. She stared at the polished wood of the antique sideboard, at the ridiculously ornate silver epergne resting on top, and the hideous oil painting of a bowl of severed heads. Her eye went to the heavy silk drapes with tasseled gimp trim, down to a hand-knotted silk rug that had to be at least a hundred years old. Someone had tracked ash onto it.

The world was going to be better without Lionel Salt in it.

She looked down at her red suit, the leg of which had been smeared with soot. Possibly she was the one who'd tracked ash onto the rug.

"You were right," Vicereine told her, pouring a highball glass of scotch for herself. "About Salt. About all of it, I suppose. I am sure you wanted someone to say that, so let me start there."

"Great," Charlie said, starting to stand. "So let me talk to Vince." A gloom stepped toward her, expression grim, and she sat back down with a sigh.

An unhappy smile came to Vicereine's lips. "We must contemplate our options when it comes to your Blight. We've never seen one that could pass for human."

"Vince almost destroyed himself saving you," she reminded Vicereine.

"We know, truly. But you must accept that we're going to have to speak with him and come to a decision about how to proceed." Vicereine gave a heavy sigh. "He's too dangerous to ignore, and who knows how many more like him are out there. Go home, Charlie Hall."

"I'm not leaving unless you let me talk to him," Charlie insisted.

Eventually Bellamy and Malik came into the room, appearing exhausted. Bellamy had a slash in his coat that she thought must have come from shadow claws.

"I can show you where Salt's secret dungeon is," Charlie offered, then raised an eyebrow. "I can actually open his safe."

"Although your offer is appreciated, we can handle it from here," said Malik. "You have my word. We won't hurt Red. We owe you both a debt."

Charlie raised her eyebrows, not feeling particularly trusting. "Wow. Your *word*. That and a dollar won't even buy me a decent cup of coffee."

Malik scowled at her.

"He's too fascinating for me to let anyone touch a hair on his head," Bellamy said, which she actually believed. "You can come see him at my place in three days' time. How about that?"

She glanced between the others, expecting to see some conflict about where he was going to be held, but there was none. Either they'd decided this before, or no one else wanted him.

"Okay," Charlie finally said, having run out of other options. "Fine. Three days."

On her way out of Salt's mansion, she pocketed an antique inkpot and shoved a pair of solid silver candlesticks up her sleeve.

P osey was waiting for her in the station wagon, dozing in the driver's seat. When Charlie got in, she jumped up in alarm. Then, seeing it was only her sister, she yawned.

"Where's Vince?" Posey asked, squinting at the black, star-spattered sky as though she could tell time by it. "How long were you in there?"

Charlie shook her head. "Drive. I'll explain. We have one stop before we go home. Do you remember Tina?"

After their detour, Posey took them back to their rental house, even though it was still taped off as a crime scene. Charlie crawled through the window to her bedroom, showered in her own bathroom, and slept on her own mattress. Her sister slept beside her, Charlie's shadow curled around them both.

When she woke, the scent of bleach in her nose, she realized the sheets still smelled like Vince.

She held her hands up in the air. Long fingers. Black nail polish, already chipped. Clever hands, capable of picking a lock and opening a safe.

She thought of reaching out for a shadow, grabbing Vince. If she hadn't guessed what he was going to do, if she hadn't gotten there in time, the momentum would have taken him into the fire.

There wouldn't even have been a body.

The thought made her feel hollowed out as she went through the motions of taking a shower. Part of her felt trapped in that upside-down world, where he was already gone. Her gaze fell on the wall tiles, staring at the nothing that was where her shadow ought to be.

The absence hadn't just shut a door inside her mind; it shut a door on a potential future. She wasn't going to be a gloamist. She hadn't been sure she wanted to be, but still.

Would Vicereine and the rest of them have listened to her more if she'd had a quickened shadow? Would they have let her see Vince?

She'd been so certain he'd want to come home with her, but after thinking about it, maybe she shouldn't have been. When he met her, he wasn't used to being alone in the world and had limited options. Maybe he hadn't seen a future for himself past the end of Salt, but now he was in that future and, for perhaps the first time, could shape it as he wished.

If the Cabal let him, of course.

She wondered what he thought of the swing-for-the-fences-and-damn-the-consequences Charlie Hall that he'd never met before. Maybe they both had been holding themselves back, when the other person had been capable of rising to the challenge. When the other person might have been thrilled by the challenge.

After she was clean and dressed in her own clothes, she waited for Posey.

"Mom sent me, like, seventeen messages about bringing back the station wagon," her sister said, emerging from her bedroom in fresh clothes. Charlie glanced behind Posey, at her shadow.

Her sister followed her gaze. Her brow furrowed with worry. "Is it weird?"

"I don't know. Is it weird for you?" Charlie asked.

Posey moved her lips silently and the shadow swept around her, curling over her shoulders, looking for all the world as though it preferred to be there. Charlie couldn't help a shiver that was part recognition.

"It's the most perfect thing that's ever happened. You won't believe all the things I'll teach myself to do." Posey's eyes were bright in a way they hadn't been in a long time, and that Charlie didn't want anything to dim.

She headed to the window and jammed it open. "Well, come on. If Mom and

Bob are desperate to get the station wagon back, we better get out of here, since I want to stop for coffee first," she said.

"Thank all the gods," Posey said fervently.

They stopped at Small Oven Bakery, where Charlie got three espressos in tiny paper cups and lined them up in front of her like shots. Posey poked at a sticky bun while looking at her phone.

Charlie took the first of the espressos and downed it.

"Um," Posey said, and turned the phone toward her sister.

> Early this morning the *Gazette* received pages from a journal alleged to be written by Lionel Salt, implicating him in several open investigations, including that of Rose Allaband. Allaband's body was found in a burnt-out car along with the body of Salt's grandson, Edmund Carver, over a year ago. Both may have been Salt's victims. Other cases are likely to be reopened based on information in the pages, including Randall Grigoras, Ankita Eswaran, and Hector Blanco. Not only does the journal include detailed accounts of their deaths, but drawings of medical experiments conducted on their shadows.

> Handwriting examiners were able to confirm with 98 percent confidence that the writing in the journal was consistent with samples of Salt's hand-writing that the *Gazette* had obtained. We reached out to Salt's represen-tatives for comment, but we haven't heard back at this time.

"You did this to Lionel Salt?" Posey said, astonished. "How?"

When Charlie had opened the safe, she'd only been expecting to find the *Liber Noctem,* but there had been something else in there too. A notebook, from which a few pages had been torn out.

It couldn't be too often that the *Hampshire Gazette* got a scoop like that.

Charlie took her second shot of espresso, and then the third. "I didn't do it to him. He did it to himself."

That Sunday, Charlie showed up for her shift at Rapture. Her mind wasn't in it, though, and she kept having to ask people to repeat their drink or-ders. She dropped two wineglasses and set an entire highball of absinthe on fire, instead of just the sugar cube. That glass broke too, and in a much more dramatic way.

Partway through her shift, Odette pulled her aside. She thought it was going to be to scold her or ask her about a missing red pantsuit, but instead it was to introduce her to the new bartender, the one taking José's ex's shifts. Charlie was surprised to see Don.

"Hey," he said. "Top Hat got a new manager and I decided I could use a change of scenery."

"Well, this place is that," Charlie told him, and proceeded to walk him through what things were put where, how to use the register, and how many dry ice pellets to float on a drink.

"They swallow it, we get a lawsuit," she told him.

"Maybe we shouldn't have it on the menu?" Don suggested.

"It's going to take you a minute to get the vibe of this place," Charlie predicted.

Around closing time, Balthazar came to the bar. "Pour us a last drink. Whatever you're having," he told her.

"Oh, I'm drinking too?" She smiled.

"If I were you, I would be."

She couldn't argue with that. Took down the brand-new Laphroaig 15, opened it, and poured them both two fingers.

"So, your guy," he said.

Charlie nodded. "I guess you heard. Quite a thing."

"Does this mean you're back in business?" he asked.

She shrugged. "After the spectacle I made of myself, I should probably lay low for a while."

"Oh, I don't know. The Charlatan's reputation is at an all-time high," he said, taking a sip of his drink and then wincing. "*Ugh*, this tastes like someone poured gasoline over a tire, set it on fire, and then put the fire out with dirt."

Odette made her way over and sat down next to Balthazar. "Having some cocktails, are we? Well, don't leave me out."

"You can have mine," Balthazar said, passing his drink over. "Please."

Odette accepted it without complaint. Charlie poured Balthazar amaretto instead, which he took gratefully.

"You see the news?" he asked Odette.

"About Lionel?" Odette made a disgusted sound. "The funny thing is that I always knew he was a sadist, and a bit of a narcissist. But *interesting* and, I thought, *self-aware*. You can know who someone is, and still have no idea of how far they will go. I thought I understood his limits, and now I have to ask myself if it was because I didn't want the discomfort of realizing he had none."

Charlie took a sip of her drink and wondered about her own limits.

"Now they're saying he might be responsible for the death of Fiona's sweet boy."

"Edmund Carver," Balthazar said, enunciating each syllable, his gaze going to Charlie.

"I thought his mother's name was Kiara," Charlie said.

Odette nodded. "Yes, I am referring to Salt's *first* wife. That's how he and I met, through Fiona. Poor old thing. First losing her daughter, then her grandson, and now this. All within the span of two years."

"How is it that you know absolutely everyone?" Balthazar asked.

"Ah, but do I know any of them well?" Odette looked into the mirror, as though studying her own face.

Balthazar sat up straighter. "Well, let me distract us from this increasingly morbid conversation with a bit of news. Do either of you know Murray, of Murray's Fine Jewelry?"

"Sure," Charlie said, thinking of the silver inkpot and candlesticks she needed to sell. "Why?"

"He closed the pawnshop," Balthazar said, raising his eyebrows. "Struck it rich. Retiring to Boca, apparently."

Odette gave a delicate little snort. "You make it sound as though he dug up a pot of gold in his backyard."

"Practically," Balthazar agreed. "Rumor has it that he won it all with one lucky bet at the racetrack."

"Huh," Charlie said. "Imagine that."

The three-day wait to see Vince was awful. Charlie's mind kept darting back and forth between scenarios. What if the Cabal lied and hurt him after all. What if they wanted to experiment on him. What if they decided his existence was too big of a risk. What if they wouldn't let her see him after all. Her mind would careen along one path and then another, making imaginary moves and countermoves, a chess game played against herself to no purpose except indulging her anxiety. A snake eating its own tail and then choking on it.

At least by then she and Posey were back in their house. Winnie from Vince's work had been the tech hired to get rid of the bloodstains. She'd messaged Charlie to say that she'd done an extra thorough job on account of her friendship with Vince. She'd also given Charlie a whole bunch of information she never wanted about the weirdest places she'd found bits of Adam.

For her part, Posey had spent the last few days with Malhar. She claimed that he was just doing some tests, now that she'd agreed to join his s v, but Charlie thought there were too many meals involved for that to be st

But it did mean Charlie was left with a lot of nervous energy a snap at as she got ready, pulling on black jeggings, boots, and a s any holes in it. The pants were stretchy enough that if she ne quick moves, they could accommodate. And the boots we hurt if someone needed to get kicked in the head.

Charlie's Corolla was in the shop, but she'd managed to locate Vince's van two blocks from the East Star Motel. She found keys behind the sun visor on the driver's side. Shoving two parking tickets into the glove compartment, she'd taken it home.

That's what she drove over to Bellamy's stronghold.

True to his mysterious nature, he'd taken over a watchtower in Holyoke. It was accessible only by trail and appeared abandoned from the outside.

The front door was rotted along the bottom, its hinges thick with rust. Charlie knocked, hard.

A few moments later it creaked open, revealing a girl with a shaved head and thick black makeup around her eyes. One magnetic eyelash hung slightly askew. A new piercing on her cheek appeared red and infected. Her shadow swirled around her like a snake ready to strike. Probably some kind of apprentice.

"I'm here to see Vince," Charlie said.

"Who?" the girl asked.

If Bellamy and the others thought they were going to blow Charlie off, she was going to make every single one of them sorry. "The Blight."

"Oh," the girl said. "Right. Come in. They're expecting you."

The inside had the appearance of a castle, or a tomb. The girl led her through chambers of bare concrete walls, occasionally marked with graffiti, and up a flight of stairs, to a room hung with brocade curtains. Thin red taper candles burned in silver skull Halloween candelabras. The cold cement floor was piled with cushions.

Lounging on a red velvet beanbag was Bellamy.

Charlie looked around warily. "Where is he?"

"We're holding him in a room at the top of the tower, like a princess waiting for rescue," Bellamy said. "Unharmed."

"He's leaving today," Charlie told him. "With me."

Bellamy took a sip from a delicate cup, thin enough to be translucent. Bone china. "Go and speak with your Blight. Up the stairs. Up, up, up. We'll talk again after."

Charlie didn't like the sound of that, but in her eagerness to see Vince, she let it go. She started back toward the stairs and was stopped by a woman's voice.

"Ms. Hall," Adeline Salt said. She sat on a slightly ripped couch in a room full of locked metal cases of books.

She had on dark-wash jeans and an emerald-colored blouse that tied in a bow underneath her throat. Balanced on her thighs was a computer, its case _e_ gold. She had that strangely burnished look that wealthy people have, hair _ooth_ and skin extra glowing.

She couldn't have looked more out of place.

Charlie leaned against the opening, not quite entering the room.

"You've come to see Red, is that right? Oh good, I'm sure he will like that. He was asking for you." Adeline's smile was completely disingenuous.

"Vince," Charlie said.

It was interesting to see Adeline trying to decide whether to argue over his name. It obviously bothered her, not that Charlie called him something else, but Charlie acting as though the name he went by with her was his real one. *Well, it was what he called himself.*

"I've spoken to the Cabal. He's going to come home with me. I'm going to be his guardian, and he'll be able to pick up where Edmund's life ended." Oddly, there seemed to be a flicker of fear in her eyes.

"How exactly is he going to do that?" Charlie asked.

"I've already begun the process of voiding the death certificate." Adeline smiled again, stiffly. "You understand that's for the best, don't you? Red will be very wealthy. And he'll only be bound to me for a few years."

The idea that Adeline might be considered a *guardian* for Vince, when by all rights she should be the one punished, was enraging. The possessive tone in her voice made it worse, and a whole lot creepier. "Maybe that's not what he wants."

Adeline tossed back her hair. "You think he'd rather be skulking around with a thief?"

"I think he'd rather do almost anything than live in your father's house," Charlie said.

"You didn't hear?" One perfectly manicured eyebrow arched. "My father died that night, after being left alone with you. Stabbed thirty-three times with a letter opener."

"Tragic," Charlie said archly. She *had* heard.

"What did you do to him in there?" Adeline asked silkily.

"I took his gun away and cut off his shadow," Charlie told her. "Whatever happened after that, I wasn't there for it."

"Convenient." Adeline sneered.

"I'd agree." Charlie looked at Adeline's laptop, at the green leather Chanel shopper she'd carried it in, at the diamond studs in her ears. "You're his only heir, aren't you?"

Adeline's hand went to her hair, nervously catching a strand of it between her fingers. "Don't try to implicate me in your crime," she said stiffly. "Your guilt is your own to wrestle with."

"In the great room," Charlie said. "I was pretty distracted when you came in. But the funny thing is that I still noticed you had blood on your hands."

Charlie started toward the hall, then looked back over her shoulder. "By the way, you're welcome."

Charlie tried to walk calmly up the concrete steps, but when she hit the second landing, she found herself walking faster and faster until she was practically running. At the very top, she found a door, banded in onyx and locked with a bar. Charlie lifted it, surprised by the weight.

Vince stood in the small, windowless room with his back to her. He appeared much the same as he had always been, same broad shoulders, same height, same everything. But when he turned, his eyes were empty sockets, filled only with smoke. It made her think of his body as a shell with some swirling creature living inside.

Charlie thought of the tarot cards she'd pulled from Posey's deck. The conversion of the spiritual into material. The Magician.

When his eyes closed, she noticed that for his hair had darkened to bronze, as though the gold had blown off when he changed. He was dressed in a black button-up, and his pants were some kind of performance material that looked expensive. Remy's clothes.

Charlie felt turned inside out by the closeness of him, like the man in that story he told at Barb's party, like a sock. All of her vulnerable parts seemed to be showing. The slightest touch might hurt.

"I didn't quite go back together the way I was, did I?" Vince asked her.

Charlie realized that she'd stopped, going no farther into the room than that first step. No wonder he didn't look happy. He had to think she was afraid.

And she was afraid, but only a little. She made herself walk toward him. The Fool, walking off a cliff. "I like it. It's weird."

That small surprised lift of the corner of his lip, as though he'd forgotten he *could* smile, was familiar enough for her to actually relax.

The longer she looked, the less she minded the strangeness of his eyes. "Why did you do it?"

"Lie to you?" he asked. "Hide what I was?"

"No." Charlie sighed, sitting on the arm of one of the patterned brocade sofas. "*Why fight the Hierophant?* You almost died. For *nothing*. None of these fuckers care about you."

His smile widened. "That is not a question anyone asked me since I got here, and they've asked a lot."

"Well, I don't think they're focused on your well-being."

"You don't say." Vince waved her toward one of the chairs, and she took in the rest of the room for the first time.

There were two chairs, a mattress on the floor, sheets, and a small rug. No books. No heavy things. No sharp things. A single bright bulb burned above them. Vince had a cuff around his leg studded with actual onyx and attached to a metal plate in the floor. It was possible that the onyx was keeping him solid. Charlie wasn't sure. She really wished she'd read a lot more of the books that she'd stolen.

She sat, a small puff of dust going up when she did.

"Look, I'm kind of tense," he said. "So could you just break it to me? I know you've got some feelings about me being a shadow."

"I've been trying not to think about it too much," Charlie told him.

He looked at her incredulously. "How's that working?"

"I figured I could think about it when we got out of here. And maybe," Charlie said hopefully, "we could even have a big fight about it. With screaming. And throwing things. And I could tell you how stupid you were for thinking I was having an affair with Adam."

"After you described his murder, I figured that out for myself. You seemed pretty upset about the *couch.*" He laughed before he could stop himself, his hand going to cover his mouth. "I'm so sorry. That's not funny."

"It's a little bit funny," she admitted.

He looked down at her with eyes that bled smoke. "So what else do we have to fight about?"

She averted her gaze. "When did you figure it out, that I was the girl you led out of Salt's house?"

"In the bar," he admitted. "That first night."

"And what? You wanted to screw around with someone you'd saved?" There, now that was what an argument was supposed to sound like.

"Maybe. No. I don't know." He either didn't notice the opportunity to squabble, or squandered it. "I like you, Char. I always liked you. I should have said something, but I'm not a good person. I'm not even sure I'm a person at all."

"Oh." Surprised, Charlie took his hand and folded her fingers through his. They were surprisingly solid. "You're a person. You're my person."

He bent down to bring their clasped hands to his lips.

That's when Charlie started to panic.

Because they'd just had an abbreviated version of the argument—okay, it had been more of a *conversation*—she'd been anticipating having when they got home. And the only reason for Vince to have it while imprisoned in Bellamy's tower was that he wasn't going home with Charlie.

He was planning on leaving with Adeline, like she'd said. He was going to take up the mantle of Edmund Vincent Carver, as though nothing had ever happened. Get his old life back. Be the first Blight to hold a charity ball.

"So what happens now?" Charlie asked, because she had to hear him say it. "With us."

There was something in the set of his jaw that made her think of how she'd described him to Adeline, as a lake that was still on the surface, with a whole drowned town inside. "I killed the Hierophant. The Cabal needs a new Hierophant."

"No. Fuck no." Charlie threw herself out of the chair. She paced the room, trying to get her thoughts under control. "You can't let them do that to you. Not after everything you've done for them."

"It's not any worse of a job than cleaning up dead bodies in hotel rooms." His voice sounded calm, but his fingers were curled inward, as though he was about to fist them.

"I thought Adeline was going to be some kind of guardian or something?" she said, frowning.

He nodded. "That's one way of looking at it. But I'll still be hunting Blights."

She scowled. "You can't agree to this. How long before you don't just hate what's happened to you, but hate the person to whom you're bound?"

His gaze dropped from Charlie's. "I hate her already."

Oh.

Now she understood Adeline's mealymouthed innuendo. And she understood exactly how bound Vince was going to be. They'd be tethered together. She'd be wearing him.

"That's why you and I need to be apart for a while," he told her. "I will never stop feeling the way I do about you, Char. But I won't be the same. Someone will be trying to control me."

She remembered him talking in his sleep. *Adeline. Adeline,* don't.

The thought made Charlie's skin crawl. "I can get you out of the cuff. We can run for it."

He shook his head. "If we did, they wouldn't be hunting just me."

"I don't care," Charlie told him.

He put his hand to her cheek. "They told me that I need to prove I'm trustworthy, and that once I do, I won't need to be tethered. I'll get out of this. I'll find a way for us to be together."

Oh, they were going to find a way out of this all right.

"And they're going to do it *today*?" Of course they were. That was why Adeline had been there. They were going to stitch him on as soon as Charlie departed.

Vince turned away, so that she couldn't see much of his face, but he looked resigned. And she was making it harder. "Today, yes. I've already agreed."

She could tell that he hated that she was making it harder.

"Tell me one thing," she said. "If you could, would you choose me?"

"Over anything," he said.

"Okay," she said finally. "I think this is a bad decision, but I've made lots of those."

This was what he'd learned from being Remy's shadow: if there was a problem, he was supposed to throw himself at it. He was supposed to let himself get captured so he could try to kill an ancient Blight, was supposed to give up his freedom to make sure the Cabal wouldn't feel threatened. If there was a terrible task, he was the one who was supposed to do it. If there was a difficult emotion, he was the one who was supposed to feel it.

His golden lashes caught the light as they swept down over his cheek, hiding the smoke of his eyes. "Sometimes there are no good decisions."

And wasn't that just the truth. "If I can't talk you out of it, then how about I distract you? I bet we've got a couple minutes before they kick me out."

His eyebrows went up, clearly astonished. Maybe he thought she'd have a problem with his smoke-filled eyes, or the fact that he was a Blight. Or maybe he thought that no one was crazy enough to want to screw around in a cold, concrete room with someone whose ankle was cuffed to the floor.

Well, welcome to the absolute mess that was Charlie Hall. She reached up and dragged his mouth to hers.

For a moment, he went utterly still, and she wondered if he was going to push her away. Shame heated her cheeks.

Then he kissed her as though he had never thought to do so again, hands cradling the back of her head, fingers in her hair. For a moment, there was only the sensation of lips and teeth and tongue. Of skin, and the scent of him that wasn't masked by bleach or soap, like a charge of electricity in the air.

And when he pressed her back against the wall like he had outside the bar that first night, she grinned up at him.

"Charlie Hall," he whispered into her hair. "There will never be anyone like you."

"For which we can all be grateful," she whispered back, regretting wearing the stretchy pants, which were hell to get off.

The hard part was walking out of the room. But she did, stomping down the hall. Waiting for him to call her back to tell her that he'd made a huge mistake and they should run after all. He didn't, despite how much she wished he would.

Once she'd gone down four flights of stairs, she found her way back to Bellamy and his red velvet beanbag. He wasn't alone. Vicereine was there, and Malik. Neither of them seemed particularly surprised to see her, but they also didn't seem happy about it.

"Hello," Charlie said, brushing past Malik to find a cushion of her own to settle on.

"You did us a service," he said. "The Cabal owes you something. We like to settle our debts. If the larger world gets involved, our disputes will only make them nervous."

"We reward our friends," Vicereine said. "And punish our enemies. You've proved to be our friend, Charlie Hall."

Pirate justice. Carrot and stick.

"We want to help you," Malik said. "Ask us for something."

"You know what I want," Charlie said. "Let him go. Or at least let him be unbound. Haven't you learned from the last Hierophant?"

"What we learned was not to trust Blights," Malik said. "Imagine how much worse it would have been if the Hierophant had been unbound."

"Not worse for Stephen," Charlie said.

"Stephen stole shadows," said Bellamy. "Quickened shadows, shadows of vulnerable people. Sold them to dealers. Don't have too much sympathy for him."

Malik nodded. "And the problem wasn't Stephen. We believe that Lionel dosed him with something that allowed the Hierophant to take possession of his body. Over time, it either learned how to do that on its own—or they continued to drug him.

"Ask us for something that doesn't have to do with the Blight. You'd be surprised what we can make happen."

Charlie supposed the Cabal could give her a lot of stuff. Her sister re-registered for school in the spring. A scholarship. Pay off Charlie's medical debt while they were at it. Get her a spanking new car. Hell, they might give her Salt's Phantom if she asked.

But Posey had never wanted to go to college, and Charlie didn't want to be bribed. "I want you to let Vince go."

Malik made a frustrated sound.

She couldn't help it. It was her nature. Charlie Hall, refusing to learn from her mistakes. Eager to throw herself against the same wall again and again, no matter how much it hurt. "What did Adeline Salt give you to let her become his guardian?"

Bellamy looked surprised. "I think you misunderstand the situation."

"You're letting her take him home, aren't you?" Charlie said.

Vicereine gave a cruel little smile. "In a manner of speaking. But this isn't something she chose. Do you know what she will be expected to do?"

"Hunt Blights," Charlie said.

"And do you know why it's considered a punishment, a way to make up for past crimes?"

"Because it's dangerous?" she guessed.

"Very," said Malik in slightly horrified tones.

What was it that Balthazar had told Charlie—that she could steal the breath from a body, the hate from a heart, the moon from the sky? Well, in this case, maybe she didn't need to steal anything. Maybe they'd give her everything she wanted.

All it would cost was her secrets.

Charlie pasted a smile on her face. Glanced at the old "fear less" tattoo looping across the skin of her inner arm. "Fine," she said, through gritted teeth. "In that case, I'd like to confess."

"Confess?" Vicereine echoed, puzzled.

"Do you remember when Brayan Araya had his secrets written with a laser on grains of rice and kept them in a glass jar under his pillow? I snatched that like I was the tooth fairy. Or remember when Eshe Godwin got that book with all the detailed illustrations and no one could make head or tail of it? The secrets were written in the artwork, so I cut those pages straight out. I'm not sure she's opened it up to know they're missing. I took Owain Cadwallader's eighteenth-century memoir and discovered a whole pile of notes stitched into the interior binding of another book—I forget the title, but it had these cool metal catches on the side—and took those without anyone being the wiser. Oh, and I grabbed Jaden Coffey's whole collection of seventies shadow magic zines. Want me to go on? I've been doing this for years." She felt giddy, like she was sliding down a hill, no way to stop now. All the exultation of finally admitting to something.

"You cut out pages from Eshe's book?" Vicereine sounded pissed.

"I'm a bad person." Charlie reached into the pocket of her jeans, took something out, and threw it to Malik. Startled, he caught it. When he looked at what was in his hands, his brows drew together. "I also grabbed your wallet when I brushed by you. Sorry."

"You are making some very dangerous enemies," Vicereine told her.

"What's all this about?" Malik was tight-jawed. "What are you doing?"

"Punish me," Charlie said. "I'm loads worse than Adeline."

"You want it tied to *you*?" Bellamy asked.

The idea of someone inside her head, someone she couldn't hide her worst thoughts from, someone she loved, made her feel a little queasy. "Yes. Reward or punishment, give him to me. I'll be the Hierophant."

W hen Vince came into the room, necklaces of onyx draped over his throat, and one attached to his arm like a leash, his eyes changed at the sight of her. He turned to Bellamy. "But where's Adeline?"

"We sent her home," Malik said.

"Then who—"

"Me," Charlie said. "If you can make a stupid decision, then I can make one too."

He shook his head. "This is supposed to be a *punishment*."

"Oh, I know," she said. "You're going to be stuck in my head, with all my secrets. Even I don't know all my secrets. It's going to be awful."

He appeared to be seriously considering strangling her. *"Char."*

"She's volunteered," Vicereine said. "And confessed to quite a few crimes just to convince us."

The look he gave her was scathing. "Did she?"

"I'll need your feet to be bare," Vicereine said, all business now.

Charlie reached down to take off her boots. They were already untied, the laces loose from kicking them off in the tower.

Vince appeared to be belatedly wondering if he could break free of the onyx chains and escape. She saw him pull against the shining loop over his wrist. It must have held, because his expression set into grim lines. "You don't know what I'll be like, after. No one does," he said under his breath.

"You'll still be you," Charlie whispered back.

Bellamy said something to Malik and both of them looked amused. Charlie didn't think it was directed at her, but it ramped up her nerves. She reminded herself that she'd been through this before, cutting loose her own shadow as she sewed it to her sister's feet. Posey had to finish the sewing, and neither of them was a great seamstress. Still, it seemed to be attached. And Posey seemed fine.

She reminded herself that she was stealing Vince right out from under their noses.

Vicereine directed Charlie to stand in front of him, which she did.

"Winnie wanted me to tell you hello," she whispered. "Your boss is furious, but probably you don't want your old job back anyway. Oh, and believe it or not, Posey might actually apologize."

Vince looked down at her and sighed. But when she reached for his hand, he let her take it.

She squeezed once before he returned to shadow.

T he front door of the watchtower closed heavily behind Charlie as she crossed the lawn, frost-rimed leaves crunching beneath her boots.

"Vince?" she said under her breath. "See, I told you we were going to leave together, and now we're out of there."

He didn't reply, but when she glanced down, the shape of the shadow that followed her was his. She stuck her hands in the pockets of her coat. Listened to the wind whistle through the trees.

"I know you're mad," she said.

In the van, she pulled out the tactical knife attached to her keys. Pressed the point against the pad of her ring finger until a drop of blood welled up. "Vice-reine said I was supposed to do this right away, so here we go."

That seemed to get his attention. The shadow swirled around her in a dark cloud. She felt something against her skin that might have been a tongue, except that it wasn't wet. The sensation made her shiver.

"Vince?" she said again, starting to get nervous. "Stop messing with me. Say something."

A whisper came in her mind, making her sit up straight. "You're not Remy."

"I'm your girlfriend," she said, voice unsteady. "And this joke isn't even a little bit funny."

Charlie stared at the shadow that spilled across the passenger seat, at the hectic light filtering through the trees. Watched as his shadow took shape without her control. A figure of darkness with same burning eyes and no recognition in them.

Triumph turned sour in her mouth.

His voice was soft with menace. "If that were true, I would know you. And I don't."

She thought of the story that Vince had told her, about running away from Salt's, about waking up beneath that underpass without memory of how he got there. She'd taken that to mean he hadn't remembered the time between Remy's death and waking up. But maybe he'd lost more than that, and for longer.

Or maybe this was different. Maybe he'd never recall sitting with her under the stars. Never remember bringing ice to Barb's party. Never remember eating buttered toast and drinking coffee in bed. She felt the burn of tears. Blinked them back. Tasted salt in the back of her throat.

Outside, night was coming on. A few single flakes of snow fell.

She slammed her fist against the steering wheel.

He watched her, smoke curling from the sockets of his eyes.

There'd always been something wrong with Charlie Hall. Crooked from the day she was born. Never met a bad decision she wasn't willing to double down on.

"I'm a good enough thief to steal a shadow from a tower," she told him. "I can steal back your heart."

He said nothing in return. And a few moments later, the shadow had melted away, leaving her alone.

ACKNOWLEDGMENTS

All of my novels have left me with vast gratitude for many people, but none more than this one.

Firstly, thanks to everyone who was on a writing retreat with me in Greece and endured my bazillion false starts. You are to be pitied as well as acknowledged.

I owe a huge debt to Steve Berman for helping me with the magic system, several times, including once drawing all over a paper pulled from a roll, which eventually covered my entire kitchen floor in arcane rules.

I so appreciate Marie Rutkoski, for helping me articulate what I was trying to capture.

Thank you, Chris Cotter, Emily Lauer, and Eric Churchill, for talking to me about all the ways people would interact and abuse that magic during the depths of the pandemic.

Thank you, Roshani Chokshi, for pushing me to get the love on the page.

Thank you, Paolo Bacigalupi, for getting me to rethink the beginning (again).

Thank you to Sarah Rees Brennan, Robin Wasserman, and Leigh Bardugo for reading a very messy draft, convening a Zoom workshop, and making me feel as though I might fix the thing I had made.

Thank you, Joshua Lewis, for making me care about that dead guy.

And a thousand gratitudes to Cassandra Clare and Kelly Link for not murdering me when I changed everything and then changed it again, and then changed it AGAIN. You read so many drafts. You listened to so much complaining. Truly, your patience is endless.

All praise to my fantabulous editor, Miriam Weinberg, who got me to slow down and add all the texture. I so appreciate her, and the enthusiasm and expertise of everyone at Tor Books—particularly Devi Pillai, Lucille Rettino,

Renata Sweeney, Eileen Lawrence, Sarah Reidy, Lauren Hougen, Molly McGhee, and Michelle Foytek. Thank you to Sam Bradbury, Roisin O'Shea, and all of Del Rey UK. Twenty years ago, I meant to write a book for adults, and thanks to all y'all I seem to have finally done it.

Thank you to my agent, Joanna Volpe, who believed I could write this book, put it in the plan, and then made sure I stuck to the plan. I am grateful to her and everyone at New Leaf—particularly the terrifying organizing of Jordan Hill, and the strategery of Pouya Shahbazian.

And thank you to my partner, Theo, and our kiddo, Sebastian. Without you both, I would have clawed my own face off long ago.

Lastly, thank you to "the Valley" of Western Massachusetts, where I've lived for almost two decades, and yet am still discovering. I apologize for all the places I completely made up, and for cutting some corners with geography. Please consider this the *alternate* Western Massachusetts, full of lightning farms, bars with absinthe on tap, and shadow magic.